Why in Paris?

Why in Paris?

HARRY F. REY

Encircle Publications
Farmington, Maine U.S.A.

Editor: Michael Piekny

Cover design by Deirdre Wait
Cover images © Getty Images

Published by:

Encircle Publications
PO Box 187
Farmington, ME 04938

info@encirclepub.com
http://encirclepub.com

For Omri, without whom I'd have no words.

And for Sandy. The world is waiting to hear your story.

Act I:
The Bohemian Revolution

Chapter 1

Paris, 1937

CLAUDE AND I, LIKE the beginning of all great queer friendships, had attempted to find romance with each other, back on my very first night in Paris in the late summer of '36. Fresh off the train from Austria, naturally the place I dropped my bags was Giovanni's bar on the corner of Rue Duperré. I'd once read this bar was a gathering place for men of my sort; that was from a discarded pamphlet I found in a certain gentleman's facilities back in Vienna. I knew one day I would make it to Paris, and on that day, Giovanni's was where I would go.

Two drinks in at Giovanni's and I'd already secured lodgings upstairs with Madame Framboise, who wrote my mother a very lovely letter in the most overwrought French, assuring her that not only would I have a soft bed and a warm kitchen as long as the postal orders lasted, but she'd even send her a monthly newsletter of how I was getting on at art school. Not to mention the insurance required by my mother, as executor of my father's estate, that I was, in fact, learning something. Art school was, of course, purpose *de jure* for being in Paris. But it was the modern medium of photography which had captured my imagination like a revolutionary theology. The very idea photography could be art being as abhorrent to the great masters as Marxism to the moneyed classes.

From Vienna, I brought the state-of-the-art Kodak 35 mm camera my grandmother had given me in 1935. I'd been too self-conscious to take more than a few snapshots of my mother and our furniture, and only when we were at home. Such were the looks, or worse, the questions, the police would heap on a quiet young man taking pictures around Vienna.

But now I was in Paris. With a twinkling in her eye, perhaps from attempting to match-make two young men together, or perhaps from the fact she was permanently pissed on gin, Madame Framboise waved Claude over from his stalking horse at the bar, leafing through *Le Figaro* in the late afternoon light seeping into our basement lair.

"I'm halving your rent," she told him, the gin licking her cheeks a strawberry red.

"Thank you, but I work alone," Claude said. He raised his eyebrow over my rough, anxious edges and the camera clasped to my chest.

"You boys belong together."

"You always say that."

"Well I think you'll bring out the best in each other."

Claude scoffed and snatched the remainder of liquor from Madame Framboise's glass, while she returned to what intrigued her most about me. The camera in my lap. "Which angle suits me best, Herr Anders?"

"At least she doesn't need rouge," Claude said, sliding in beside her, dusting strands of loose hair behind Madame Framboise's ears. Even a fraud masquerading as an amateur could capture the love between these old souls. It flowed right into the lens, as the two of them embraced tighter than my mother had ever hugged me. The two of them laughing operatically, cheek to cheek, the glorious friendship between a middle-aged woman and a boisterous young queer itself a study in still-life. Only Giovanni's grumbling that my snapping pictures would 'frighten the gents' as he brought us a steady supply of drinks turned me slightly off. But I was having too much fun with new *chéries* to worry about Giovanni. There was also the matter of Claude's fluttering lashes and hands constantly tapping my own as I drank or wound the camera, such indelicacies leaving a trail of electric sparks that led straight up the stairs, to our attic room on the corner of Rue Duperré.

Give us our credit. Claude tried, and far harder than I. We both knew the drunken cloud where romances are birthed would not offer us cover for long. We must link ourselves together now, or be damned to the sins of friendship for all eternity.

But we were simply a couple of negative charges. The bottom ends of two magnets, constitutionally ineligible to consummate a marriage of *mignons*.

And so, my trans-continental voyage to dip my toe in the virgin waters of a long-overdue sexual awakening free from my mother's yoke dried up like… "Like Madame Framboise's pussy," Claude said the very next night at Giovanni's bar—essentially, the downstairs living room of my new home.

In a dark, sheltered corner of the smoke-filled basement bristling with men on the prowl come evening time, Claude hushed the lay of the land directly into my ear, never breaking eye contact with the man he hoped to lead into the alleyway where he conducted his business.

"You're one of us now, darling," Claude said, already loosening his belt in the hope to be there and back in the time it took me to bring us another drink. "And there's three things all us Montmartre boys must know: get the money upfront, never suck a dick in your own stairwell, and…" Claude stood from the table, grabbing the front of his trousers to keep them up as the man he'd been winking at openly beckoned him to hurry up, "a shot of absinthe is like bleach for the throat."

Our romantic relationship, such as it was, manifested itself with him pouncing on my bed at two in the morning, his voice lacquered in absinthe; purely to harp on about the finer details of the French Wars of Religion.

"You see," he'd say with a languid hoarseness while attempting to relight the stubby end of a *gauloises* with a burnt match, "if one's mother was Catherine de' Medici, how could one *not* have issues with women?"

For Claude, all great histories were littered with the untold stories of our homosexual forbearers. When we took flight through the Tuileries, arm in arm, he would recast the entire foundations of Western civilization in a lavender hue.

"It all started with Charlemagne buggering his way across the continent," Claude explained, his arm linked through mine as we wandered through the Parisian autumn. "He wanted to be Caesar reborn, or Alexander the Great,

3

so he had to re-birth an Empire in order to give himself the power to fuck whomever he wanted."

Claude lit yet another cigarette as we stopped in front of an imposing equestrian statue of Philip I, King of the Franks. I took endless pictures, too many for what little amount of film I could afford, trying to capture the majestic monarch in the fading light. But the long shadows cast from the bronze hunk, and the puffs of cigarette smoke, interrupted any chance of a decent shot. The better image was of Claude gazing up the statue, preparing to recant some other great revelation of the mighty queers of Europe.

"You know his story, right? Philip the Amorous."

"Well…"

"Oh Anders! Sometimes I forget you never met another queer till you met me." His cigarette cast clouds of smoke around us, as if a great sorcerer was letting me in on the secrets of the universe. "Every age has a beauty. One human being so magnetic all the artists, painters and poets of the age can do nothing but spend their lives attempting to capture their heavenly essence. Once in a generation, the gods will gift us such an idol. And in case you were wondering, that, my friend, is the meaning of life. To seek out that beauty wherever it may reside and praise it with things unattempted yet in art or prose or rhyme."

"That's the meaning of life?" Claude wasn't listening. This was a monologue.

"The undisputed idol of eleventh century France was a young beauty called Giovanni." Claude explained as we marched through the Tuileries. "His hair was golden and curly, like a Roman. He had the body of Neoptolemus, piercing blue eyes and skin the color of a Berber. The Archbishop of Tours, a man named Rodolfo, took this lad as his personal lover and every Sunday, Rodolfo would dress Giovanni up in all the Church's finery and have him stand by the altar for all to see.

"During Mass, a squad of actors dressed as Jews would burst into the Basilica and rip Giovanni's clothes off while yelling obscenities in a dramatic reenactment of the Passion. The crowds loved it, and one day the King himself came to visit and watch the show. He asked the Archbishop for a private audience with this Jesus, and fucked Giovanni senseless. King Philip returned to Paris boasting of how not even the son of God could resist the

4

king. But then the dour St. Ivo got all up on his high horse and bitterly complained to Pope Urban II about this debauchery in the church and the court. Do you know what happened next?"

"They...were all burned at the stake?"

Claude laughed. "The Pope said Ivo's slander had no basis in fact. Rodolfo had the King appoint their favorite boy Giovanni as bishop of Orleans, where he ruled for forty years, by the way. And Rodolfo continued to be a well loved and respected figure in France to whom young men would line up outside his Church, hoping to be cast as the next sexy Jesus. So don't let anyone ever tell you us queers have no history. We *are* history."

This brought Clause to the ultimate hero of the modern queer—Napoleon— dashing around Europe, tearing down medieval walls and liberating the subjugated with Revolutionary ideals. "After all, that's what revolution is really about, isn't it?" Claude liked to say. "Lust. The right to love whom and what we want. Democracy, communism, republicanism. All great political upheavals have lust at their heart. Lutheran, Parisian, Napoleonic, the Russians. Revolutions occur when we decide to lust after something greater than the threat to our own life. Napoleon endures because he understood the fundamental truth that to love our own liberty is greater than anything this side of Eden."

"We'd do well to remember our histories," Claude would mutter when after a long day of schooling me on the true story of Europe, I'd finally coax him into his own bed, so to avoid being woken by the death-rush footsteps of Madame Framboise climbing the stairs with the morning's baguette, lest she think we'd spent the night together. If she ever thought such a thing, the entire clientele of Giovanni's bar downstairs would know by dusk. And the rest of Montmartre by midnight.

Claude would also sacrifice a good source of income since the men who frequented Giovanni's would now think Claude was giving it away for free, and I'd lose the air of mystery which followed me around. Sometimes I wondered if the reason Madame Framboise so enjoyed a drink with us was so she could judge the two of us together, and get the dirty on that most masculine of activity she loved to hear about.

The room we rented from Madame Framboise was more of an attic really.

Once upon a time Rue Duperré in Montmartre had been the beating heart of the Bohemian revolution—artists and painters living in the shadow of the sacred hill where Saint Denis had his head lopped off.

But this village within a village had long drifted from the heart-stopping citadel of hallucinogenic machinations it had once been a generation ago. The barren world painfully present in every photograph I developed of the scenery around our arrondissement. Empty chairs at café tables where once Toulouse-Lautrec got drunk. The watery doorways on rain-soaked cobbles that had once whispered inspiration to Cézanne and Gauguin. These days tourists ventured up here to take Mass at the Sacré-Cœur, gaze upon the flamboyant windmill atop the Moulin Rouge, or visit one of the ladies and gentlemen of independent means, as Claude described he and his coterie. Often all in the same day.

Ossified, gentrified, putrefied? Perhaps. But Montmartre was the reason I had come to Paris. And Claude was the friend, the brother, and sometimes even the self I'd always dreamed of being.

If only Claude and I could have found romantic love with each other, things would have been simple. And my story might never have been told. If love for men like us was as straightforward as love for men like them, I have a feeling so many of the stories Claude told me, would never need to be told. We queers are, like it or not, living history.

*   *   *

I saw the money Claude made. It was impossible not to, because he flashed it around like his fantasy was to be robbed in broad daylight. Which could very well have been the case. The pickups he entertained for fifteen minutes in the unlit cobbled alley behind the bar were not the source of Claude's riches. Far from it. The handful of francs he brought back to our table from each adventure merely covered room, board, and the wine we got drunk on.

No, it was the weekends Claude spent inexplicably away that brought home the big bucks. He'd leave without warning, leaving behind a note on my pillow that always started the same way.

In the likely event of my death, you may collect my remains from…

Followed by the address of some swanky hotel, or a villa in Le Touquet or Calais. Once he simply wrote *the south, I presume*, and returned with what sounded to me like a rather tall tale of a ménage a trois with a Spanish marquess and Italian duke in Monaco... but also a fistful of cash.

"We must invest this at once!" He'd declare, and drag me, arm in arm, up and down the boutiques of the Champs Elysée.

We played the same game each time. Claude would strut in first, hanging up the bowler hat he'd once swiped from a British lord, and announce to the clerk my impending arrival.

"The nephew of the last Austrian Emperor requires a tailoring for a rather special affair this evening. I need your full attention and best men on the case. We have only hours."

I'd watch Claude through the window, my hands clasped behind my back or thumbing the camera strung around my neck, pretending to browse the suits and shirts on display like the last Romanov, cousin of the Kaiser, or whatever else Claude was selling me as.

The clerks would snicker, or ignore him, or occasionally, yell at this oddly effeminate, practically malnourished young man to exit their shop immediately. At that moment, Claude would thump his bursting billfold on the counter like a prime piece of meat, and I would wander in and ask Claude, in overly accented French, if we would still have time to take tea at the Ritz.

Perhaps the clerks saw us for exactly what we were—a common whore and his admirer, spending ill-gotten gains as quick as we could. I wonder if we wore it so conspicuously. But money spoke louder than snobbish prejudice ever could. Their moustaches would twitch, eyeballs engorge, and with a snap of the fingers and a flick of the measuring tape, I would be ushered inside as the doors locked and Champagne was placed in our hands.

We had discovered early on in our affair that we wore the same size, apart from in the foot, where Claude was half an inch larger. I believe this was the nucleus of his scheme, following the one and only disastrous attempt to spend his earnings on a fine meal.

Those closed-door haberdashers and tailors were perhaps the only places in Paris Claude and I could truly be ourselves, outside of Giovanni's. There was no suspicious maître d' watching for a slip up in our silverware usage—

no patronizing waiter asking us if we could afford the meal we'd just ordered. Here, Claude had pre-paid for our ticket to luxury, and we reveled in every moment of it.

In the privacy of a men's dressing room, Claude could be as camp as the queer Kings of Europe he so admired. And more often than not, the clerks and the tailors would let their own guard down, and feel just a little freer in the presence of at least one screamingly obvious homosexual.

"The world is run from behind the closet door," Claude whispered to me once after a rather raucous laugh with an aging yet illustrious Italian jacket maker.

I pondered on his comment as I stood in my undershirt in front of the dressing room mirror and listened to Claude and Carlo debate the best way to accentuate my backside. Claude offered a commentary on the angles of my body, poking one butt-cheek while Carlo helped himself to the other.

"Carlo, it's a perilous time for European royalty. With all this fascism nonsense there soon won't be any countries left looking for a monarch to rule over them. We must marry off our young nobleman well, and this suit can make that happen. Look here." Claude snatched my camera from the dressing table and held it up to Carlo's eyes like a pair of opera classes.

"*Sí, sí*," Carlo agreed, as if agreeing that I didn't photograph very well, as he tightened up the fabric pinned around my inner thigh.

My life in Paris was lived almost entirely around homosexuals. Upstairs with Claude, downstairs at Giovanni's. Almost every professor at school, and of course the cliquey students who barely gave me the time of day. In all of my twenty years in Vienna I'd never even come close to encountering the number of us I interacted with on a daily basis here in Paris. And it was utterly wonderful. We were all outsiders. All of us feeling that little bit of difference, and that pressure and tension maligning itself into the most wonderful creativity, or fiercest tongue, or insatiable appetite for the flesh.

But the latter was a hunger I could not bring myself to satisfy. I subsisted on a diet of Claude's tales, imagining the scenes, picturing the bodies. Like some tale from Hades where the hungry man can only every smell the cooking— but not try it—I ingested every word and dove into the fantasy as soon as I was alone.

The frightened rabbit inside me took this for safety. I did not have to go and explore the world of men, because Claude could do it for me. He could describe his encounters in such vivid, lurid detail that I'd often need to share some of his cigarette afterwards.

"I am lucky," Claude told me on the occasional night we went all in on a bottle of something that could wipe the varnish from a table, "I am lucky to have moved away from the street and out of the parks. We're fortunate to live in our time, you and I."

"How so?"

"The Great War wiped a generation of men from this earth, and we are the sons of fallen fathers, the sons of single mothers. Raised free from the paternalistic dictatorship of our parents and grandparents. Even the men who did return came back broken, either in body or spirit. In all my life I have never been told off by an angry, older man, have you?"

I thought about it, but not for very long.

"No, actually. Even my schoolteachers were women."

"We are the forgotten generation. We can live in whatever way we want. Luckily for me, the way I want to live is entirely funded by the fathers of the generation that was lost. They no longer have sons to pass on their wealth to. Many more lost the rest of their pennies in the Depression. The world destroyed their dreams, then destroyed them again, and now they live out their days, giving in to every dormant whim and vice on offer. And *chérie*, I'm an all-you-can-eat buffet."

Claude lifted his wine glass and clinked it against mine, then downed the rest of it, let out a burp and clicked his fingers in the air.

"Giovanni, another bottle. Tonight we are drinking to the age of whores."

*   *   *

The weather grew colder, and we spent all our time downstairs in Giovanni's drinking right through to the end of 1936 as if it would bring the true summer closer. The basement bar saved up all the heat from the rest of the building via an old-fashioned wood-fired furnace that Giovanni himself kept constantly lit, the wood being brought in by strapping young men who would work at the chore in exchange for a drink and a night away from the cold.

I'd commandeered one of the catacombs as a dark room, hanging wet images from husks of firewood and between stacks of bottles, giving each image I developed a distinctive white blotch in the top left corner, my calling card perhaps. When I'd finally mastered the process, I was so excited by my alchemy that Madame Framboise framed one of the first images—a substandard shot of the Eiffel Tower taken from the Trocadéro—behind the bar with a proud nod. Gaily, I then had her critique the pictures I'd taken of Claude done up in his latest finery. I showed the photos to Giovanni when he was in the right mood, and to all the regulars Claude had, at one time or another, rejected *even if they offered me all the francs in France*. It was rather easy to elicit feedback on my composition, depth, and interplay of negative and filled space when the subject was the person they all loved to pass judgment on. When I showed Claude images I'd taken of Madame Framboise, his response was:

"She looks like an old whore."

"Oh dear. I wasn't intending to—"

"No, Anders. You've done it. You've captured her true self."

As she mopped up tables, scrubbed floors, and scratched entries in Giovanni's books, I realized where else would an old whore retire to than Giovanni's bar? There was something wonderfully familial about that place. It could've been the weathered faces of the elderly men who treated the bar like a social club, or the chipped, dirty mirror that ran along the length of the bar, creating the illusion of being in any other *tabac* anywhere in France. Or it could've been Giovanni himself, a swishy, mustachioed gentleman never without his red velvet waistcoat, whatever hair he had left slicked back with oil.

He greeted us all with a distant pleasure in his eyes, as if he knew and loved each of us individually, like a great uncle. But he wasn't a soft man, far from it. One quiet evening, the bar shook with fear as a police constable, complete with cap and cape, entered our establishment. He slammed the door shut, laid one hand on his truncheon, and glared around our little crowd with a superior smirk.

I was retching with fear, while the older sort began to drink up. But not with worry, more so with a sense of they were used to what was about to happen, and preferred to finish what they'd paid for.

Giovanni gave no quarter to any sense that something bad was about to befall us. Claude, who was born without a healthy fear of authority, began dictating a letter to my mother, gaily informing her of my arrest for debauchery. As I turned a horrendous shade of nipple pink, Giovanni smoothed down the thin hairs on his upper lip, refolded the towel across his arm, and addressed the officer of the law thusly:

"*Bon soi, monsieur.* I trust you are aware of the type of establishment you have walked into?"

"I believe I can gather the gist of it, yes," the officer replied, tightening the grip on his truncheon and narrowing his eyes at each of us. I thought I was going to be sick and looked around for an empty glass or dish while Claude kept asking why I wasn't taking down his version of my descent into vagrancy.

"Wonderful. May I fetch you a drink while you wait?"

"Wait? Wait for what?"

"Why, your turn, sir." The policeman's face became whiter than mine. Then he looked ready to smack Giovanni square in the mouth for even the slightest insinuation. "We are a fully licensed brothel, as I assume you know," Giovanni said. "But unfortunately we're a little understaffed at the moment. And what with the economy being what it is, finding a good woman to take care of my regulars is easier said than done."

The policeman glanced around at all of us once again. An assortment of a dozen men, sitting around doing very little but drinking our wines and waiting. Waiting for something that would likely never come. The love of our life, or the love for merely an evening. The policeman stayed silent; all his words had been stolen.

"I can take you to my office and show you the paperwork if you wish? But I've been running this establishment since 1910 without so much as a gentleman being shortchanged."

"Well, you have no women."

"That's my business, sir. But I assure you, Monsieur Proust is not hanging around these parts."

The officer considered his position. Giovanni stood before him, confidently smiling. Probably because he could see Claude sitting right next to me, so there was no risk in finding something incongruous occurring in the back alley should the policeman decide to poke his nose in.

Whatever he'd expected to find—men dancing together as a gramophone played or wandering off into a darkened room—wasn't happening. Even if the officer had found something worthy of an arrest, although the chance would be a fine thing at Giovanni's, the brothel license granted by the Parisian authorities covered all manner of sins. One could run a cock-fighting opium den without raising so much as an official eyebrow. As long as homosexuals were not openly copulating, and again, Claude was right beside me, our little bubble was, in theory at least, legally secure.

* * *

"Anders," Claude asked me one evening as we climbed five flights of creaking, spiraling stairs from Giovanni's to our attic room. "Why did you come here, of all places? Your mother could've sent you off to art school far closer to home. Why in Paris?"

I thought about my answer as we pulled ourselves up the last few breathless steps. Inside our studio, our freezing breaths further frosted the room. I dived under the blankets and wondered once again if throwing open the window would let in some warmth.

Claude began to ready for his night shift. Our schedules overlapped at Giovanni's. He slept most of the day and came down around eight or nine, as I made it back from school after wandering through yet another part of Paris, my camera at the ready. In those hours before I went to bed and before he headed out as a fully formed creature of the night, our friendship flourished.

Dragged up in all the fine clothes his immorality had accrued, I perfected the art of capturing the complexity of human life from behind a Kodak lens. In those roaring nights when Giovanni's came close to capacity, I was Claude's personal photojournalist, practicing visual tension in the anticipatory glances between Claude at the elderly man's lap he was about to sit on. I learned texture and contrast from the gnarled hands of an old shipman sliding up Claude's slim thigh. I studied movement and composition from monochrome portraits I took of Claude dancing on tables and Giovanni's backhanded threats to get the hell off them. But as much as our nights were filled with hijinks and my awakening quest for the pursuit of true beauty, we also used those sacred hours for discussing the very broadest mysteries of life.

Art, the Church, the Revolution, the Paris Commune, monarchy versus oligarchy, Franco, Da Vinci, the Thirty Years War; there was no concept nor notion we could not touch. No footnote too obscure, no theory too abstract, that could not have a home in our nightly salon.

All…but why I had come to Paris.

To ask me now, after so many months, of why I had come to Paris, seemed even more intrusive than the time he'd asked me to check his piles. Perhaps this is how we might come closer. For our friendship to dive off the cliff of mutual intellectual interest into a pool of deeply personal waters. The dark and murky kind which threatened to pull you under should your arms ever tire of keeping you afloat. Yet falling for Claude, like drowning, was not the way I wanted to go.

"*La Vie Bohème,*" I said with a sigh. The reasoning I'd so carefully constructed should the need ever arise to justify my presence here. I hoped it was good enough, there was no reason it shouldn't be. But still, my heart skipped as if a border guard was taking too long inspecting my papers.

But Claude did not turn away with a dismissive smirk or laugh or question me at all. He glanced over from the mirror where he was tying a bow tie under a starchy white collar, hands turning blue despite his insistence of never feeling the cold. With his blond hair oiled back, coat-tails dangling and white cotton gloves waiting patiently on the bed to be pulled on, he could have passed for a prince. Or at the very least, an earthly, monied lord.

"*La Vie Bohème,*" Claude chuckled. "Let me tell you why I think you're here." He returned to his own subdued reflection in the mirror, and I was glad he could not see the blood drain from my body like he'd pierced every artery with his genteel cackle. Illuminated only by the candle we kept for late nights after Madame Framboise had shut off the electricity, Claude straightened his tie. I watched his face turn somber, like he was dressing to perform the role of

13

pallbearer for an uncle he hated, rather than preparing for a night of guzzling overpriced champagne and playing with overpaid cock.

I closed my eyes in anticipation of the blow. It was coming, I could feel it. Claude was about to rip my carefully fabricated life apart.

"Henri Murger's *Scènes de la Vie de Bohème* was the first proper book Herr Anders read in French," Claude said, not untruly. I stayed silent, heart still pounding. "The young lad jerked off in his Lederhosen to fantasies of a wild Bohemian life, flirting with artists and sucking the dicks of the young, wild, and free of Montmartre.

"Then our little Aryan discovered Puccini, probably with his mother, at one of those fancy opera houses you Viennese love so much, before they all got draped in Swastikas." Claude, now satisfied with his bow tie, slipped his icy hands inside the white cotton gloves as I breathed out. He had not hit the mark.

"All the other boys with their *Mutters* are getting hard to Mimi, but our hero is fantasizing about Rodolfo, up on that stage in skin-tight leggings. And as he weeps over Mimi's death, our little Herr Anders concludes he must go to Paris, no matter if he cannot write nor paint nor draw. The Bohemian life is his calling, and he will go wherever it doth lead."

Claude turned around and stared at me with a sour face. Not angry, but weary. Like I was an ignorant child whom he'd had enough of for the day. He was ready to depart—dressed in a soldier's finery, prepared for battle on the field of love. His weariness was not for me. If anything, perhaps my green-eyed optimism had given him life these last few months. His weariness was for the world. Like a street cat no longer afraid of trucks or people. What was the point of being afraid when there could be treasures buried deep in those waste bins? This was Claude. A scrappy tom who quite literally survived on his ability to fear absolutely nothing.

"You're right, Claude. What can I say? I came to Paris to become Bohemian. Or at least be a tourist in this world. Even for a while. I don't know if I'm cut out for it, but at least I know I've found the best place to try."

"I hate to be the bearer of bad news," Claude said softly, sweeping a fur-lined cape around his shoulders and making for the door. "But Bohemia is dead, sweetheart. You're a generation too late."

14

Chapter 2

I HATED ART SCHOOL. Endless studies on perspective—class after class of still lifes that had the ironic effect of making me want to be enthusiastically dead—filled my dreaded days. I could barely hold a brush, let alone turn the strokes into anything even the most radical abstractionist could possibly decipher.

"Anders, what are you even doing here?" The impressionists master hissed at me after I'd fallen asleep in a lecture by some landscaper I was meant to revere.

I didn't have the wherewithal to tell him I never really cared for *traditional* art. My mother had simply been looking for a way to use her inheritance to get me out of Austria, and I was primarily concerned with traveling as far away from her as I could in order to lose my virginity—a feat which was inching ever further away from me the more time I spent with Claude and the frothy members of the homosexual working class he entertained in our nightly encampments at Giovanni's.

"Perhaps painting is just not my medium," I told the school masters. But my mother had already paid in advance for my two years of study. It was now incumbent on them to find an outlet for me.

Someone had gifted the school a state-of-the-art filming camera. The sort they used to make cinema. Nobody had a clue how to use it, or cared to learn, so it sat in the storage room, becoming the concern of the school secretary, who eventually introduced it to me.

"It's a Vinten Model H," the elderly clerk told me as he muddled around the cluttered shelves of wax fruit and mannequin parts, the camera waiting in the corner, moored to a tripod. Its double ears and lens like a nose faced the ground, giving it the air of a depressed dog in a world of cat worshipers.

"What does that mean?" I asked, wiping dust from it and the stack of virgin reels by its side.

"Damned if I know. But you look like a smart kid," he said, not looking at me, "I'm sure you'll figure it out."

Claude was right about one thing, or at least three. I could not paint, nor write, nor draw. And I had little else to do with the Vinten but film the lectures. Operating the camera at least kept me conscious. One day, I was setting up the clunky machine in a light-soaked studio. There's such a thing in moving image recording as too much light, which is less of a problem for still images. Too much sun turns the resulting movie into a harshly white, almost opaque scattering of figurines who were once people. Movies need far more of an artificial set-up than photography to capture reality.

I was rolling down shutters and blocking off windowpanes to keep the Vinten happy, when students began to file in. Classmates of a still life course I'd already been excused from. While I fiddled with blinds, wondering exactly what kind of movie I could make from filming a bowl of fruit or whatever it was they were supposed to be drawing, a stocky young man, chalk-blond with a creviced smile, walked into the studio. He disrobed in the manner of every other run-of-the-mill model, and sat his hairy backside on a stool in the center of the room while the students dampened their brushes and mixed their oils. But I didn't have an easel to hide behind, or a blank canvas to distract myself from the humongously handsome naked man in the room.

There was no hiding while handling a filming camera. The model's gaze wouldn't leave me, nor the Vinten, alone. I wondered if he thought I'd start shooting bullets from the barrel. Within the confines of that class, I learned to apply the visual arts to the moving arts, without prejudice to the resulting image. Unlike most of every one of my pictures which would be scoured over by Madame Framboise, Claude, or any of the assorted gentlemen at Giovanni's, none of the school masters had the remotest interest in viewing the results of what I shot on the Vinten. None even knew *how* to view the hours of lectures I'd filmed on the impressionists. The reels sat on shelves, gathering dust. As would the full-frontal movie of this model. I played with close ups, tracing beads of sweat down abdomen riverbeds. I broke the rules of composition, measuring my own erotic response to when the model's cock was in full view, to when only a hint of inner thigh was captured through the lens. Then the horror-like shock when, after minutes of stillness, the model stole the quickest scratch of his balls.

Happily, I left the Vinten set up in that very studio, and captured hour after hour of human nudes, running my own private masterclass on still life captured through film. With each reel I loaded and unloaded from the Vinten, I was ever more convinced that a single, perfectly captured frame is worth an hour of film. I longed to capture that singular elusive image, and I knew it wasn't going to come snapping pictures of Claude dressed in ill-gotten clothes.

Hot with anxiety at first, I stopped cowering under lampposts, hiding my camera like a kitten. I ventured and strode around the bustling anonymity of Paris, armed with my camera and my own sense that, despite what the school masters said, photography could be art. I could easily lose a day in the city's photogenic atmosphere. People talk about the night-time lights of Paris, the gas lamps covering the bridges or the electric bulbs on the Eiffel Tower, but there's nothing like the light from a Parisian sun on a bright, clear day. The sky is so impossibly wide, an unending vista from atop an Alpine peak.

In Paris there's no sea or mountains to encroach on the view. The endless open space is only pockmarked with the grand designs of great masters. Architecture birthed from an imperial mind, Napoleonic scenes in all their shocking glory.

I had fallen in lust with the Parisian style. More accurately, I'd fallen for Baron Haussmann. His touch had the breath of familiarity. The wide-veined boulevards in Paris directly inspired modern Vienna, in particular the *Ringstrasse* which circled the city.

The newness of Paris dropped against a city so old in spirit electrified me like a streetcar. The Paris of my imagination drawn from the pages of Henri Murger was of tightly woven streets draped over cobblestone alleyways. A

Victor Hugoesque labyrinth that bred revolution and fire. The capital of Bohemia, and all its people.

But that was not the only Paris. There was another city, generally hidden to the casual observer, that bloomed in the most unexpected ways. Hidden Paris existed like a re-founded capital constructed on the ashes of the old. To the untrained eye, modern Paris was birthed from the marble-white mausoleum dreams of Napoleon III, a city constructed atop forgotten ghostly graves of revolutionaries and the damned. But there was another Paris, slithering in and out of sight. Slight suggestions of what the city had once been, carried on the backs of those who'd once torn down great empires from these narrow streets. The secret city fascinated me. Capturing that spirit, the essence of something lost, became an obsession I freely obligated myself to in want of any pleasures of the flesh.

I would walk down Rue Lafayette all the way to *L'église de la Madeleine*, seeking out the secrets hidden between marble colonnades. And every so often I would spot it. An old, decrepit widow crossing the boundary of a modernist road like a ravaged mouse slinking across a marble floor. Gypsy children playing amongst the quadratic lines in the Jardin des Tuileries as mites would dance around a stained-glass lamp. Even the clawed, spindly walls of a long-lost hovel sinking beneath concrete reminded me of a Ship of the Line frozen in an Arctic wreck.

These people who felt like they did not belong, but did not know why. Indigenous Parisians infused with the blood of a storied city, unable to find their way about. The rebellious zeal of the populace, floating away in the masterful drainage system. An entire metropolis designed for armies to march triumphantly down the avenue, or artillery to park themselves at the intersection of a revolution and blow the sans culottes to smithereens.

But my attraction to Paris, and its depths of light magnificently draped over newfangled art deco buildings stuccoed against baroque spires, was quite different to the way Bohemia stirred my soul. Yet here they were together, on my very doorstep. Two worlds in one, filled with a million lives.

Plato says man has three parts to his soul: *logos, thymos* and *eros;* reason, emotion, and desire. On the surface, the city of Paris drew me in through reason. I grasped the subtle intimidation of wide streets or the Gothic beauty of Notre

18

Dame through logical enquiry. Its beauty sprang from the mind of a genius.

Bohemia stirred my emotions. A longing for freedom, beauty, truth and love. Abstract concepts lived out loud, beyond the strict lederhosen world I'd grown up in. It was beautiful because it was inspiring. Even the haughtiest traditionalist, my grandmother, for instance, could appreciate a good counter-cultural play, even if she did so from her private box wrapped in a fur.

Desire… well I hadn't given it too much thought. Proximity to Claude, perhaps. Nights at Giovanni's with one eye on the door, waiting for someone to step inside, take my hand and make love make sense.

Spring was breaking through and my desires achingly no closer to being fulfilled. With the growing length of the days I could venture farther with my camera and take advantage of all the light I could in between school, Claude, and processing my rolls of film in Giovanni's cellar.

Desire would have to wait. Man can survive on just one element—*logos*, *thymos*, or *ergos*—he can take his pick. He can live quite happily with two out of three. Many millions do so without complaint. But man cannot thrive without all three. This I knew as well as the breath in my lungs. Paris was reason and emotion, but absent of desire.

Until I met Jean.

* * *

I was hanging around the Jardin du Luxembourg after venturing all the way across the Seine on one particularly bright Saturday in early March. Claude was away all weekend on business in Le Touquet, and I'd decided to make the most of the pleasant afternoon light.

I'd been taking pictures of *le marchand de masques*, trying to catch the illumination of Zacharie Astruc's sculpture as the light bled through the still-bare winter trees. But I wasn't convinced I was having much success. I wanted to catch the sun shining against the bronze face of Victor Hugo, but the shadows did not work in my favor.

At least I was alone in this tract of the park with only the spindly trees and watchful crows for company. I stood back and lit one of the rare cigarettes I smoked, wondering whether to wait for the sun to set.

19

With my camera slung across my back like a musket, the fur of my coat keeping the chill from my neck as the smoke curled into the air, I felt like a lonely soldier watching the frontier. The last thing I was expecting was for someone to sneak up on me.

"*Avez-vous du feu?*" I spun around in slight surprise. A resplendent man stood a little too close, burning my eyes with his incandescent allure, even though he was only asking if I had a light. The man's skin as black as ink, and he wore a tweed jacket and flat cap like an English country gent. He raised a solitary cigarette in the air just like the sculpted child grasping the disembodied face of the great Victor Hugo. He was smiling, broadly, showing off the whitest teeth and an impish grin I was already bewitched by. My smiling back was mere enchanted reflex.

"Yes," I replied eventually. "Of course. Here you are."

I handed him a matchbook. But he didn't cast his used match to the ground like Claude always did. Instead, he dropped it in his coat pocket, smiled at me once again, and asked:

"Are you a German spy?"

"I beg your pardon?"

"Out here taking pictures." He looked me up and down as if searching for evidence that would prove my innocence. "You're clearly not Parisian."

I knew that was true but wondered how he knew. I'd barely spoken a dozen words.

"Oh?" I said, shaking out my finished cigarette and casting an eye for a place to properly dispose of it. If this man could so casually accuse perfect strangers of being foreign agents, then what might he to do those who threw their waste on the ground.

"Parisians pronounce *oui* as *weh*." My accuser took a long, leisurely draw and stood like he was leaning against an invisible tree. "You don't look English, or German either for that matter. But there's a note of something about you, almost Eastern European."

"And what makes you so perceptive?"

"When people spend so much time staring, you stare back. You notice things. That's what I do. Observe people, and notice things."

"It does rather sound like you're the one who's the spy," I said.

He smiled and stuck out a hand. I expected a firm, bone-crunching grip, but his touch was potent energy, coiled in the breathless, two-toned shade of his elegant hands.

"I'm Jean."

"Anders. From Vienna, as it happens. And I'm a photographer."

"Yes, I figured from the camera. Funnily enough I'm in want of a portrait or two."

Jean spoke the words into being with a smile that would not retreat. From atop the high structure of his statuesque face, a look of wonder bathed me in excited delight. The spark imperceptible to brutish men who crashed through the delicate world us others inhabited. This second city, alongside the obvious one. A city of lingering glances, soft handshakes, and gentlemen asking each other for matchbooks.

"Well it seems we should talk," I said, sticking my hands in my pocket while still holding the butt. I felt the friendly distance between us shrink, then spark with a tension I could only guess was sexual.

"Well, Anders, it seems we should. Care to join me for a stroll?" Before I could answer Jean moved forward and linked his arm through mine. My heart racing, I glanced behind, but there was no one around.

"I'd love to."

*   *   *

"I want to be a model," Jean told me later that evening over gin's at Giovanni's. "I know it sounds stupid... shallow. But it's always been my dream. It's not even about the clothes. It's the fact..."

"What? Tell me."

"No. It sounds better in my head."

"You can tell me."

"I've never seen anyone like me modeling clothes. At least not for men." We'd talked our way across half of Paris, all the way back to Montmartre. Jean knew all about Giovanni's, not that I'd had any suspicions to the contrary. That night it was busy, with the kind of bustle and hustling Claude and I tended to duck out of. We sat at the bar, the corner between us, soaking up

21

the coveting glances those falling in love are too oblivious to notice.

"You certainly have the look for it," I said sincerely. Without his cap and coat, Jean radiated beauty like a sun. No wonder he covered up so much in public. Every feature of his face could have been carved by Donatello out of pure onyx. Every word he spoke tempted me ever further towards luscious burgundy lips.

"I'm serious, Anders. I know how vapid it must sound, but I know how I look. I've seen how people stare. A beautiful woman can walk into any boutique on Avenue Foch and be on a catwalk in a fortnight. A man like me can't even get through the door."

"That's horrendous. How can they ignore you like that?" I said, not even caring if I was nothing but a business opportunity if it got me one inch closer to tasting Jean's lips. But the idea of lost dreams distracted me even from the potential for a kiss. "I can't believe they behave in such a way. Even in Paris?"

"If I have a portfolio, then I can mail it to the designers. Show people at the fashion houses. Someone else could drop it into the boutiques for me, maybe even you."

I told him I'd be happy to. Claude and I were in and out of enough of them.

Jean gazed at me with something beyond wonder. Perhaps for him it was the magic key of the camera resting on the bar, perhaps for me it was the elixir of a man seeking me out, subtly offering the promise of his skin. Jean's gaze was enchanting, and I longed to be spell-bound. Giovanni's could have been full of the men of my surface-level dreams, but next to him, I did not care to turn and look.

Still, some part of me understood this transaction. I was an easily manipulated young man with a camera, he was a stunning sculpture with a desire to be looked at. I could be staring down into a pit of unrequited love. But there were Jean's lips inducing me to dive in.

"Like I said," my voice barely a whisper. "I'd love to help."

"Thank you, Anders, truly." He clasped my hands in his and our fingers weaved into a checkerboard. But then he slipped away before I had a chance to commit the grasp to eternal memory. Jean sipped his gin and cast a probing shadow around the raucous bar I'd all but forgotten was there.

"Why don't we start first thing tomorrow?" I asked, not wishing to leave our next meeting to anything resembling chance.

"Are you sure?"

"Of course. The light is best in the morning, and tomorrow should be as clear as today. We could start at the Sacré-Cœur and work our way down to the Boulevard de Clichy. I'm imagining you standing in the center of Pigalle while the traffic circles around. I think it could be quite stunning."

Jean smiled. That's all I wanted.

"It sounds like you have quite an eye, Anders."

"See that picture," I said, pointing behind Giovanni who had been studiously ignoring me all night, perhaps in solidarity with an absent Claude, I wasn't sure. "That's the first picture I successfully developed here. Well, second really. It's nothing special. I went up to the *Trocadéro* at night and truly saw why Paris is the city of lights. I'm sure some aesthete would walk in here and call it essentialist, or just derivative, but after a week of duds and too may ruined rolls of film to count, I was quite relieved to get the process right."

"It's stunning," Jean said with every note of sincerity. "The way you captured the movement in the lights, the reflections from the puddles, the people taking in the view. It's like a Matisse, but... real."

"Matisse painted in color." Giovanni suddenly chimed in, apparently eavesdropping, his thin moustache twitching around the aroma of scandal. "Another round, boys?"

"No, not for me," Jean said. To my horror, he got up from the stool and took his jacket from the hook under the bar. "My photographer here wants me up bright and early for tomorrow's shoot. I'd better get home before it's time to return."

I could've cursed Giovanni from now until the end of time. I felt the sands of my chance slip through my fingers. A chance for what I hadn't yet figured out, but I didn't want it decided for me.

"You can stay here," I blurted out, to a raised eyebrow from Giovanni but a grin from Jean.

"Are you sure?" Jean asked, holding his jacket and glancing briefly at the Italian as if waiting for permission.

"Why not?" I said before an objection could be raised. "I live right upstairs, and my roommate is away until Monday. We can get an early start before the crowds come for Mass."

"Wonderful," Jean said, hanging his jacket back on the hook. Before sitting down, he pulled out his billfold and slapped a twenty franc note down on the bar. Giovanni could disapprove all he wanted, but money talked, and he skulked away. "Oh, what was the first?"

"First?"

"Yes. The first photograph you developed successfully?"

"You don't want to see that."

"I do."

I sighed, but as an excuse to glance around the bar. Most of the collective attention had gladly drifted away from us, knowing we were a closed circuit and a waste of time. From my own billfold I pulled a creased picture. Jean wiped down the bar with his sleeve.

"My mother and grandmother." Jean nodded as he gazed with me, backwards in time and across the continent. The two women smiled back, lounging on the couch with our broad window behind them, streetlamps reflecting back. They both held schnapps glasses and cigarettes, having agreed to pose only because I repeatedly asked. "It was all lights and movement in our apartment that night. I'd only started with the camera so didn't particularly know what to do. This is the only picture that made it."

"They look like fun."

"They are. My mother, though, she's deathly afraid of war and wanted me to be as far from any front line as possible."

"Do you miss them?"

"If I returned home, I fear I might miss Paris more."

* * *

"It's freezing up here," Jean said as I led him upstairs.

"Believe me, it gets worse."

I flicked the temperamental electric light on, illuminating the attic Claude and I shared. Clothes were heaped on his bed, the mound of silk shirts and cashmere sweaters piled higher than the metal bed frame.

"My God," Jean said, "look at these clothes."

"And there's a whole wardrobe more behind you," I said, pointing behind.

"But this is a custom-made Madeleine Vionnet," Jean said, clutching a beige cardigan like a dying child. "And… Chanel? I didn't think she even made men's clothes." He held up a double-breasted blazer Claude had me fitted for after a week in the Dardanelles with a particularly generous duke.

"What we save on rent he spends on clothes."

"I can see."

Jean pawed through a lifetime savings' worth of garments as I collapsed onto my bed, the champagne he'd insisted on, to celebrate our new partnership and spite Giovanni, rushing to my head.

Slowly—because I was quite drunk—a scheme fomented in my mind.

"Why don't you try some on?"

"Are you serious?" He asked, glancing around as if Claude might burst out from under the bed and catch him red handed.

"Sure," I lunged for my camera, knocking my elbow sharply on the bedside table. "I wear them all the time. And we can send the designers a few shots of you actually wearing their clothes. Good idea, no?"

"I suppose." Jean's attention drifted back to the clothes. He picked up the blazer again.

"No, no," I said, climbing back onto my feet. "You need a whole outfit. Here, I'll help."

Together, we sorted through Claude's things like a couple of thieves. I knew if Madame Framboise caught the light on at this hour, and for this long, she'd be up here like a shot. But I didn't care. Jean was already unbuttoning his shirt.

I didn't have the sobriety to keep from staring, and I'm not sure if he had it to notice. His body had been on my mind since the moment we'd met, and now, the flesh was appearing in front of me, piece by piece. He stripped to a perfectly white undershirt that clung like a second skin to every sinew of muscle across his broad, sculpture-smooth torso.

Even with my eyes closed, I would've been aroused. The hints of his scent my nose had been chasing after like a bloodhound throughout the day intoxicated my senses. Claude always smelled like the perfume counter in the Galerie Lafayette, and the men I used to spy on in the gymnasium in Vienna either stank of stale sweat or waxy soap.

Jean was all man. Pure leather mixed with sexual desire. Arms bare, he didn't reach for the clothes we'd agreed on. Instead, he kicked off his boots and dropped his trousers in a smooth, faultless motion, revealing a pair of undershorts even whiter than his vest.

"Stand right there," I said, taking a much-needed step back. Jean looked at me straight on. His mouth dropped into a deadly stare—a lustful pocket of dangerous desire that catwalk models perfected. He stood still, arms folded, as I began to photograph him in the sharp electric light. I took pictures like this could be my last night. The continent was spinning and a war could break out to serrate our lives before we even had a beginning, let alone an ending.

We both lost ourselves to our respective fantasies, connected on either side through the lens of a camera. I shot him from every angle the room would allow, in every pose, wearing almost every item of clothing on Claude's bed. Each time he asked if I'd had enough, I quietly asked for another pose.

More lips, more hips. Less head, less leg. Look at the camera, look away. Lean towards the window, lean back. Jacket open, jacket closed. Top off, legs spread, spread even more. Turn away, turn back, bend down, get closer... get closer.

*   *   *

"Anders... Hey, Anders?"

Sun was pouring sharply through the window. My head was thumping and a figure who I simply knew was not Claude was gazing down at me.

"You slept well," Jean said. I tried to recall the night, working forwards from the last thing I remembered. We talked for hours downstairs, until Giovanni turned the lights out. I took him upstairs, and...

I glanced over at Claude's bed. All the clothes that had been scattered over it like thousand-franc bed sheets had been neatly folded and placed back on the covers. The bed itself looked like a legionnaire had made it. Jean had slept there. I just hoped it was not due to my foolery.

"I hope we got some good shots last night," he said, staring out the sunny window, shirt buttoned and ready for the day, "and the weather's nice."

Simply as himself he looked divine. Jean was one of those people who didn't need a single thread from a designer. Claude did. Without the fashion-house satins, he would fade away into a crowd. Disappear into the background like a gossamer postcard on an amphitheater's stage.

Jean, on the other hand, took up all the space available with some simple threadbares. He didn't need an outsize presence or a cruel, cutting visage disguised as wit. No, the little quirks of personality the members of our community must cultivate to stand out from the crowd was as much needed as Zeus needs a suit of armor. Jean had that one true quality one need not dress up, pimp out or inflate—magnetic beauty. An attraction that shone through in spite of even the most expensive and exotic silk. I was convinced it would be apparent in the shaky projections of the Vinten, too. I had been dying to ask him to get in front of the film camera. But I feared inviting him to live model in a class where I didn't even paint would be too coarse a question, make it too voyeuristic of me. Particularly when art school remained the purview of proper society—of professors, of my mother and my late father's money. Jean was that second city. The secret world that, for so long of my life, had only played out in my mind. It scared me to slam those worlds together.

"Ready?" He asked with a grin that sliced through my hangover. If he'd asked me to sell all my worldly possessions, along with Claude's, I would've responded the same way.

"Yes."

*   *   *

I passed the next few days locked away from the world in my dark room. I didn't want to see a soul until it was time to show Jean how the photographs turned out. Lucky for me, school was broken up for Easter, for I would not have even pretended to concentrate, or even show up.

Finally, the hour came—for I measured my developing time in hours—to show Jean how the pictures turned out.

On a cloudy Thursday, with my mood stormy and nervous for the coming evening when we would meet for only the second time (as I counted our first nineteen hours together as one complete event), I pulled the final images together in a leather binder previously holding my matriculation certificate.

"You left some important documents lying on the floor," Claude said coolly as I crept into our room. He was perched on the edge of the bed, blond locks wrapped in a towel turban, applying foundation to his cheeks while holding up a hand-held mirror.

Since he'd returned from his weekend away, I'd felt like a guilty husband creeping around a suspicious wife. Claude had come back to a perfectly made bed—clothes piled neatly, floor swept and sink bleached. I daren't breathe a word about Jean. Giovanni had been on the receiving end of some rather harsh looks, which had sent him the same message to keep quiet. Yet still, Claude demonstrated a chilly distance.

"I put them under your pillow."

"Oh, thanks," I said, saving myself from starting to wonder if he was holding them hostage.

"What's in the folder?" Claude asked with no other reason than to fill the silence as he dabbed at his cheek bones with a sponge.

"Nothing interesting. Just some pictures for a client."

Claude turned to me with a great big grin, like he'd suddenly uncovered some great secret.

"A *client*? Herr Anders! Well I never. I did wonder what you got up to while I was away. Now I guess the cat's out the bag."

"No, no, no. Nothing like that. I'm not prostituting myself." Claude returned one raised eyebrow. "Sorry, that's not what I meant."

"I should hope not." He returned to dabbing powder on his face. "Your accusations are a legal fiction, Monsieur Magistrate. A man cannot register as a prostitute under the laws of France."

"So that's how you've walked out of so many court houses."

Claude grinned, and the tensions between us thawed instantly.

"Now who is this mystery client of yours? And more importantly, what kind of photographs have you been taking?" Claude asked with a naughty, knowing smile. He'd often, in a somewhat drunken state, begged me to take images of him in the nude, or even with a client or two. 'For posterity!' He'd declare. 'I won't always be so young and comely.'

28

"He's coming to pick them up very soon, actually. And I shouldn't show them to you before he's seen them. It's not right." I thumbed the folder, nervous to see them myself under a normal light. "It's a shame you're working tonight, otherwise you could have met him." I breathed out a sigh of relief at the hint Claude would be coming nowhere near Jean this evening. I was hoping this trip up to my room might lead to a little payback.

"Well you're in luck!" Claude said, snapping the mirror shut. "The bishop telephoned half an hour ago to cancel. So, I'm all yours, my darling."

"Oh… wonderful."

"Let's see if this client is impressed with your skills. And who knows? I might commission you myself. Did I tell you I've been considering taking out an advertisement in Le Monde?"

"Le Monde?"

"Yes, the newspaper. With only a picture of my face and the words: 'Do you recognize this man? If so, send a banker's draft of one thousand francs or the world will learn of how you like to get spanked with a leather belt.'"

"Just finish powdering your nose; he'll be here shortly. And you take some time getting used to."

We took our usual spot downstairs. Claude had to bring the drinks as I was a bundle of nerves. My eyes kept flicking to the door as if I'd been tipped off to a raid. The folder of photographs sat on the table between us—a weight dragging our conversation down.

"Aren't you the nervous Nancy," Claude said, smiling gleefully. "I do wonder why. I bet the photos are pornographic." I checked the clock, already five past six. I was too nervous to even shake my head. "They're filthy, aren't they? Pictures of naked bodies writhing in and out of each other. My, my, I did wonder what you got up to while I'm away."

"They aren't pornographic."

"Well darling, maybe they should be? That's not a bad business. I myself would pay handsomely for such an album. I could bind it in hardback and—"

"There he is," I said, relieving myself from the interminable conversation with Claude and rushing across the empty bar to greet Jean. As he planted a third kiss on my cheek, a look of laughable surprise swept over his face as he saw who was sitting behind me.

"I say," Claude said as we approached the table, "look who it is."

"Claudia," Jean said with a smirk drenched with caustic disdain.

"You two know each other?"

"Like syphilis," Claude shot back, sipping his wine. "Anders, how on earth did you become acquainted with this vagabond?"

"He approached me in the park, actually," I said as I slid back into my seat, very aware of the hard-edged silences and chilled smiles.

"Hmph," Claude snorted, "speaks volumes."

I glanced quickly at Jean, then harshly at Claude.

"I think the pictures turned out not too bad, actually. Jean, we can take a look and you can tell me how many copies—"

"What are your intentions with young Anders here?" Claude asked like a suspicious father investigating a future son-in-law.

"Simply business."

"Charging him by the hour, are you?"

"No," I said, still not quite grasping the subtext, "I'm providing the service. I agreed to photograph Jean for his modeling portfolio."

"Modeling?" Claude scoffed again. "The only thing he can model is a thirty-centimeter dick. And believe me, half of Paris has already seen it."

I didn't know what to say.

"Oh behave," Jean said calmly, "you're scaring the poor boy. Now drink your wine and let's take a look."

I opened the cover of the folder where my certificates of achievement should have been. The art shows I'd competed in and swimming competitions I'd won like any normal boy from Vienna. In truth, after removing my gymnasium transcripts, there'd been little else to show for my life. And as I'd peeled back the film to place the photos of Jean inside, I couldn't have cared less about my anonymity. Capturing this man's beauty was worth a lifetime's accomplishments. It was undeniably satisfying to smooth the film back across the pictures, corner smudges included. Softly to myself, I smiled. Even if my life amounted to nothing more, at least I'd captured one frame of beauty.

"Is that it?" Claude asked, peering over my shoulder at Jean dressed in clothes I eagerly hoped Claude wouldn't recognize. "Perhaps you truly are a bohemian," Claude said, getting up from the table, throwing back the dregs of his wine. "Obsessing over trash and dressing it up as treasure."

In real life, Jean was head-turningly handsome. I knew not just from my own eyes, but those of the men who'd crowded Giovanni's last Saturday night. Each one stabbing us with bayonets of jealousy as we laughed and joked and drank.

And then I understood the thing Claude once told me in front of a statue of Philip, King of the Franks. Life had no other meaning than the race to capture the fleeting beauty that lit this otherwise dark, cruel world like a warm fire.

Claude mercifully found a man by the bar he hadn't yet propositioned. Finally alone, Jean and I leafed through the reams of photos, picking out the top three he would take to the fashion houses.

"Only three?" I asked, worried at the thought of being judged, and not Jean being judged, but me. His beauty was undeniable. My skill with a camera, a little shakier. Untested, like that of a hastily repaired chair. "But you have so many different looks. And so many we didn't yet try."

"Like what?"

"Well…" I tried to clear my throat. I wanted Jean to say it, not me. "Like more of just… your body." Jean tinkled with quiet laughter. I was keen to test the skills I'd learned exploring the human form with the Vinten. That it's not simple, face-forward beauty the photographer, or film operator, is attempting to catch, but the *promise* of more beauty to come in the next image or frame. The magic is in anticipating what's not yet been shown. A striptease and a life model achieve the same end, but through wildly different means. Means I dreamed of trying out with Jean. If I couldn't ask him as a man to unbutton his shirt and remove his pants, at least I could ask him as an artist.

But instead, I turned the cardboard page.

"This is a good one, with the scarf," I said, sinking my teeth into my lip so I would not say any more.

"Oh yes. Although I'm not sure what Coco Chanel would make of me wearing her scarf."

*   *   *

Hitler seizes Austria. German troops march through Vienna as Treaty of Versailles lies in tatters.

An elderly man at the table beside us smoking a pipe ruffled his newspaper, attacking me with the blaring headline.

We didn't speak as Jean ordered us coffee near Les Invalides one spring morning. We were taking a break from shooting. Yet everyone was now under siege by headlines at every newsstand and *tabac*. Jean and I had been living for many weeks in a fantastical world, in perpetual hope that the next shot, angle, setting, would deliver a modeling contract to Jean. Everything we shot and developed leading further away from reality and towards that second, sub-rosa city of French Bohemia. And suddenly here was that hard, material world crowding in.

"What's wrong with you?" Jean asked, raising his collar against the bitter wind.

"Nothing," I mumbled, and took one of his cigarettes. Nothing but headlines, I could have said.

"Ah," Jean said, lighting up a cigarette as our coffee arrived. I seized the cup with both hands, letting the warmth unchill my fingers crisp from the camerawork. "All your family is in Vienna still."

"My mother and grandmother," I said, keeping my voice low for an unfathomable reason. I was in Paris, not Vienna. There were no Nazis marching down the street. Riding bicycles along the road, their baskets stuffed with baguettes. Or sitting with a pipe and a paper, or serving us coffee, or directing traffic. These were Frenchmen. In France, I was safe.

"Your mother doesn't approve of Nazis?"

"Not really. She's a socialist. Was a socialist, at least. Back when there used to be elections."

"And your father? Was he also an Austrian socialist?"

I smiled. "I don't know, actually. We never met. He was an officer in the Imperial Army, and he died before I was even born." I don't know why it made me feel wistful, talking about him now. But it did. My childhood had been filled with second-hand stories of my father. I'd pieced together the image of a heroic but foolhardy man, utterly brave and incredibly loyal, sacrificing himself on a field of carnage to protect his men. The evidence of him delicately laid out in my mother's glass-doored cabinet. The medals he won, the saber he wielded, his hat and the stripes of his rank conferred upon him by the Emperor. I tried to let the rational logic of it sink in. My father's memory would surely afford my mother whatever protection she might need with the authorities.

"My father was a soldier too," Jean said. "One of the Senegalese *Tirailleurs*. I met him a few times when I was a child. After the war he came to visit my mother, and me." Jean began to laugh. "He wanted to take us back to Africa to live with his other wives! My mother was none too keen."

"I should say."

"Especially since my mother's whiter than even you." Jean drained his coffee and stubbed his cigarette out in the ashtray. "Funny thing, fathers. They say an absent one is the cause of our abnormality. A lack of masculine influence, so I've heard. But if it wasn't for war, your father would still be around. And mine, well, I'd probably never have been born. So who's fault is that, then?"

"Fault?"

"Yes, fault." Jean kept staring at me like I owed him an explanation. "The reactionaries who've seized the state and sold off the Third Republic!" He said, grinning and slapping my shoulder. "The capitalist fat cats made us this way. They cause the wars and pocket the profits, they take fathers away from sons, leaving us to grow up among our mothers and grandmothers, so we never know what a true male role model looks like. And of course, what choice do we have but to spend our lives trying to fill that father size hole in our hearts with love from other men whose fathers were also absent, and also left them wanting. We're all just lonely men, looking for another lonely man to make us feel a little less lonely."

"You're lonely, Jean" I drilled into his eyes like I had nothing left to lose. I did not prefer to dabble in the Jew-baiting conspiracy echoed in Jean's regurgitated readings of the communist newspapers.

"I have you," he answered with a smile.

"You've never had me."

"You've never offered me what I want."

"And what's that?"

But Jean didn't answer. He stood up from the table, stretched and sighed as if I was already five minutes over my time.

"Come," he said, throwing down a few francs on the table, "we've got pictures to take."

*   *   *

"You know I never saw your cock when we tried to have sex?" Claude said from his bed while puffing on a long thin opium pipe, as he sometimes did when the weight of the world eclipsed his normal good cheer. I'd only just stepped in the door from my day with Jean; I hadn't even taken my coat off or unhooked the camera from my shoulder. Perhaps news of the Anschluss had affected him, too.

"I, uh, don't really recall."

"I do. It was the first night we met. We were drunk, you more than me. Madame Framboise whispered to me it was probably the first time you'd ever been drunk. We went upstairs and I kissed you."

"Oh?"

I remembered every moment of that evening. How could I forget. New and alone in a strange city, in a place I'd always dreamed of. Letting myself be swept up in the potential to be someone else. To write one's own story, free from the expectations of others. There are only a few precious moments, hours even, when one is dropped into new surroundings with such a chance. One must hold fast to that new identity; to seize it, to embrace it with all one's might and let it devour any last vestiges of the person one used to be.

I had tried, but ultimately failed to recalibrate myself in these new surroundings. I reverted to the person I always was, always would be. The one watching life through a camera lens, Jean drifting further from me with every shot I took of him. My love remaining ever unrequited, desires ever unfulfilled.

"You didn't know what to do with a man," Claude continued. "Giovanni didn't think you'd even kissed one."

"So?" I swallowed sharply, flushed with all the pinpricks Claude jabbed at me. Unable to bat them away and wondering for what greater purpose he was skewering me so.

"Well we did kiss," Claude said and took another puff from the pipe, "I remember."

"Then you ran your hands over my body like you'd spent all your twenty-one years waiting to do so. You grabbed, you pinched, you acted like a vulture ripping apart a carcass, terrified that the next bite might be your last."

I remained by the door, coat still on, camera still under my shoulder, gasping for shallow breaths as I tried to sniff out the threads of questions Claude was asking.

"I stripped off," he said, his glassy, opium-dilated pupils staring at me from across the room, "and you couldn't stop watching me. I thought, there's someone who's never willfully been so close to another naked human being. I let you take me in your mouth because I felt sad for you, Anders. Even though you were all teeth. Actually, you probably weren't that bad. I just know how good I am."

Claude blew out a ring of smoke as he grinned. Not at me, but past me. Like I hadn't already heard all about his special skills.

"Anyway, after that you fell flat onto the bed, on your stomach, pulled down your pants and said do whatever you want to me. Now, I can penetrate. Believe me I can do all manner of things you can't even comprehend. But I figured trying to fuck you after you'd so spectacularly failed to even suck my cock wouldn't be the best start to our friendship."

"Does any of this have a point, Claude?"

"I'm getting there. And in all the time we've known each other, you've consummated your obvious feelings for men exactly zero times. Am I wrong?"

I said nothing. Whatever his game was, I didn't feel like playing along anymore.

"I'm not wrong, am I? You're infatuated with Jean, I understand that. I understand why. But a whore doesn't give himself up for nothing. You had half a chance when you started taking his portrait. Not anymore. Now the two of you are in business together, and while a whore might, on occasion, sleep with a man out of simple attractiveness, he certainly won't sleep with a fellow whore."

"I beg your pardon?"

"You are a whore, Anders. True, you may not take your clothes off and do unspeakable things for money, but you enable them. You take pictures of Jean and he distributes them up and down Rue de Sebastopol, sticking them inside telephone boxes and lavatories with a post office box written on the back."

"I… I didn't know."

"What, you thought he was trying to model? Did you really believe he was waltzing up and down the Champs-Élysées handing out his picture to the great fashion houses of Paris? Not really. But Jean has broken boundaries. He's the first whore in Paris with a personal photographer. He's taken his business off the street, and into the almost respectable world of postcards and money orders. So you've done one thing, Anders. You've revolutionized the business of prostitution in Paris."

"I'm… sorry?"

"Oh, I don't care. I've got a client list as long as Jean's cock, I'm not taking on new business." Claude began to grin again, and then laugh. "But just so you know, the whores of Paris have found a new enemy, and he's known only as the cunt with the camera who takes stunning portraits of the man we all know as Jean. So bear that in mind the next time the two of you go off on your next little adventure. If they don't try to smash your face in, they'll want to pay a small fortune to have their own picture taken."

"This is your point?" I asked, a little confused by the anti-climax from what I feared. "Giving me, what, business advice? Suggesting I become the official portrait taker of the Parisian street worker?"

Claude stopped laughing. His face dropped to deadly serious, and he clutched the pipe like foil, jabbing it in my direction.

"My point is, Anders, why in Paris? Disposing of one's entire life to start from scratch in a far away city may seem like the stuff of opera, but it's utterly reckless, and you're not the type to be reckless for no good reason.

"It's clearly not for the sex, because you're not having any. And what, there's no whores in Vienna to take pictures of? No Aryan bodies to spy on in the swimming pool? And don't give me that nonsense about being in love with Bohemia. You're as far from being a Bohemian as I am from being pope. So why, Anders? Why are you here?"

"I'm going to leave," I said quietly, "and return once you've put away your opium pipe."

Chapter 3

IN THE LATE SUMMER sunshine, I passed many a pleasant afternoon by the banks of the Seine. War becoming a distant impossibility, something to worry screaming newspaper columnists, not ordinary folk. Notre Dame stood behind me, as imposing and gaudy as ever, just as it had for a thousand years. But instead of pilgrims, these days it drew tourists in a never-ending wave. Like the Huns throwing themselves against the walls of Rome, they came. The Italians in their linen suits, the English in their bowler hats, the Americans with their Kodak cameras yelling loudly where to get a hot dog.

I even noticed Germans. Tall, blond Aryan couples speaking quickly together in low, hushed tones behind a paper map lest someone hear their guttural speech and chase them from the cobbled streets.

As one more street vendor on the *Île de la Cité*, I saw it all without a care. I did little else but sit back on the folding beach chair I brought with me every day, displaying my wares on the miniature trestle table which folded into a suitcase to carry home when the sun set, or until I had sold all my prints.

I called my collection 'Hidden Treasures of Paris.' Every day I hung a dozen different prints. Some were scenes of Paris in the winter rains or images of light and dark playing against the grand, romantic backdrop of the city's sites. The others were of Jean. Jean bare-chested and soaking his feet in a fountain in the Jardin du Luxembourg. Jean smoking in a doorway in the Latin Quarter. Jean running up the steps in Montmartre. Jean laying down like a crucified Jesus on the tiled floor of the Pantheon, his famously large member clearly visible under the raggedy cloth.

That one I kept in the suitcase and only offered to those who stopped to enquire about the man in my pictures.

Paris was the backdrop, but Jean was the absolute star of the show. Tourists came, allured and aghast by the juxtaposition of this beautiful Black man against the backdrop of the famous landmarks they'd traveled all this way to see.

I had a few detractors, of course. Sanctimonious Germans with their Nazi armband stitched onto their coats who'd mutter about *Entartete Kunst*. They'd nod politely at me as they pretended to browse my collection while actually bemoaning the racial impurity of the country they'd paid to visit. I used to enjoy waiting until the very end of their conversation, after they'd told me '*merci*' with a duplicitous smile, and turned to leave, then I would jump to my feet and yell back in German: "This is France, and Frenchmen come in every color!"

But yelling at passers-by was not the correct temperament for one who worked the street. Some days Claude would come sit with a flask of cold tea or a picnic basket filled with cheese, pate and cognac and he'd teach me the tricks of the street trade.

"Watch this couple over here," he said through a mouthful of baguette, and pointing across the street with the rest. "Look how the man is always four or five paces in front of the wife. He only stops when he has something to point out, explaining whatever uninteresting piece of secondhand knowledge he picked up at the bowling club while she clutches her hat and tries to pretend she understands a word he's saying. Look at that silk around her neck and the pearls in her ears. English for sure. He's landed gentry, she's an industrialist's daughter. The class difference between them is miles wide. He has no respect for her. If I saw them in a hotel bar, I'd wait until she retired upstairs and he lit an evening cigar, and I guarantee he'd be paying me every franc he has play a tune on my skin flute."

"How insightful, Claude."

I learned that having Claude around was a dampener on sales. Sitting together on a promenade, sipping wine and gossiping about 'the trade' made us look like two homosexuals selling pictures of a third homosexual. Not the sort of art seller most tourists cared to buy from.

Yet on my own, I could pass quite easily as the languid sales boy, caring only professionally for the wares I flogged, answering only the questions, not the critiques. Never once did I mention I was the photographer. But people did not ask whom the photographer was. They asked: "who is the artist?"

"They're photographs... from a camera," I answered in my first few rounds of circular conversation, doing a double take to check my stock had not been swapped with someone else's watercolors.

"Clearly," some would reply, casting quizzical eye upon the simpleton I'd made myself out to be. "But photography is also art, is it not?"

Whatever they might say, I could not begin to identify myself as an artist. Art was still to me the medium to which I was a keen observer. The topic I could write a thesis on, yes. The concept I could speak about for evenings on end, comparing cubists to romantics to impressionists. But not something I practiced.

One night at Giovanni's, Claude and I befriended an Englishman. Claude had propositioned him, of course, but he wasn't interested in paying, and we both found him increasingly attractive. As the night poured itself down our throats, the three of us playfully batted around a suggestion this John would "give us both a good seeing to," which Claude had rather inartfully said I was in dire need of. But as we finished off our final round, the sanctimonious John of England repeated a quote from the most bourgeoise of queens, Oscar Wilde: "All art is quite useless."

"Because its aim is simply to create a mood," I said, repeating the explanation Wilde had given of that infamous line in *The Picture of Dorian Gray*. "Art is not meant to instruct, or to influence action in anyway. I believe that's how Mr. Wilde described the thing."

"As if Mr. Wilde would be a surrealist," Claude added. John did not like that. The night could not be salvaged, at least not for me, and I retired upstairs, swearing to live a life of celibacy before I gave myself up to a man who would or could not understand human achievement had no greater purpose than the love of art.

"You didn't miss much," Claude told me later that evening. "Confirms my suspicion why an Englishman is always on time: his lovemaking never lasts more than two minutes."

So I lived in Bohemia, but I was too much the Austrian to identify as a Bohemian. On the sunny banks of the Seine, the only answer I would ever give to the inquisitive eye would be: "the artist prefers to remain anonymous." When prompted, I'd say the same thing about the model, too. That caught their attention.

"But he is so striking," they'd say. "Handsome, alluring."

"Beguiling, captivating? Trust me, I know. The ultimate form of man, I have heard some say about him." This wasn't a spiky lie, every word I said about Jean was truth. "Isn't it a privilege to simply bear witness to this singular moment of pure beauty, frozen in time?" After telling them that, I'd always make a sale.

* * *

The streets were quiet thanks to the mid-week storms which had kept most of the tourists off the blushing wet cobblestones. Madame Framboise had a foolproof weather forecasting system that involved counting the number of spiders visible from her window ledge divided by what time the old alley cat cleaned his ears. She'd assured me it wasn't going to rain for the rest of the day, and so I sat in my usual perch, Notre Dame to my back, grey clouds moving fast above my head, and not a sale to be had.

With my chin buried deep inside my scarf, there was little else I could do but close my eyes and think about Jean.

What the people who bought from me did not know was that I knew intimately every photograph I sold, because I'd dreamed of it a hundred times or more.

My favorite shots of Jean were, unsurprisingly, the ones where he bared his flesh. We trotted off to the sites of Paris at first light, when he'd be free to roam around the gardens or the steps without his shirt, his shoes, or even his trousers. None of the photos were nudes, of course, but some were about as risqué as one could openly sell on the streets of Paris. At least on the streets around the *Île de la Cité*. No, in the time Jean and I had been acquainted, I'd yet to properly see the generous appendage that according to Claude, made Jean famous. And every time we met, that dream drifted further and further away. With every roll of francs I gave him for the cut of that week's sales, every set of negatives we looked through, every time we chatted about the weather on the way to a location, we became less and less familiar. Friends becoming business partners, lovers regressing to roommates.

Jean never talked about his 'other' profession. Not even to acknowledge that it was fact. Claude, on the other hand, reveled in his status as a *gentleman of independent means,* telling everyone who would listen about what this 'nameless ambassador' or that 'anonymous deputy' liked to do, or have done to them, in bed. This all fit quite nicely into Claude's worldview that most, if not all, of the significant characters in history had been homosexuals. And given the roster of high-powered men he'd allegedly been through, I wouldn't be surprised if Claude's historiography turned out to be true. Just last month an acquaintance of Claude's had invited him to Germany to be of service to a high-ranking Nazi. It would have netted Claude more money than he'd made in his entire life, but Madame Framboise has filled his head with worry that war with Germany could break out at any minute, and being stuffed with a Nazi dick was probably not the safest route to go down.

"Rumor has it," Claude told me one evening the second I got home from a long day of shooting, "your friend Jean is a favorite of married couples."

"Oh come now. Don't be ridiculous."

"How dare you take me for a liar. From what I've heard, certain men from those dizzying circles enjoy watching an African savage their wives, and they pay a fortune."

"I'd imagine the wives aren't complaining, either," I said, more thinking out loud. Claude looked at me oddly as I snatched his drink so I'd have something to blame.

"I hope he's paying you well, Anders. He can afford it with the amount he works." While Claude prided himself on being an escort of the highest class, Jean, as Claude always delighted to inform me, was a more garden-variety whore.

41

As Jean and I met for our weekly photo shoots I started to disbelieve Claude. Jean seemed like the exact opposite of the type of person who could do such a job. Although he took some of his clothes off for me, he was shy when not around the camera. He even buttoned back up as soon as we heard footsteps or the roar of a motorcar coming to disturb us.

I thought it might have all been one big character assassination or attempt to dissuade me from spending time with Jean for some archaic reason, until one afternoon near the Louvre. A handsome looking couple who clearly had money were taking a stroll when they spotted Jean posing by the Pont des Arts. I was standing further up the street, taking pictures, and they did not notice me there.

The wife rushed up to greet Jean with a loving hug, while the husband vigorously shook his hand with a broad, polo-player grin. Jean looked startled, almost uncomfortable, as the couple merrily spoke at him, clearly trying to talk him into meeting with them again. Eventually Jean pointed to me standing a little away, playing with my camera lens to seem busy and not like an eavesdropper.

The couple took the hint that Jean was not in a mood to talk and bid both of us adieu. The husband nodded and tipped his cap at me, but the wife, well, she taught me never to doubt Claude again. She came right up to me, greeting me as one would the unknown third party of a dear friend. She clasped my hand into hers, folded a card into my palm, leaned in close to my ear and whispered:

"Come to me if you have any photographs of his cock. I'll buy them all."

Jean and I never spoke of that incident, but I listened a little closer each time Claude wanted to fill me in on the street-gossip about Jean.

Subtly, I found myself questioning the foundations of the life I'd not so much built, but stumbled into. What if one day my mother and grandmother came to visit Paris, and we were taking a stroll on the Pont des Arts, and that same woman remembered my face and approached me with the same question. Perhaps with more urgency, since many months would have passed. *I simply take the pictures*; I might say in some line of defense. I can't imagine my mother buying that for a single second. Whore or whore-enabler, what was the difference? So I didn't have sex, but I took the money all the same.

Worse, I couched the entire operation under the rubric of *art*, when the grand heights of my so-called artistic achievements were nothing baser than debauchery, modernized with a camera.

* * *

The weeks drifted by, sandwiched between manning my stall and the hungrier poses I directed Jean to take. There was no better classroom than the marketplace to learn what the people want. The fistfuls of francs, hundreds a day sometimes, were undeniable. Risqué sold. Was it art? I didn't pretend to consider the question anymore. It was popular. A facile conversion of Jean's body into image then into paper currency.

The trick was in playing with the eye. Structuring the image to make it *feel* like a nude, even if it wasn't technically pornographic. The story told in the parts not seen. The intoxicating idea of what the sensuous figure was about to do, or what delights of the flesh the lens had seen, but never printed. Those uncaptured images lived in my head as much as it left with those who came to browse, then returned to buy, sometimes the whole set I had on display.

Capturing Jean naked might have done wonders for my business, but less so for my state of mind. For it was all I thought about. Truly, Jean naked was all I saw, whether in the stall or striding through the park together to find a secluded place for another shoot.

Then finally the epochal changeover came. It was the day after Bastille Day, when Paris had already emptied for the summer. We took a stroll through the Parc de Bagatelle, sweltering in the heat. As we came across the water and saw no one else was around, Jean immediately informed me he wanted to swim. He stripped off, left his clothes in a pile and dove right into the water. He had shown himself in full, his holy body and sublimity between his legs, as I blanched and scrambled up to him to get the right angle. Crouching in the grass, shifting behind a rock or a tree as he frolicked by himself, it was easy to enter the mindset of a nefarious voyeur.

I made thousands of francs from the photos we took in that single afternoon. Jean took a handsome cut too. A picture of him standing up in the tree-lined lake, the water rippling around his abdomen. Another I took of his intricately lined back, a strategic branch obscuring his otherwise on display buttocks. The one that stalked my nights though was ostensibly of a gnarled old tree. Jean was close, but out of focus. Half his body was out of shot, but the part inside the frame offered a tantalizing fissure of bare thigh. My armor stripped bare. The truth of our *Entartete Kunst* plain for every tourist wandering under the shade of Notre Dame to see. Claude's sage words echoed with nihilistic precision as I settled into another day of whore-mongering. Nestled into my chair beside the portable photographic display, I closed my eyes against the often disturbed looks of passersby.

"Look at this, darling," a strong male voice said in English. The accent was American, but heavy and thick, like the New Yorkers from the movies.

I opened my eyes and watched a bright, golden couple gaze delightedly on the photographs hung up on my display. They were both exquisitely dressed, looking almost like shop mannequins. The lady could have stepped straight out of a catalog. Her long silk-white gloves draped up to a tightly laced bodice. Golden hair cascaded down from underneath a bonnet, while a parasol built for any weather rested against her shoulder. Passing her on the street, she would land briefly in the mind as a woman of modest disposition, but certainly not of modest means. The richness of her attire masked a rather plain face, but the sheer butchery of color and fabrics she wore bedazzled the eyes until one looked past the spectacle and realized that each item she wore would find itself at home in a bordello. She'd just decided to wear them altogether.

The gentleman was as tall as a swimmer, frightfully blond under his summer hat and he wore a baby-blue striped suit that would make him blend in amongst beach furniture. He was a man for whom a suit, or any clothes for that matter, did him no favors. He was quite simply a roughly hued paragon of the male form—a Michelangelo animated by Mary Shelley, a creature of the divine.

Together the pair looked almost comically out of place. Like a pastiche of a Parisian couple who'd just stepped out of a Noel Coward play. Yet he enchanted me. She was the supporting actress, but he was the Hollywood star with Californian skin and a Roosevelt voice.

"I say, aren't they exquisite?" the lady responded, spinning her parasol and leaning over to investigate the pictures further. I had to leap from my chair so as not to be squished by her bosom which seemed to take on a life of its own under the bodice.

The gentleman looked at me with a curious smile.

"They're all originals," I said in English. "Very contemporary."

He unhooked a photo from the display board, in itself a violently American thing to do. I'd seen no other buyer reach through the seller's divide and touch the goods. But it made me sure they would buy something. I quickly tried to remember the price of the dollar, wondering how I might inflate the price and be done for the day so I could go home and imagine this Hercules ravaging me.

"You have a good eye," he said rather unnervingly. I didn't know if he meant to accuse me of being the photographer, or simply the curator. I peered over the lady's parasol and saw the photo he held was one of the most sensuous I dared display. Jean was sitting cross-legged on a rock after bathing in the *Bois de Boulogne*. His skin was still wet, and he was clearly naked, although by trick of the light there was nothing to be seen.

"From where are you?" I asked in English, trying to change all manner of subjects.

"Jewish?" The gentleman asked.

I froze. Speechless. The blood might as well have stopped pumping through my veins. I had an unquenchable urge to run my hands all over myself. To dash to the fountain and check my reflection. To understand exactly what in my clothes or on my body had prompted this life-altering question. Did it mean Paris was no longer safe? Did everyone think this of me as they passed me on the street? Was I Jewish to them all?

"What… what makes you say that?"

"Oh, no reason," he said as casually as if he'd said nothing at all and replaced the photo. "I'm from Brooklyn, and Jewish, of course, and I've only ever heard other Jews ask in that way."

The lady turned to me with a kindly smile and said: "'Where are you from?' is the correct way to say it in English."

"Funny story," the man said, talking to me like I was his cousin at a wedding, "my Hebrew teacher was actually born in Palestine. Hebrew was her native language and she always talked that way. It's because she was translating the Hebrew in her head directly into English. It's quite amazing, isn't it? Here we are discussing the finer points of Hebrew grammar on the street in Paris like the language hasn't been effectively dead for the last two thousand years."

He gazed off into the distance. They both did, actually. They stood quite still, savoring the moment. I clandestinely wiped the prickling sweat from my forehead.

"I'm David, by the way. Where are my manners?" he thrust a hand out and I quickly wiped the sweat off my palm before grasping his. "And this is my wife, Hella."

"How do you do?" she remarked. At least she wore gloves.

"Anders," I said, cautioning a smile. David's eyes caught me. "So," I said, turning back to the pictures. "Can I interest you in any of the pieces?"

"Actually," David said, "I'm more interested in the person behind the camera." He was prodding me to come forward and admit they were mine, but I said nothing. "The subject speaks for himself. But then there's the picture taker, and I'd say he has designs on his subject. Don't you think, darling? As if we ourselves have stumbled upon the man bathing, but are actually left to question the watcher himself. And our position as voyeurs. What do we do, push the bushes aside and run towards beauty, or slink away for fear of rejection? Truly, Anders, these pieces you're selling are stunning. Photography may be a fairly new art form, but trust me, I've yet to see anything quite like this."

Still, I didn't own up. I nodded and reviewed the photographs alongside him.

"What I enjoy," I said, quickly clearing my throat, "is the idea of movement in the photographs. The picture could be a still frame from a film camera and uh, *the photographer,* is inviting us to think about the next scene in the set. We're part of a... movie film. We're recalling snippets of scenes from a wider tale. After all, art is useless if we don't remember any of it, isn't it?"

"How astute. Tell me," David said after more closely inspecting yet another topless shot of Jean, "do you have a relationship with this model?"

"Yes, well, uh, I mean, only professionally." The question had caught me off-guard. But immediately I was relieved. He'd drawn me into admitting something I had trouble saying out loud.

"Wonderful. I have a bit of a business proposition for you both. We have a good number of friends who might be interested in some exclusive shots. Here," he said, fishing for something in his jacket pocket before pulling out a delicate printed card. "This is my address. It's right across from the Jardin du Luxembourg. Hella and I have a lovely studio, don't we darling?"

"Hm?" She looked up from a series of shots of Jean at the Arc de Triomphe, his shirt completely unbuttoned and flapping in the wind. "Oh yes, it's wonderful. Lots of light."

"Come by with your model friend tomorrow afternoon and let's all discuss it over a few vodka martinis. How does that sound?"

I was speechless. I held the card, staring at the printed address as my eyes glazed over. *Anglo-Atlantic Productions*, the card read.

"And of course, I want to buy your prints, at least as a good faith gesture." David pulled out his billfold slowly, as if giving me time to digest all this.

"Oh, of course," I mumbled, pocketing the card while running through all possible ways to phrase this offer to Jean, bouncing between one foot and the other as the agitation got the better of me. I needed Jean here, now, before the opportunity crumbled. 'A smart, rich American wants to see more of you. Think of his friends. Think of who else might see you. Fashion houses. Parties with Coco Chanel, and you, and I. And maybe you'll see what I've done for you, give up this whoring life and love only me...'

"Which picture would you like?" I asked, ignoring the tumult in my stomach.

"All of them," David said. I didn't quite understand. I glanced at Hella, expecting her to start laughing like this had all been one big ruse.

"This one would look lovely on the staircase, don't you think?" Hella asked her husband, linking her arm into his. "Cover up that frightful space where the Dalí used to hang."

"I was thinking the exact same thing," he said, and kissed her on the cheek. "I don't want to deprive you of all your stock, so why don't you just bring them round when you come tomorrow." David unhooked himself from his wife, and began counting out bills in denominations of fifty. "How's a thousand francs for the lot? This is three hundred now as a deposit, and I'll give you the rest when you arrive. Seems fair?"

He folded the cash into my hand like I could get him the best seat in the house. How clever of him to turn this obvious set up into a transaction I could not refuse. The exact same sensation I had as the train pulled out of Vienna lodged itself in my throat, when I watched my old life from the window of a carriage disappearing into the distance as I traveled into the unknown. I didn't quite know how, but I felt the ghoulish hand of history on my shoulder.

*　*　*

"David and Hella?" Claude said in disbelief. We sat at our usual table on a quiet Tuesday at Giovanni's, Claude to the left of me, Jean to the right. Fortunately, this was our normal night to meet at the bar, split the cash and plan the next week's shots. Sharing hundreds of francs between us was rather out of the ordinary, and both Jean and Claude had sat, jaws open, as I recounted the day's earlier events. All minus the Jewish question. That I buried as far back in my mind as it would go.

"David and Hella Roosevelt?" Claude asked again.

"I knew them when they still went by Rosenblatt," Jean said with a smug smile.

"Way back in the nineteen-tens, was it?" Jean responded sharply, never liking to be out of the know.

"I think it was in the late-twenties they stopped going by Rosenblatt, or maybe it was before. Wait, when did FDR become governor of New York?"

"We don't expect you to know that, Jean. I didn't think they had newsreels in the silent picture days."

"Anyway, that's them," I said, shifting uncomfortably at the blatantly Jewish name. "But how do you know them?" I glanced sideways at Jean, wondering if this was another couple he'd been a guest star for.

"Their parties are famous," Jean said, taking the entire story as one great compliment while Claude squirmed with seething resentment.

"More than famous," Claude added, "they're legendary." The shock of the news seemed to have locked these two into a truce instead of the low-level war of attrition our weekly meetings tended to be. "I once fucked an actor who was there. He paid me to wait all night in his apartment while he was at David and Hella's with his fiancé. He returned at five in the morning, drugged on everything you can imagine, and wouldn't shut up about all the 'avant-garde' in attendance."

"I heard Ezra Pound once sucked off Ernst Hemmingway at David and Hella's," Jean said.

"No, you didn't."

"I did too! And Max Jacob got banned for always inviting whores riddled with the clap."

"Friends of yours?"

Jean ignored the barb, turned to me and said: "The real reason they're famous is Josephine Baker."

"Oh, everyone knows that!" Claude said loudly. "That's why they started hanging out at David and Hella's in the first place. Everyone wanted to be the next Josephine fucking Baker." Claude cast a long, suspicious eye over Jean, speaking untold volumes between them that I'd never hope to understand.

Sometimes, when I talked about Claude to Jean, I caught a wistful, drawn-out look of longing across his face. As if they were actually estranged brothers, both too proud to apologize. In those moments, Jean's face was at his most expressive. Riddled with melancholy that he actively tried to mask. More than once I'd stopped him in those moments to take his picture, capturing the entire tragi-comedy of Paris in one over-the-shoulder look from a West African Frenchman.

Despite my wish to sit quietly, observe and learn, the silent stares from both of them became a little too overpowering.

"Who's Josephine Baker?" I asked with trepidation.

"She literally invented pornography," Jean said.

"No, no." Claude scolded. "David and Hella invented pornography, she was just the first star."

Jean conceded the point with a shrug.

"David knew her from New York, so I believe," Claude explained to both

49

of us, although Jean sat with a subtly bothered look like he could tell the whole thing better. "She was the last girl on a Broadway chorus line, but always upstaged the performance by running around like she couldn't remember the choreography."

"I first met her when she was performing at the Folies Bergère," Jean said, pleased as punch to get one over Claude, who retreated behind his glass at Jean's first-hand account. "I was working there as a stage boy, and the second she noticed me backstage she jumped right out of her chair, screeched to high heaven and started babbling away in American Negro slang." Jean burst out laughing. "I nodded along for ten minutes before finally butting in and telling her: '*Madame, je suis désolé. Je ne comprends pas!*'"

Claude rolled his eyes. Audibly, somehow.

"We hung out before every show. I taught her French slang, she taught me how the Harlem boys speak. Came in very helpful with my American clients. And, I used to take Chiquita out for a walk before every show."

Claude scoffed.

"He means her pet cheetah," Claude said. "A woman as marvelous as Josephine Baker keeps a pet cheetah."

I nearly spat out my drink.

"If she wasn't properly walked, fed, and rested before Josephine went on stage, Chiquita would get frightened by the commotion and dive into the orchestra pit. That's how I learned medicine, too. Some of the orchestra would need to be patched up after the show."

"Well my friend Paul was at her wedding last year," Claude cut in. Glaring at me as he said it in the hope of wiping the aura of amazement off my face. "And my friend Carlos was her paid translator while she sat for Picasso."

"Huh," Jean responded. "*Paying* friends of yours?"

Claude fumed. For a moment I thought he was going to chuck his drink in Jean's face, but it would be unlike Claude to waste good gin. "Perhaps your future work will be studied by racial eugenicists," Claude said bitterly. "Anders," Claude turned to me, "you can send the photographs you'll take tomorrow to Monsieur Hitler in Berlin. Tell him there's an uppity Negro in Paris who's abnormally giant cock is worthy of scientific study."

Jean shrugged and grinned. Although my face went in the opposite direction.

"Wait… what do you mean the photos I'll take? Of Jean?"

The pair of them glared at me like I'd singularly failed to understand the entire point of the conversation. Evidently, I had.

"What…" Claude said, sharing a smirk with Jean. "What do you think they wanted you to do?"

Suddenly I couldn't hear anything over the pounding of my heart. Not the clink of glasses Giovanni was polishing behind the bar, nor the subdued conversations of the old men in the background, and not the laughs of Jean and Claude, gasping for breath at the expense of my obvious naivety.

"Dearest Matter," Claude shrieked, doing his favorite bit: dictating the weekly letter I wrote to my mother. "Things are going quite well in Paris. I've taken up with a *schwarze* boy and a Jewish-American pornographer. That camera grandmother bought me is proving quite useful, but I shall need a wider lens. Regards to the Führer."

They both burst out laughing, and I slunk behind my drink, cursing my pursuit of beauty, and the need I had discovered to always be nearby it. The fire was warm, but it burned, too.

Chapter 4

I KNEW I WOULD not sleep at all that night. I retired early, feigning the need to clean my camera, but was in fact sick of this newfound camaraderie between Jean and Claude. What I hated about Claude's street-cat smarts was how quickly he could turn against me when the tide commanded. Someone who he could whisper poison about for weeks on end could, in the flick of money clip, become the best thing Claude had ever set eyes on.

Claude had subjected me to months of dirty looks every time Jean's name came up. Every time I talked about a day that included him, plans that he was part of, something amusing that had occurred on one of our tours of the city, Claude would respond with at least a pout, and if he was feeling energetic, an eight to ten minute diatribe on the failings of Jean and how he personified the problems afflicting the institution of street whoredom.

Now I had become the common enemy. The butt of a joke mending the ties between two former enemies. Perhaps in time it would work out for the best, with the two most important people in my life healing the rift that had kept them apart. But for now, all I felt was annoyed.

Claude came upstairs around midnight, having merrily sent Jean on his way home. As he readied for his evening's shift while stumbling about the room, I faced the wall and wrapped the covers around me, making it clear I did not wish to talk.

"You're going to have a fabulous time tomorrow," Claude said without expecting an answer. "Who cares that David and Hella are a couple of faded starlets, desperately trying to recreate the magic from a decade ago when *les années folles* were in full swing. Honestly, what's an anachronistic party couple to do but attempt to cling to relevancy with a last gasp effort at making themselves the center of any world that'll have them. Why not male pornography? There's certainly a market. Jean, I, and all the other boys of Montmartre can attest to that. Why not photograph our bodies and record our actions on a movie reel. It's only the next logical step in our profession. Technology and invention come to us all, Herr Anders. Even the common whore must adapt, and adapt we shall. I would offer you a shot of my absinthe to toast this new age," Claude paused to take a swig directly from the bottle, then spluttered and coughed, "but I can see you're pretending to sleep. Very well, but I must be off. This common whore hasn't retired into the movie business just yet. But at least you'll finally get your wish to see Jean's cock." The door creaked open and he headed into the night which belonged to him, and never me. There was no greater indication of the vast difference between our lives than this moment. "Why don't you keep a set of prints for under your bed, I know it's as close as you'll ever get to the real thing."

*   *   *

The next day I got to the Roosevelt's house early. I'd spent the preceding two hours in a café knocking back coffees until the waiter said I should probably slow down and brought me a free beer. But there was no point in putting off the inevitable. I'd practiced my excuse *ad nauseum*, I needed to understand the lighting in the space before Jean arrived, I had to block the poses, to feel the space, rearrange the furniture.

Those things I would have to do for any indoor shot, but more than that, I had to understand the nature of this position. Each of the last twenty-four hours kept revealing yet another layer to this gaping pit I sat on the edge of.

I couldn't find their name on the buzzer, and immediately started to panic. The rush of caffeine and lack of sleep played havoc with my constitution. I asked three different passers-by if this was number seventy-five, and each one of them grunted that it was.

53

It dawned on me I'd been pacing up and down the street corner of a known pornographer for at least ten minutes while nervously clutching a camera. I'd spent all this time practicing my excuses for David and Hella that I had none ready for a police constable.

Finally, I approached the heavy wooden door obtruding from the curved stone, freely sweating and checking once again the list of ten unknown names on the buzzer. With a deep, terrified breath, I prepared to start from the very top.

Then the door heaved open, and an old, whiskered man stood in my way looking perturbed. Or from his perspective, I was standing in his way.

"Pardon me, but I was looking for—"

"Their entrance isn't this door. They have their own one, over there," he growled, jostling his capped head further down the much quieter intersecting street of Rue Royer-Collard.

I wanted to stop a moment and tell him who I was looking for, but he'd already brushed right past, slapping me with his shopping bag and letting the heavy wooden door slam shut in my face.

A few paces down the street I found another door, nondescript, battered and wrought of heavy iron. Passing by, one would probably not consider it a door at all, but a blocked passageway of some old servants' entrance.

There was a name on the side. One single name beside one single button, engraved in shining brass bolted to the stone. The name was unmistakable, as was the amount of times a finger had slid along the end of the plaque in search of the buzzer, whittling away the bronze over years upon years of excited, inebriated party guests turning up in the corner, bothering the elderly neighbors.

I sucked in what felt like my last breath; taking in just a snifter of the scent of Bourbon roses that floated my way from the gardens across the street. Suddenly I wanted to do nothing more than turn away and race to the gardens. To take off my shoes and point my camera at the pretty little flower beds. I could tell Jean the whole enterprise was off. I simply did not have the ability for it. I'd continue to sell his portraits, but I'd branch out. Perhaps take still-lifes of the flowers of Paris, or the Eiffel Tower from the damn *Trocadéro*.

There were many excuses I could come up with. The one thundering loudest in my head was that I wished to experiment with color. That was the best I could come up with, and even that felt pathetic.

Yet I had come this far. And I had waited this long. Even if only to share the beauty of Jean with someone else who could appreciate a good-looking man, without dripping in disdain like Claude.

Swallowing hard, I ran my finger along the brass name plate, feeling out the indents of the letters smudged from famous fingertips. One more breath, and I pushed the buzzer. It gave off a metallic ring that echoed deep inside the house, chiming the faintest sound of a copper bell somewhere above.

I stared at the nameplate as I waited, meditating on the word and all its subtle meanings. The active de-semitization one more thing I'd thought I would escape in Paris, but inevitably catching up with me.

For the name inscribed on the home of David and Hella Rosenblatt was not their own but spoke all manner of things. Like the crypto-Jews of the Bolivian plains my mother had told me stories of, who hid their customs for hundreds of years to escape the inquisition, the sign on the Rosenblatt's door reminded me only of that. The name they'd chosen to hide in plain sight was utterly in keeping with the character I'd determined they had. The brass plate said simply:

Roosevelt.

The door buzzed, loud and clicking. I opened it, took a deep breath, and gazed up at the narrow staircase, examining the sharpness of each step. If a man were to fall down these stairs, or was pushed, his life would surely end, if not be placed in mortal danger. The preposterous, uncanny sense that my life would end on this staircase stalked me as I stepped off the street.

* * *

I crept up the concrete stairs. The middle of the steps was a lighter color than the edges, as if a carpet usually ran down the narrow stairway to the street level but had been removed for cleaning. The bottom edges of the warm purple wallpaper were bleached and frayed, the sign of a well-used entrance way. But the most intriguing aspect illuminated by a single yellow bulb was the array of framed pictures that raised a fellow's eyebrows as he ascended to the solid wood door at the top. A spectrum of Parisian society was on display. A few faces I felt I should recognize, and more that I didn't. Plus an empty frame staring at me where Jean was supposed to go.

I'd somewhat dismissed the stories Claude and Jean had told me of Josephine Baker. But as I climbed, her outsize presence on the Rosenblatt's stairwell was unmistakable, gazing sensually at me in several images encased in black and white. The pictures alternated between her dancing in a banana dress and her posing with a plume of feathers and nothing else, reclining on a chaise lounge, brilliant pearls around her neck. And then, after a run of dull, dry men photographed next to the effervescent David, there she was again in the very last picture at the top of the staircase. Ms Baker grinned out at me, sitting in what looked like a Sultan's harem with the purring Chiquita laying like an oversized house cat in her lap.

"Anders!" I was startled as the heavy wooden door flew open and David loudly declared my name while his lips sucked on a pipe. "Come in, dear boy." He threw an arm around my shoulders, wrapped in the softest velvet I'd ever had rubbed against my skin. He was even more handsome in his natural habitat. The smoking jacket trimmed perfectly to broad shoulders. A swimmer's chest with a smoker's laugh. Hair held high and treated, yet pillowy and soft as golden strands on Jason's fleece. Yesterday David had been clean-shaven. Today light stubble graced his cheeks in a manner that left me imagining David topless in a marble bathroom, brushing foam on his face and whistling a jaunty tune.

I lost my breath and nearly my balance as we entered the palatial Aladdin's cave. Hallways spun off in every direction like the entrance to an Ottoman maze. Green carpets and red lamps uncovered more art and statues against every wall than most minor Habsburgs ever would have seen. There was even a brass telephone hanging proudly on the wall when barely no one else in Paris had one.

"This is your home?" was all I could say. David chuckled and led me towards a door bursting with natural sunlight beyond.

"Home, studio, workshop, entertainment venue. We're all things to all people here at the humble Roosevelt abode."

Now would have been the perfect time to ask him about the name. But to do so felt crass, as if talking to a friend who was clearly under dressed for the event and asking whether they realized it.

I followed him into an ornate sitting room at least thrice the size of Giovanni's bar. Fresh light from the Jardin du Luxembourg flooded the room through the bay windows. One could barely find a route through the patchwork of couches, armchairs and little corner tables made of glass and ivory that spread across the room busier than a hotel lobby.

"Come, take a seat."

Where? I thought to myself. David answered my unsaid question and plopped down in the middle of a plush green couch with carved wooden inlay in the center of the room. It was one of four identical couches around a large square coffee table made from four tusk-white elephants holding up a heavy piece of glass. As I took a seat on the couch across from David, I noticed the dozens of seating areas in the room were laid out in such a way that all routes led to this central inverted pedestal. I imagined the room full of Parisian royalty, the conversation ever flowing into the central hub where David and his wife held court.

He sat cross-legged, puffing on his pipe and utterly at ease, as if we were nothing but two strangers waiting for the same train. He picked up an English newspaper from the table, the *Times*, and clicked his tongue at the headline. I turned my head to it and there it was: a striking portrait of Hitler.

David stared at me from across the table like my thoughts on the matter could carry weight.

"What do you think about this Sudeten business, then?"

"I…" I tried to form the words which would not make my ignorance appear to be so blithe. Truly I didn't remember the last time I'd picked up, or even taken in a newspaper headline, beyond the one-sentence parsing of the world which blared from the mouths of ragged French paperboys.

"Hello, you two," David's wife Hella said, entering the room just in time with a tray of things for tea. She was dressed a little less frilly than the day before, yet together these absolutes still managed to pull off the sensation one was watching two very skilled performers dallying through a comedic act.

57

"Ah, darling. We were just discussing the Sudeten crisis." David said, gesturing with his pipe.

"Oh, do leave the poor boy alone," Hella said as she made her way effortlessly through the knot of chairs. She placed the tray on the table with a sloppy clatter, and fell into the third couch, conspicuously leaving the fourth one empty for our eagerly awaited guest.

"You'll have to forgive my husband. He continues to see the best in people."

"Not exactly, my darling. I just believe our kinfolk will be safer if we don't declare war on Hitler. Let him rule the German speaking world, what do we care? Himmler can give us all a free ticket to Palestine."

I shifted uncomfortably. I tried to find some point of interest on the wall, some talking point to steer the conversation far away from the territory these two seemed to constantly circle around. Hella poured us all tea while lovingly ignoring her husband, but my flustered silence began to take on a life of its own.

"Ah!" I said, louder than necessary, "here are your prints."

I'd all but forgotten the pictures I'd brought, my primary reason for coming, and pulled out a brown envelope from the satchel that held my camera and four extra rolls of film in preparation for whatever task they would have me up for.

"Wonderful," David said, smiling kindly and leaning across the table to take the envelope from me. Hella busied herself with the tea but glanced over as David spread the portraits of Jean out on the glass. The landscapes of only Paris, he left inside the envelope.

"Stunning. Simply stunning." Hella quietly nodded in feminine agreement. "You certainly have an eye for composition. I trust you saw the ones on the staircase on your way in?"

"Of Miss Baker, yes of course, they're wonderful."

David pulled the pipe from his mouth for the sole purpose of slapping his leg. "The boy knows his stuff!"

"I took those," Hella continued, still leafing through the portraits of Jean on the table. "A long time ago now, but she does so enjoy showing them off to guests whenever she's here. You should come and meet her one time, along with your friend, what was his name?"

"Jean," David said.

"That's it. Speaking of," Hella glanced at the clock on the wall shaped like Louis XIV's Medusa-style sun, "he should be here any minute."

"Actually," I offered, feeling glad to finally add something of use to the conversation, "Jean used to take Chiquita out for walks when Miss Baker was at the Folies Bergère."

"Aha!" David yelped, pointing wildly with his pipe and practically jumping from the couch. "What did I tell you, darling? This boy is it!" He tapped on a picture of Jean, "the next great star of the erotic stage."

Hella seemed indifferent to her husband's excitement, but that didn't stop him. He got up from the couch and began to pace around it, puffing on his pipe while he thought out loud.

"The seductive nature of the male form captured on camera. *Le garçon noir de Paris* anointed by the great Josephine Baker herself. I'm telling you, darling, the crowds are going to love him."

I let out a reluctant cough and cut in: "I understood we… were doing a photo shoot? What crowd would there be?" Claude and Jean had done a good job of preparing me for nudity, yes. But the picture David painted seemed far beyond anything like that.

David and Hella passed a look between themselves as if they took my unease as a personal affront. David put his pipe down on the table and leaned on the back of the couch.

"We are chroniclers of the avant-garde. Protectors of Bohemia. Patrons of the artistic revolution," he said, without so much as a fleck of irony. As serious as a professor.

I stared, hang-jawed and quiet like I'd come face to face with the very noumenon of my reason for being. The solitary nature of chasing beauty dissipated as David clasped his hands behind his back and began to pace, laying out his vision of an artistic revolution.

"Artistic freedom, if its boundaries are not continually nudged and pressed, will contract. For freedom of expression is not in itself a natural state of humankind. It's the antithesis of authority; the freedom to follow the longings of one's heart. Reactionaries do not fear red flags on the barricades so much as they fear artistic freedom, for it's art that heralds the revolution. Would the Paris Commune have ignited if Victor Hugo had not scratched out *Les Misérables* on revolutionary kindling? Never. It is only ever the artists who forge new ages of man. Wouldn't you agree?"

I nodded frantically. In one breath he'd said out loud what I could not in a lifetime form, even in the quietest part of my mind. I began to understand the magnetic forces of history—how the great heroes of the past can bind other humans to their cause, to the point of laying down their life. David was silencing the vicious doubts that crept into my mind every time I lifted my camera. The nasty cry of 'whoremonger,' repeated in Claude's opium-tinged tone endlessly inside my head dimmed enough to truly hear David's words: *The boy knows his stuff.* Like a starving man being led to a feast, bountiful praise was genuinely given, by both of them. Why should I not gorge on it?

"We are in the business of artistic revolution, and I believe you, Anders, and your little camera, could very well be Robespierre incarnate."

My shaking leg went completely hysterical. My breath narrowed and chest tightened as the echoes of David's wide smile filled the room. This went beyond the simple meeting of like-minded souls. More than just hearing what I wanted to be told. Claude made me laugh, Jean made me hard, but David uplifted me beyond earthly desires. The Platonic soul with its *logos, thymos* and *eros*—reason, emotion, and desire—encapsulated in a single man, with a singular vision. Offering me a part in this new world he was creating. Hella, too, with her direct line from Ms. Josephine Baker to a camera to the pictures on the staircase towards this mansion which had swallowed me hole. The few Bible stories I could remember told by a bearded old uncle rang in my head like alarm bells. Jonah being led to the sea. Abraham being shown a new land that would make him a great nation. David offering me and my camera a place by his side.

We stared at each other across the dazzling room. David's scholarly, handsome face bathed in Parisian sunlight. The line of his eyes tumbling down his broad, Semitic nose and pointing straight at me, a hurricane of excitement bursting behind glassy eyes. I wanted to serve him, kiss him, and be held by him all at once.

From every phenomena around me; the chintz couch, the expensive furnishings inside an exquisite apartment, the stories from Claude and Jean rattling around my mind, even the sense of change David and Hella brought from the moment they cast a shadow across my simple picture-selling stall—all of it pointed towards the truth of the creed David spoke.

Hella began to giggle and waved her hand in my direction. "Oh, he does love to self-aggrandize. Don't pay him too much heed. It shouldn't come to bloodshed, I wouldn't think. But Paris isn't what it used to be. One can't simply exist on being *avant-garde*, not these days anyway. We have a number of friends abroad who can't come and enjoy the gaiety of Paris themselves, so we help bring that gaiety to them."

"By sending them pictures of models?" I asked, sitting forward and ready to pay attention to every word she spoke next so I could defend my own involvement in the truth rushing rapidly towards me like an oncoming train.

"Well, yes." Hella shifted in her seat, and I felt bad probing a woman to discuss something so impolite. She was not Madame Framboise who reveled in the coarse language of Claude, far from it. "We're a bit like a subscription service. We send our friends the latest trends from Paris—people, I mean, as opposed to fashion."

"Executives in motion picture studios in Hollywood are particular fans," David added. "Always hunting for their next starlet."

"Our catalog is a little thin when it comes to men. Modeling is not a particularly masculine trait."

"Jean's dream is to be a model," I said.

"Well there we go," Hella agreed with a grin. Just then a bell rang from somewhere inside the house. "Ah, that must be him now." She got up and smoothed her dress down. "I'll show him in then leave you boys to it." She said it with finality, like I would not see her again today, then fled the room.

David busied himself with relighting his pipe, and I quickly stood, feeling that I should make some show of spending time on the lighting and composition of the shots as a photographer should.

I was a little relieved a friendly face was on its way. Even to act as a witness to reality, that the Paris I had dreamed of, waging revolutionary war through the medium of the male form, was real. What a disconcerting suspense there was now, creeping up my gullet. *He's elevated whoremongering to an art form!*

I heard Claude screech. But David was blasé about things like shame. For David there ought be shame, not in his Jewishness or the demi nature of his interest in men alongside his wife. Maybe schoolboy Anders could choke on guilt, but not Herr Anders the radical.

* * *

"That's it," David said, leaning over the back of a plush armchair as Jean, bare-chested and shoeless, stretched out on the chaise lounge and I scurried around him, capturing every angle I could.

After Jean arrived, the pleasantries had not lasted for long. I had been anxious to get started while the light was still good, and through David's efficient finger-snapping direction, we had turned and twisted Jean into every conceivable pose and angle.

"Excellent, excellent. Now look away from the camera. Perfect. Now Anders, get right in there with the feet."

"Feet?"

"Yes, feet!" David yelled. I slunk to the floor and maneuvered to the end of the low couch where Jean's obtrusively large feet were dangling. His trousers were also not long enough, and with him stretched across the furniture it gave the appearance of him being giant-like.

"Now Jean, listen carefully. Anders is going to start from out here," he pointed to a spot beside him like he was commanding a hound, "and approach you. I want you to undo your belt slowly, but don't take your trousers off. Just leave them undone with your hand slipped under the waistband. I want to get a shot of the hair underneath."

He directed, and we both followed. The pose was perfect. Perhaps the most erotic thing I had yet seen since first meeting Jean. The late afternoon light illuminated the natural ribs of his slim frame in wonderful fettle which I tried so hard to not concentrate on. But as the tight rolls of black hair tangling from Jean's flat abdomen downwards rushed into view like a receding tide revealing an ancient wonder, it was all I could do to keep clicking the shutter lest I throw myself on his body.

Considering him as a statue made it easier. I was in a museum, casting my eye on an epic beauty of the age. The only difference being this one was alive, moving, gently grasping the thing which made him famous.

I'd never sweated so much inside a museum. Perhaps I should think of the scenario more like a piece of Bohemian theater—a living celebration of the male form I was lucky enough to document.

"Perfect Jean, perfect. Now slowly edge your trousers down and look straight at the camera. Anders pull out. The perfect shot is when it pops out and we want to see the size of this thing in proportion to his body."

I was behind the camera. Jean was looking at me. The filter of glass and mirror notwithstanding, he was looking at me as he stroked himself under the thin beige cloth standing between us and artistic revolution.

Never had I seen photos like the ones I was taking. The very idea of the existence of such pictures seemed an anathema to what I knew as being possible in this world—as far beyond the concept of plausibility as men walking through the canyons of alien planets.

Yet here we were. The means of this pornographic production were my own. I could envisage desires into reality. My mind fractured as I snapped the sensuous, slightly open mouth of Jean. I hummed with quiet anxiety as Jean slipped both hands into his trousers, the button undone. The offer on display. The images establishing my very conception of man, one I would be expected to turn into thousands of copies. Each one to be stamped with an intended destination. *Entartete Kunst* made by my own hand, on its way to every corner of the world and a man's desires as quick as a telegram.

"Pull back," David said to me, his voice as distant as a guide in a gallery, calling out across a sea of people gasping to take a peek at the masterpiece.

Jean's eyes did not leave mine as the great reveal occurred. Like some impossible feat of physics, the gift Jean had been birthed with expanded across the horizon. Who could imagine such short trousers could contain such magnificence? It was everything Claude had promised, and more.

"Wonderful," David's voice cut through the dream like my mother waking me for school, "now bring one hand behind your head, and let the other do what comes natural."

I sucked in a nervous breath, and thankfully Jean broke our gaze. He closed his eyes and drew his head back while I captured every movement.

But the thing that echoed most in my mind, the thing I knew I would never forget, was the words Claude once said:

"Every age has a beauty. One human being so magnetic the artists, painters and poets can do nothing but spend their lives attempting to capture their heavenly essence. Once in a generation, the Gods will gift us such an idol. And in case you were wondering, that, my friend, is the meaning of life. To seek out that beauty wherever it may reside and praise it with things unattempted yet in prose or rhyme."

Claude was utterly, utterly right.

*   *   *

"So, what's it like?" Claude asked one slow night at Giovanni's.

"What's what like?"

"Jean's cock of course. Can he really suck it himself?"

"I don't know, I haven't seen it." I defamed myself with such blatant falsehoods. Jean's naked form must be second only to Michelangelo's David in terms of sheer numbers of eyes who'd gazed upon it by now. If only David knew a way to transmit nudity by radio signal, Jean's body would surely be more seen, and more lusted after than any other in history.

"Oh, you lie. You've been there almost every day for more than a month now. What are you doing, taking pictures of him in funny hats?"

I shifted in the seat and took a gulp of stale beer. I hated lying to Claude, mainly because I was so bad at it and he could smell an untruth like others can identify sour milk.

"And you haven't shown me any of the pictures you've taken," Claude said, gleefully laying his trap.

"I don't have a dark room anymore," I replied quickly. "Giovanni needs the cellar back for an air-raid shelter, so I haven't anywhere to process the film." Like all great lies it was based on a kernel of truth. I'd heard Giovanni mutter about German bombers soon to come with the war everyone seemed to be expecting but David.

Each day before our session, David would roll out yesterday's *Times* and say something like: "Look, Chamberlain has gone to meet Hitler to solve the Sudeten crisis." Or: "The French don't want war, the British don't want war, and certainly the Germans don't want war. This is all silly posing over a territory no one cared about." Then finally, yesterday as I sat back on David's couch while Jean showered off after our session, he waved the front page of the paper at me and triumphantly read aloud: "Peace for our time."

"Giovanni *does not* need an air-raid shelter," Claude said. "We're about as likely to go to war with Germany as you are to marry Jean."

The truth was I'd confessed to David my worry about processing the film in the less than secure location of Giovanni's basement. With glee he'd given over to me a small, windowless pantry just off the kitchen they used exclusively for catering their parties.

Amongst the crates of vintage champagne hung all the shots of Jean drying under a red bulb. We hadn't been shooting every day, unlike what Claude believed. A handful of times, in a variety of positions, had been more than enough to gather ample material to keep Hella running back and forward to the post office multiple times a day.

"With all this time you're spending with them I thought they'd at least invite you to one of their parties."

"They haven't had yet," I answered honestly. "Hella says it's not quite the season."

"Well when they do you must get me an invite. All my business is drying up. I almost considered coming down to the Jardin du Luxembourg with you and whoring myself out in the bushes just to feel the touch of a man."

"What are you talking about?"

"This is the worst time to be a whore, in the stormy times when a war might be brewing. Times of real peace and actual conflict are the best in my profession, but this in between-ness just makes people afraid of a penicillin shortage."

Chapter 5

I SAT WITH DAVID in the entertaining kitchen, upon stools by the marble island I imagined being crowded with champagne coupes and silver trays of hors d'oeuvres. Instead, the counter was covered with the results of Jean's last visit which had certainly launched an incursion across the borderlines of artistic freedom. Even David had gasped when he first saw the results.

"I have to say I feel rather uncomfortable giving these to your wife."

"Oh, don't worry," he chuckled, "she takes them purely at their artistic value."

"Do you… think they have any? Artistic value, I mean."

David glanced over an image of Jean's bare backside, gently touching the edges of the paper as if it was round flesh.

"My boy, I can honestly say that not since I made Henri Matisse sit down and share a couple of gin rickeys with Pablo Picasso, right here in this very kitchen, have I made more of a contribution to the world of art." I blushed, thinking he was making fun. But his mouth stayed still and serious. "Forget cubism, futurism, dadaism and all that derivative, navel-gazing nonsense. This… this is something utterly unattempted since classical Greece. The eroticization of the male form, for the pleasure of men who can appreciate a good, firm backside." He slapped the image on the marble counter, causing me to jump.

"Aren't you afraid customs will open these up and the police will show up here? Or at the addresses of the people you're sending these to?"

David lifted one particular image he kept coming back to of Jean on his back, legs spread wide, with a thick phallus carved from pure ivory inserted halfway in.

"What's that? Oh no, not at all. All the envelopes are stamped with a diplomatic mark."

"Does that work?"

"Has so far. And when your name is Roosevelt, neither the police here nor customs there tend to ask too many questions." He picked up another image, this time of Jean staring at the camera while licking his own fingers covered in the end result of the photo shoot. "So much more useful a name than Rosenblatt, don't you think?" David laughed to himself, and I wasn't sure if it was from what he said, or the almost comical look Jean was giving the camera. "When we first arrived at Calais the poor border inspector couldn't make out the handwriting on our papers. Anyway, I had a book by Teddy Roosevelt in my bag, and showed it to the fellow to try and point out some of the letters. Well, he simply copied the name down, stamped our documents and that was it. Ellis Island in reverse, Hella called it. Returning to the old world and getting an upgrade from a couple of penniless Jews to American royalty. And ever since Franklin's been President, well we get half the post of the embassy anyway."

I listened intently, then we returned to our silent review of Jean captured in many ways. The early reviews had proved popular, and in fact had expanded their subscriptions threefold, all of them men, and all with addresses David could identify as expensive parts of cities spread out across the North American plain. Fifth Avenue in New York City, Beverly Hills in Los Angeles, and even the street in that Washington David assured me was the location of Congress.

The envelopes that arrived stuffed with checks and postal orders also contained various requests. Some were beyond the realms of human decency, but most were simple inquiries for what seemed like the most logical direction of our artistic adventure. The photographic revue of sex between men. A descent into an abyss I could scarcely pretend we weren't already deep inside.

"The trick is not to blow our wad too soon, so to speak." David had told me when I first broached the subject of an increased fee should I actually become an out-and-out pornographer, as opposed to the artistic revolutionary I hoped to consider myself to be. "We must create the demand first; have the word spread far and wide that from Paris comes the celebration of the male form, in a little brown envelope, delivered by the Post Office of the United States."

But we were not there yet. David still believed there was far more mileage to be gained with Jean. I, on the other hand, believed in Claude's Paradox. Fully seeing what Jean had to offer only spurred a thirst, it did not slake it. The more Jean's beauty was sexualized, debased like a gold standard, the more it became like a desire that could be quenched by anyone. Bearing witness to Jean as an auto-erotic creature fractured the illustrious truth of his ageless beauty. *It's hardly my paradox*, Claude told me when I broached the subject. *It sounds like yours.* "If only he could fuck himself," David said wistfully, biting his lip and looking over the dozens of pictures across the marble top. "What's next? What can he do?" He tapped his cheek, and with more trepidation than I expected, said:

"I think he's done."

David looked at me quizzically.

"Have you ever seen a more beautiful man in all of Paris?" I half expected David to laugh, but he didn't. Eventually, he shook his head.

"I must admit, I have not."

"Any other model we find would barely hold a torch to Jean. And I mean that sincerely."

David smiled. "I know you love him."

"What?" If I had been drinking tea, I would have spit it out.

"And I think he loves you, too. I see the way he looks at you. You can say no other model would compare to Jean, and that might be true, but even if we were to find a man as beautiful, or as enchanting, or as well-endowed as him, nothing could replace the look of love."

I glanced back over the pictures, trying to spot this look he was talking about.

"I saw it from the very moment I set eyes on your collection outside of Notre Dame. The existential force between the photographer and his subject no Kodachrome or colorization process could recreate, the unmistakable look of desire. You want him and he wants you, and what stands between you is only the camera." David went silent, watching me as I processed the words which secretly made sense. "That's why we have to capture Jean in every conceivable position and with every possible instrument we can, before you two have sex and break the spell. But I do take your point that there might not be much more we can humanely do with him."

It wasn't like Hella was sitting here to make me feel ashamed. I felt more myself around David than anyone else, including Claude. Around him, it was fine to desire Jean, because it was desire we were trying to capture. But there was a marked difference between the externality of arousing pictures of a haunting man, well endowed, to the heartfelt, intimate feelings for him I feared to speak out loud. The spark lit from our first spring meeting had faded over the summer months to a transactional, collegiate one where if he was to stop posing or I was to stop photographing, we might not see each other for many months.

Now in autumn with the bare truth revealed, there was even more reason to part eternally. One does not often visit the same whore, again and again, for the very same reason one does not re-read the same book, nor watch the same movie reel. Transactional relationships are inherently finite, and I believed, quite appropriately, in my mind, Jean and I would never rise above the muted stasis of situational friends. From the moment we'd met, his draw to me had been business. The camera I clutched meeting the figure yearning to be photographed. I was a fool to think a man like him could find my naivety attractive. That we were friends was a blessing in itself; and I'd let him down even at that. We had not risen above the supposed purpose of the pictures, to find Jean a modeling job worthy of his beauty. We had only descended, leaving his dream misplaced, like a man's billfold on a tram. It stung, and since it was half my fault, Jean would only ever half forgive me.

"I guess it isn't wise to fall in love with one's friends," I said, gazing out the kitchen window at the yawning entrance of the Jardin du Luxembourg as the trees swayed beyond the iron fence topped with golden spears.

"Quite the opposite." David said sharply. "Where else is one meant to find love?" I felt his eyes on me until I turned to meet him face on. "In the changing pavilion of the *Bois de Boulogne*? Out there in the park between the bushes?"

I didn't have an answer, but I had a question. "Is that where you used to look?"

David sighed. "For some, that's all the love they will ever know. Five minutes, if even that, in the dark, between men who think themselves as dirty. And if they think of themselves as filth, then filth they will always be. They will give nothing, only take, and be ashamed of it every moment before and after. Those men out there in the parks and in the pools think of their lives as shameful and those five minutes are the only times they feel alive. Imagine that. To feel alive for only five minutes, then spend the rest of your existence believing that when you felt most alive is the most shameful thing of all. And to tell you the truth, Anders, those encounters are shameful. Because there is no affection in them. No love, no passion. Only friction and spit. So yes, young man, I know what I say because there I looked, and forgive me but I found that empty life wanting. Judge me as you will, but I married a woman who makes me laugh and we each have sex with our good friends. There is not a lover of mine who has stepped foot in this house that my wife does not know, male or female, and the same goes for she."

Now David stood up, a fiery anger in his eyes, defending his interpretation of the revolution.

"I will forever choose spending hours with loving friends over five minutes of affectionless nothing. Take to the bushes if you please, Anders, but do not expect to find love there." He headed for the door, angrier than I'd ever seen him. But his anger was righteous. I agreed with every word he said, in principle. He was the revolutionary leader and I was the boy who didn't even know the touch of a man. In this long summer as the world swept to war, I was stuck reading theory while my comrades campaigned. The plots slipped away because I still feared my own truth. Who I was and who I perceived myself to be still very much divided by the camera lens. I'd known as a Biblical certainty that my desires could only be found in public facilities, or bushes of the Jardin Du Luxembourg. Now I could see they existed in expensive suites for fistfuls of cash, or on plush satin couches while a crew directed the scene. I would not reach out and touch it any more than I might one day switch places with Jean and have him photograph me.

David might be able to defend his grandiose vision of Bohemian love, but I was mere poseur, an Austrian Jew hiding out in Paris.

He opened the door from the kitchen but turned back to face me, his eyes not devoid of kindness but still full of exasperation.

"So yes, have sex with your friends. Have sex with Jean. Spend your time in the company of people who believe the same things you do, if that's what you truly believe. I have no shame in who I am or what I do; not as an American, not as a Parisian, not as a bisexual and certainly not as a Jew."

He left me alone. A tear crept suggested itself in my eye. The falseness of sitting at the right hand of a revolutionary while remaining petrified of the chaos change would bring.

* * *

By now I had been through the Jardin du Luxembourg many times at night. Indeed, I knew Paris just as well after dark as I did in the day. From the bright lights and crowded bars of Montmartre to the tourists dining on pavement cafés crushed together in the Latin quarter. But I had never seen the city through a filtered eye. Through the view of one hunting for illicit treasure between hidden spaces. Each rustle of a tree or crack of a branch that followed my footsteps I spun to see what shame it might be hiding.

David's words had struck harder than I'd ever imagined—for just like the first time he spoke of his idea of artistic revolution, and he spoke out loud the truth which had always been buried in my mind, so now he gave veracity to the knowledge that had always been in my soul.

Sitting on a bench in Vienna for hours on end and staring at the men who came and left the gentleman's facilities was no way to find love. It's why I had never indulged, despite the times I entered after building up the courage, only to shrink back like a shy young boy from even the vaguest suggestive look from either the top-hatted or flat-capped men inside.

Equally, I'd failed to find the draw in Claude's way of doing things—to go out to the back alley with any man who smiled his way at Giovanni's, or traverse Western Europe on the franc of old and lonely men, vampirically sucking out all they could of his young, vibrant life.

Both would bring the same, unsatisfactory dead weight of hurried trysts, devoid of emotion, blanched of love. Nor did it seem the happy middle David so superciliously spoke of was in my immediate grasp. He'd climbed mountains to get to himself—open and free and shameless. There was no guidebook to get to that destination. Even to give David the camera and have him photograph from the side while Jean did the things I dreamed deeply of was no substitute for emotion, connection. David , not I, was the one with friends who approached the erotic self with such open, reformed, and progressive morality that they could move between the clothed and unclothed state with all the care of shaking a cocktail.

Those people I would like to meet. I would like to see that in action. Those people I would like to study and learn from.

As I walked through the park, thinking those thoughts to myself on what felt like the last unfreezing night of the year. I pulled off my gloves, stuffed them in my satchel next to the camera and lit up a cigarette as the pathway unfolded towards the park gates and out to Rennes Metro station.

Alone on the dark path, I stopped for a brief moment, the sound of scuffling footsteps stopping with me. I fell onto a bench and smoked, as free and alone as that one black goose who chooses to stay behind during winter.

A light caught my eye, flickering behind the trees blowing in the wind. I thought it perhaps from the city beyond, the *noir* of Paris glimmering in sophisticated awe. Instead of a hard bench I imagined myself among those lights, under a restaurant canopy. Smoking with Constantine Cavafy, Josephine Baker, Jean and Claude. Stroking Chiquita under the chin while David brought us a round of drinks. Instead, I scuffed out my cigarette on the silent ground. Sore muscles devoid of touch screamed in protest as I rose to reluctant feet. They felt heavy. Clamped to the ground like I was chained in irons. Through wisps of chilled breath, I saw the light's trick. It was not the city after all. No provocative conversations at the café courts of the avant-garde. The sparkling light through waving spindles of dark trees a sign for a *toilette*, pulling me inwards to its hellish clutches. Satanic choirs might as well have been trumpeting around me—buffeted with the consternations of David the Prophet, castigating those men who chose to find release in the dark anonymity of the unknown. The irons did not release from my feet but dragged me forward, sliding rough across the park's path, falling, twisting into a sinkhole. The world became devoid of both light and life, the hidden city swapping places with the Paris of truth and light. Darkness and sin dragged me towards the gates of hell.

I lit another cigarette to give my wild hands something to do. In three quick drags the entrance found me. Flickering in electric light, reflected in a puddle by the men's entrance. It had not been raining. Breath heavy and chest tight, I glanced around at the encouraging darkness. Trees hid me from the rest of Paris, from the wider world. Only the orange light of a cigarette called out across no man's land that I was here. I snuffed out the flame with a boot against gravel and stepped inside. There was no door, no lock. The facilities never closed, as if the city was providing a public service—a non-stop playground of hungry men with a roof to protect the patrons from the elements, and even a dull electric bulb providing just enough light to find one's way around the wooden stall doors and white porcelain sinks.

Between the plopping drips of a leaky pipe, the unmistakable sounds of heavy, labored breathing drifted from the row of stalls. The cold steel of stubbornness my mother always said I'd inherited from my father hardened my spine and spirit. David, Claude, Jean—damn them all.

*   *   *

"Mother, what's hell?"

"Quiet, Anders, eat your strudel."

Amongst the clattering of plates and conversation in the grandest coffee house in Vienna, I ate the poppy seed strudel my mother always gave me when we came here with my grandmother. It wasn't just the buttery pastry or the thick, sticky sweetness of a million poppy seeds clumped together I loved, it was the way my mother told me each and every time it had been the favorite dessert of my father.

"You're ruining that child," said the stern, thin-lipped mouth of my grandmother. "Listen to him, asking about hell. This is what happens when you don't give him a proper Jewish education."

"And what would you have me do? Send him off to *Hashomer Hatzair* twice a week to get beat up on his way home? It's not safe, mother."

"Nonsense. And even so, what lesson is that to teach him? To let bullies win? Ignore his heritage, his family? Really, Alice."

With one smile, as warm as fire, as sweet as strudel, my mother deflected my grandmother's sharp tongue. Her white-gloved hand stroked my hair as I ate and drank my hot chocolate.

"Hell's a place where very bad people go when they die."

"*Some* people think so."

"I wasn't finished, mother. Yes Anders, people who go to church believe hell is a punishment for the wicked."

"What do we believe happens after you die?" I said.

"Who cares," my grandmother said, leaning across the table and wiping chocolate froth from my lip with her handkerchief. "What matters is what we do in this life, how we treat other people, how we take care of our families. Don't worry about death. It's life that is precious, Anders."

*   *   *

"I've been thinking about our little Jean problem," David said the next morning as we buttered croissants in the other kitchen I'd rarely seen. It was in what David called their private apartments—the living quarters of this royal couple, as opposed to the public rooms at the other end of the apartment.

Although this brass and dark wood kitchen was at the back of the building, looking out across private gardens instead of the park, the morning sun poked infrequently through the clouds. The old iron stove and red painted walls gave the place the air of a country cottage somewhere deep in the Dardanelles, instead of central Paris. Still, I took the invitation to join them for breakfast, instead of going straight off to the dark room as usual, as an apology.

Yet I felt like I owed Hella an apology for questioning her husband's morality. The rules they lived by might be new to me, but that didn't mean it was wrong. Far from it, they could very well have been the most morally upstanding couple I'd ever met. My own apology, running in my head like a broken Vinten, remained unspoken among the respectable politeness of their breakfast table.

"Our Jean problem?" I asked, pouring us both more coffee from the *cafétiere*.

"Wait, David," Hella chimed in, "before I forget, come to us next Friday night, won't you?"

My breath caught in my chest and I coughed up a piece of croissant. I could only imagine the next words as being an invitation to a *Shabbos* dinner. They would simply bypass the awkward question of my perceived Jewishness and jump straight into the detail.

"I thought it was about time to throw a little soiree now we're well and truly past summer and all that war in the Sudetenland nonsense has settled down. I thought you boys might like to show off some of your photographs."

David and I shared a subtle look which itself felt transgressive.

"Wonderful idea, darling. We'll call it, *le nouveau homme.* Invite Jean, won't you Anders? Everyone will adore him."

"Of course."

"Yes, do," Hella agreed, "and whoever else you'd like."

"Well my friend Claude—"

"Yes, yes, bring him too." David said, excitedly jumping from his chair and draining the rest of his coffee. "Now," he said, dashing to the door, "about my idea. How do you feel about really pushing the boundaries of the artistic revolution?" David said it with the widest grin I'd ever seen on him.

"M-more so? More than what we've done?" I got up from the table and wiped my mouth while Hella, job done, buried herself in yesterday's *Times* and buttered another croissant.

"Let me show you."

* * *

David led me down carpeted corridors to somewhere between the public and private parts of the Roosevelt mansion. We stepped inside an odd, 'L' shaped study with a couple of leather armchairs pushed up against overstuffed bookcases. Without saying a word, he moved a drinks cabinet, bottles rattling, to reveal a door I hadn't noticed until he opened it up.

"Welcome to the guest bedroom," he said with a sly smile as he flicked an electric light switch on.

The room was a windowless cube, the ceiling lower than the rest of the apartment and the flimsy looking walls clad in faded green wallpaper like a hastily arranged movie set.

I suppose the large film camera standing on a tripod and pointing down at the neatly made bed gave such an impression.

"A movie camera," David said, shuffling sideways through the narrow gap between the bed and the wall to get to the camera. This Vinten I knew well. It stood like some gargoylic piece of equipment from Dr. Frankenstein's laboratory. David tapped proudly against its metal and leather exterior. "A gift from a friend a few years ago. He burned down a studio to collect on the insurance money and thought it was a shame to let this be destroyed. So, he gave it to me," David played with the axle and the hinges squeaked as he swiveled it around the tripod. "We nearly set the place on fire, twice, the first time we tried to use it, and since then it's just been laying around," he sighed, "a good idea with no way to execute it. I thought you might know someone who—"

"I know how to use it." The words fell out my mouth before my mind could register they'd been said.

"Really?" David stared at me from across the bed with an impish grin, like a child up to no good. We both were. There was no hiding now from the true meaning of pushing the artistic boundary. I could tell myself all the stories I wanted, but none was clearer than a cinema-quality camera pointed straight at a mattress.

"Yes," I climbed over the bed to get a good look at the lens, "I learned at art school." I investigated the camera. Everything seemed to be in excellent condition. A little dusty, but a quick blow sorted that out. "I couldn't paint or draw, but they had one of these, so they set me to work recording Picasso and Dalí when they came to lecture." I didn't mention my secret reels of still-life models. "Kept me from falling asleep."

David watched in silent admiration while I familiarized myself with the one thing I'd learned at that place.

"It's not that hard to use," I told him. "You really don't need me. Maybe I could cut together some of the reel but… where do you want to show it? Don't tell me you have a projector back there too."

"Oh goodness no. Back there," he knocked on the hollow wall, "is just the pantry. Well I suppose your dark room now. No, no. One of our friends in Hollywood sent me a telegram after seeing Jean's pictures. Apparently, they caused quite the scandal among certain gentlemen's clubs up and down the California coast. Actors and stockbrokers alike are coughing up hundred-dollar bills just for facsimile copies of *le garçon parisien noir*. I figure we have this camera, and someone over there can surely get their hands on a projector. Just imagine," David put one arm around my shoulders as his other wrapped around the Vinten, "in one of those Santa Monica beach houses," he registered my hollow look, "it's where all the big shots in L.A. live—"

"Aha. I understand."

David returned to picture-painting: "in the clutches of the homosexual underground, in a sea of white faces, silk ascots and canvas loafers. Where to get an invite, one must have a seven-inch billfold and spend all your time in the gymnasium." Again, I looked at him blankly. "Trust me, Anders. I know the type all too well. Our host cracks open the metal tin casing and behold. Ten minutes of movie history. These men who've suffered through a lifetime of girly magazines and god-awful pin up broads finally have objects of their desires projected on the sponge-painted walls of left-handed high society."

"Can… can we do that?"

"Well it's never been done before, so I don't see why not."

I took in the entirety of the room which barely fit the two of us and the history making camera. "We'd need more lighting, that's for sure."

"Done."

"And I'd want to strip the walls. Or paint them, I don't care, just not this awful caterpillar green."

David's face dropped like he'd been the one to pick out the wallpaper, but only for a moment.

"Also done."

"And we'll need to move the camera, or the bed, or something. It's far too close to get a decent shot." I stepped towards the foot of the bed, counting my paces. "If only we could have another meter or so here, then the camera can face the head of the bed."

"I could knock the wall down? There's only a few feet of dead space behind this wall." David said like he had a sledgehammer ready to go. I didn't want him to go to such drastic lengths, especially since part of my mind was not fully committed to the idea. Although I'd already seen Jean in every conceivable state one man could get into, and taken hundreds of photographs in the process. What was so different about recording a film? Jean might find it different.

"You don't need to do that," I said, tapping on the flimsy, hollow board. "What if we just cut a hole for the lens and put the camera behind it? It might make the whole experience feel a little more natural for the performer."

David's mouth drew into a wide grin, and his eyes, and his cheeks, and every part of his face and body. As though I was finally thinking like him, like an artistic revolutionary.

"Well, my little director." I returned his broad smile. Finally feeling like I had something to offer this new world. Photographic whoremonger had never sat right with me. Video pornographer, well, that truly was pushing the boundaries, as David said. It didn't matter what perverted actions took place on that mattress. Making history was in the act of filming. Doing what Claude had always told me was the meaning of life: to create things unattempted yet, in prose or rhyme or the moving picture.

David beamed. "The whole world will know us."

Chapter 6

WE WALKED BRISKLY THROUGH the moon-lit Jardin du Luxembourg, Claude to my left, smoking, and Jean to my right, complaining about the state of the Third Republic. He'd been doing little else since Claude and I refused to come to a Communist rally with him last week.

"The problem with the French is they don't want to acknowledge I'm Black."

Our breaths and the tobacco smoke mingled together in the chilled night air and ghostly silver light. The ongoing gas strikes had quietened the streetlamps, but the electricity had returned at least. One could tell from the fiery yellow glow emanating from the Roosevelt Mansion, drawing us in like moths to the flame.

"But that's the beauty of France," Claude said. "We're all Frenchmen. I'm French, you're French, he's... Well he's Austrian but never mind. The Republic values absolute equality before the law, blind to color."

"Don't you see? That's exactly the problem. Refusing to acknowledge difference, in class or creed or skin, makes matters worse. We don't all stand equal before the law. I stand as a Black Frenchman, you as a white. What color is the magistrate? What color is the officer who arrests me for soliciting because I'm walking through the park, but allows you, a known prostitute, to cavort freely around the hotel lobbies of Paris?"

I glanced behind me with some nervousness, fearful of the police while in such company.

"There's no law against prostitution," Claude said, blowing smoke across us both.

"Nor against sodomy, but how many nights have I spent in jail, and how many have you?"

Claude shrugged while I wondered if and when I should intervene. The last thing I wanted was to enter the party with my guests squabbling.

"I wouldn't be complaining about discrimination if I had a cock the size of a school ruler."

Jean snorted. "I might be thirty centimeters long, *darling*, but you're half a meter deep."

Quickly I muffled a snort of laughter.

"Oh, think it's funny, do you?" Claude threw his cigarette to the ground and pointed to himself. "Well it was this hole that paid for the coat you're wearing."

"No one's throwing a party for your hole though, are they?" Jean muttered.

"Oh, they certainly are. You're just moving in the wrong circles. I've been to many a gathering honoring my *hole*. I might as well be a fucking fertility goddess."

We walked in silence through the remainder of the park, although I sped up as we passed by the public *toilette*, its electric light flickering, the portal to hell continually on offer. I knew of the demons inside. My personal demon taking the form of a bearded man. He could have been an artist, a painter who sold postcards in a stall next to mine. He wasn't handsome. He stank like a rummy and stumbled, too. But he'd known what I wanted without me saying a word. With a forceful hand and a fiendish grin, he brought me to my knees on broken tiles. I did not rise again until the sour taste of shame dribbled from my lips. I had stumbled, knowing there was so much further to go.

A gendarme had been watching from a cubicle. He was young. More nervous than I. With his hat on, he brought me up, not down, and sucked the air from my lungs as we kissed; long and deep, leaving my lips red and raw. I wasn't sure if he led or I, but in a flutter of moments, I leaned against the tiled wall, trousers around my ankles, as a stranger's breath burned the back of my neck and he bored into me. In a matter of hurried minutes it was all over. He pulled up his trousers and walked out without even a nod, leaving my virginity congealing on the broken tiles.

Was the *toilette* any different from where we were heading? It's simply a degree of wattage; one old bulb against a spectacle of illumination emanating from David and Hella's private rooms. True shame are the actions we do not want others to witness. For a man cannot live entirely shrouded in the darkness of shame for very long, or very well.

Neither Claude nor Jean lived in shame, nor David, nor Hella. Every spotlight on the stage could shine upon them, and they would cry to the crowds to bear witness and be smothered in roses by the last curtain call. Why did shame follow only me? Why did I insist on living my life behind the curtain, trapped in the shadows, watching all the other players dance?

"Anders, why are you running?"

I looked back at them both; they were rushing forward, confused, trying to catch up with me as I slowed to find my breath again. I had to get out of the park. I had to leave this shame behind.

By the time we left the park, the wild, brassy beat of jazz and laughter drifted down from the top floor of the Roosevelt Mansion like a painting come to life. Black silhouettes danced across the dazzling orange windows as we stood below, gazing up at the *joie de vivre*. An artist could not have envisaged a more Parisian scene. The critics would slay a filmmaker for indulging in such pastiche.

"They don't do them like this anymore," Jean muttered, looking up and quietly contemplating a time Claude and I could only imagine.

"Come on then!" Claude yelled, bounding for the door with the brass plaque and well-pressed buzzer.

I leaned over to Jean in the brief few seconds we now had to be alone. "Does it bother you? All those people up there, looking at those... *pictures* we took."

There it was. The shame. It drifted over from the park like a poisonous gas and swirled around my nostrils making me want to choke. Whatever the guests upstairs would think was by my own hand. I studied his face for any hint of regret, the slightest blush of anguish I recognized in myself each morning I looked at my sullen reflection in Claude's chipped mirror.

Yet all Jean did was grin, then grabbed my hand and placed it squarely on his crotch. There it was—the thing teasing me for months. The thing I'd wanted the most but had been too ashamed to ask for. My heart fluttered in my chest and the cold closed in around my ears as blood rushed to the point of contact. His smile the first beam of sunlight breaking through a heavy sky.

"That's meant to cost ten francs," Claude called over from the doorway. There was a twang of suspicion in his voice. "Don't give it all away for free, my dear." Claude said as he held the door to the stairway open for us both. "People might realize that's the only color you come in."

*   *   *

"Sorry we're so late," I said to Hella as soon as I found her treading in a wash of people, drinks, music, conversation. The mansion was packed like a brasserie before an opera debut. Hella was perched on the couch we always took tea on, the party guests breaking over her like waves. She wafted her cigarette holder to one side as I leaned down to kiss her three times on the cheek while kindly holding back the engorged feather flopping from her hat.

"I never knew the rich smelled so good," Jean muttered behind me.

"You've found it, darling." Claude shot back, "the perfect way to introduce yourself."

"There's hardly any trams because of the strikes," I continued, stepping sideways to present Jean and Claude to our hostess.

"Oh. You didn't come by motorcar?" Asked a woman sitting next to Hella. She wore her black hair in a short, severe bob—the kind that had gone out of fashion with the Depression. Her eyebrows were drawn on with pencil, and she spoke by pointing her prominent nose directly at us. I shook my head in response, feeling the first pricks of the class-based uncomfortableness I'd feared.

"Darlings," Hella said to us, "this is my good friend Kiki, the queen of Montparnasse."

"That's funny," Claude said, barging by Jean and me and clasping Kiki's black-gloved hand. "They call me the queen of Montmartre."

"And did you also come by tram?" She asked him with an interrogating look, one self-proclaimed monarch testing the other.

"No, of course not. I cantered here accompanied by the horses of apocalypse."

"Isn't it four horse*men*?" Hella asked.

"Very correct darling, and I had all four of those men mounting little old me on the way here. So if you wouldn't mind, I'd quite like to sit down and rest my weary haunches."

Kiki threw her head back and shrieked with laughter. "Come join me on my throne, then," she said, patting the velvet between her and Hella. "And we'll discuss our reign."

Claude seized the opportunity to curl up in a position between the two grande dames of the evening, squarely cementing his place as the third dame they didn't know they'd been missing.

"Darling," Hella said to me, "go find David. He's been waiting for you to arrive. He wants to present you as the maestro behind these photographs everyone's come to see. I think he's over there in the kitchen."

Leaving Claude to his perch, Jean and I slunk away. It would have been easier to whack through an equatorial jungle with a butter knife than make it through the throng of people oozing out of every crevice of the room. Like some greatly intricate dance, the bodies weaved between chintz chairs and throw pillows, following the flow of champagne like a bubbly tide. If war was on their minds, they'd determined to go out dancing.

Even through the mélange of conversation, we could hear the band reaching a crescendo. Bass and sax and trumpet and drum, interspersed with the chiming notes of a mighty soprano, an entire musical spectacle occupying the space normally reserved for photographing Jean *sans-culottes*. A short woman who owned the gigantic voice was finishing up a French tune, holding the final high note longer than I'd ever heard someone do. The entire crowd swayed with her, gasping in awe as she accomplished the triumphant climax of the song. The Black man on the saxophone flittered out a final brass note, and we all leapt into applause.

"Édith!" a thin-faced man with curled hair and his suit hanging off his bones called out, squeezing between us. "Oh, Édith darling, that was simply wonderful." He quickly clapped his hands then kissed her on both cheeks—two times. Together they looked quite the pair. She as petite as he was gaunt. "We must find time to talk. I have the most wonderful project for your talents."

The crowd watching dissipated during their conversation, leaving only Jean and I standing blankly, openly watching these two to talk on the makeshift stage while the band had a whiskey break.

"Aren't you two a handsome pair," the man said, inspecting us both like a prime cut of meat.

"Aha," Édith said to Jean, her expression falling back into a damp melancholy now the song was over, "you must be our model. Come," she took his hand like a schoolteacher, "Josephine's been asking for you all night. I think she's in the kitchen."

"Miss Baker's been asking for me?" Jean squealed, snatching Édith's hand and leading her off to the kitchen instead.

"Well," the man said, "I guess that leaves the two of us. Monsieur Cocteau, if you may, but my enemies and lovers call me Jean." He stuck out a hand and shook mine firmly. In his suit it felt like we were conducting a business transaction. "Which one will you be?" He asked with a twinkling of his eyes like a warlock casting a spell. His magic struck with a sharp current. More shocking than a Vinten model H set up in David's secret boudoir. More breathless than when I'd first spied Jean naked. Shaking my hand was the unsurmountable, unimpeachable, and unrivaled bastion of the Paris set. Monsieur Jean Cocteau. The man who spat sarcastic epitaphs at Hemmingway and could close an art gallery with one cutting comment passed under his thin moustache. No leader of the French Republic, no visiting writer or star of the Folies Bergère had a hope in hell to survive in the Paris social scene without paying homage to the novelist, the filmmaker, the poet, the playwright, the artist and the very embodiment of the avant-garde, Monsieur Jean Cocteau.

I didn't know how to respond to his heavy wink, so I just mumbled: "Pleased to meet you, Monsieur Cocteau. I'm Anders."

"From Vienna; oh yes I know. David's been going on and on about you for weeks. Hasn't let me see a single one of your pictures yet, the beast. Well, let's get a drink inside you, shall we? See where that takes us."

I followed him through the crowd, conscious of the eyes upon us. Jean Cocteau seemed to be the man everyone wanted to speak to. Their unspoken thoughts moved across silent lips as he nodded away those who might dare and interrupt the path we walked. But like an emperor, Jean Cocteau was not a man one addressed without a formal invitation.

We made it to the far corner of the room where a few couches were arranged around a table covered in an assortment of glasses and bottles in various states of repletion. A distinct scent of recently smoked opium wafted in the air. Two men sat lazily together, but talking seriously. The closer one had his foot up on the table, delicately surrounded by the half-empty glassware, and looked vaguely familiar, as if I'd sat opposite him on a tram and remembered his beauty for later.

"Anders," Cocteau said, standing me in front of the two men and interrupting their conversation, "this is Emmanuel," he pointed first to the one sitting further away. "Apparently he's a photographer of some note, although I don't really care for surrealism myself."

"Ha, ha," Emmanuel said, standing up and vigorously shaking my hand. "Pleased to meet you, Anders." His American accent was far more pronounced than David's. I imagined he was fresher off the boat than most.

"And this," Cocteau said, pointing to the strikingly handsome man with his foot indifferently on the table, "is my lover, the disgustingly talented Monsieur Jean Marais."

I couldn't not be taken aback by the casualness with which Cocteau introduced this stunning man awash in wavy blond hair framed by a chiseled, clenched jaw perfectly proportioned for the big screen. Next to the wiry, Slavic sallowness of Emmanuel, Jean Marais was a Gallic god, and strangely familiar.

Marais didn't move from his comfortable berth. He nodded at me briefly and said only: "*Salut*," before looking past me to Cocteau and asking: "Are Salvador and Gala here?"

"Haven't seen them, why?"

"Paul is over there," Marais said, pointing with a bottle of Russian marked vodka I hadn't noticed him cradling.

Cocteau glared across the room. With his hands still on my shoulders like a father to a son, there was little else I could do but look too. Whispered gossip I was not yet privy to whipped between the men. It involved figures I could not see or did not recognize, slipping between the drawing room and the hallway in fine dress soaked in cocktails at the cuffs.

I slunk into the chair beside Marais. Or more accurately, was guided firmly by Cocteau. I had to crowd my legs to one side because Marais refused to move his leg from the table, as if wanting me to stare directly at his crotch.

"I know you!" I said suddenly. "You were in *Nights of Fire.*" It was the first film I'd seen in Paris with Claude. Marais vaguely conceded the point with a smile of bleached teeth so angularly aligned they could have been sculpted by a master.

"Marcel L'Herbier utterly butchered Tolstoy," Cocteau said, still standing, but handing me a drink. "Never trust a straight director with a Russian novel, that's what I say." I sipped the drink suspiciously, unsure what taste to expect. Its harshness burned my throat and my lips convulsed into a splutter.

"Looks like the boy's not getting along with the vodka," Emmanuel said, chuckling at my coughing fit.

"Well it's an acquired taste, after all. But when you've gone to bed with as many Russians as we have," Cocteau said, "acquire the taste you must."

"I'll drink to that," Emmanuel said. Marais responded by taking a swig from the bottle. His eyes darted between me and Cocteau, now perched on the arm of my chair. Marais wore the broad, distant mask I knew from Claude's dabbles with the opium pipe. But his cloudy haze was about to lift, and soon he would enter the plateau of epiphany.

"And how was it for you?" An uncomfortably smooth voice washed in acid said from behind. I turned to look as Cocteau leapt up from the arm of the chair and greeted this newcomer with the standard kiss. Grease was all about this man. Grease smothered his black hair, making it stick to his scalp like it had been glued on. Grease swathed his long, thin moustache. Grease oozed from the pores of his skin.

"Doctor Mélenchon," Cocteau declared, wrapping an arm around the man's stiff neck. "Meet my new friend Anders. He took those hush-hush pictures David *dragged* us all here to see."

"How do you do?" Mélenchon offered a limp hand that left my palm slightly damp. "Seems it worked quite well indeed," he said to Cocteau about Marais who had clearly left the plane of existence the rest of us were occupying.

"Oh indeed it has. I assume in twenty minutes or so he'll be bouncing around the place."

Mélenchon handed Cocteau a small cube wrapped in, quite ironically, grease-proof paper. "For the come-down. Fresh in from Oran."

"Wonderful. I'm glad you switched back to Algerian hashish. The Tunisian one was awful."

Mélenchon flashed me a sly smile I didn't like. "Let me know if you're ever in the market for a fix," he said with a wink.

"I'm fine, thank you."

"Are you in Paris for long?" Cocteau asked him.

"No, no, Just till next week. Salvador is coming down to Perpignan with me. Wants to spend Christmas in my studio."

"Or sampling your latest imports."

"Perhaps. Although he'll make a pleasant counterweight to the politics of my usual dinner guests these days."

"How goes the civil war?"

"A nightmare. I do wish Franco would hurry up and take Barcelona already. All we hear at night is the damn artillery and incessant gunfire. The Languedoc has become worse than the Eastern Front."

"Ha," Cocteau laughed, "everyone up here is pissing their pants about even the suggestion of war, and you're down there living it."

"For three years!" Mélenchon kissed Cocteau on the cheek and began to slither away, but not before turning back, pointing at Marais once again, and saying: "Do let me know if it makes him a better fuck, will you?"

Cocteau laughed politely and shooed him away, turning back to us even though we'd been listening to their entire conversation.

"How many fascists are you friends with?" Emmanuel said as soon as Mélenchon was a safe distance away. Cocteau swung round on the arm of my chair to face his accuser, throwing his legs over the other arm and essentially trapping me underneath.

"He's not a fascist, just a sympathizer. Anyway, I'm a friend to all, my dear. One shouldn't discriminate based on political opinion. What is it you Americans say? Freedom of expression and all that."

"And freedom of assembly," Emmanuel responded. "Meaning we're also perfectly free to kick Dalí out of the surrealist movement, and any other autocrats."

"Thank you, I did read Paul's diatribe against Salvador. It was in itself a rather surrealist thing to do, excommunicating the greatest surrealist who ever has, or probably ever will live." Cocteau let the barbs soar over the strung-out Marais and land where they lay. I didn't expect it, but his words sent a previously congenial Emmanuel into a man sizzling with displeasure.

"I even sent back a copy of the letter with a few corrections," Cocteau continued, sensing he had the upper hand. "One should never write while blinded by anger, remember that," he said to me, tapping my shoulder, "but while full to the brim with opium, and slightly before commencing a long night with a good hard cock." He gave Marais a soft kick with the toe of his shoe, but the actor barely moved at all.

Emmanuel laughed, but it was strained laughter, barely concealing a seething resentment that had either been papered over long ago, or was due to erupt very soon. Either way, the distance between them was far greater than the space around the coffee table.

"What do you think should be done with fascists, Anders?" Emmanuel asked. I sensed the attempt to draw me into one side of this festering wound between them, so I coughed and mumbled and pretended to think of an answer.

"You can't ask him that!" Cocteau cried. "He's Austrian."

"So what?"

"So, there's Nazis all over the place. What if they heard him?"

Emmanuel scoffed at the suggestion. "What do you mean all over the place?"

"Well there's two by the door," Cocteau waved in the general direction of the rest of the room, but I couldn't make out who he might be pointing at specifically. "And I'm one, according to you. Plus isn't that Dalí over there?"

All of us, even Marais, sat up a bit straighter and peered towards the kitchen where Dalí was allegedly to be found. I could only see a gaggle of people exiting the kitchen, laughing and holding recently filled champagne coupes, and then David ushering them all out.

"That's not a fascist, *darling*," Emmanuel said, mocking Cocteau's intonation. "Just one of David's ghastly old hat stands."

"Everyone," David called to the room, taking center stage as the band trumpeted down into brassy silence. "If I can have your attention for a moment. Thank you all for coming this evening to celebrate yet another milestone in our never-ending exploration of the boundaries of art. A few months ago, my lovely wife pointed me in the direction of a humble street merchant selling the most eye-catching images I'd seen in a long time."

Immediately I shrank into the chair, attempting to sink beneath Cocteau's legs before David forced me to stand up in front of the crowd containing an unknown quantity of fascists. I caught only a glimpse of his gaze. But it made him pause for a moment, as if reassessing what he was about to say next.

"You all know of my fondness for vagrants and vagabonds. After all, why else would you all be here?" The room chuckled with light laughter.

"Out in the hallway we've set up the fruits of our recent labors. The very first presentation of striking, highly erotic images catering entirely to the sensibilities of a certain type of gentleman. Well, you all know who I'm referring to. The queers!"

"Hurrah!" A cheer rose from Cocteau, and a good dozen others around the room I couldn't identify.

"Ladies and gentlemen, please make your way out to the hallway as we present to you the artistic revolution that is *l'homme noir homoérotique de Paris.*"

The room burst into applause. David shot me a wink, both of quiet congratulation and acknowledgment that I did not particularly want to be so publicly acknowledged, at least in this speech, to this crowd, at this moment.

I followed the party out into the hallway, now adorned with copies of prints of Jean in all his glory. I tried to see them objectively—soaking up the saturation and purity of tones like I was a neutral observer. A shining ivory phallus held its own rhythmic light against the dark hues of Jean, who was squatting on it while he faded into dark corners like a Caravaggio. The composition of this particular image was a deliberate nod to Jesus on a cross. The colors and the context completely inverted. But the most important thing was for me not to turn bright red from shame. Jean certainly wasn't. He stood at the top of the hallway, greeting his admirers at the turn where the viewing line moved from one side of the impromptu gallery to the other.

I swayed a little awkwardly around the hallway, not quite knowing where to put myself. I couldn't find Claude, and I certainly did not want to take any credit away from Jean. This was his body; it should be his victory.

"It feels rather *déclassé*, no?" I heard Emmanuel say to Cocteau. "I try to avoid ever having to see another man naked in real life, why would I want to see him in art?" I drifted towards their orbit, peering between their heads to see the picture Emmanuel did not like. Jean was sitting naked on a stool, his legs spread wide, cradling his unrepentant erection with both hands. I liked the shot. It reminded me of a similar image of Mary cradling the baby Jesus.

"It doesn't give me vertigo or cause me to vomit involuntarily, so it's certainly not one of your self-indulgent, surrealist-for-the-sake-of-being-unique pieces, but I think it's breath-taking."

"You're only saying that because you like seeing pictures of naked men."

"Of course I am, just as you only dislike it because you don't like seeing pictures of naked men. Such is the privileged position you hold over me." Cocteau let his words hang in the air and sipped champagne. It took Emmanuel a few moments to understand he was not, in fact, being given a compliment.

"So my opinion holds no weight?"

"Not really, no. The entire artistic universe is constructed around giving men like you, what's that English word, your *jollies*. Titillating, tantalizing, teasing you. There is simply no end to what people will do to themselves to advance the cause of heterosexual arousal. You yourself have contributed to that canon no end. But when we deign to take one small corner of the world for ourselves, you have the audacity to stand here and—"

"Psst," someone whispered behind me. I spun and found Claude, his face a twisted mess of anger. Kiki of Montparnasse was attached to his arm, leaning away from him and laughing at another conversation. "I thought you hadn't seen his cock?"

"What?" I whispered back.

"You told me you'd never seen Jean naked. Not only is he naked, but... coming Kiki!"

She was dragging Claude by the arm and turned to see why he was stuck. I thought she was grinning at me, so I smiled back, but with a flush of embarrassment I realized she was looking at someone else.

"Sweetie, there you are," Emmanuel said, casually but harshly pushing me aside. "I've been busy having my taste questioned by an opium addict."

I looked over my shoulder and saw Cocteau had already drifted away. Kiki remained attached to Claude as she partially stumbled into Emmanuel to greet him with a kiss.

"It's all a bit vulgar, isn't it? Don't worry, my love. Size isn't the only thing a woman needs."

"Not the sort of thing you'd want performing at L'Oasis, is it?" Claude asked her, but was speaking directly to me.

"My God no. That Jean belongs in a menagerie."

I wanted to say something in retort. If not to defend my work, then at least my interpretation of Jean. There was a truth in what I'd heard Cocteau say, and Claude was only turning on me, I knew, because he was annoyed. There could have been a mountain of praise heaped upon the pictures, but a slice or two, from a name people knew, was enough for the critique to be lodged forever in my mind.

"You know," I began, stopping Claude, Kiki and Emmanuel in their tracks.

"Anders!" David called from across the hall. He looked to still be relaxed and genial, but I sensed a sour note in his tone—like tasting an expensive wine you were too afraid to say had gone sour.

"Excuse me," was all I said, and left Claude with a look of being stung.

David pulled me into the doorway of the main room, standing on his toes to gaze over the murmuring crowd still enjoying the display.

"You see that man over there? The one drinking the schnapps?"

I followed David's line of sight and spotted exactly who he was talking about. If I'd been offered a prize of a thousand francs to pick out the one German at this entire soiree, I would have bet it all on the German being this distinguished looking fellow.

His blond hair, slightly receding, swept back from sharp blue eyes and a clear face ending in a short little yellow moustache in the style of many

91

leading Nazis. I thought I spied an Iron Cross under his stiff collar, but then he turned his back to me.

"I see him. Who is he?"

"The prince of Hesse." David whispered with a breathless urgency, as if the very act of speaking aloud might itself invoke an invasion. I turned and stared at David, finally witnessing the crack of fear across his face. It was the same fear I refused to acknowledge, despite all signs to the contrary. The fear of being a Jew in mainland Europe in late '38 while the governor of a German province sipped schnapps in the hallway.

"What does he want?"

"Two things," David said. "First, to keep his wife occupied for the next half hour." I looked again and noticed a slight, soft-featured woman chatting with another distinguished couple. "Your little whore-friend doesn't speak Italian, does he?"

"I don't think so."

"Fuck. That would've been useful."

"Why?"

"She's the daughter of the King of Italy."

"Okay," I said, starting to sweat a little myself at being in such close proximity to two individuals who could reach both Hitler and Mussolini within the hour. "Wait, why do we need to keep his wife occupied for half an hour?"

David straightened his waistcoat in a vain attempt to salvage some sort of decorum amongst us both. "Now for the second thing. The prince would like a private audience with Jean."

"With Jean?" I asked, then immediately regretted opening my mouth. David shot me a sharp look. This was not the time to be dumb.

"Leave the wife to me," David said. "You get the prince into the study at the end of the hallway. I'll send Jean in when the coast is clear. Then—"

"Then?" I whispered through a heart already thumping at the thought of being alone with, or even speaking to, a high-ranking member of the Reich. "What do you mean then?"

David leaned down close to me, so close I could smell the dampness of his skin. "I hung a painting over our little camera hole in the wall, but I cut a hole out of it, the painting I mean, and replaced it with some light cloth to keep the camera lens a secret… more or less."

"David, why in the hell did you do that?"

"Jean Cocteau and I were thinking of doing an experiment with Marais. I was going to ask you to hang around later and turn the camera on but… never mind. It's all set up now."

"Set up for what? Cocteau knows about this?"

"Shh!"

"David," I tried to summon all my sincerity, but I feared it came out as little more than a whimper, "what the fuck has your secret camera room got to do with me talking to a fucking Nazi?"

"This is a massive opportunity we have here."

"Have you been smoking opium? What opportunity?"

David cleared his throat and gripped my shoulder. We'd already been standing in the doorway for longer than was probably polite for the host and the photographer.

"Listen. Once Jean and the prince are alone in the study, show them the room where they can get acquainted. Tell them you'll be waiting right there in the study and they won't be disturbed. Then turn the gramophone on, slip out, and lock the door." He placed a key in my palm and wrapped my fingers around it before I could say a word. "Come through here, into the kitchen and into the pantry where your darkroom is. Slip through the crawlspace, get the camera running and… *voilà*."

"*Voilà*?"

David breathed a nervous sigh. "We'll have a film reel of Victor Emmanuel's son-in-law and the Führer's aristocrat doing the dirty with a Negro man. *Voilà* isn't the half of it."

"David, have you thought this through? What if—"

"What if Prince Philipp of Hesse turns out to prefer being a Roman instead of a Greek? Yes, I thought about that. Let's hope Jean is a professional." He slapped me a bit too hard on the shoulder, pushing me involuntarily forward towards the crowd parting like the Red Sea to the unknown shore of the German prince casually stealing glances at the pictures of Jean. "Worst comes to worst, we'll send you in," David said loud enough to end our private conversation.

I did the only thing I knew how to do when finding myself in a situation where I wanted to die—breathe through my nose, shake my head, and imagine I was taking the first fateful steps towards the Bohemian revolution.

* * *

"*Erlaucht Landgraf,*" I said to Prince Philipp in German, addressing him by his proper title and adding a short bow for emphasis. He looked at me, slightly surprised, but immediately gave me his full, aristocratic attention. "Would you mind coming with me for a moment? There's an urgent telegram for you from Berlin."

"*Meine Landgräfin,*" I said over-politely to his wife, nodding as I walked silently with her husband down the hallway towards the less public section of the Roosevelt Mansion, and then the study. We passed by Jean leaning against the wall and laughing flirtatiously with a middle-aged bald man I didn't know. The prince didn't look at Jean once, let alone twice. He wasn't pretending to ignore Jean, he simply didn't acknowledge his presence.

How easy it was for these men to lead their double lives and keep their secrets. I thanked whomever I could thank that I was here in Paris, surrounded by every notable queer in the city. For if I had lived in any other time where my life depended on playing a role as wonderfully as the prince was able to play his, I would surely have been put to death long ago.

Jean watched us walk and for the quickest second our eyes met. A question flowed from him to me. Jean mouthed a less-than-subtle "*who's that?*"

I shuddered at how badly this could have gone had the prince not been a better actor.

"Right in here, sir," I said quickly, bounding forward to open the study door. The prince went inside. I spun around, hoping to see David calmly gliding the Italian princess away. But I couldn't see him, nor had anything changed in the crowd. His wife was still chatting politely to guests perfectly content even without her husband to prop her up.

So many things had to happen all at once. David needed to send Jean in. Jean needed to agree. I'm sure I'd be a sore disappointment for the esteemed Landgraf. Then I had to maneuver myself into a crawlspace between two walls and secretly operate a gargantuan piece of machinery, completely unnoticed. All on pain of... I didn't want to think of a fate worse than what would befall me when they caught me filming the sexual escapades of senior Nazis. I closed the door, receiving a look from Jean as I did.

"Fuck," I whispered to only me.

* * *

Eight-and-a-half minutes later, the prince and I were sitting on the only two chairs in the small 'L' shaped study listening to the clock mark each passing second of our growing discomfort.

I'd already refreshed his drink and swallowed mine in one gulp. Thankfully, he knew better than to ask about the telegram. But talking about anything else was quite out of the question.

"What brings you from Austria?" He asked, picking up on my accent and the fact that not speaking was, at this point, more embarrassing than anything he or I might say.

"Photography," I answered, and immediately regretted it. In this context, that only meant one thing.

"Ah." He smiled. "They're very good, I must say. Of course, officially they're degenerate trash, but between you and I, I'm rather taken."

"Thank you very much, sir. I appreciate that."

"Do you know the model well?" He probed, and I wondered if he thought I might be Jean's gatekeeper, or perhaps pimp, and in fact he had to make some kind of offer to me to move the transaction forward.

"Just friends. I mean, not really friends. Colleagues, you know. Model and photographer."

"It's all right. We're not all knuckle-draggers. Germany is just going through a stage of—"

Fortunately, the study door opened right at that moment and Jean entered, saving me from my inability to smile through a round of Nazi rationalization.

"This better be good," Jean said to me, seemingly not noticing the prince sitting in the corner. "I was this close to getting Max Jacob to paint my portrait in exchange for sucking my—"

"Jean," I said loudly and stood up, "let me introduce you to Prince Philipp, the next Landgrave of Hesse."

Instantly Jean turned his charm back on. "*Guten abend,* my prince."

The prince stood up and shook Jean's hand. "Nice to meet you."

The three of us fell back into silence. Jean grinning at the prince, who looked slightly bemused, and me suddenly remembering I had a key in my pocket.

"Well…" I started but stopped before saying *enjoy* or *I'll leave you to it.* So I said nothing, and just left the room, forgetting to open the door to the private quarters. Back in the hallway I breathed an enormous sigh, but it gave no relief. The hall was mostly empty; the guests had returned to the main room as the band played an upbeat tune, and most importantly the prince's wife was nowhere to be seen.

"Oh fuck," I said again, and rushed back inside the room, slamming the door closed and startling Jean and Philipp who had moved to within half a meter of each other.

"Sorry, sorry." I rushed over to the drinks trolley while nearly tripping over my own feet. The two men watched in silent wonderment as I moved it out of the way and opened the door in the wall to the bedroom. "This might be more comfortable," I said, flicking on the light and stealing all the looks I could at the picture David had hung to hide the camera hole.

The boudoir was smaller than I remembered it. The bed, beautifully made, stole the center of the windowless cubby tucked into the Roosevelt Mansion. Being behind two locked doors, to the study and then to the secret room, it imbued an aura of secret silence. Only the faintest thumps from the band beyond could be heard. I glanced anxiously at the walls; various pictures hung to deflect from the utilitarian bareness of the room. It wasn't hard to spot the Picasso David had hung to cover up the hole in the false wall, behind which was that fucking Vinten. I almost wished I didn't know a thing about it, to let some other patsy risk life and limb in this maddening enterprise. I only ventured a few brief glances at the Picasso. It was rather second rate. A hodgepodge of brightly colored shapes and half-faces probably left unsold from the art shows David threw for him. Anders, look at yourself, I thought, almost on the cusp of a chuckle—before art school, before Paris, I would have never known you could criticize a Picasso, or how it could be done, on what grounds, or that there were such things as good Picassos and bad Picassos or good Matisses and bad Matisses and so on for all the titans. Fortunately, this effort's garish muddle of colors and shapes hid quite well the cloth covering the camera lens. I couldn't spot it myself. I only hoped Jean and the Nazi were more interested in each other than the fixtures and fittings.

"I'll be right out in the hallway, so… um… take your time."

With the exact same indifference with which the prince had walked past Jean in the hall, he walked past me, then Jean followed him into the room. I grimaced and shivered at the cold-blooded irony that I'd come to David's, and brought Jean with me, to make art, not whoremonger. And here I was, whoremongering behind art. Oh what a world I was in.

As Jean closed the secret door, he gave me a toothy, nervous grin, but I couldn't help but feel I was feeding him to the wolves.

But the door to the secret room clicked shut, and the countdown started. By myself in the study, I quickly put the gramophone on, then spotted the remainder of the Landgraf's drink. A golden whiskey. Scotch of an ancient vintage. David's private collection, the sort Americans are drawn to in the way the French collect bottles of wine which once graced the cellars of Napoleon III. I never had a taste for whiskey, but I downed the remainder of Prince Philipp's glass in one grimacing gulp. The gramophone was at least doing its job and started playing some Duke Ellington; jazz would have to do. I darted back into the hallway, locking the study door.

"Why were you in there with Jean?" It was Claude. My mind froze. The hallway resplendent with Jean's naked photos still remained, although most of the guests had drifted back into the drawing room, where the band could be heard full force from here.

"I… uh. There's a…"

"I don't know why you keep lying to me, Anders. You told me you'd never seen Jean naked, and yet suddenly there's dozens of photos you've taken of him far more than naked. You're always whispering with David and spending all of your time here without ever telling me why."

"Claude, I'm sorry. I have to—"

"Go, yes of course you do. Well you know what Anders? So do I."

97

His face was lined and furrowed, not with anger, but sadness. I saw the blackness around his eyes more than I ever had before. It marked the hollow spot, the empty space he now had from having to give so much of himself away in order to survive.

"What? Where are you going?"

"Away. The south. A lovely gentleman named Doctor Mélenchon suggested I spend a few weeks away from winter in the sun. He said it would do the world of good for my health, and I agreed. I was going to invite you to come down to Perpignan, but…" The verge of tears rushed towards him, but he swallowed it back. "You're the worst kind of hypocrite, Anders. You silently judge me for smoking a bit of opium or not being afraid of men or sex, as if you inhibit some virginal quality. Yet here you are, hanging around with Jean Cocteau and his drugs, sucking off Jean and doing God knows what with David. Judge me for being a whore all you like, but at least I live the full measure of myself. And… I'm fine with it."

Claude turned and marched straight down the hallway, not daring to look at the pictures of Jean so overtly on display. Claude was right, about everything. From the opium-fueled inquisition in our shared attic bedroom when he'd questioned my reasons for coming to Paris, to this very moment, calling out my hypocrisy. Every self-serving lie I told—about my secret love for a prostitute named Jean, to sating my shame-filled view of sex by living on the depraved stories Claude told me, to hiding my Jewishness even from another Jew, right up to this farcical evening where a painting by Picasso was butchered to make way for *Entartete Kunst* caught on film. I ran after Claude, yet slowed, surrounded by my own renderings of Jean's erotic gaze.

"Claude, wait. Please. Don't go yet. Claude. At least don't leave like this. Let me say goodbye."

Claude whipped open the heavy front door. A chill blew up the stairs. At the bottom the greats of Paris were taking their exit from the Roosevelt Mansion, their vibrancy seeming to beckon now to Claude. A few magnificent voices tinkled up, over the balling strings of the lively band. Claude, simply shook his head. Not just disappointment, but a sense of loss. Of what we'd had together, before I rammed Jean into our lives and set myself on a path to win unattainable beauty. Claude was sure I should have listened to him. And let the beauty just be. To watch it from a safe distance, and not chase it through the streets of Paris, like a madcap botanist trying to catch a singular butterfly. And I was ready to admit he was right. Claude's eyes reddened.

"Goodbye, Anders."

The front door of the mansion slammed shut, yet I heard him clomp down the stairs. But I had not even a moment to contemplate my loss. No time to take a breath. The band played on, and time ticked down.

I rushed through the main room where slightly less people than before were hunkering down for the night. Kiki and Josephine were dancing by the makeshift stage. I looked around and calmed down just a little when I saw Hella sitting on the couch in the middle of the room with the prince's wife. They were laughing. She looked relaxed. Things might be okay.

In the kitchen a handful of waiters were stacking cleaned glasses and silver trays, and David was laughing with a couple, but his eyes when they saw me were anything but smiling.

"Linda," the woman said, still laughing and vigorously shaking my hand. She was dressed in trousers and a coat like she'd only this moment returned from safari in the heart of Africa. "And this is my good friend, Roland."

"How do you do?" The jovial Englishman shook my hand far less hard than she had done.

"I was just telling David," Linda continued, "how wonderful your photographs are. I've never seen anything like it. I have a studio on the Left Bank. I mainly do models, but you should come by if you'd ever like to collaborate."

"Oh do," Roland added, gripping my shoulder, "I would love to see more of your commercial work. Perhaps we can arrange a small opening for you in London."

"Thank you, honestly. I think the general consensus might be that they are all a bit vulgar."

"You must never pay any mind to an art critic, particularly an American in Paris," Roland said. What is it they say about Americans and Paris? Once here, they can never find happiness again, and what good is an American who isn't happy."

They all chuckled together, but the vein on David's forehead was cracking, and my feet were on fire, dancing from one to the other as I mentally counted the articles of clothing Jean had taken off the Landgraf by now… or the inches they'd already covered.

"What's your secret to happiness, David?" Linda asked him. "I don't think I've ever seen you frown in twenty years in Paris."

"Only your company, my darling," he said through gritted teeth.

With a hand on either of their backs, David shoved them gently towards the door, and they accepted his prodding.

"Nice to meet you, Anders," Linda called back. David waved like they were departing from a dock. Then he turned to me, his face like thunder, and grabbed me by the collar.

"Where the hell have you been? I sent Jean over twenty minutes ago."

"Sorry, he only came—"

"Get in there!" He pointed to the pantry and I bolted there before his raised foot could kick my backside. Inside, I flicked on the red lamp. The latest batch of pictures were still hanging from the wire, Jean in various stages of self-satisfaction.

Now two doors away, the live jazz band was muffled, but I could hear the recorded jazz from the gramophone still playing from the study. That was some relief. At least they had not finished yet.

I snuck between crates of bottles that shielded the entrance to the crawl space, knelt down, and slid the wood panel along the wall.

The light seeping through from the bedroom was enough to see the Vinten, standing in all its glory.

I turned the camera on before daring to look through the hole in the wall. The Model H whirred up far louder than I ever remembered, and I held my breath tightly while trying to get the tape rolling before the inevitable banging on the wall from an enraged, entrapped Nazi.

Only with the camera rolling did I dare glance at David's handiwork. Just as he'd said, the lens was pointing through a cloth. The hole cut in the wall was perfectly sized for the camera, so I couldn't see what was actually going on unless I looked through the scope.

Now there was no reason not to. In fact, I put my ear closer to the wall, and heard the subtle sounds of moaning.

Carefully, I stepped around the tripod and looked through the scope, still holding my breath, I realized. I let it out and it fogged up the eye glass. Terrified of the thing collapsing, I ever so gently wiped it with my sleeve, and held my breath again. I couldn't see my feet in the darkness, either, meaning I couldn't move or risk kicking the Vinten. Keeping painfully still, I moved my face only an inch to the scope.

The cloth made the picture darker and a bit grainy, but the sight was unmistakable, and now so were the sounds. The prince of Hesse was resting on his forearms and knees on the bed, trousers pulled down and shirt and coat pulled up, blond hair still smooth, and his face a measure of secret satisfaction.

I thought seeing Jean like this would destroy him for me. I'd worried about it before our first photo shoot, the night I'd decided to take my life into my own hands and give up my true virginity to a tussle-haired stranger and a gendarme in the *toilette* of the Jardin du Luxembourg. Yes, the deed had been done, and I could still taste the once sour, now sweet memory in the back of my throat. I'd been fucked, and the world had kept on turning.

Now, as I watched him please a man who counted both Hitler and Mussolini as close colleagues, if not family, all I felt was the strange pangs of quiet resentment, and one question reverberating in my mind. Why was I not on that bed, with Jean groaning behind me?

*   *   *

After the deed was done, I skipped back through the house to unlock the study, at least this time without distraction. I waited in the hall like I'd been standing there keeping watch and the prince's privacy the whole time. Prince Philipp left the room first, a little red in the cheeks, but otherwise thoroughly unperturbed. He only said to me:

"Do you know where the washroom is?"

Keeping my face straight like my life depended on it, I pointed down the hall.

Inside the now unlocked study I found Jean with his legs swung over the arm of the leather chair where the prince had sat, smoking a cigar that was clearly not his. I replaced the drinks trolley back in front of the secret door to the boudoir, and sorted the bottles, thinking carefully about what exactly I was feeling. Jealousy was there, but subdued, very much as if I had witnessed the whole thing through a glass lens and a stretched piece of cloth.

The dominant sensation stretching across my lips was an enhanced sense of naughty satisfaction, like hearing a hilarious anecdote while drunk and remembering it the next day. We had pulled off the impossible: David, Jean and I. I had no idea what David planned to do with the reel next, but that was beside the point. Now in the world existed documented evidence of Prince Philipp, the next landgrave of Hesse, in the most compromising position any man or Nazi could find himself in.

"Drink?" I asked Jean.

"Why not?"

"What would you like?"

"Whatever's most expensive."

I assumed it was a bottle of scotch with '1896' written on the label, so I poured us two glasses and sat down on the other chair.

"*Eugh*," Jean declared after taking a sip. He got up and added seltzer to the brim. "That's better. What are you smiling at?"

"I don't know, really. Just… this whole evening."

"Why? Did you learn some great truths about humanity?"

"I doubt that. No, I guess I'm happy about you."

"Me?"

"Yes, I think you had a good time and I'm… proud of you." Jean slunk back in the chair, staring at me like I was speaking German. "People couldn't have been more complimentary about the photographs, most at least. You reconnected with Josephine, and you buggered a Nazi."

Perhaps it was the whiskey, or Marais' second-hand opium, or the fact that I couldn't care less right now that Claude had stormed off in a huff, but I burst into uncontrollable laughter.

"Careful," Jean said, jumping off his chair and taking my glass from me. "You're spilling expensive scotch all over the place." That made the whole thing funnier, and he burst out laughing too. He stood close to me. Closer than he'd been for many weeks. My chest heaved and my head swam. From the drinking, the laughing, the satisfaction of pulling off a heist. I slid deeper into my chair, spreading my legs as I did.

"You're drunk, Anders."

"So what. Kiss me."

Jean looked away and smiled, softly shaking his head. The white-toothed grin stung. He looked around the small study, from the secret passage to where the deed had been done with Prince Philipp, to the door to the rest of the mansion where the party was in full swing. He looked as one does before crossing a busy highway, before finally leaning down towards me, hands on the arm rest, holding himself just far enough from my face that I couldn't yet kiss him. Thank God I *was* drunk, because it hurt to see the only desire was my own, reflected back at me.

"You smell like Claude."

"Well… you smell like a Nazi."

In single moments the world can turn. Lifetimes opening and closing in the bat of an eye. I could see his supple dark belly. The hardest thing was not to dive in and kiss it. I waited, slunk on the chair, ready, willing and able to do whatever he wanted. Jean threw another vinyl on the gramophone, hopping around to a fluttering beat as I watched, wondering if he would return to take me into a wide-lipped kiss I could almost taste. Instead, he investigated the drinks trolley.

"We really need to take some more pictures for my modeling portfolio." I thought Jean was joking, but he investigated the bottles with the utmost serenity. "Did you hear how they talked about me? Handsome this, stunning that. An English guy, Roland something, said he could see those pictures in a color supplement or a magazine. Well, not all of them I suppose. But some. Did you hear, Anders? Did you hear how they talked about me?"

Bottles clinked.

"I heard." I heard them perfectly well. I silenced myself from naming the bubbling rupture between photographer and model, always simmering beneath the surface of any venture. Aficionados are taken by one thing or the other. Model or photographer. The choice is binary, not both.

"Scotch from the 1870s?" Jean said, still basking in the warm glow of borrowed compliments. I didn't make a move to take them back, for I knew where the truth lay. "Sounds disgusting, no?"

"I'm game if you are." I saw Jean smile at the words. He uncorked the bottle, smelled it and made a face. Glancing back at me, he took a swig, then coughed like the consumption had caught him.

"Heavens to Betsy," Jean said, grinning through the occasional splutter. "That's something David would say, right?"

"Sounds about right," I replied, relaxing into the clearest signal there could be that Jean would not be making love to me, at least not tonight. I could envisage how it would happen but couldn't see it ever happening.

"This really needs some seltzer too." Jean tempered the whiskey with sparkling water. "You want?"

"Sure."

"I must get the taste of that Nazi out my mouth, but straight whiskey is worse."

I burst into a shrill laugh as Jean gargled with David's expensive scotch. No, our relationship did not need another level of complication. We could drink to a successful night, a heist well-orchestrated. As the music played on outside and the night ebbed away, there was little else to do but laugh and drink.

* * *

"Anders," someone was shoving me awake. I'd fallen asleep on the chair, and Jean too. Darkness and quiet had settled over the Roosevelt Mansion. But David was beside me, dressed in a silk robe and slippers and disturbing the early morning calm. His blond hair a mess over his forehead, but it only made him appear more handsome and intriguing, like he'd recently finished a night of boisterous lovemaking. "Come with me."

Yawning, I followed him out into the hallway strewn with the remnants of the party: a stream of glasses and bottles littered the floor like crystal boules. We stepped into the main room softly lit by the first streaks of dawn spilling in through the windows. Even more bottles and glasses were in evidence here, along with the sound of snoring coming from more than one couch.

"How much did we drink?" I said, rubbing my eyes and trying to remember how the room looked when I last saw it.

"Shh," David replied and yanked me into the kitchen. That was even more of a mess. Trousers and undershirts were piled and flung all over the place. Clearly the party hadn't truly got going until after hours.

"Take the reel," David whispered, voice hoarse and twisted far from his normal breezy tone. "And take my bicycle," he dropped a key into my hand, "it's locked up around the back. Ride south to the Meudon forest, it should take you an hour, and bury the reel there."

David disappeared into a cupboard, then returned with a small satchel. He stuffed half a baguette from the counter inside, some cheese and a small canteen, and shoved it into my hands.

"Don't forget where you bury it, all right?"

"I won't," I said, filling myself quickly with resolve. The job wasn't quite done. Burying the evidence would bring some finality. I already looked ahead to the afternoon when the mission would be complete and I could forget this episode had ever happened. "I'll return later and photograph the spot."

"Good idea. But not today, in case you're followed. You know what, keep the bike and cycle back on Sunday morning. That's the least suspicious time to be seen taking photographs in the forest. In fact…"

He disappeared again into the half-light of the kitchen, rummaged in a drawer then came back and shoved a pair of miniature binoculars into the satchel.

"Buy yourself a book on bird-watching."

Chapter 7

THE OPENING MONTHS OF 1939 were good to me. Claude was out of sight, but not of mind, and his petulance seemed to have started and ended with disappearing to Perpignan with Doctor Mélenchon.

He wrote me frequently, sometimes twice a day, with updates from what had become the front lines of the dying days of the Spanish Civil War. Perhaps so I would know it was always him writing, Claude addressed each letter in the way only Claude knew how to do.

My Dearest Toulouse Lautrec,

Barcelona has fallen, and Republicans are streaming across the Pyrenees. Mélenchon drove me to the beach to see their encampments. These men are in a terrible state. Many walked with barely a shoe between them. Mélenchon did what he could for the wounded, as did I. Although passing out opium is about all we can do to ease the pain of the worst of them. The Red Cross is nowhere in sight, of course…

To Paul Cézanne, my one true love,

Camps have opened all across the beaches. A handsome young

Catalan artist called Jorge has arrived to stay with us, fellate Mélenchon and draw sketches. Jorge goes to the beach every morning to draw, and comes back every evening even more full of praise for Franco. I have never met a man who could hate his injured countrymen more than he. I meanwhile have fallen madly in love with another Catalan, this one a Republican fighter named Jordi...

Good day, Eugène Henri Paul Gauguin,

Jordi has died from sepsis. I am terribly distraught, but am being consoled by his brother Iker. Jorge has departed to Rome, thank heavens, and I am assisting Mélenchon in his fundraising efforts for the refugees. I hope you are looking after Paris for me. She can expect me back sometime in the spring...

While Claude was busying himself caring for the last remnants of the Spanish Republic, I was chronicling the headiest days the French Third Republic had ever seen. The perpetual cusp of war put the artistic class of Paris in a party mood, like a stench of smoke wafting from room to room through Nero's palace.

The Roosevelt Mansion hopped into life on a Thursday evening, and often remained full and alive until deep into Sunday afternoon. A casual soiree would evolve into an exhibition or a reading, then flow seamlessly into a party before turning back into a brunch and lecture from one of the many literary cabals.

I photographed them all. The laughs, the cheer, the conversations had beneath a cloud of cigarette smoke. I also took Linda up on her offer to come by her studio. I assisted her with a few fashion shots of stick-thin models which was entirely uninteresting to me, but far more useful was watching her process of developing, which taught me more than art school had ever tried. When she returned to London with Roland, she entrusted me with the keys and told me to keep her studio working.

Now with a proper place to develop my pictures, I could move the dark room out of the Roosevelt Mansion. It was just as well as we needed the space to store reel after reel of blank film David was procuring from all the corners of the earth.

"I don't think there's enough whores in Paris to fill these reels," I said, after helping lift yet another crate up the stairs, through the house and into the kitchen.

"I'll worry about that," he said, "you just worry about keeping them secret."

Although Jean often made an appearance at David's parties, he was far from the only star of the *films cachés*. Every so often, David would catch my eye from across a crowded room. He would give me two winks with his right eye, that was the signal for me to sneak into the pantry, past the waiters clattering around with glasses and trays, sneak into the crawl space to get the camera rolling.

I did not watch most of the performances from the hidden room. An old man with a young woman, as famous as he might be and as pretty as she, was not of interest to me. I would pass the time by placing bets with myself on how long the man would last, then mentally calculating what part of the film to cut. Once I came close to needing to change the reel, but I figured forty minutes of spanking was enough to hold against even an Italian politician. Then at first light, I took the reel wrapped tightly in Hella's clothes from last season, the bike, binoculars and bird watching book, and cycled to a place outside the city to entomb the evidence in a shallow grave. I would then stand atop the buried treasure, the coffin-like case wrapped in silk or satin like an Egyptian mummy, and take a photograph of the twisted tree or moss-covered statue to cement the reel's place in my mental map of Paris.

Once in March, David asked me to go and dig up number twenty-three. It was a duke from the House of Savoy, the one who had been spanked for forty minutes by a voluptuous Spanish woman called Isabella. I'd cycled all the way to the Bois de Vincennes Zoological Park to bury that reel on a grassy knoll beyond the gates which overlooked the hippopotamus watering hole. I cycled there at dusk, packing a small picnic to nibble at, the bird watching book open and the binoculars laying on the grass as a pod of pelicans flocked around the hippos, enjoying an evening bath. As darkness fell and the crowds left, I took the small trowel from the satchel and dug up number twenty-three to the sound of birds squawking.

In Linda's studio, I sliced three frames from the reel and developed the pictures which David then sent by courier to Rome. I don't know how much David asked for, but he gave me two thousand francs for my troubles and sent me back to re-bury the reel. Nothing was said of it again, but the rest of the reel was not required.

Spring was when Paris began to prepare for war. Gas masks were given out by the city, and David responded the only way he knew how, by throwing a 'gas masked ball.' The rest of us might be breathing quicker and sleeping less with our war anxiety, but David had never seemed more enamored with the brilliance of his own idea. His handsome, full face damp with exuberant confidence. Blond skin blushed with an apple-red sheen whenever he was particularly heated up, like now. He was Claude on opium, except without the bitter tongue and melancholy.

"Perhaps we'll burn hashish and dim the lights, it will give the house quite the atmosphere," he suggested an hour before the party as I sat in the kitchen, cleaning my camera. He brushed back dancing hair as he strutted where other men would nervously pace. He swung off his evening jacket to reveal only a see-through shirt and loose cravat. Brown nipples from tight pecs I hadn't quite noticed before shone through white cotton. Even the way he stood now that he'd stopped pacing—leaning back on the marble counter, bulge first, was laced with provocation. None so much as the smile on his face, though. "And anyone who wishes to stay sober… or anonymous… can keep their gas mask on."

I smiled weakly, saying nothing. In fact, I did not move from my perch, slightly in the way of the waiters who clanged around more than usual given the fact David insisted they wear their masks too. No hashish ended up being burned, but I took a little for myself, and sat perched on the windowsill of the kitchen, the window open a crack, smoking. The noise of the churning party made me feel queasy. David's mansion no longer worked as a shield from the outside world. The gas mask planted a realness that made me feel sick to my stomach. Nor did the hashish help to calm my nerves. I gazed out at the dusty evening sky, the shredded light fading beyond the park turning the world into a mustard-gas colored hue, and I sat on the thought which had been sneaking into my mind for a while now. I would never leave Paris.

Survival felt so complicated. Should war come, one would have to survive the raising of armies shipped to the trenches and likely blown to smithereens within a day or two. If the Germans managed to break through the lines instead of digging in along the fields like last time, one would then have to survive the siege. Months, years it could go on. Our food would dwindle, and the populace would head straight to the zoo for those tasty animals. Then the cats, then the rats, then… who knew? Then there was the aftermath of the siege to make it through. The last time the Germans had withdrawn from their bombardment of the city, the populace erupted in revolution and the Paris Commune staggered around for a few months before being crushed in an orgy of blood and summary executions. In other words, whatever happened, my Paris was doomed.

I sighed, watching from the window as the guests arrived, laughing beneath their masks. Survival seemed so utterly exhausting. I heard Jean's voice from nearby. If we were a couple, perhaps I could have fallen into his arms, tearing my heart out at the melancholy of the terrible prelude to history we found ourselves in. He might kiss me on the forehead, squeeze my middle and say whatever words one lover says to another when the darkness makes them afraid. But lovers we weren't.

Finally, the party was in full swing. I'd done a few rounds with the camera, snapping pictures of people I didn't know posing in their pearls and gas masks. I gandered near the kitchen, stealing a full glass every time a waiter emerged into the main room with a silver tray. David had told me earlier there was an English lord who was a huge fan of Jean's and had requested an audience. So I waited for the signal, which did not seem imminent, since Jean was dancing up a storm with Josephine Baker and an actress friend of hers. Their masks forgotten as the music flowed completely through them.

When Jean danced, he was a different man. He cast off the tall, quiet dignity that I'd always felt he carried around with him and which came through so naturally in his portraits. It's the singular quality which made him such an enchanting figure to photograph. Not many men when nude and erect could pull off a majestic loftiness like some Mesopotamian god-man. But when Jean danced, the heat of his blood changed. He lost himself in a beat which he grabbed with both hands. Jean's face split into a grin which did not leave. While it was so easy for others to bop casually around for a song or two before the self-consciousness overtook them, Jean had no such trouble. Every movement his body made was perfectly in time with the music like it had been written for his bones alone. It was the same way I saw him make love to strangers; he led, and they all had to follow. A picture was but one frame of his beauty.

"No one in Paris is content to be a spectator," Cocteau said from behind, startling me. Beneath the gas mask he appeared even more hollow than usual. He removed the rubber contraption, and we drank together while leaning and watching those three soak up all the attention the room had to offer. "Apart from you."

I nodded but said nothing. Jean Cocteau was the one person besides David and Hella whom I saw most of all. I'd learned quite quickly this is where he conducted most of his business—from casting for his next film or play to seeking out a publisher for his next manuscript.

Cocteau once told me how hard he had worked to insert himself at the center of the artistic world, and now he was here, had no plans to leave.

"I am happy to watch," I said.

"A voyeur of life."

"I suppose."

"In a city where everyone wants to be an actor, Anders, you cannot act. He will never love you the way you want."

I watched Jean dancing and laughing between those two women, every facet of himself filled with enjoyment. He was positive, alive, glowing, bright. All the things I did not know how to be. I could love him from afar, but I had nothing to offer. Nothing at all.

"I'm not worthy of his love," I responded, hoping to encourage Cocteau on with bare faced truth. He responded with a kind hand on my shoulder. Kindness and warmth, I realized, was all he had ever shown me. To David I provided a service, to Jean a means to an end, even to Claude I sometimes felt I was little more than a one-man audience for his monologues, and that if it was not me, Claude would have shoehorned some other fellow into his life, to send letters addressed never to my name, but to all the people he wished that I was. Yet Cocteau was humane, a gentleman, and to him I was meaningful.

"Marais and I are getting out of the city this weekend," Cocteau said, "I need a break from all this war mongering and air-raid drills. Come with us to Le Touquet. At the very least you can take some nice pictures of us strolling along the promenade."

I turned away from Jean, laughing and holding Josephine Baker's hand as she spun around and around. Cocteau's face was small and certain. "I will," I said. And I meant it.

*　*　*

I traveled with the couple in the back of their motorcar, happily spectating at a sight I had never before seen—the intimate moments between two men in love.

Cocteau drove us north, sunglasses on, to the town they called *Paris-Plage*, or Paris by the beach. Marais sometimes had his hand on his lover's thigh, sometimes lit a cigarette for him, but more often than not faced backwards to talk to me.

I had assumed from our previous encounters Marais was the quieter one. But out in the countryside away from the eyes of the world that was far from true. He'd just been high on opium the other times I'd seen him. They were equally at ease in themselves and with each other, engaging in charming banter, pointing out memories the other had forgot as only couples with a chunk of years under their belt can do.

"You like Vienna," Marais reminded him. "It's Venice you swore never to return to."

"Oh, that's right. I had a bit of a bad breakup there," Cocteau said to me, turning to the back seat as we hurtled through the bumpy country roads. "I had to say goodbye to a lover. Raymond. He was a beautiful man. Bonkers, but beautiful."

"Baby doll," Marais said, playing with his hair, "he shot himself on the steps of the Santa Maria della Salute after you left him. Bonkers barely covers it."

"After you've been with me, there's not much point in living," Cocteau said to me with an obvious wink.

"Why don't we keep our eyes on the road, shall we? Before your list of ex-lovers begins to resemble the death toll of a Sicilian feud."

In Le Touquet the hours were long but full. Time seemed to slow down, with every moment between the three of us as all-encompassing as a single-shot feature film. We ate and cycled and took pictures along the chilly shore, all in the first afternoon. Cocteau paid for my own room at the Westminster hotel while I looked around the lobby, I didn't even know he'd done so before handing me a key.

"Dinner in an hour," Cocteau said, casting a watchful eye over my reaction. I wondered what he was trying to catch me out on. I didn't need to see the dining room to understand the sort of dress which would be expected.

"Wonderful," I said, quickly snatching away the key. "I've been waiting for an excuse to wear my dinner jacket. No one ever seems to invite me out to eat in Paris."

I knew Cocteau was watching as I walked away.

After dinner, Cocteau and I were sitting in the smoking lounge, enjoying a cognac together while he puffed gently on a cigar.

"It's funny," I said, swirling the golden liquid around the glass as an unseen pianist played a familiar tune I wished I was cultured enough to name, "I never smelled cigar smoke before coming to Paris."

Cocteau pulled the thick brown thing from his mouth and dabbed off some ash into the silver tray beside him.

"In Paris they smoke shit. Dried grass and hay. This thing," he rubbed the cylinder under his nose, taking in the aromatic scent, "is pure heaven direct from Havana. I introduced almost all of Paris to them back in the twenties." Cocteau admired the cigar, and the work he'd put in to cultivating a story behind it, like there was for every object in his life. "Did your father not smoke?"

"I never knew my father."

"Ah, of course. The forgotten generation." He puffed away, staring into the middle distance as I imagined a father might when readying to tell his son some great truth. "I drove ambulances during the Great War. So much beauty ripped limb from limb. I was your age, perhaps a little older. It's not until one's mid-twenties before one casts off the horny excesses of youth when even a table leg will make you hard. I was at the age of truly appreciating a handsome man. The shape of his nose, the broadness of his shoulders. The fact I prefer a smattering of hair on the chest and navel to nothing. Those little idiosyncrasies as peculiar as taste buds. Like how some people despise all kinds of legumes for no particular reason, or will always choose red meat over chicken." Cocteau stared at me. "Do you know what I mean?"

"Maturing one's palette," I said with a smile. "Like developing a nose for cognac."

"Indeed, my boy. Although you would sleep with your friend Jean in a heartbeat, but not David, am I right?"

I think I blushed a little at the suggestion.

"I mean… David is my friend, my… my employer, practically. I've never even considered—"

"But if he offered?"

"I… I don't know."

"But Jean on the other hand, with whom you also have a financial relationship, you would fall to your knees at the slightest suggestion he wanted you."

I shifted in my seat, a little uncomfortable at the line of questions. The answers, after all the tumult in our affairs, not as clear to me as I would have thought.

"You can have a defined type, Anders," Cocteau said, crossing his legs and blowing out a ring of smoke. "Just don't let the type define you. You'll never know how many leagues of men have wasted their lives searching for the prosopopoeia of their boyhood fantasies. This one is too short, that too fat, this one too provincial, that one too urbane. Finding love is not about thwacking through the forest of life with a twisted map and a broken compass, hoping to stumble across the buried treasure."

Cocteau let the words hang in the air like his cigar smoke. I took a sip of the cognac, sitting with a haunting sense this conversation had been given to a version of me, by a version of Cocteau, the younger and the wiser, the novice and the master, a thousand times before.

"How does one find love then, father?"

"My own father killed himself when I was nine years old, so do not take what I am about to say as some second-hand saying borrowed from the garbled summary of an amateur philosophy heard from a friend of a friend of a taxi driver. What I know is from what I experience, over and over and over again. Love is not the thing you dream of, nor the unknowable ideal constructed entirely in your mind. Love is, and only ever will be, the person standing in front of you, day after day, offering you love, and love is what you feel inclined to give in return. Justice balances the entire world, Anders. You can pour your heart into Monsieur Jean, you can have his image do unspeakable things to your body in the dead of night, don't think he does not see that. Because a boy in love is like a firefly streaming through the darkness. We can all see it. But until the day he stands in front of you defenseless, open, asking to be loved. Until he hands you a gun and says: 'to me you can do your worst, as long as you are always mine,' do not waste another night watching him from the sidelines, not when so many others are watching you."

We sat quietly after that. Cocteau drinking from his glass, and I from mine. A snifter of guilt from my night at the *toilettes* roiled down my spine. I'd been invited into the beating heart of the avant-garde, yet was somehow disappointing them by not engaging in some wild, scandalous affair that could be whispered about at David's. And being manhandled on some damp hard floor was hardly a love story worth repeating. It was true I did not know what fatherly advice was. And perhaps it was also true that Cocteau did not know how to give it. But given it he had, and sat with it I did.

"Where's Marais?" I asked eventually without much reason except I hadn't seen him since we left the dining room.

"Oh, probably upstairs doing a bit of exercise."

"Exercise?"

"Yes, he knows I'm not really in the mood after such a big meal, and well his appetite is insatiable."

"It doesn't bother you?" I asked, not really sure why I should have expected two men who broke all known bounds of conventionality to uphold the promise of monogamy.

"Anders," he said with a world-weary tone I was used to hearing from Claude. "Imagine for a moment trying to drive from here to the Cape of Good Hope, with no map, no directions, no road signs, and knowing you

115

can never once stop and ask for directions. Not only that, but everyone you know is watching how you get on. Some are hoping you'll get lost, some are sneaking out to lay traps on the road, and others are simply curious to see how far you will get.

"We used to have costumes to dress up our love. The church, the navy, the stage. You've seen the play 'The Trial of Oscar Wilde?'"

"I have. Last year. It was excellent."

"My good friend Maurice Rostand wrote it. We used to be something of an item. In fact, when I first spotted that gorgeous hunk of seafood hanging by a grand piano under a shell-shaped sconce in one of those striped-wallpaper bars, I said to myself Miss Marion Davies you have met your piece of trade for life. Ha! We barely lasted a season. Perhaps because our version of sex was attending every party and funeral dressed in a different outfit inspired by the Lord herself, Miss Lavender Wilde."

Cocteau looked beyond me, like he was looking at time passing.

"My favorite part of that play," he continued, "and the best scene Maurice ever wrote is at the climax, during the court case. Wilde refuses the weapons of lies and demagoguery which his adversaries have used to skewer him throughout the trial, and delivers a vibrant, heart-wrenching plea for art and freedom. A man alone, he wages a heroic war against ignorance and intolerance. This," Cocteau said behind weary eyes. "This is the strength it takes to love another man. All of us are warriors, fighting for nothing more than survival. Nothing more than love. Nothing more than freedom."

Tears pricked his eyes, but he swallowed them away. I did not dare offer comfort. It was not the thing two soldiers did during a battle-break.

"With war comes wounds, and wounds become scars, and scars are parts of ourselves our lover must accept, and even come to love."

"You too have scars?"

"More than most. Marais accepts the things I hate and love about myself. And I try to do the same. That is the essence of love between men. We are imperfect, broken, angry, scarred, mean, selfish, brutish, coarse creatures, and we must accept each other as we are, our farts that punctuate the silence of the bedroom and our occasional bad moods which must be catered for. This is the road we are on."

Cocteau finished his drink as I saw from the corner of my eye Marais appear in the lounge looking freshly showered.

"One day I believe the road will be full of cars rushing along paved highways lit with electric lights and bright blue signs. But for now, we are the only ones on the road, driving over bumpy terrain through a night which sometimes feels like it will never end."

"You spoke of love like it was the man standing in front of you, asking to be loved, and now it sounds like it's the man you're trapped alongside in the car," I said, my eyes still on Marais slinking through the tables to us. His cheeks were blushed like Claude's after returning from the alley behind Giovanni's with a fistful of francs. I couldn't decide if Cocteau was truly at peace with what his lover got up to, or was simply acting that way since it was what a true Bohemian would do.

"Love, like fate, will not always walk up to you in a park and announce himself so boldly. He will sneak in between the margins of life, bursting upon you when you least expect it."

If I had known what it was to have a father, this is where my childish intransigence would take over. Fate had walked right up to me, in a park, across the street from the Roosevelt Mansion, as it happened, and love had struck me. Perhaps all I would ever get from it was a thousand pictures, but that could be enough. That was more love than I ever imagined would be possible.

Marais came over to join us, surprising Cocteau with a kiss.

"Anders," Marais then said, leaning down to brush my cheek on both sides with the smoothness of a clean-shaven actor. Soft hair draped over my face, and I searched inside myself for a feeling. For any feeling. Marais was handsome, they both were, but the only person I desired to be sitting across from, the only scent I wished to bathe in was of Jean. My Jean, not these other two imposters, as polite as they were.

"Well then, my love," Marais said. "Are we ready to retire?"

"I think so," Cocteau stubbed out the end of his cigar and stood heavily, clasping Marais' arm.

"Goodnight, my dear," Cocteau said to me. "Remember we are driving home tomorrow. Maybe next time you can drive us."

* * *

I saw David a few nights later when I went round to drop off a new set of obscene prints of Jean I'd developed at Linda's studio. He was sitting in the 'L' shaped study, smoking with the lights off.

"Are you feeling all right?" I asked as I nudged inside. "Shall I fetch Hella?"

"No, I'm fine." But he clearly wasn't. "They've dug trenches all around the city. And through the Meudon forest." David crushed out the end of the cigarette, then pulled out a new one from his silver tray.

"Do you think they might find—"

"I don't know," he snapped back. "But don't bury them out there again. It will be better if you stay nearby. You have a whole park over there to put them in. It is deserted at night, more or less. If we fall under siege the last thing we need is Germans digging up all the dirt we have on the French establishment."

"I will, of course." I nodded quickly and left the envelope of pictures on the table and turned to leave. The darkness and the stench of dirty smoke was making me dizzy. Not to mention David's rapid change of heart. He had clearly been sitting here for some time, stewing in the mess he'd made by blackmailing his party guests, and figuring out how to shift his guilt onto me.

"David… the forest is huge. The chance of anyone digging up a reel is… astronomical, surely. I hope you aren't losing sleep over that."

"Not just that," he responded with a soft smile. "These anxious days get even to me."

"Is there anything I can do for you?"

"No, my love, no. I will be right as rain the next time you see me and ready to be lashed to the wheel of pleasure."

I waited for no real reason. Not knowing what to say, but feeling uneasy about leaving him alone in the dark. I snuck a glance around the room, looking out for the glint of a revolver.

"Perhaps…" David said.

"Yes? What is it? Anything I can do, please tell me." Cocteau's words about David stirred inside. What if I cast it all off, my inhibitions, my clothes, and dropped to my knees in this dark room. When first we had met, I had looked upon David as a Bohemian general, calling me forth to a new revolution. Cocteau was right about one thing, though. The image we constructed in our minds never found footing in reality. David did what he did because he knew how to do it. I stepped forward in the smoky darkness, less cautious than I ever had been before.

"Perhaps you could pour me a drink?"

"Certainly. Would you like a scotch and soda?"

Momentarily forgetting his sadness, David sat straight up in the chair, glancing at suspicious eye through the whiskey bottles Jean and I once drank from.

"How dare you. That single malt cost more than Mary's virginity."

"Gin?"

"Why not."

I side-stepped to the drinks trolley and added tonic to the gin.

"Thank you, dear, I am parched." He took the glass and drunk long and deep.

"Why is Hella not here?"

"I prefer my wife not to see me during these bouts of melancholy."

I wanted to say something, to offer some protest, but David cut my thoughts off.

"I don't want to hear it," he said. "Our marriage is our business. Non-traditional, as you understand. But it works. So I ask you not to pry."

"Very well," I said, feeling my way back towards the door.

"Oh Anders, wait. Jean asked me to give you this." David got up from his chair, pulled something from the bookcase and handed me a letter.

"Jean?"

"Yes."

David sat back down, and the room briefly illuminated again as he struck a match to light another cigarette. I hadn't noticed him finish the first. It was too dark to open and read the letter here, and it was clear that David preferred to be alone now. I bid him a brief goodbye and cycled all the way home, the unopened letter in my satchel. The moment I got home I would have Giovanni pour me a glass of wine, and I would retire to a lonely table in the bar, or even straight up to my room if there weren't any tables to be had, and read the letter then where I could give Jean's words the peace and contemplation they deserved. Pulling over to the side of the street and scouring his handwriting by a gas lamp was not what Jean deserved.

I walked into Giovanni's, greeted by warmth and light and scribbled words from Jean.

Dearest Anders

I wish I could have said this to you in person, but we never seem to find the time to talk these days—

"Well if it isn't the Viennese Paul Cézanne."

The letter dropped to my side as the old Claude, except with a healthy-looking tan, greeted me at the entrance to Giovanni's distaste.

"Claude, you're back!"

"Absolutely I am. Imagine the war breaks out and I'm stuck down in Perpignan."

"You don't prefer to be somewhere safe?"

"And sacrifice my fortune? Darling, don't be ridiculous. I'd camp behind a marching army, if I could." He spun around to the half empty bar. "That's right, Claude is back in Paris and open for business. Spread the word. Giovanni, be a doll and pour us a couple of drinks, will you? And clear away the boxes you've left out the back. My office hours are open."

"God, I've missed you."

We mounted the bar like noble white steeds as Giovanni hurled drinks our way. Jean's letter unread in my hands, hidden under the brass.

"I saw my first platoon of soldiers at the train station today," Claude told me, then thumped a silver pocket watch on the table. "Those that can't pay in cash pay in kind. And what about you? What's new at the Mansion?"

"Not much. I saw Édith perform last night. Her voice is breathtaking. The way she—"

"Oh I know," Claude dismissed me, throwing back a shot of absinthe. "And how is our mutual friend?"

"Oh… well…" the sweat in my hand coating the letter. "Actually, I just cycled all the way from David's. Let me go and… powder my nose and I'll be right back. Don't move."

I darted upstairs. Falling onto the bed, my lungs collapsed as I pored over the tear-stained paper, wishing I could rush to the end and know what happened.

Dearest Anders

I wish I could have said this to you in person, but we never seem to find the time to talk these days. I thought you would be here tonight, but David said you were spending the weekend in Le Touquet with Cocteau and Marais. Perhaps it is easier to write these words down.

From the moment I met you, I have loved you from afar. I wanted so many times to take a step towards you, but I never could. For I never felt I was worthy of your love. You know me. You know what I am and what I must do to get by in this world. It has always been different for you. I am not saying better or worse, but your life is not like mine. You came to Paris to pursue these lofty ideals of art and Bohemia, while I dream of leaving this cesspit far behind me.

For brief moments in the story of our friendship, I thought we might grow into love. Not the sort that's bought and sold, but solid love. The kind that makes a life, a partnership. I spoke to you often of my dreams; to be a model. I was never expecting to spark a revolution, to strut down the catwalk wrapped in Chanel, but a picture or two in a magazine or catalog, it is not beyond reality. In fact, it is reality. And it could have been mine, but I didn't press for it, you didn't press, and here we are. You learned you could have me take my clothes off instead, and make money by the Seine. In all honesty I do not know how to love another man. Truth be told I did not know it was even possible, before I met you. But I know one man selling another is not love. Nor close to it.

And then David came into our lives. Like all the men I met, he wanted me for my body, and for what my body could do for him. I accepted it, because that is the only way I have ever known a man

121

to want me. And, I am afraid to say, it is even how you want me.

I wished for the longest time that you might want only me. Not for one night, but for all nights to come. I thought you might be someone to whom I could share my dreams with, and be a harbor for yours as well, like Cocteau and Marais. But that dream, like all my others, has drifted away. I never expected David to treat me any differently than what I am, but I did not expect it of you. Spending time at David's has become no different to the parks or the baths. It is another way to make money, another way for men to profit from me.

I know you have made tens of thousands of francs from me, and I am glad to share the wealth. That you have profited from my body as I have. But I do not want this life anymore.

No, that is untrue. I do not want this life with you. To watch you, Anders, fall out of love with me. To see how you look at me after every rendezvous David tells me to do, is too painful. I cannot stand the disappointment in your eyes. I am what I am, that is true. And I have been who I have been, there is no changing my past.

But I thought that you might be my future. I dreamed of a different life, in Paris or elsewhere, where we were together, alone together. In love, together.

I am leaving Paris. I don't think I shall ever return. I have said my goodbyes to everyone else, and now this is my farewell to you. The war is coming and all the fun we've had and our business at the mansion will be gone in the blink of any eye, and I want to get ahead of all that when it comes, before you up and abandon me. Truthfully, I no longer want to pine over what our relationship could have been, but never was.

Farewell, my dear Anders. I will never forget such times as these that I loved you.

Yours in love,
Jean.

Why in Paris?

*   *   *

The summer of 1939 bubbled like a ruined stew. The continent was on the precipice of something disastrous. All the bad decisions were catching up with us, swirling towards a perfect storm that no one man could protect the other from.

My own poor choices, my failures, my insecurities, had left me alone. Yet I saw Jean everywhere. In the back of heads, in the endless crowds of soldiers fresh from the African colonies. In all the places around Paris we had been together, in every photo we took.

I never knew how quickly someone in life can go from real to ghostly. And Jean haunted my every step.

I never breathed a word to Claude. He asked, on occasion, what Jean was up to, and I answered truthfully—I don't know. David asked only once, and I told him matter-of-factly Jean had left Paris. David's only comment on the matter—glancing up at me with sad eyes from half-moon reading glasses—was that we had better find some new boys if we wanted to stay in business. Or else I could teach him how to use the Vinten and I would take Jean's place on the other side of the wall. I didn't know if he was kidding.

I told Cocteau, though. And Marais. Two weeks after I received the letter. They took me out for dinner and cracked open the steely exterior wrapped around me.

"Your first heartbreak is always the worst," Cocteau told me, and Marais agreed. "But each one is a little easier than the last."

"The trick," Marais added, filling up my wine glass, "is to lock your affections away, but keep those other parts of you wide open. The right one will know exactly where to hit." He winked at Cocteau.

"Just don't forget where you left the key."

I tried those things. One feeling removed from real emotion, I did it all. I slept with Cocteau and Marais that night. And again, both separately and together. I slept with so many of the boys David brought for me to film and photograph. I even slept with someone I met at Giovanni's. Claude was out for the night, and I was downstairs drinking alone—which is exactly what I normally did when not at David's, or when I wasn't digging up plots of

123

land to bury state secrets around Paris.

He was handsome, silvery blond and German, as it happened. I noticed the accent and terrible French straight away and helped him order a beer. We spoke at a distance about nothing in particular, like the way two strangers from the same land do when they meet far from home.

His name was Eilas. Although only twenty-seven, he dressed like a magazine advert of a newly minted professional, stiff collars and sleek suits. He worked at the Citroën car factory at Quai de Javel under the shadow of the Eiffel Tower—a job secured for him by his father, a civil servant in Berlin—one who had survived many purges and loyalty parades.

Eilas, along with his employer, were now only waiting for the day he would be sent back home as a risk to national security.

The bar grew empty. Giovanni turned off the lights. That Eilas would stay with me was *fait acompli*. He had never intended to leave the bar that night, at least not alone. That was fine with us both. With all the time to spare that two exiles have, I led him upstairs and we took the night to explore each other. I was getting pretty good at it by this point. My tongue searched around all parts of his body. I grew more desiring of him with every moan I put into his lips. Watching him lay back on my pillow, holding my head in his hands as I relaxed my throat the way the boys had taught me. For the very first time since not having Jean, sex, and something on the same road as love, swirled around in a heady mix of saliva, sweat, and touch.

In the silence of my room in the middle of the night, Eilas whispered to me in my first language, one element of my boyhood fantasy. He pulled my mouth off him and straight to his face, kissing me open-mouthed. Eager as one who knows his desires will be gone with the daylight.

Strong German arms spun my body around. On my stomach, on my bed. Eilas's tongue tingled down my spine and delved into me, a ravenous beast. I buried my face into the pillow as he guided my body up, and himself inside. All of me he took, because all of me I gave.

In the bright spurts of morning, I watched from the bed as Eilas put his suit back on. I'd woken alone, with him already standing naked by the sink, washing me off his body. And now I watched him straighten his tie in Claude's dirty mirror.

"You're the most beautiful Jew I've ever seen, either inside Germany or outside of it," Eilas said, leaning down to kiss me.

"I'm—"

"Anders, come on." He glanced down at my covered crotch wrapped in the sheet. With a playful growl he ripped the sheet from my legs. We tumbled and laughed together on the bed, but I stopped it before his tie became tangled up. Eilas rested his head on my chest as I smoothed down his hair, and suddenly he seemed intensely sad, spinning our night together into a feeling of being under siege as the dangerous outside world encroached, clouds gathering in the summer heat.

"Just… stay out of Germany, all right? Stay here in Paris, where it's safe."

Our time was over. From the door, Eilas blew me a kiss as he left the room and I stretched out naked under the sheets still smelling of him. I looked at Jean's letter propped up on the chest of drawers where it had sat for so many weeks now, this constant reminder of my broken heart. But I could not look at it any longer. I got up from the bed and quickly stuffed it in the drawer, under all my winter socks. I let out a sigh, and my body exhaled so much I did not know I'd been clutching my heart. Paris is where I would be safe, and what had Jean done but abandon me here. Eilas had seized what he wanted, whereas Jean had shrunk from the fight. But more than that, as the tune of the world drew closer to the part where the drums boom and symbols clash, Jean had left me alone. To abandon the people we say we love is to declare that love for them non-existent.

*   *   *

It happened on a Friday morning, the first of September, 1939.

I was at the Roosevelt Mansion, along with Claude and a handful of other young men who had stayed the night. It wasn't a party, far from it. Hella was away for the weekend in Calais, so David had decided to throw a small get together for the dozen or so of us who had become regulars in rapidly expanding David's global pornographic subscription service. Thomas, Gabriel, Louis, Alexandre, Lucas, Martin, Hugo, Nathan, and a few more I didn't know well who were friends of Claude.

The evening before we had drank and smoked and, with David as our maestro, looked through the stacks of pictures I'd taken throughout the preceding months. Some of the boys alone and some of the boys together, while David highlighted the bits and pieces of feedback clients had sent.

"Felatio is very popular, perhaps more so than Lord Byron style." David explained. He'd moved one of the couches in the main room to set up an easel we were all gathered around. I switched between a series of pictures he wanted to highlight while he gestured with a schoolmaster's stick.

"You see here how Hugo is staring up at Thomas? This is what we want. It allows the client to picture himself in either position. Contrast it to this one where both Louis and Lucas have their eyes closed, and how much harder it is to picture oneself in either position.

"So, the next phase is to do a series for each of you performing felatio on everyone else and then having it performed on you, and then an additional series with two on one, three on one, and so forth. There are literally thousands of combinations which will allow us to send the clients something new every month, particularly as the subscription list grows ever longer, I might add. Claude will be keeping the schedule, so please speak to him about your availability over the coming weeks."

"Oh, fuck," Thomas said, "we're out of champagne."

"Already?" David replied with the exasperation of a scout leader. "Fine. We'll finish this then I'll bring out some more. Honestly, you boys are drinking me dry. Right, where were we? Oh yes. The Lyon trip is scheduled for next month. I've secured us the use of a villa, and it has a pool,"

"Ooh!" the boys all said together.

"Anders will be bringing the movie camera and the famous Jean Cocteau has agreed to come and direct. But remember, film reels are expensive and limited, so I need everyone to be ready to perform and get it right on the first take. That means no clients for seven days before, and no extra-curricular activities, I'm looking at you, Martin." Martin gave a faux-shy smirk, then slid from the back of the couch where he had been perched into the space behind his lover Hugo. "Right, if that's all then," David said, and glanced at me for the all clear before continuing. I nodded. "Let's get drunk."

Sometime after ten p.m. that night, the doorbell rang. Figuring it was another boy, I sauntered into the hallway, drink in hand, to answer it. But the two men who came to the top of the stairs were far from what I expected. They were dressed in the long overcoats and felt hats of the men all us boys in Paris feared.

"Good evening," the one with the moustache said. "I'm Inspector Georges, and this is Inspector Roussel. We're looking for a Negro man who goes by the name of Jean. Is he here?"

"No. I… I haven't seen him."

"So, you know him?" Roussel, without the moustache said.

"Yes, I mean, used to. Not really. Not anymore. You know, not for a long—"

"Can I help you?" David interjected from behind me, to my muted relief.

"Yes, I hope so. I'm Inspector Georges, and this is Inspector Roussel. We are looking for a Negro man who goes by the name Jean. He's in his late twenties. A number of our enquiries have led us here."

"Many people seem to believe we could find this Jean through a man called David Roosevelt or David Rosenblatt."

"It's Roosevelt," David said firmly, "and I am he."

The inspectors poked their heads further through the doorway as the high-pitched screeches of the boys drinking and laughing shot like bullets from the living room.

"If you wouldn't mind coming with us then, Monsieur Roosevelt." Georges said flatly.

"Not at all. Let me just get my coat and hat."

"Of course, sir."

David didn't even look at me as he walked smartly to the hallway closet and wrapped himself up. I shivered worse than when Eilas had called me a Jew. Worse than when I read Jean's letter. The threat of the law was finally catching up to us all.

I stood awkwardly by the door, in spitting distance of the officers who blocked any escape. With their handguns. And motorbikes. And cars. And dogs. And prison. And deportation. My natural instinct was to bolt down the stairs, out into the night, and never return.

"Shall we, gentlemen?" David said, reappearing at the door and also carrying an umbrella. Still without a glance at me, he pushed between the two inspectors, and they followed him down the stairs.

I closed the door as the world spun, then staggered back in and called out for Claude.

I pretended with the boys, for a while. Listening, smiling, and drinking heavily. I admired and envied Claude's ability to put every worry aside and enjoy the moment, and he did it without the slightest sense anything at all was wrong.

What worried me most was that Claude did not joke. All the other times I'd been afraid and he not, he'd laughed, made fun, pretended to write to my mother or run through all the advocates he knew and their associated fetishes, so I could have the best legal representation possible in my upcoming trial.

As the hours ticked into the first of September, there was no time for jokes. We could only sit together in silence, long after the other boys had gone home, gone to clients, or fallen asleep, and wait for David to come back. It was eight or maybe nine in the morning when he finally returned home.

"It's bad," he told the two of us in the kitchen as soon as he arrived. Although he said it, his face said otherwise. Like this was nothing but a scare, a warning we could bounce back from. I hoped with all my might. "A group of city workers digging a trench in the Meudon forest found something round and metal."

"Oh my God," I said involuntarily, clutching the marble countertop for support.

"Yes." David said.

"What?" Claude asked. "What is it?"

"A film reel of Jean fellating, fucking, then fisting the German ambassador to France."

Claude's mouth dropped at David's words. He looked at me, then back at David, but this was not the time for complaints about who had seen what. I gulped, remembering the high forehead and full moustache of the man I hadn't even realized was German until later when Jean told me. He'd explained everything he wanted done to him in great detail, and in flawless French.

"It got passed around to several cinematographers for several weeks," David said, now pacing around the kitchen in the low, cloudy light. "No one knew who was on it, or even if what was happening was some sort of crime. You can relax, by the way, apparently it's not a crime unless it is shown publicly, so let's not do that."

But I didn't feel any better.

"Eventually the reel made its way to the police, who, for some reason decided the Negro man must be a prostitute and the older man someone wealthy who was somehow in danger of being entrapped. In their enquiries, the police spoke to journalists, hoping someone might recognize the face in the film they believed was well known."

"And did they?" Claude asked.

"Why yes, Claude. They did. Jean of course is nowhere to be found, and the other party is currently occupied in the diplomatic corps of the Third Reich while we all stare down the barrel of war. But, satisfied no one was at risk of harm, nor any crime of blackmail was in the cards, the police closed the case, and the journalists are now free to publish the unspeakable details of the private life of the German ambassador. Speculate at what possible social function these acts occurred, and harangue all of the guests we've ever had for lurid details of the next—."

"So what did the police want?" I asked, feeling myself quietly shake.

"Only to warn me that this Jean might be trying to entrap or blackmail others, and if I see him, I should let them know."

"That took all night?"

"No. That took five minutes. I spent the rest of the night tracking down the journalists and newspapers who know about this story."

"And?" Claude said. "Did you find any?"

"Yes, Claude. Several."

David unfurled one of the many newspapers he had brought home with him and pointed at the headline: *German offensive in Poland. Warsaw bombed, many reported killed.*

"In two days' time this paper like every other is going to be full of the scandal of the Nazi ambassador to Paris getting fucked and fisted by a Black French whore in *my* home, under *my* roof, at *my* parties. And every politician, actor, financier, diplomat, cleric and ambassador who ever had their fetish fulfilled in that room is going to send every thug in Western Europe this way to track down those film reels and kill us all in the process."

David screamed out loud and threw the newspapers to the ground in a fit of rage. I jumped, we both did, but mainly I wanted to smack myself in the mouth. My own foolishness, stupidity, or just downright bad luck had opened the door and let in the gust of wind which was ready to knock down everything we had carefully constructed.

"How could you be so stupid, Anders?" The words caught me wrong. I stopped mid-sulk, and stared back.

"This was your idea."

David rushed towards me, finger pointed in the air and face twisted in anger. I wanted to be punched. Let him smack me a new one, teach me a lesson, end this farce that what we had been doing was okay.

I thought he was going to. Claude's face showed the same—an unreal sense of fear lit through a cloudy grey sky. The overcast sky foreboding a war overdue.

I scrunched up my face, waiting for the blow to land. When it didn't, I squinted and saw David hunched over the countertop.

"Did they say when they are going to run the story?" Claude asked, trying to diffuse the tension and focus on practicalities.

"As soon as this German nonsense in Poland blows over," David mumbled, then trudged to the door like a man to the gallows.

"You better hope there's a fucking war," David said, "otherwise we're all dead."

Act II:
The Age of Whores

Chapter 8

Paris, 1941

LIFE UNDER OCCUPATION WAS akin to living in some opium-induced fever-dream of Salvador Dalí. Daily life painted in the surrealism of cycling past the giant red and black swastikas hanging from the Hôtel de Ville or atop the Eiffel Tower. Reality itself had been replaced by a dadaist existence, a bizarre conflagration of German and French, where everything French was being Germanized, swastikas everywhere, the Wehrmacht patrolling boulevards. Many days I felt like I'd fallen into a coma and woken up in an absinthe dream. Gothic-font German letters of my schooldays appeared around the landmarks of my recent memory. The places Jean and I had stopped by now a marking point on an occupied tourist trail.

It was as if the subject of my first photos of Paris had come grotesquely to life. People wandering the streets in search of what they could no longer find. The shop that could no longer sell them cheese. The bakery shuttered. The shoe shop shut down. An indigenous population unable to feel at home; people who had lived all their lives in a city transfigured into a waking nightmare.

As the slow, decaying drudgery of days, weeks, months began to pass, with an anxiety we had grown accustom to bearing, I often thought about David, and the first night I'd been at his party. How virulently Cocteau had dismissed the surrealists and shred Emmanuel's defense of their movement and expulsion of the fascist sympathizers. If only that could work once again.

"I pronounce you exiled! Huzzah!" Cocteau had said to Emmanuel. Neither of them moved from their seats. *"Now I shall walk to the kitchen and say hello to Señor Dalí."*

Ebbinghaus—the only German philosopher I'd ever given any credence—said we tend to remember the first and last things in a series of events the best. Life at David's was a series of events. The first night anchored in my mind, the music, the beginning and unraveling of conversations, the jewelry on bare necks, our mad dash to get the Vinten up and running; and the last night anchored there too: I couldn't get the last thing David had said to me out of my head.

The war, as it turned out, didn't blow over. After Poland collapsed, the newspapers busied themselves with actual news, and not the scandal. Although I flicked through their pages every day, watching and waiting for the story to break. I had nothing better to do since I was no longer welcome at David's, although I heard from the boys the parties continued despite the war, but less frequently, and each one quieter than the last as the avant-garde abandoned their city one by one. But the story never broke.

The shocking autumn turned to tense winter. All of Paris, and the world it seemed, waited for Hitler's next move. The harsh winter that year offered a modicum of protection from the feared invasion. Claude busied himself with entertaining the French soldiers passing through Paris to reinforce the Maginot line. I cycled around the city documenting the construction of snow-covered defenses with my camera, sending what I could over to Linda and Roland in London, and even selling a few shots to the newspapers here.

I never asked any of the editors or journalists I met about the film reel. And sometimes I wondered if what the police had said to David was true, or if what he'd told us was true, either. Perhaps those two inspectors were nothing more than a couple of his friends, dressed up and spinning a story so he could rid me, Claude, and all the rest of us from his life. No, I realized that was just more war-borne hysteria, as talk of France being Hitler's next trophy spread through us bystanders.

Then the terrifying thaw began. Frozen ground melted into pathways ready for the German invasion. The city watched the newspaper headlines as well as the horizon. They would often publish multiple editions a day, and sometimes just print out a new front page with a quick digest of the day's events one could lay over the rest of the paper like an updated summary sheet.

The city woke up one warm day in April 1940 with dread from a finally vanquished winter. The mornings' papers screamed the one thing we all feared: *Denmark invaded.*

On the same evening, a new front page hit the newsstands. Only one word had changed. *Denmark surrenders.*

I believed with every fiber I had, with everything I knew to be true, someone would now publish the story of the German Ambassador. Painting a gigantic target on Jean's back. I didn't even know where in France he was to help him. That story would surely open the floodgates. Ordinary Parisians taking picnics and pickaxes out to public parks, hunting for incriminating reels. Of the last Bourbon. The leader of the Radical party. A deputy mayor of Paris. An Italian duke. The Soviet *chargé d'affaires.* Prince Philipp of Hesse. And countless generals, parliamentarians, industrialists, Nazis, Brits, Americans, Spaniards, and all their relations with the revolving door of gentlemen of independent means we delivered for their enjoyment and our own blackmail, night in, night out. What else had the papers to lose? Why not fire every piece of ammunition they had at the advancing enemy, even if a few of our own were among the injured?

But the press abandoned their positions quicker than the retreating government. *La drôle de guerre*—the Phony War as it was called—dragged on for eight interminable months from September of 1939 until the Germans finally crossed the Western Front on May 10. The government's plan had been to sit and wait for the invasion all along. After the Dunkerque evacuation in late May, the city realized no help was coming, least of all from the feckless government who played musical chairs with aging Great War generals.

On the morning of Saturday, June 8, I sat in Giovanni's reading the paper. The Allies had evacuated Norway. Madame Framboise was in a state, out of cigarettes, nerves everywhere. Then we heard the rumbling thunder of distant artillery fire. In a fit, she threw bottles of gin in a suitcase and rushed by foot all the way down to Gare d'Austerlitz, still in her dressing gown. Along with all of Paris, it seemed. She returned that evening. Trains crammed with citizens had left the station with no destination known. Not just trains but trucks, wagons, carts, bicycles. Madame Framboise hadn't much fancied a slow march to nowhere in her slippers, so she returned, having at least traded Giovanni's gin for cigarettes.

Four days later, on Wednesday, the government, having fled south, announced on the radio that Paris was undefended. An open city. Two days after that, Nazi tanks rolled through the streets on a chilled June day. I almost breathed a sigh of relief. I stood by the side of the street watching the soldiers march down Baron Hausmann's avenues. I wanted nothing more than to cycle down to David's and tell him all would be well. No one would know what we'd done, and now no one would care. The world had greater problems than the sex lives of a deposed government and conquering officials.

But I never did. The thing that stopped me was a creeping terror I tried to wish away. This was Hitler's Paris now, and Jews would be wise to keep their distance from each other, and the enemy, and themselves. On the morning of the next Monday, June 17, 1940, huddled in the bar with sunlight streaming through the grates into the basement, Claude, Giovanni, Madame Framboise and I listened as Marshall Pétain said the fighting must stop. We were to surrender. It was news to no one.

The nightlife of Paris was but another victim of the occupation. But it did not die, at least not entirely. Like green shoots growing out of the thickest mud, what it meant to live in Paris found a way to thrive around and about the curfew. One simply had to arrive at one's destination before the sun had set and be prepared to last till dawn.

Fortunately for Claude and I, Giovanni's contained all the entertainment we needed.

* * *

The truest thing Jean Cocteau ever said to me was this. There are certain places in every city, pit or peak, take your pick, where queers will always gather.

Why in Paris?

In Rome it is the Via San Giovanni. In Madrid it is Chueca. In Amsterdam it is, well, Amsterdam. And in Berlin it is, or at least was, Schöneberg. Cocteau knows because he visited all these places, and many more. In the early '20s, he traveled around Europe with a young novelist called Raymond Radiguet. Cocteau was in love with Radiguet—deeply, madly in love. But it hurt him so terribly that Radiguet did not return those feelings.

Cocteau dragged him to every queer bar and bathhouse and midnight park on the continent, throwing every kind and form of man in front of Radiguet to better understand how to please the boy. But it was all in vain. Radiguet remained a closed book, with Cocteau no closer to understanding the source of the young novelist's true desires or sexuality, nor able to admit nor understand that the unknowableness of desire can be a sexuality all in itself. When they returned to Paris in the winter of 1923, life took its course. Radiguet came down with tuberculosis and died, aged only twenty. Coco Chanel arranged the funeral, which Cocteau did not attend.

Nevertheless, Cocteau understood from the entire experience the stark difference between a fully-fledged queer man, and an ordinary bloke who doesn't mind the occasional dipping of the quill. The queer will always, without a doubt and most likely in the space of an evening, find that one place in a city, the bar, the park, the bathhouse, where he may gather among people of his sort. Whereas the bloke, while he may also happen upon these places, will usually require a guide or even a map to find the place, because at the end of the day, the bloke can take it or leave it. A true queer has no such choice.

"So as a goose always knows how to fly south for the winter," Cocteau told me, "so a homosexual's erection will always know where to lead him."

In Paris, that place was Montmartre. More specifically, Giovanni's bar, was the nadir into which men sank, or the apex they sought to ascend.

Cocteau spent several nights a week with me at Giovanni's. He liked sitting with me because I could eavesdrop on the conversations between the soldiers and relay what I heard.

Every German soldier was promised *Jeder einmal in Paris.* Everyone once in Paris. They came like an invasion of tourists, walking around the city holding maps and cameras, their Karabiner rifles slung over their backs as they took a break from conquering Europe.

Giovanni's did not appear on their maps or in their guidebooks. Montmartre itself was only mentioned as the 'artistic quarter' of Paris. But despite the logistical difficulties, each and every night Giovanni's was packed with German geese who'd found their way to the right watering hole.

"How long did it take you to find Giovanni's?" Cocteau asked me one evening as we watched Claude hand out numbered tickets to soldiers who wanted more than just a drink, in order to form a more orderly and efficient queue.

"Oh, I came here straight from the train station," I said, only after realizing exactly what that meant. Cocteau laughed and we clinked our glasses together as Claude called out from the stairs: "Number twelve! *Nummer zwölf, numéro douze.*"

A rather plump but excited looking German officer who'd been sitting alone at the bar jumped up from his stool, ruddy-faced and sweating under his dark green cap, and rushed to the stairwell where Claude greeted him with a *mademoiselle* smile and led him by the hand upstairs.

"We must find a man to love only you," Cocteau said, "and not the entire Wehrmacht."

Claude was not the only one servicing the Wehrmacht. At first, he'd insisted that every Reichsmark go through him. And for a while, it did. But barely a month after the occupation began, no one man could supply the demand of the German army.

So to Giovanni's came Thomas, then Gabriel, then Louis, Alexandre, Lucas, Martin, Hugo and Nathan, and a few others who'd hung around the Roosevelt Mansion. I cycled around Paris like a resistance fighter, knocking on attic doors and basement windows, bringing these boys out of forced retirement caused by the flux of invasion. If this was to be the age of whores, better that we were together. Still no one knew how David and Hella were. Not since the Germans rushed over the Maginot line and anyone with the means to attend a party decided instead to flee the city. But after the occupation had taken hold and things had settled in, much, though not all of Paris's moneyed population drifted back from their second homes in the south. A true Parisian is always drawn back. It never crosses their mind to live anywhere else. A Parisian found beyond the Île-de-France is in perennial exile. They measure time not in how long they've been away, but how many days, months, years even until they return. Wherever they go, for however long or far, a true Parisian is forever on their way back to Paris. And so I heard, not from the boys, but from Cocteau, that David and Hella were doing fine, and like many of Paris's well-trod establishments, had re-opened to a new clientele. Giovanni's had, so why not them?

"How are things at David's?" I would ask Cocteau every so often, but he would only shrug and say:

"You know, *popular.*"

I knew what he meant. David had apparently discovered quite the niche in occupied Paris. Just as Giovanni's had turned into a twenty-four-hour working brothel for German men of a certain sort, so the Roosevelt Mansion had become a hangout for the upper crust of the officer corps.

Somehow, the officers of the Wehrmacht had got the idea that David's encapsulated the spirit of true Paris. When the troops had finished doing their circuit around the Champs Elyse, they went to the house on the corner of Rue Royer-Collard and Boulevard Saint-Michel expecting a party.

I always wondered how the Germans got that idea. Had the generals gone and visited every famous writer and artist in Paris, and asked them where they could spend an evening experiencing this *joie de vivre* they'd heard so much about?

If irony had its way, the idea would have come from a certain aristocrat, from whom someone had heard the place to go in Paris was a beautiful apartment overlooking the Jardin du Luxembourg. There, the champagne flowed freely, the company was riveting, and there was always a singer with a song, a band with a tune, and the next great artist with something to show off. Perhaps even a whore or two for the right guest. This was the Paris of their imagination.

What the Germans would never understand, of course, was the spirit they sought after was freedom itself. The passion of Paris in all its many forms and contradictions: Bohemian and suave, modernist and surrealist, avant-garde and traditionalist, republican and revolutionary. The dream of Paris did not live in neatly dressed ashlar buildings or broad, Haussmannian boulevards watched over by wrought iron balconies. It could be found only in that second city, the hidden Paris which was only truly on display at night.

It was the time the city showed itself. All the greatest people who ever lived here lived nocturnally. They rose at the absinthe hour and slept come dawn. The writers wrote by candlelight, the dancers danced under electric bulbs. Perhaps only the painters painted by the sun, but I knew for a fact they had all their best ideas while letting the bottle lead them through the darkness. The occupation killed the night. It killed passion. It was anti-life. Dadaist surrealism, as coined by Cocteau's great rival Tristan Tzara, rejects the idea of art, so occupation rejects the idea of freedom. So Paris had to reject the night, and the city bled in the daylight hours.

In this Nazi choke hold, in this bleeding day and dead night, David, much like Claude, much like the rest of us, had to keep performing tricks to survive.

But one should not judge the actions of others under stresses one can never understand. I had never fought in a war, so I never allowed myself to think much of anything about the decisions of those who had. The stories of heroism some liked to share after a drink or four washed over me like the horrors they spoke of, too. I could not say if I would run across the trenches, hide in the nearest shell-hole, or shoot myself in the foot just to get out of there.

If I were David, if I were Claude or Cocteau or even Giovanni, and found myself drowning in a nightmare of found objects—hotels, landmarks, dirty streets—repurposed into the machinery of Nazi occupation, I don't think I could do anything else but do my best to carry on.

* * *

On a warm evening in the spring of '41 I was at the bar, patiently waiting for Giovanni to serve me, as we were secondary to any German who wanted a drink. I always tried to make myself invisible, avoiding eye contact with anyone around in case they got the wrong idea and tried to redeem their ticket with me.

As I waited, investigating the cleanliness of my nails once again, the conversation of the two soldiers behind me turned interesting. Even when Giovanni finally approached me, I shrugged him away so I could hear the end of it.

With a purposeful languish of a spy master changing trains, I brought Cocteau his drink. He glared at me as I sat down.

"What took you so long? I've been hit on by two captains and a lieutenant already. I can't keep—"

"Yugoslavia fell last week, and Athens was occupied yesterday."

"Good God."

The days lengthened and spring only brought more bad news. I heard from a clutch of regular infantry who'd been in Paris since May they were being sent to the East. Not to reinforce Poland, though. They were preparing for something else.

One evening Claude was sitting with us, taking a break before starting up his late shift. Cocteau was upset. He hadn't heard from Marais in several days and was doing everything he could to stay calm. Claude was not someone one could easily stay calm around.

"That one over there," Claude said, pointing over our heads to a tall officer leaning against the bar and chatting with a Luftwaffe pilot, "has the biggest cock in the entire officer's corps."

"Have you no shame?" Cocteau cried out, banging his fist on the table and causing a few of our occupiers to look around.

"Shh," I hissed.

"Do you have a problem, old man?" Claude snapped back.

"What about France?" Cocteau whispered, keeping one eye on me.

"What about it?"

"Where's your loyalty to the Republic?"

"Look," I said, growing increasingly nervous about the volume of patriotism being expressed. "I'm not sure this is the right time for—"

"Loyalty?" Claude asked, his cheeks glowing with incandescent redness. I'd never seen him so furious. "Loyalty to a republic that's spat on me since birth? Loyalty to a nation that spews lies about liberty, equality and fraternity but offers me none of it?"

"Listen, I really think—"

"Shut up, Anders." Claude yelled, knocking the chair back as he jumped up from the table. "I'm not finished with this pompous prick. You think, Monsieur Cocteau, because you're wealthy and well-connected and bourgeois you have some inalienable right to set the rules for the rest of us. People like you care about the things that don't matter, because the things that do matter are so frivolously gotten by you. I care about having enough cash in my pocket for my next meal, keeping a roof over my head and not getting shot to death on some grim battlefield fighting over a strip of land nobody's heard of.

"I don't give a shit if the Tricolor, the swastika, or the goddamn union-jack flies over the Eiffel Tower, just give me bread for the day and a bed for the night."

"You seem to have no trouble finding a bed for the night," Cocteau responded, at least quietly.

"Too right I don't. I might speak French, but my hole is international, a real brotherhood of men!" He sat back down with a thud, and gradually the heavily armed eyes drifted back to their own business. I smiled nervously around the bar, breaking my no eye contact rule to show I was on top of keeping the peace between these two. Despite the glances, the conversations among the men remained steady and loud, the occupiers confident in the knowledge they could pass around secrets and gossip and not be understood. I could hear it all.

"While you've been yelling," I said, "the Germans have invaded Russia."

"What?" They both said together. Cocteau leaned across the table and said: "When did this happen?"

"I don't know," I said through gritted teeth, "because you were both yelling so loud."

"Well then," Claude said, getting up from his seat and dramatically stretching, "I better go and *gather some intelligence,* so to speak."

"At least your hole is good for something," Cocteau shot back.

"I think you'll find it's *holes,* plural. And yes, darling, I'm a one-man fifth column."

Chapter 9

CLAUDE SAID HE'D HEARD from a soldier who couldn't get hard, and so spent forty-five minutes sharing his life story, that there was a bakery in Saint-Denis that supplied croissants to the officers, and thus the bakery was allocated unlimited quantities of real butter to bake with. This soldier's job was to collect the croissants and *pain au chocolat* from the bakery and deliver it to Nazi headquarters at the Hotel Majestic, nearby the Arc de Triomphe. The baker always gave him a couple of extra for the journey, and he said to Claude they were the best thing he'd ever eaten.

One morning, as I helped Giovanni clean tables and mop the floor in the dead hours before the first batch of horny Germans arrived, a soldier appeared at the doorway, the warm sun blazing in from the street above masking his round features.

Giovanni had taken garbage to the back alley, so I got up from the floor where I'd been scrubbing off a beer stain, threw my rag into the bucket and focused my mind to make sure the French I was about to speak did not have the slightest trace of German in it.

"Is Claude here?" The soldier asked in French.

"He is, yes. But I think he's sleeping. Shall I wake him for you?"

"Oh no need, but please, give him this."

He handed me a small package wrapped in a red-checkered cloth. It was warm and smelled like buttery heaven.

"I will."

The soldier nodded and left, and I quickly unwrapped the bundle and gazed on the most perfectly formed croissant, the first real one I'd seen in well over a year.

"Where in God's name did you get that?" I heard Giovanni gasp.

"A German dropped it off for Claude," I said, then quickly explained about the bakery in Saint Dennis that baked with real butter.

"He'll never know," Giovanni said, practically salivating at the mouth.

"He will. Fritz will come back, ask Claude how it was, then shoot the both of us for theft."

"Or just you. He never saw me."

Giovanni lunged for the croissant, and I feared this was no longer a joke.

"Go get him up," I yelled, lifting the precious pastry out of his reach. "We'll share it."

Claude laughed when he finally came downstairs and I told him the story.

"It's a shame," he said, wafting the aroma towards his nose, "I think the poor soul is in love with me."

Giovanni seized Claude by his silk dressing gown. "You'll let him piss in your mouth if he keeps on bringing these."

Claude glanced at me and smirked. The image of this little man getting so worked up over a croissant was the best laugh we'd had in a while.

"Generally, that costs more than a croissant, but all right, keep your toupee on. Next time he's here I'll ask if he can bring one all for you." Giovanni relaxed a tad and released Claude. "I have some real coffee upstairs I've been saving for a special occasion: looks like that's today."

Giovanni nodded quietly but look perturbed. Like he'd had to retreat from a position he never thought he would have to, being reduced to such selfishness. It took me a few moments to appreciate just how out of character this was for a man who had, with little more than a twist of his moustache, turned a neighborhood queer hang-out into the primary location for the homosexual contingent of the German army.

"Coffee, Anders?" Claude asked. "Or do you prefer the taste of piss Giovanni seems so keen on?"

* * *

A few days later, the soldier had come and gone again. Claude told me he'd figured out why the young man couldn't get hard the last time. He was passive.

"It was so simple," Claude told me one morning as the first lights of dawn approached and he readied for bed. "I should have known as soon as he started talking about his damn mother's baking. That's the difference, dandies will talk and talk till you shove a cock inside them."

"You managed it?" I asked. I didn't think I could. Claude grinned.

"*Blitzkrieg baby you can't bomb me,*" he started to sing and dance around the room.

"Tell me!"

"Something something neu-tra-la-ty." Then he threw himself onto the bed and buried his nose in the crumb-stained checkered cloth he now kept by his bed.

"What's his name?"

"Hans," he sighed like a girl in love, flipping onto his stomach and lifting his feet into the air. "Hans the submissive lad from Hanover who only wanted to be a humble baker, but his father made him join the army. Anders, teach me how to say 'I love you' in German."

"*Ich liebe dich.*"

Claude shrieked with laughter. "Well that makes three of us!"

"Where in Saint-Dennis is this bakery, then?"

"He says it's around the back of the basilica. Monsieur Bastidon I think was the man's name. Why do you ask?"

"I have an idea," I said, grinning back at Claude. "How many Reichsmarks do you have?"

"Thousands." He pulled out a steel box from under the bed and hurled a roll of notes wrapped up with string at me. "Take. What do I need them for, I have my Hans to bring me pastries and bread and his sweet little hole."

* * *

145

I cycled all the way north to Saint-Dennis. Curfew had broken with the dawn, but the streets were still empty. No one knew where to go these days. Even the basilica seemed locked up, like God was also under occupation.

I found Monsieur Bastidon's boulangerie exactly where Claude said it would be. The front door was locked, and the shutters closed, but I could smell the melting butter from a kilometer away. An alley ran alongside the bakery's back door, open ajar to let out the heat. I left my bike on the corner, and stepped gingerly along the cobbles, towards the light and aroma pouring from inside.

"*Guten morgen,*" I called out as I slipped inside the kitchen, parroting the harsh, clipped, yet oddly polite German the occupiers used on us locals. An elderly man in dirty whites was layering beautiful golden dough over a countertop. The rest of the kitchen was cramped with trays of unbaked pastries ready to slot into the ancient ovens, and around my feet boxes of full of goodies already baked.

I'd startled the man, and he stared at me with a shock of fear I don't think I'd ever caused in another human in all my life. Although I wasn't in any sort of uniform, I'd side-parted my hair and shaved with such military precision I could have come straight from the office of Otto von Stülpnagel, the military commander in France.

"Monsieur Bastidon?" I asked.

"*Oui... uh, ja, mein Herr.*"

I smiled and approached him slowly as one might a wounded dog, desperate to tell him not to be afraid. The confusion at my civilian clothes was also evident, and I had to be careful not to appear to be who I really was.

I took the roll of cash Claude had given me from my satchel and stepped forward holding it in front of me.

"Your baking," I said to him in thickly accented French, "*c'est magnifique.*"

"Oh, ah... *merci,*" he said, red cheeks now nervously stretched in a polite smile. "*Merci beaucoup.*" Inside the bakery was sweltering, but an extra layer of sweat was now excreting from his skin thanks to my presence.

"May I?" I pointed to the goods, "a few, to take with me?" I held out the cash again, and he got the message.

"*Oui, monsieur, oui.*"

He snatched the roll of notes and stuffed them under his apron, then hurried around the kitchen gathering up a pastry or two from each tray, along with irregularly shaped ones that would likely have gone to his family. He threw them all onto one of those red checkered cloths, constantly glancing past me to the door, in case this was all some cruel trap.

"*C'est bon?*" he asked, wrapping up the cloth and tying it into a bag.

"*Oui. Très bien. Merci.*"

He nodded, seeming relieved to have survived this test. He thrust the cloth full of hot croissants into my hands, then shooed me towards the door which slammed shut as soon as I was out.

Pleased with myself, I carefully put the cloth in my satchel, swung onto the bike and headed for home.

I even let myself get excited for a decent breakfast. It was certainly worth waking Claude up for. Taking the steps down to Giovanni's two at a time, I pulled the cloth out of my bag and began to unwrap it before I even got inside.

"Giovanni! Madame Framboise! Mademoiselle Claude! I have a surprise for you all."

Something was off, though. The room seemed too quiet, with dirty glasses still piled up on the counter. Giovanni would never leave the bar such a mess before going to bed. Nor was he out in the alley, because the back door was shut.

"Good morning, Anders."

I spun around, dizzy from terror. There he was, sitting calmly at the corner table I usually occupied with Claude or Cocteau. The man I'd never expected to see here.

"David, what are you doing here?"

He didn't answer, but got up and walked towards me, sniffing at the pastries.

"Seems I came on the right morning." He took one from me. But he didn't seem angry, or mad. More resigned to his fate in life, as if coming to me was the one thing he'd promised himself never to do. David smoothed back his knotted, straw-dry hair once shiny and slick. He fretted with his hands, looking skeletal in the cheeks. Less from hunger, more from fear. "Got anything decent to drink?"

*   *   *

The shock of seeing David again for the first time since the outbreak of the war was like the occupation itself—a confusing morass of color and shapes and frightening images. Great monuments of Paris now thinned out and afraid. David stood before me, a man hollowed, inverted. As if Emmanuel had crafted a dadaist portrait of the *bon vivant* I'd once known, then displayed this anti-art before us all, proud of his achievement while Cocteau scoffed in the corner, saying: *No, darling. He's just sick as a dog.*

Before we could even get down to the business of discussing whatever it was he'd come all this way for, I heard Giovanni squeak from the cellar door.

"What were you doing down there?" I asked him.

"I heard an unfamiliar voice calling out your name, and I thought they'd come for you."

"Come for me? What do you mean?"

"You know," Giovanni said, cautiously coming towards us like a frightened mouse. "Because you're a Jew."

I wanted to run, to leave everything behind rather than deny the undeniable… But with David standing right there, peering over my shoulder, hands clasped behind his back and flecks of croissant on his clean-shaven cheek, I would feel more the fool than even I could handle.

"I'm the Jew," David said, making me jump in surprise as he leaned over and offered Giovanni his hand. The old Italian shook it rather confusingly, glaring at us both. "Very nice to meet you, finally."

Giovanni had the same look on his face from when he said only I would be shot if the German found out we'd stolen the croissant meant for Claude. I suddenly saw this short, plump and usually smiling man in an utterly different light—as if the photograph of him in my mind had gone from negative to technicolor. And I sensed that I could no longer trust him, if, indeed, I ever could have.

The entire structure of my life in Paris, the security of where I lived, the faces of the people I'd never questioned counting on, all of it crumbled like a bomb had gone off under the foundations.

"What…" I said, swallowing, "what made you think I'm a Jew?"

"Oh, I don't know," he replied, making his way over to the pastries, "I think Claude thought you were, so I just assumed." Giovanni glanced over his shoulder at David, still tall and baronly despite heavy eyes, an unknown factor in this equation. "Not that it makes any difference to me." He added hurriedly.

"Claude thought what?" Claude said from the stairs, emerging into the bar wearing the same silk dressing gown I'd seen him in that morning. He yawned and his eyes were dark, as if he'd been asleep for the hour and a half it had taken me to cycle to Saint-Dennis and back. "David!" Claude bounded across the room and leapt into him with a great big hug. "What are you doing here?"

"I've come for Anders' bar mitzvah," he said, grinning at me.

"Jewish humor," Claude said, noticing the pastries, "I'll never get it. Shall we eat?"

We didn't simply eat, we feasted. David and I dragged tables together and wiped down chairs still damp from the sweat of last night's coterie of German soldiers. Claude aired out an old, checkered cloth and polished chipped plates with his silk gown. Giovanni brought out a bottle of flat champagne he'd hidden away, and we squeezed an orange in to improve the taste. This was us: three queers and a bisexual, enjoying a breakfast of mimosas and freshly baked croissants, the war be damned.

I kept thinking about one of the first lessons I'd learned from Claude. We are history. How many gays in how many generations had faced the same, or worse? How many had breakfasted, laughed with friends, held hands with lovers as the spiral of history conspired against them? How many Jews?

David gave us all the brief update I already knew from Cocteau. The highest-ranking Nazis of the occupation army had commandeered the Roosevelt Mansion for their own pleasures, chasing away the usual suspects but trapping David and Hella in their surrealist role as entertainers-in-chief.

"Picasso still comes occasionally to sell them some of his paintings," David said as Giovanni picked uncouthly through the crumbs. "He figures the Germans could seize his work if they wanted, so why not make a buck."

"You haven't seen Jean, have you?" I asked with more trepidation than I expected from myself.

"Oh, he still comes often enough," David said flatly. I sat back, shell struck. "That's how I knew where to find you."

I stared at David confused. "Jean Cocteau?"

"Yes."

"Ah. I meant my Jean."

"Your starlet with the massive cock," Claude added, biting a chunk off a *pain au chocolat* for emphasis.

David returned his smile weakly. "Yes, I know who he means. I haven't Anders, I'm afraid. Well then, shall we talk business?"

I found the abrupt change of subject rather disconcerting. Because it undoubtedly meant some new challenge. David glanced at Claude and I, and then Giovanni still picking through the crumbs. Claude got the message.

"Giovanni, darling. Don't you have to go and order wine and beer from the military quartermaster?"

"Oh yes, I suppose so. It is Tuesday after all." He sighed and got up from the table, wiping croissant from his fussy waistcoat. "I never thought time could move slower."

"Boys," David said as soon as we were safely alone. "The Germans have drunk all my wine, scared away all my friends, and listened to all my records. I am soon to become useless to them, and I for one do not want to find out what the Germans will do to a useless degenerate Jew such as myself. But I've got one thing left to offer them. The officers don't like sharing brothels with the men, nor does the high command like sharing brothels with the officers. But the high command doesn't have anyone to cater just to them."

"All right," Claude said, "I get the picture. I can't say I haven't been shared among the men, but they don't need to know that."

"Not you," David said, almost laughing. "They're Nazis, not queers. At least not most of them. I'm talking about running a proper bordello. With women and such. But not like a seedy brothel." David openly sized up his surroundings. No one could say the rooms upstairs where Claude and the boys swapped numbered tickets for Reichsmarks had the kind of class the high command expected.

"I've found my numbered ticketing system works quite well, actually."

Claude said. "Germans seem to enjoy waiting their turn. Individually, I mean. Less collectively."

"I'm not talking about running a raffle here. It'll be one big party, like in the old days. We'll pretend the broads are guests, make sure they dress fancy and drag it on throughout the night so the generals will feel like they're being flirted with, not like they're waiting for their number to be called. I've already converted the library to a guest room, and I commandeered two of the neighbor's iron bed frames since she took off to Marseille. That makes six workable bedrooms."

"Six?" I asked, nervous to know if he included the secret room in his calculations.

"Seven, at a push," he added with a grin. The thought turned my insides out, but on some level it was nice to see David come alive. "We'll cap the guest list at sixty. That means a minimum of twelve working broads per night. Giving them half an hour to dance with their German, twiddle his medals, then half an hour with his boots off."

"That's being generous," Claude said.

"On average. Two girls sharing the use of one room, working through one German per hour. We can start at eight and be closed up by two."

"I mean it's generous to think they'll take their boots off. These men do everything like a *blitzkrieg*."

"What do you want us for?" I asked, fearing he might mention the Vinten camera.

"Who better to run a bordello than you two?"

"Well that's true," Claude said. "We know all the best whores in Paris. Plus this one can eavesdrop on their conversations."

"Exactly," David said. "Just imagine German high command all in one place, drinking and gossiping with each other. The Resistance will pay a fortune for that kind of information."

"The Resistance?" I said, suddenly terrified.

"The Resistance," David nodded. "I'm banking on that money to keep the booze and broads flowing. Oh, don't worry Anders, we're not going to poison them or anything. But we can keep our ears, and our eyes..." he let his gaze linger on me, and I knew he was thinking only one thing. "It's

151

settled then," he said. He lifted his glass, as did Claude, then I, reluctantly.

"To the best bordello in all Paris!" Claude declared.

"L'chaim!" David responded. I felt sick.

Chapter 10

IT TURNED OUT THE occupying army was a gossiping sort. Word spread like a forest fire around the soldiers that a new brothel was opening in town, and every madame in the city had been asked to send pictures of their best women like a casting call. Only a few would be selected to attend the most exclusive party in Paris where a guest required the rank of Oberst or better to attend.

David had talked to a few of the old gang—those who were still in Paris at least—to come next Friday night. The military government had agreed all the guests would be given an *Ausweis*, a special transit pass personally signed by General Otto von Stülpnagel, which would let them out at night after curfew.

Even the promise of a coveted *Ausweis* tempted very few, however, as David bitterly complained one morning at Giovanni's. We'd established an impromptu planning committee at the bar; David, Cocteau, Claude and I would meet early in the morning after the dregs of the previous night had drifted back to their base and long before any self-respecting soldier would bang on the door of a brothel.

"There's rumors Reichsmarshall Goering is coming," I said, bringing the rest of yesterday's croissants to the table. The deliveries had become a regular occurrence. Hans had fallen hard for Claude, so it seemed, and he brought not just pastries when he could, but pate, cheese, marmalade, and even a side of beef once—anything he could scavenge from the military headquarters in order to win round the unwinnable Claude, like some ancient shepherd boy trying to claim the town harlot with bushels of wheat and goats. A real gay folk tale this all was, and the provisions provided the perfect fuel for our meetings. "And Field Marshall Erich von Manstein who's coming straight from the Russian front."

"Goering, really?" Cocteau asked me, looking up from the array of photographs of prostitutes which had been delivered in droves. On the back listed their 'special skills' which at first had been funny to hear read out loud, but now was a little hard to stomach with breakfast.

"That's what the men are saying."

"Well that does pile the pressure on, doesn't it?" Cocteau ripped up the photograph of a topless, full-bodied woman laying on a chaise lounge he'd been holding. "We're going to need far more talent than a broad who can put her legs behind her head."

Cocteau scratched his head, nervously lighting up another cigarette. He didn't eat much these days, or certainly none of us ever saw food pass through his lips. Only the stubby end of a cigarette or the spout of an opium pipe.

"Do we have enough opium to handle Goering?" David asked in between scratching down numbers in his notepad.

"We should," Claude answered seriously, as if it was more important than the champagne supply. "I can ask Mélenchon to send some up from Perpignan."

"Mélenchon, perfect." David said, "tell him to come to Paris, will you? He'll draw a few of the artists in if they know they can get a free hit. Can you ask any of *Les Six?*" He asked Cocteau, referring to the crowd of sculptors, musicians and poets Cocteau had gathered around him back in the day.

"Perhaps Auric, but it's doubtful."

"Try, will you? Right now, the biggest name we have is that actor fellow Robert-Hugues Lambert."

Cocteau glanced sideways at David and stubbed out the last of his cigarette on a picture of some other girl not good enough for a Nazi soiree. "Shall we try and limit the number of flagrant homosexuals running this show? I think we might have saturated the market on that front."

"We're not *all* homosexuals, Jean."

"Oh, aren't we? How is your lovely wife? Knee deep in labia, I would imagine."

David flamed with anger and Cocteau dragged his chair back. The last thing we needed was a fight, as I was sure Giovanni would denounce all of us just to save his tables and chairs.

"Who else can we invite?" I said loudly, trying to settle the tension. "What about Kiki de Montparnasse?"

"Ha," David scoffed. "She fled long ago. Along with that stick insect Emmanuel. Bunch of collaborators."

Cocteau nodded in agreement, face barely containing disgust at the mention of Emmanuel's name.

"Collaborators?" I said, "What do you mean? They're helping the enemy?"

"Of course they are," David yelled. "Fleeing Paris before even a shot was fired, abandoning their city, leaving her lonely and wounded in the moment of her greatest need. I hope they're all shot the second this war is over."

"Jean Arp has also gone," Cocteau said, albeit with slightly less bile. "Tristan Tzara's fled to Marseille along with the rest of those surrealists. Ironic they no longer want to live in the nightmare of their creation."

"How about Miss Baker?" I suggested.

"Also gone south," David said, flicking through crossed off names in his notebook. "Marie Bell could come. Although she's not a whore."

"Hmm," Cocteau said, "how will the Germans be able to tell who's available for their use?"

"Perhaps they could wear some sort of badge?" David said. "A black and red armband, perhaps."

"Oh, very good, David," Cocteau said, waving away their fight. "Fine. We'll sort out the details later. Let's find some women first of all or this idea of yours will turn into... well, this place." He held up two photographs of naked women in front of me, "which one of these is more to the taste of a German field marshal?"

I stared at both the images, trying to focus on something other than evaluating the composition, the clever use of space to draw the eye to, well, the supposedly good parts.

"I, uh... am not really sure—"

"Why am I asking you," Cocteau said sharply and looked around the empty bar. "We need a straight man."

Silence. I looked to David, who looked to Cocteau, who turned around and glanced to Claude by the bar pouring himself another breakfast drink since Giovanni was still asleep. Not that Giovanni could fill that role, either.

"Madame Framboise?" Claude offered.

Cocteau sighed, shaking his head as if he disapproved of our collective inability to know a straight man well enough for this task. "She'll have to do."

* * *

Evidently the rumor of Hermann Goering planning to attend the launch of a swanky new evening club for the sophisticated officers was based on far more than speculation. The military commander's office got in touch with David several times to move around the date of the launch party.

It was a testament to the reality of life under occupation—a sullen boredom locked in the knowledge that only material events of a dialectical scale would end the tedium of the struggle for survival, and not necessarily for the better—in such conditions even the whisper of a fresh idea sprung into a life all of its own.

A successful city thrives on a potent clash of many cultures. Vienna used to have it, when it drew in all the peoples of Austria-Hungary to suave around the remnants of the Holy Roman Empire, like sophisticated Visigoths enjoying opera in the Colosseum. From the day of the Armistice, Vienna ceased to exist, or so my grandmother always said. Berlin took on some of the mantle that Vienna abdicated, but more so than any other place, Paris emerged as the next center of the world.

The imperial capital of the artistic universe, its storied streets were soon traversed by Romanovic emigres, Italian fortune-seekers, Armenian survivors, Czech and Slovak entrepreneurs, and all manner of other forgotten nationalities struggling to keep a page in the rapidly flipping books of history.

During the interregnum between the wars, for every thousand Parisians, at least a hundred were foreign born. This was a greater proportion than any other built environment on the continent since perhaps imperial Rome.

It was precisely in this collision of societies, a forced fusion of many worlds, a brutal collaboration of a thousand histories all sharing the same resplendent space echoing with Napoleonic glory which truly made Paris the center of the world.

There are many forms of occupation. By a foreign power or brutes closer to home. By a siege army or a deadly famine. It doesn't particularly matter. What matters only is a shrinking of personal freedom to almost nothing. Occupation is the opposite of dynamism.

We as victims and they as aggressors were on opposite sides of the war, but both of us were under occupation. Hitler had seized the German nation as much as he had seized the rest of Europe. He had captured their minds, held hostage their spirits and besieged their beliefs.

Many Germans sacrificed their freedom willingly, as one might join a movement when there's no other movement to join. Most of us do the done thing. We follow our peers, fit in with the crowd and go along with whatever makes our lives easier. It doesn't mean we don't miss the other thing, however.

The Germans under occupation, even the leaders of the movement, still yearned, somewhere in their twisted logic, for a breath of space, a bit of room to flirt with another who took their fancy, but still return home to kiss Hitler on the mouth.

This was why David's party had blitzkrieged the imagination of the occupying forces. Away from their wives, they were free to indulge in harmless flirtation with an exotic mistress, do something anti-Aryan, something decadent. Indeed, the wife at home knew all about it, and while she might not approve of the details, she understood the needs of men at war.

This party at David's would give the once dynamic elements from both sides a little room to breathe. It would be a renewal of Franco-German values that were bravely forming a whole new world. A conjugation of artistic femininity and military masculinism, celebrated in a consecration between conquered and conqueror, as Jupiter might have seized the wives and daughters of Zeus.

So, the date for this seizing of the *best* of Parisian women with the *best* men of the Reich was fixed for the first of September 1941, two years to the day the whole world changed.

*   *   *

The Nazis did everything in their considerable power to welcome this new addition to the crowded but static Parisian bordello scene. A red carpet was literally rolled down the stairs and out onto the street. The heavy iron door to the Roosevelt Mansion propped wide open, as for what possible purpose would it need to be locked? Two soldiers flanked the doorway, but they were merely decorative since half the arrondissement had been shut down in advance of the arrival of the high command in Europe.

"You think they'd all come in one car," Claude said to me as we peered out the kitchen window at the steady stream of arrivals. I didn't answer. In fact, I couldn't. I poured myself a glass of water, but dropped the glass then smashed the water bottle as I swept it up. Claude bandaging my cut finger like mother *tsk-tsk*ing her clumsy toddler. I tried to light a cigarette but set my bandage on fire. As if living in the belly of the beast was not bad enough, here we were inviting as many beasts as possible into the mansion, and for what purpose? To help the generals relax so they could be more efficient killing machines when they returned to work?

As much as I wished this wasn't happening, I also knew there was no other course of action available. Not to David, at least. When the Germans ordered you to throw them a party with the best whores in Paris, all you could do is hope for it to be the best one they'd ever attended.

In place of the white jacketed waiters I remembered, now there was a clutch of soldiers in feldgrau uniforms scurrying around the kitchen, preparing champagne and arranging *hors d'oeuvres* on David and Hella's silver trays.

Hella was playing the hostess, dressed grimly in black with a lacy vale, as if to separate her from the throng of heavily made-up women sitting around the couches acting mostly ignorant of each other like too many big cats in the one cage.

Claude and I had been here since dawn, ensuring every inch of the mansion was beyond reproach, supervised by an officer from Nazi Headquarters at the Hotel Majestic and Hans, who'd driven him. The officer's surrealist, high camp performance of peering through his monocle while white-gloved hands inspected every surface for dust would have made me laugh if I wasn't so focused on figuring out my backstory. Who was I meant to be? David's worker who inexplicably spoke French with a heavily German accent? I decided it was best to say nothing at all. Even when we endured a slight crisis mid-afternoon, when the officers who had come early to set up announced that five Black men had arrived carrying all manner of brass instruments.

"There was no Aryan jazz band available?" Cocteau yelled at David before rushing downstairs to shoo them away. He commandeered a car and an army driver, and drove straight to *Le Sphinx*, formerly one of the city's best brothels which surely the Roosevelt Mansion now rivalled, if only by sheer numbers of employees alone. There Cocteau found Édith Piaf drinking a sherry and readying to perform for the middling officer class, but Cocteau bundled her and her pianist into the back of the car, gave the madame a chunk of Reichsmarks in exchange for the last-minute booking, and stuffed Édith with champagne and caviar earmarked for Goering until she was no longer against this brutal collaboration.

In the main room she was humming with the pianist, providing a background aura to dampen the clattering of trays from the kitchen and the nervous silence which hung in the air.

Nobody was quite sure how this would work. In a normal brothel one either arrived and went straight to business or would be plied with a few drinks to get the courage up and quicken the pace, so that women were never occupied with one man for too long. At busy times, or if one's preferred person was occupied, one had either the option to wait, take someone else, or return at an appointed time.

Le Sphinx and Le Chabanais had even installed special telephones connected to the military network for officers to call ahead and make a booking, such was the demand during these *années erotiques* when sex was about the only thing one could make a decent living from. Sometimes it felt like the entire city had been transfigured into one big romping ground for the Germans. Just as the eastern front was for killing, so the western front was for fucking.

But this was a party, or at least it was supposed to be. Field marshals and *Reichmarshals* were not looking for the ordinary type of slot machine experience their inferiors indulged in. They wanted to feel like they were in some bygone era, invited to an evening where getting off was simply a side effect, the real eroticism infused throughout.

"Dance competition," David said at five that afternoon. "We'll have a dance competition."

"You already suggested that half a dozen times and we all already said no," Cocteau said, massaging his pulsing temples.

"Do you have a better idea?" None of us did. "We'll have dances for half the hour, then give them a chance to mingle and start the next round. Hella and I will keep the scores, along with Picasso when he comes and Édith. The lowest scoring couple is out of the competition, so it will give them an excuse to sit out the remaining dances and go off with whomever they like while the rest of us get on with the next round of dancing."

Reluctantly, and with no more time left, we had to agree.

"How many rooms are there again?" Cocteau asked.

"Six. All the beds have been turned down."

"What about that other one? Inside the study?"

David glanced quickly at me, then back to Cocteau. I didn't know what that meant, if I was meant to pipe up and say something or leave the room.

"That one's for Goering. Or von Manstein if he wants it. Let everyone subordinate to them know it is strictly out of bounds and reserved exclusively for field marshals or better."

"I'll give you the signal," David whispered to me after we'd all scattered to finish checking over our last chores. I could smell his cognac-soaked tongue as he leaned into my shoulder. Drinking was probably the only way for a Jew to survive this night. "You sneak off into the pantry, get the camera on, and make sure you get it all, and on one reel, okay? There's no time to bother with splicing the film. One take with one of these bastards. That's all we need. One time. One bargaining chip. That'll be enough. No more after that."

I breathed out heavily. Mainly because it was the only way to breathe.

"What's the signal?"

David staggered away from me, then back again with a play-acting grin and laced his arm around my shoulder.

"Oh Antoine, there you are." I glared at him. "What? Do you prefer I introduce you to the Nazi high command as a Viennese Jew? No? Then listen. Oh Antoine, do we still have that magnum of Gosset in the pantry? You'll then run in and get the camera rolling before I send them in, so they won't notice any change of noise."

I didn't share David's confidence.

"Oh, buck up," he said, slapping me on the back. "The sour face makes you look like a Jew."

* * *

During the dance competition it seemed as if both Hermann Goering and Erich von Manstein were far more interested in winning than they were in scoring. The two-dozen other senior officers let their superiors steal the show, cheering on Goering in particular who proved himself quite nimble on his feet.

Édith's performance was as masterful as David and Hella's. She sang her very lungs out while Hella acted as the ultimate madame, swishing around the room making introductions between lonely-looking Germans and the suite of women of every shade and sort dressed up to the nines. David had done them well. Actually, it was a combination of Hella and Madame Framboise, a fifth of gin, and an endless collection of clothes, curtains and even Giovanni's best tablecloth stitched into a bustier. The women might look like they were ready to waltz on stage at the Folies Bergère alongside Miss Baker. David's mantra come to life: the illusion was all that mattered.

Despite the opulent surroundings, the free-flowing booze and the good-natured atmosphere, the entire charade sickened me. David kept yanking me out of the kitchen, forcing me to wander around and freshen drinks or direct certain couples to an unoccupied bedroom.

There was no point in me being here. The Germans did not exchange one useful word between them, not that I could overhear, anyway. So like a lamb in a terrible fox outfit, I was needlessly walking a tightrope across a gorge.

Let me hide in my room, coming down only to help Giovanni serve drinks to soldiers with secrets who, even if they somehow found me out, I would at least be in some position to negotiate with.

161

Here, any single one of these men could shoot me on sight. For fun.

Surprisingly, and it was genuinely peculiar since I fully expected to die or at the very least be arrested, the Germans were the paragon of Teutonic politeness. The language of the evening was English. David introduced himself, the singer and pianist, and us as the staff in his smartest American brogue, joking that when the time came to invade America, he would happily take the place of that other Roosevelt in the White House.

Between the ladies and the gentlemen, I heard only English, and that's what they spoke to me. I realized how much easier it was to pass in a third language than it was in a second. Jean had sussed out my French after half a dozen words, and my native German dialect was very much of the Austro-Bavarian variety. A young male Austrian found idling in Paris was probably the only type of person who'd be done for quicker than a Jew. So English brought me some measure of security.

As the night and the dance competition wore on, there was no sign of either Goering or von Manstein coming close to retiring to the room. Meaning all we had done was throw them a party, which they had enjoyed, and thanked us profusely for.

"Never mind," David whispered to me in the kitchen as Goering suspiciously won the dance competition to a ten-minute round of applause, "we've established ourselves now. It's only a matter of time before a big fish swims into the trap."

Perhaps David was right, but the last thing on earth I wanted was to be around for the next time. Walking this tightrope again, playing the subservient host to a circle of hell. I'd rather drop my trousers in front of the lot of them, recite the *Shema* and have it over with.

By two in the morning, only a handful of Germans remained. The soldiers in the kitchen had packed up and left long ago, taking every spare morsel of food with them. One Nazi officer was occupied with a woman named Aubrey, as he had been since midnight. Another was drinking all the whiskey he could find, and one more had fallen asleep on the spot where Édith had sang all night.

Their escorts weren't going to tell them to leave, at least not on our account, but there was a staff meeting at seven a.m., one of the drivers said, so if they weren't all out by three, then the escorts agreed to round up the sleeping Nazis and take them home.

Claude, David and I danced silently around the remnants as we cleaned up, Hella having already retired and Cocteau long gone as well. Some girls left with their officers, others had been given a lift back to their homes by a randy driver, but despite their *Ausweis's* a few hadn't gone for whatever reason and were sleeping on the couches. We'd cover them in blankets as soon as the last Nazi left, and I myself wanted nothing more than to curl up in a ball and drift off into a dream world where things made sense.

As I scrubbed mud from the carpet in the hall, a thudding knock made me jump. Von Manstein had returned, and alone. I froze on my hands and knees in shock, wondering if this was the end.

"Oh, good evening again, sorry to bother you." The commander of the Russian front said to me, while I grasped a sponge and tried to clean off the dirt he and his men had dragged in. And he was apologizing to me. For disturbing me. "I uh, seem to have left my…"

I wasn't sure if his English was failing him, or his words. Part of me wanted to speak to him in German, if only to spare the embarrassment of this rather bumbling man stuffed inside a green-grey uniform.

"Ah, Field Marshall," David said from behind as if he'd been expecting him all this time. "Right this way, if you please." David kicked me back to life and flashed his teeth in an angry grimace. "Antoine, the Gosset in the pantry? Do we still have it?"

"Don't go to any trouble on my behalf," von Manstein said. "Two glasses earlier this evening was quite enough."

I froze. Unsure whose instructions to follow. David glared at me. Wasn't he worried the Nazi would hear the camera without the background noise of Édith Piaf wailing or the gramophone? Or even the lull of background conversation? The hush around the house accurately reflected the time of morning. Two a.m. has a certain sound of silence even in the noisiest bar or dance club. As soon as the noise fades away, the blackness of the night, the physical absence of light dampens the atmosphere like a sudden storm.

163

"I'll, uh, go check," I said, if only to scurry away from the threatening scene.

My heart thundered and clattered; my skin cracked and stretched across my rib cage as I heaved and huffed without ever having the satisfaction of oxygen.

"Anders?" I heard Claude say. But his voice was diluted, like he was speaking to me through a dream. The floor swirled as my vision flashed red and black, red, and black. Swastikas everywhere. Giant black metal arms and sharp edges, cutting and scratching me as I fought past chairs, scraped past walls, and made it into the kitchen.

Like I had countless dozens of times before, I slid into the pantry, glad of the pitch-blackness which chased away the red flashing sirens of Nazi symbology. I crouched down and slid open the trap door, the Vinten camera standing quietly in the crawl space, waiting for me like a lover. I would not be getting out of Paris alive, I assumed.

I found acceptance in the acknowledgment of that simple, verifiable truth as I turned the camera on, shooting the still-darkness of the secret bedroom. The casual chit-chat of David I could now hear drifting through the flimsy wall from the study. My heart, my chest, my crunching bones and labored breathing washed away like the inevitable tide.

I would die in Paris. Perhaps tomorrow, or the day after, or the month after. There was no hiding from death. It was inevitable. By torture, by firing squad, by starvation or hard labor in a camp, the only calm I could find was in the certainty of dying. In fact, I should have died quite some time ago. Had I not left Vienna, only one of two things would have happened to an otherwise fit young man without discernible skills. I would have been conscripted into the army, or my Jewishness would have been uncovered, and I would have been, or on my way to, forced labor. To even inquire about mother and grandmother would raise a flag of suspicion, if not outright reveal me. For now, I was alive, but this once trivial fact was coming at higher and higher cost.

Thus every day I breathed I shortchanged death. I lived beyond my shelf life, spat in the face of fate. When death is inevitable, what is there left to fear? As the camera reels spun, capturing darkness, I no longer had to care about the things which normally keep the living awake at night—namely the unknowableness of death and the unanswerable question of if their life would matter. This was my legacy, a visual record of the secret sex life of a senior Nazi.

In a war which had already killed millions and would likely kill millions more before the last shot was fired, my death might mean one small thing. What else can a casualty of conflict ask for?

I breathed out, lifting a layer of dust from the lens. An unfamiliar sort of calm landed upon my shoulders. I couldn't tell if it came from a good place or not, but it was there, nonetheless. And I accepted it in.

Nothing, however, could prepare me for what came next. Not if von Manstein walked right up to the ruined Picasso covering the hole in the wall and gave me a poke in the eye.

"Right in here, Field Marshall," David said as the door to the secret bedroom swung open and the light flicked on. Inside stepped not one of the remaining women, but Claude. Smiling. Holding a glass of wine.

The Nazi had already lost his hat, jacket and shirt, and Claude tackled the buttons of his breaches with one hand while sipping from the wine glass with the other.

David closed the door, from the inside.

* * *

Burying the reel had been far easier than I expected. As soon as dawn came and curfew was lifted, I walked straight across the street to the Jardin du Luxembourg. I was alone in the mist. The hour was too early and too still for anything that needed guarding.

Unconsciously I was drawn to the spot where I'd first met Jean, by Zacharie Astruc's sculpture of *le marchand de masques*, the cherubesque child holding out the scalped face of Victor Hugo. As I dug in the chilled, dewy ground with my little hand trowel, I stared up at the smiling child atop his plinth of faces.

What an odd thing to sculpt.

"Everything all right?" David asked as I returned and found he and Claude drinking real coffee in the private kitchen. They were both in robes, with wet,

165

combed hair and sitting across from each other with the wireless tuned to the BBC like nothing at all had happened. But this was the only way to play it. Nothing *had* happened. Not unless every inch of the Jardin du Luxembourg was ripped apart by exploding shells. And if it was, then by that time it wouldn't matter what *had* or *had not* happened because the Germans would pulverize the city and all its inhabitants in the hellish fire of the end times that would be the fall of Paris.

"Fine," I said, and filled a china cup from the cafétière.

We sat quietly, with only the low English drone of the false weather reports the BBC broadcast throughout the early hours to keep the utter silence at bay.

"I think last night was rather an unparalleled success," David said eventually. "Apparently they want to extend the dance competition to some kind of a league."

I didn't shake, nor feel fear. Save the for the slightest bit of uncomfortableness like a thunderstorm on the horizon. Death would come at its appointed time, I had to remember as much, and there was nothing else to do but sit and wait for the weather to change.

"Same time again next week?" David said to us both. Claude nodded enthusiastically, I less so.

"I think next time," Claude said, "let's invite more active Romans and less passive Greeks."

Chapter 11

I TOOK A PICTURE of every place I buried a reel. All throughout the remainder of 1941. And there were many, The Roosevelt Mansion became the hit attraction of Paris. We even made the magazine of the German occupation force.

The Roosevelt Mansion is a sight not to be missed—if you can get an invite, that is. But you'll need to be a Generalmajor, or have a friend who is, to get you in. The Roosevelts, cousins of the US President, have some of the finest champagne in the country, and you'll rub shoulders with the artists, poets and painters who made Paris famous. Not to mention every type of woman a man could desire is on hand to make this stop the most exciting in Paris.

Although we never really spoke about it, Claude, David and I, the system worked, so to mention it out loud in any place, at any time, was to tempt an unnecessary fate none of us could afford to get on the wrong side of. That 'one time' David had promised disappeared as the thrill of cheating death hit harder than an injected drug. Oddly we all felt this similar compulsion, once a little risk is taken, why not more?

We also knew when to not get greedy. Sometimes a big fish would swim on through, a general or a high ranking Oberst, but find a different room all by themselves. To say to them anything, that we had another room specially prepared for someone of their rank, would cause anyone with even the slightest suspicious mind to take a second glance around that wooden box with terrible wallpaper and wonder what made the room so special.

Often too the most senior officers, the field marshals and generals did not care to indulge. They had their mistresses follow them around, so had no need for a casual encounter at a whore house, no matter how expensive the furnishings or free flowing the champagne. Some of them came because they seemed to genuinely enjoy themselves.

David found a more effective tactic was to home in on an eager young Nazi keen to rise up the ranks. They were easy to spot; they had won the Aryan genetic lottery and so in the racial theocracy of Nazi Germany expected blond hair and blue eyes to be all that was needed to ascend the ranks. Their uniforms were freshly pressed, never so much as a button out of place, and they refused any alcoholic beverage, at least in front of their superiors.

David would latch on to one of them and treat him like he had the direct ear of the Führer.

"We would love to host more regularly, but of course champagne supplies are so limited. Let Berlin know, will you? And tell the Führer if he is ever passing through Paris again, we would be honored by his company. Oh, and have you met Picasso? He isn't here this evening, but you simply can't leave Paris without visiting his studio. Are you sure you don't want a drink? Very well, I have some excellent scotch in the study; here's the key. I've kept it locked for your personal use only this evening. Field Marshall von Manstein himself told me to make sure you in particular have a key to what I call the private chamber. Last time he was here, he couldn't stop telling me about this young up and comer in the Wehrmacht. And look, here you are in the flesh. Do let me know if I can make an introduction to any of our other guests. There's a hidden door in the study that leads to a private room. It's reserved exclusively for the use of whomever von Manstein requests, and you need only point in a vague direction and I'll have whoever it is sent straight there for your enjoyment."

David would lure them in, and I would make my way to the kitchen, through the pantry and into the crawl space where the camera stood and start filming. I saw all manner of perversions occur in that room. Or I should say, there were few levels of sexual debauchery a human mind could imagine that I had *not* seen in that room.

Why in Paris?

Usually it was a woman, or two, occasionally three, involved in the entertaining. The Vinten struggled to capture the bouncing of breasts and giggling spanks doled out to every higher rank in the Wehrmacht. If Hella and Madame Framboise deserved an Academy Award for the costumes, all too quickly discarded on the floor of the secret room, these girls deserved best actress for the performances they gave to an audience of one, hidden behind a ruined Picasso. Since the secret room was reserved for the most senior officials, they often felt entitled to the best of everything. They sauntered in with the most expensive scotch and the prettiest girls, diving beneath their skirts with skills learned from a lifetime of brothel going. It was always a bit disappointing to watch good, conventional sex happen in the secret room. A general performing oral sex on a shrieking broad, twisting her tits then grunting on top of her for three to six minutes. Should the reels get out, they might be personally embarrassing, but good old-fashioned sex would hardly bring down the Reich.

The woman who most often appeared in the secret room was conventionality personified. She was an English woman named Darla, who spoke French, German and Spanish well enough to be a spy, and had a matronly look about her that I kept waiting to swerve into whip-cracking humiliation, but it never did. Darla was the quintessential 'every-woman'. The typical mistress when the wife at home had all dried up. She spun the officers on top of her, hoisting her thighs across their backs as she threw her head back on the pillow and encouraged the men to explore her body with their fingers, tongues and even toes. The secret to Darla's popularity seemed to be that she genuinely enjoyed sex; she wanted, almost needed, to be pumped unconscious, nightly, and longed for the right Übermensch to deliver her thusly. In this way she wasn't so much a whore as a traditional courtesan. Forced by hard times to take up residence at a place such as David's, but waiting for the right general to take her back to Berlin full time. Sometimes the men would get caught up in the dream. Their sweaty, red bodies lying next to hers as they spoke of dinners with the Führer and holidays on the Black Sea. Perhaps that was Darla's secret, and David's genius. It all seemed like a dazzling love affair, over and done with in the space of an evening.

Although Claude was always around, and one or two of the boys from Giovanni's to serve drinks and make up the numbers, no one ever went off

169

into one of the ordinary rooms with a boy. But in the safety of the private study, where one could genuinely be perusing the books on the wall, the drinks on the trolley or hatching a plot, a horny Oberst could request just about anyone he wanted. Those were the times I could appreciate David's genius. While Darla's bottomless canal might cause little more than a raised eyebrow back in Berlin, a boy was a different story altogether.

Claude was by far the most popular. His thin frame, blond hair, and chirpy, saucy smirk broadcast loud and clear he was an individual of many talents. *Half a meter deep,* as Jean once said.

I never imagined Claude to come so alive as when he was in a bedroom. A mechanic might find satisfaction fixing cars, but after the thousandth engine fixed, there is surely only so much satisfaction to be gained. But Claude was not like that. He was more a poet. He loved his craft, and every layer of verse he sat down to write he fully and utterly committed to. Every line he wrote with love, and it only made him a better poet.

"My first love was Marshall Hubert Lyautey," Claude would tell his client in the perfectly pronounced German words I'd taught him as he stripped off. He was referring to 'France's most distinguished—or infamous—homosexual' as Georges Clemenceau had called the Great War general. The French empire builder notorious across the continent for his flagrant, boisterous love of young men. As if telling that to the German officer would somehow dissuade him from any lingering violent guilt he might feel about this indiscretion, like Claude was a kind of modern-day Philoctetes' bow, fought over by Greek and Trojan, providing strategic advantage to whichever side he was in the possession of.

"There's nothing you can't do to me, or I can't do for you."

Inevitably, the request came for another one of those boys out there to join in. I think less than half a dozen times Claude entertained a Nazi who didn't want another male involved in the encounter, and that was usually because they had finished so quickly or could not finish at all.

Certainly, the number of odd pairings when Claude was involved in the transaction outnumbered the even parings. Every time I watched through the lens as Thomas or Albert or Martin joined the fray, I understood that men, in their nature, will never change.

Gay, straight, Black, white, French, German; men look at satisfaction in terms of volume. How many women, how many boys, how much money, how high a rank, how many kills. How odd that in a world run by and for men, the very thought, the very notion, of two or more of these creatures choosing to love each other could cause such a rip in the fabric of society it must be stamped out and disavowed lest… lest what, exactly? That men decide to start collaborating instead of competing? What a world that would be.

* * *

"Bend over please, Albert," I said to the young fair-haired lad standing stark naked in our bedroom. He did as he was told, spreading his cheeks far apart for me to take a picture. I would have asked him to do it anyway, but he knew the drill by now.

"Yes, just as I suspected," Claude said, shining a torch onto the boy's hole. "Warts."

"Oh, fuck," Albert said, standing back up again and pulling on his shirt, but no bottoms. "So I can't work here no more?"

"Of course you can, darling," Claude told him with a warm smile, "just make sure it's the trick's last night in Paris before you let him screw you, okay?"

Albert nodded, valiantly accepting his war wound, then, still naked from the waist down, plopped down on my bed.

"No need to send that picture to the doctor," Claude said to me, thinking I was about to ask him what to do with the image when the real thing was squatting on my sheets. "Madame Framboise has some tea tree oil that'll make them a bit less angry. Now," he said, clapping his hands, "off you pop, there's customers downstairs."

Albert pulled his trousers back up and scurried out the door like a child escaping from a school doctor. I still had the keys to Linda's studio, and I spent a great deal of time there, developing and making copies of pictures of the boys and what state the Germans so often left them in. I felt, somehow, making these copies on all the paper I could scavenge, made each extra day I could live worth it. One day soon, I could be dead, and someone, somewhere, at some time, would have to come to this studio and see an entire record of a thousand lives lived in the lowest years we'd ever faced.

"Shame we can't take him back to David's anytime soon," Claude said, scratching his chin in Thinking Man style, "they went crazy for him. Even the straight ones." Claude, in his sheepskin slippers, shuffled to the door and yelled: "Next."

Lucas trod into our room next, already taking his shirt off for the inspection. The dark-haired Belgian was one of the few naturally masculine men we had at Giovanni's. It turned out that was one of the hardest jobs to have.

"My God," I said, staring open mouthed at the deep red scratches all across his back and chest, some wounds still oozing puss, while his shoulders, ribs and stomach glistened black, purple and blue like a freshly beaten night sky. "What the hell happened to you?"

"He was rather upset after," Lucas said with all the emotion of a bored waiter sick of talking about the rat soup special. "It's happened before."

"You're lucky," Claude remarked without much sympathy. "If it was out on the street you could've ended up like Gabriel."

I started to document the horrendous state of Lucas' body with my camera as Claude dabbed a brown bottle of what smelled like bleach onto a cloth. "Our Gabriel? From David's before the war?"

Claude nodded, investigating which of the wounds looked the worst.

"Lift your arms, please." I said to Lucas, snapping pictures of him from every angle. True, doctor Mélenchon needed only a couple of decent images to make a diagnosis. But Lucas wasn't suffering from warts or syphilis, only a vicious beating. There wasn't anything for the doctor to diagnose.

I remembered Gabriel quite well. We'd had a thing. Well, hardly a thing. But close enough. He looked like Jean. Handsome, strong-armed and broad shouldered. Deep Guyanese skin with tight-curled chest hair and a thick smile that made one want to kiss him and never stop.

He'd never worked out of Giovanni's, but I saw him once in a while when he came to drink with some of the boys. He always made a point of saying hello to me, sharing our secret inside joke, both of us remembering how he'd fucked me over the countertop in David's kitchen one night long after everyone had left, but finishing just seconds before David entered with a tray of empty glasses. I was glad his beauty existed in the world, and I'd been glad to have it. If it wasn't for Jean establishing himself as the undisputed beauty of this age, I could have imagined myself chasing Gabriel across the city to capture every muscle movement of his with my camera.

"He was with a trick around the back of the Gare du Nord," Claude said as Lucas seethed from the burning bleach being wiped across his wounds. "Keep still. The trick got mad or didn't want to pay—I don't know—blew his whistle and turned on Gabriel, saying he'd been on a routine patrol and found him prostituting himself, so they arrested him."

"What? When was this?" I said, shocked that this was news to me. Although it did make sense. I hadn't seen him in a while.

"Last month."

"Have they released him yet? Where is he?"

"They sent him on a train east a few days ago."

There was no point asking to where. Gabriel had been sent to the place no one returned. He wasn't the first street boy to disappear. Sadly, I knew he would be far from the last. Disquiet in the ranks of Parisian prostitutes began in the winter months of 1940 and, unusually, affected the men far more than the women. The man would be seen one day, around the back of a train station or mulling around the park, with no trace of him come dawn. We used to joke that he'd struck lucky, taken up with some general or bishop and had been whisked off to Berlin or Rome, but it was a mask for our fear. Rumors abounded in the void created by no body, no note. One fellow would say he'd seen the missing man shoved on a train going east, another insist he'd been arrested, or simply murdered and chucked in the river. In the vice of occupation, between the Germans and the French, the male prostitutes of Paris were the easiest to squeeze. Hardly a respectable soul acknowledged our existence, and certainly not our disappearance.

A lump got stuck in my throat, holding a back a flood of emotion I wasn't sure I wanted to open, not when I couldn't be sure if I could get it closed again. I tried to swallow it away. Gabriel was but one more casualty. One more lamp snuffed out, another life extinguished.

We were silent, save for the gritted groans of Lucas being brutally cared for by Claude. I fiddled with my camera; the realization Gabriel wasn't coming back a solemn reminder that neither was Jean.

I would never get to see him again. There was no way now. No telling where in France or in the world he'd got to. The one man I had ever loved would never know it. Before diving into the *toilette* and being set upon, I feared to die a virgin. But that was nothing compared to ending my days without saying 'I love you' and meaning it.

"Theo's also gone," Lucas said, slipping his shirt back over his battered body.

"Really? I thought he wasn't in the business anymore."

"He wasn't. He was hanging around the toilets in the Jardin du Luxembourg just for fun. The police swooped in, rounded them all up, took them to the banks of the Seine and shot them all, one by one."

"Shame," Claude said, placing the brown bottle of bleach carefully back on its place on the shelf, "he was a lovely guy. Very funny."

"Yeah," Lucas agreed, a broad grin spreading across his face. "You ever meet him?" He asked me.

"I don't think so."

"You'd remember if you did. He'd shake your hand, then whip out his hip flask and rinse himself off soon as he turned around."

"Or say 'Oh, I would but I don't know where you've been,'" Claude added.

"Yeah, or 'I know where I've been, and I wouldn't shake that if I were you.'"

"They don't make them like Theo anymore."

"That's for sure," Lucas agreed, heading for the door. He opened it and Madame Framboise was standing there, her hand ready to knock. "Oh, hello."

But she said nothing, only looked straight ahead like there was a man holding a gun to her back. Slowly, her head turned towards me, staring like a ghoul.

"Anders..." her voice barely a whisper. "There's an officer downstairs. He's looking for you."

All that talk of death. That's what brought the jinx to my door. The *ayin harah*, the evil eye, as my grandmother called it. We'd talked about the men we would miss so much that it was only reasonable for death to seize another.

Claude ran to the window, throwing it open and peering out at the soaking wet sky as if to suggest I jump. "You'll never make it."

Lucas backtracked to the closet, throwing the doors open to see if I could fit inside. If these were to be my last moments, at least my friends had done all they could. Even if it had been Giovanni who'd turned me in.

"Don't," I said, a quiet sense of final peace flooding over me, running down my spine like a last shot of morphine jabbed into a man as a final act of kindness. "You'll only get yourselves in trouble."

Claude, Lucas and Madame Framboise looked at me with a hushed awe, the kind reserved for watching a funeral procession. I couldn't look at any of them, although I wanted to hug Claude. I felt like I shouldn't, as if to do so would add a finality to the proceedings, sharp enough that I might as well jump from the window.

Perhaps this was nothing. An officer looking for a friendly chat or a date. Yes, and perhaps I would wake up from this surrealist coma the second the bullet entered my body.

I took the stairs slowly, counting every breath and savoring it like it would be my last. The other three followed, but with some distance, as if they were afraid I'd be shot on sight and some of the splash back would hit them.

The bar was busy, swirling in soldiers and the plain-clothed boys who sat on their laps, ruffled their hair, kissed their cheek then led them upstairs by the hand as soon as a room was free.

Coming towards me was Albert, closely followed by a bulky private with a giant, Germanic grin across his red face. He looked like he would snap Albert in half, and take pleasure in doing so. Albert glanced my way and gave a half-smile as he and the trick passed me on the landing. Now the only thing I could think of was Albert's ass hole, covered in warts, and this grinning Nazi who, in a week or two, would no doubt find himself freezing on the Eastern Front or sweltering in North Africa, his cock itching so badly he'd have to drop his gun or lose his aim to attempt some semblance of relief.

We didn't need to fight a war or bother with a resistance. We could just infect every whore in Paris and in a month or two the entire German army would collapse.

The thought made me smile.

I looked around for the men who'd come to take me away and started to weigh up the evidence for and against this being Giovanni's fault and if I should finger him as an informer and at least try to take him down with me. But I failed to find the crowd of solemn soldiers, or anyone who looked remotely like Gestapo.

The only man who seemed even slightly out of place was standing by the door, his back to me and wearing a uniform of black and silver instead of the standard feldgrau. He was casually eyeing the place, taking in the framed photos of old Paris on the wall, memories of my early work.

The stranger reached up to take off his hat, and, glinting in the light, were two silver cuff bands, the terrifying sleeve diamonds of the SS.

The SS man was naturally blond and slim. Like most SS members he could wear the hell out of a uniform, as opposed to the standard Wehrmacht conscript who might as well have fought in a sack of potatoes. He kept turning, looking out for me, of course. I stood on the last step utterly conspicuous, mouth hanging open.

Like a peckish fox coming across an injured rabbit, he found me, then smiled across the room and waved, the SS cuff bands reflecting in the light. I knew this man. Or at the very least, he knew me.

"Anders!" He called out while he fought his way through the crowd. He didn't have to fight much, though. Every soldier shifted to make way. Nobody wanted to get in the way of the SS. No one wanted the SS to have your name on their lips either.

Then it all came back. Three years ago, nearly. The German who'd worked at the Citroën factory. What was his name? Oh Lord Jesus Moses HaShem what in the mother-fucking world was his fucking na—

"Eilas," I said, filled with a sudden rush of life-affirming joy. I dived off the last step and threw my arms around his neck, hugging him tightly as I would hug life itself.

"*Guten abend, Herr Anders. Hast du noch eine Kamera?*" I had the strongest sense he'd been thinking about me and my pictures since February 1939.

"Shh, not down here." One German knowing about me was more than enough, I didn't need to out myself to the entire bar. "Upstairs."

We rushed up the steps like a couple of raucous kids desperate to get outside and play, squeezing between Madame Framboise, Claude and Lucas who all looked like they'd seen a ghost. I tried to communicate to Claude with a shrug and pointing subtly at the SS man taking the stairs two at a time that I was not yet done for.

Panting, we rushed into my room and slammed the door shut. Eilas' hat complete with skull and crossbones flew to the floor. His jacket came off, then his boots, his breeches, his shirt.

Strong hands held my sides and practically lifted me through the air, slamming my body against the door while he sucked on every open piece of neck he could get his lips around. I remembered how he loved me back then, exactly like a German would—straight to the point.

French men, Spaniards, Italians, Belgians, even certain Americans tended to infuse sex with a certain tropical vigor. They believed in passion, not just because they were turned on, but because in their minds, sex was not complete without a fiery, almost philosophical commitment to shared intensity.

Back then, Eilas had fucked me the German way—repeatedly and efficiently. Yes, there had been a sort of frenzied eagerness which raised our tryst above the perfunctory mechanics German sex was supposed to embody, but not by much. In the interceding years I'd come to know, and to expect more, and indeed it seemed that so had he.

He flipped me around and I moaned and banged on the door as if calling for a rescue, but in fact I had never felt so free. Ten minutes before, I feared Eilas might have been the end of me, but now the hands of an old lover were tugging down my trousers, spreading, spitting and thrusting inside like a much needed cigarette sliding into a gasping mouth.

*   *   *

"I hoped I wouldn't find you here," Eilas said as we lay together in bed, my head resting on his naked chest. I passed a Galoise to him, and he took it carefully with the hand that wasn't wrapped around my shoulders.

"Why's that? Am I a bad influence?"

"Yes," he laughed and took a draw. But then turned more serious. "But I told you last time to leave. It's not safe here."

"No," I took the cigarette back. "You told me to stay out of Germany."

"And this is now Germany."

"I think you'll find this is still Paris. You may have occupied France, but you can't turn it into Germany just by hanging a few swastikas on things."

"Not yet," he grinned at me like we were comparing handball teams.

I sat up and pulled away, taking in Eilas and his Aryan beauty. I hadn't remembered him this way, a blond paragon championing Nazi racial supremacy with every perfectly formed line of his square jaw and angular nose. It was as if he had ingested the uniform, stitching the swastika onto his skin like a horrendous tattoo.

"Eilas, why are you in Paris?"

"Why are you?"

"You know why I'm here," I said quietly, not wanting to voice the obvious, not with his SS uniform crumpled on the floor. Eilas sighed, but artificially, like he was mocking the very need to sigh itself. He turned and rested his elbow on the pillow.

"I used to think about you a lot, after I got back to Germany. My father made me join the party and got me this job working for a very senior SS commander called Reydrich. But I'd always think of you. Sweet little Anders from Austria, taking pictures of Paris and waiting for someone to fall in love with him."

I wanted to take the words at face value, to pretend this reality was not ours, and we could be simply what we are. Two men, neither so young these days, who speak the same language, enjoy each other's company, and slot together sexually. I wondered if this is how it worked for the heterosexuals. One day the woman looks at the man next to her and thinks, 'yes, he'll do nicely. Not perfect, but not bad at all.'

"You didn't answer my question," I said sharply." Why are you here in Paris?"

"I hadn't finished. I thought about you often as I was doing my job, well, helping Reydrich do his. After France fell, I hoped, I hoped harder than anyone has ever hoped before, that you'd got out already."

A sadness yawned across Eilas' straight-edged face. It made him look softer, warmer, less sharp and pointy. If we could have built a life together, then this sadness, the kind one has when having to put down a badly injured dog, would make me draw that little bit closer to him, to hug him tighter and kiss him harder. He walked his fingers up my bare chest, stroked my chin and smiled through the pain. But I did nothing.

"Reydrich is hunting Jews, Anders. He's making lists, undertaking surveys, having the French police comb through all the documents in existence. We're cross-checking census lists with baptismal records to identify Jews who might otherwise have hidden themselves in society. It's coming. The end."

"So will you have me taken away?"

"I came to protect you. I walked through those doors and asked that fag behind the bar if you were here. I wanted him to say no: you were long gone, or he'd never heard of you. Then I'd have been on my way."

Somehow that didn't make me feel any better. "On your way to hunt down other Jews?"

"What do you want me to say?"

I looked away. Truthfully, I didn't know what I wanted him to say. There was nothing I could hear which would alter the rules.

This would be my fate. Making myself fascinating enough for an SS man who was turned on by transgression, and like the Arabian nights, praying to keep his interest alive long enough to keep my life. I was in his claws, and there was no escape.

"I'm not going to let anything happen to you, Anders. Trust me. I would tell you to flee, but the safest place for you is right here, so I can watch over you."

Following his lead, I laid my head on his firm, Teutonic chest, listening to the slow, sullen thump of his heart. At least it was not the other way around, for all he would hear would be a thundering beat that would alarm any doctor.

In that moment, I understood everything Claude, Jean, and the rest of the boys went through. How it felt to lie with your body, to make a man fall for you in order to keep food on the table, a roof over your head, and breath in your lungs.

Chapter 12

THE OCCUPATION EXTENDED ITSELF into 1942, and life became increasingly filled with frustrating complexities. I had to juggle the nights at David's, which were happening twice, three times, sometimes four times a week, along with my shotgun marriage to Eilas.

Since Hermann Goering put the Roosevelt Mansion on the map, every officer in the city wanted an invitation to the famous dancing competition. Generals passed them out as rewards, and we were forced to operate a waiting list.

"There's simply not enough women to dance with upstairs, I'm sorry," David or Claude or Hella or even I would have to tell the men who would gather downstairs, the ones with the highest ranks pushing to the front. We could have, of course, done away with all pretenses and simply become the brothel everyone knew us to be, but like my relationship with Eilas, we preferred the imperfect illusion over the grotesque truth.

Some nights, Eilas would come to Giovanni's for sex—that was a given— but other times, it felt like he truly wanted to be around me. On occasion he would turn up to Giovanni's during the day, mingling with the lunchtime crowd until I arrived back from David's or from burying yet another reel in the metropole, then invite me out.

This sort of surrealism I almost enjoyed since I had given up thinking I would outlive the war. Eilas would bring me a uniform, sometimes an ordinary soldier's or one of his own SS outfits so we could go out on a dadaist date. First we'd go upstairs, fuck, then he'd watch me change and off we would go, galivanting around Paris in the very car he used to drive *Gruppenführer* Reydrich around. The Jew and the German, out enjoying snails and cognac.

I sat in the passenger seat, window down, cap in my lap, the air rushing through my hair and the too-big uniform of another man to shield me from evil. I imagined Reydrich, whomever he was, in this very seat, pointing out the next synagogue he wanted to blow up.

What would David think of me? Or my grandmother? Or any of the other countless relatives, the family I had never met. What would they say? Was this just what I had to do to survive—drive around in a Mercedes-Benz, dressed in a Nazi uniform so I could go and drink wine with my German lover?

At what point did I end this charade of existence? When Eilas took me to dinner at the hearth of pure evil? When he handed me a pistol and said it was time to prove my loyalty to the Reich?

We passed a clutch of Jews on the street. Old and young, it didn't matter. They all had stars stitched onto their clothes, doing their best to keep some measure of dignity. Eilas kept driving. He probably didn't even notice until it was time to liquidate them.

I saw the face of my mother in that crowd. It was only for a second, less than a second. The measure of time that the eyes of two strangers meet on the street. But it's that kind of time which is endless. For while it barely strikes a note on the clock, the moment will live forever in the memories of strangers.

I would never forget the face of that woman as we drove past. Her hair was wrapped in a scarf, even though it wasn't cold. Her overcoat was manky and disheveled, but when she caught my eye, her lips parted in warmth, not anger nor fear. This woman who looked more like my mother than my actual mother saw me, saw all of me, and she knew I was an imposter.

What if the time came when Eilas would hand me a gun and tell me to shoot my own mother? Whenever that day came, perhaps I would have my gun, and hopefully enough bullets for every Nazi in that room.

*   *   *

We sat at an outdoor café enjoying the spring sunshine, along with half of the occupying army. It was the type of establishment which used to display utterly perfect patisserie in the window to draw the passer by in, then serve them a barely cooked pile of mush no self-respecting Parisian would feed to their dog.

I used to pass those cafés, clustered particularly around the *Île de la Cité*, every day on my way to sell Jean's portraits, and would never hear a word of French come from their wooden tables and rickety chairs. Tourist traps, Claude called them. The sort of place foreigners with sore feet would happily pay triple the price for a mediocre coffee or stale beer just to have the memory of sitting on a pavement café and watching birds fly over the Seine.

Germans are the ultimate tourist. Every foreign land they travel to, even as invaders, they perform the age-old rituals of a sightseer with a religious fervor. Breakfast must be had early, and fully dressed. One will never see a German drinking their morning coffee or smashing their hard-boiled egg dressed in anything other than the clothes they picked out the night before. By eight a.m., the German will already be on their way to the first sight on a double-sided list placed between the correct pages of the guidebook which they study as if for an exam.

Austrians are exactly the same, but don't like to be *seen* doing these things. It's some arcane holdover from Habsburg sensibilities. When an Austrian is a tourist, he should act as if he is not a tourist, but in fact knows the city incredibly well, and is simply retracing long-remembered steps.

An Austrian would be appalled by the scene at this café. Fifty German soldiers sitting on semi-comfortable seats, all facing the street, cowering over the propaganda rags or watching a group of other tourists-with-rifles wander past the café, note it was full, and resolve to return another time.

One benefit of being dressed as an SS officer, and accompanied by one, was that a couple of our subordinates vacated a table right on the street the second they saw us. I couldn't care less that we'd forced them to finish their break quicker than they had planned.

Eilas and I drank wine while I explained to him the difference between Germans and Austrians abroad. But he seemed distracted, and eventually I gave up trying to generate a laugh from him. I pulled out my cigarettes, then, realizing I didn't keep a lighter in this SS jacket, started looking around to ask one of my fellow Nazis for a match.

"You can't smoke," Eilas hissed.

"Why not?"

"You're in the SS."

Confused, I slipped it back in my pocket. "Well no one told me."

"This would be a lot easier if you *were* in the SS."

"Have you lost your Goddamnned mind, as they say?" I glanced around, keenly aware we were speaking German in a place where even the menus were written in German these days.

"I can arrange it," Eilas promised, keeping his voice low but casual. "A few fake papers, an orphan from Vienna but with a flawless pedigree, not that it matters so much these days. No one will need to know. No one ever would. You can work for me in the archives. Plus, you speak French, and that's incredibly useful." Eilas stared at me with the sort of look one gives a strained lover, when trying to convince them to give things another tempestuous go. It would never happen, but he would be remiss of himself not to at least ask.

But like the fool who returns once again to the man they know will never change, the offer was on the table. To survive living inside the heart of darkness, working for the SS. Alive, yes. But dead inside.

"Do you expect me to read through the census and mark off Jewish-sounding names?"

Eilas shrugged and sipped his wine, as if to say, 'that's the job.' I let the momentary disbelief at the suggestion fade and started to imagine what being in such a position would allow me to do for the resistance. Could I burn the documents I found? Rewrite the names of Jews to hide them in plain sight, like a certain David Rosenblatt had so deftly done?

Here was Eilas handing me the gun and offering me the option to waltz right into a place where I could do some serious damage. Not that his agenda matched mine. He just enjoyed having a place to park his dick every few days and someone to share a meal with.

It weighed heavily on my mind. So much so that I barely said another word. A stranger passing by would think us two men forced to share the same table, not a pair of lovers, and certainly not an SS officer offering a Jew the clandestine chance to save one other life, if not his own.

But that's not the opportunity Eilas was suggesting. Not really. I knew he would expect me to do it for real. To be, for all intents and purposes, a man who did the job of those who wore hats with skull and crossbones emblazoned on the brim.

"Constantine Cavafy used to write in this café," Eilas said, for want of something else to say.

"Do you think you can hurl dead homosexual poets at me and I'll be impressed?"

Eilas shrugged. That habit of his was getting tiresome. "He's one of my favorites. I had all his books."

"I'm so happy to hear."

"But then they got burned."

"Naturally."

After that, silence, it seemed, was the better option. We drank the wine and looked at the world around us. I searched for the beggar woman I always used to see in these parts, panning for pennies in the tourist traps around the *Île de la Cité*. So much of what made this city alive had already been stolen. Had they taken her too?

She used to drag her bad leg around like it was wooden, or dead. The woman seemed as old as Notre Dame itself and swept around the streets like this was her personal domain. She must have been here for a century to claim such a prime begging spot as this. With a haggard, mean gaze she'd approach a couple or a family, it did not matter, although never the street vendors, and spew out words in unintelligible French until they dropped a couple of francs in her tin, and she shuffled away. It occurred to me I hadn't seen her since the occupation; perhaps they shot her into the Seine like so many were these days.

I knew the queers who had gone. One day soon I would know the Jews. But who would know the beggars? In the years to come, when insanity faded from the world once again and people indulged in the obscure profession of memory, who would remember this beggar woman? What name would be carved on a memorial to her fallen kinfolk?

That thought shattered me more than any other. Who will remember the dead ones forgotten about when they were alive?

"You don't have to give me an answer now," Eilas said, shaking me out of my hovel of pity, "but I've something to ask you."

He kept his eyes straight ahead, on the trickle of people on the street now becoming a passing stream. Soldiers came off the street and mingled amongst their friends in the café, pulling up chairs and passing around drinks. The whole scene reminded me of those parties in Santa Monica David told me about, where rich, plush queers gathered to watch movies of Jean pleasuring himself—a world of men still, but with different rules, praising different things.

And here was I, always the outsider. An Austrian among the Germans, a queer among the straights, a Jew among the gentiles. Perhaps the life I should build was with vagrants and the whores and the outcasts, the only people who had ever shown me any kindness. The ones I'd spent my life in Paris photographing, setting their features onto paper. The immortal vagabonds, the real aristocrats of Paris, covered in her soot, sapped by her modernity, resting nightly in her concrete bosom. My shooting them and those wild nights at David's now seemed like the most important thing I could have done with my one life. For if I'd never bothered, nor ever been here, so many moments and so much beauty would pass from the world unknown, uncaptured, unpraised, marched out of existence, nothing but decayed bodies washing up on the Seine.

I realized in that moment, sitting in the center of more Nazis than I could ever shoot, exactly what these people were. Cold-hearted bullies. It seemed so simple I wanted to burst out laughing. These were the boys on the schoolyard I'd never cared about being friends with. These were the boys so terrified of being labeled a fag, a Jew, a sissy, a traitor, a communist, a Catholic, or whatever else the insult of the day was, they'd march off to genocidal war to prove their manliness in front of their friends and fathers.

Eilas sat across from me in the SS uniform, but I didn't see it. I saw only that naked twenty-seven-year-old who'd made love to me in the early months of 1939 and whispered how much he didn't want to go home to his father, or to Germany, but stay with me, in a chilly attic on the Rue Duperré, wrapped in my arms.

How grateful I was at that moment to never have had a father to please. As Claude once said, we were the fatherless generation. They were dead, we were alive. Eilas was trapped, but I was free. For one day when this war would be over, if I wasn't dead, I would still be liberated. When the war was over, if Eilas wasn't dead, he would still be under paternal occupation.

"What did you want to tell me?" I demanded. "I haven't got all day."

"Look at your uniform."

I looked. At the silver buttons and lightning bolts on the cuffs, the incomprehensible badges on the shoulder, all of this Nazi drag like I was readying to perform in some perverse play.

"Now look at mine."

I looked.

"What about it?"

"You notice the difference?"

"Not really, Eilas."

He shrugged off my attitude, but with effort. Like his patience was running thin. Let it, I'd had quite enough.

"You outrank me."

I stared at him silently, trying to figure out why I should care the uniform he'd given me put me up a rank or two than him.

"So? This is the one you gave—"

"Wait, Anders. I mean everyone here can see you're a lieutenant colonel. I'm only a lieutenant. In fact, you outrank everyone in this café. That's why they gave us a table."

I kept on staring blankly, daring him to tell me why I should care, and thinking of all the thing I could say to show I absolutely did not. All this speaking German and talking about rank was getting old, and quickly.

"I wanted you to feel unafraid of what I'm about to say," Eilas continued. "I didn't want to compromise your answers with a sense of inferiority. I want you to know that you could slap me clear across the face right here, and every single soldier would rush to your side."

"I don't believe you."

"Believe me. We're trained to follow orders. An unfollowed order from a commanding officer means death. Every man in the Wehrmacht knows that."

186

"Nice you have these justifications ready for when you're on trial for breaking the laws of war."

Eilas ignored my comment. Still looking at me, he reached into his breast pocket and pulled out a folded, faded photograph.

"I need to ask you something. And I'm only asking for your own protection." He slid a picture across the table. "Do you know this man?" I looked it over like a cheating husband being confronted with evidence of his affairs in a divorce trial. It had been taken from inside a car parked across the street from the Roosevelt Mansion, clearly there to spy on those who were coming and going. In the picture, David was going inside.

"Of course I know him. That's David Roosevelt. He's a good friend of many people who also outrank you, by the way. But what made you think I know him?" If Eilas had a picture like this, surely he must know my whereabouts and movements, the comings and goings of mine between David's, Giovanni's, and dug up places around Paris. But I gave nothing away.

"There's a lot of prostitutes who congregate there. Regular, and… queer. Given the company you keep, I assumed that—"

"You're a queer." I said it quietly enough that Eilas could safely ignore me.

"We don't care about the prostitutes. But, we have reason to believe his real name is not Roosevelt. That in fact, he and his wife Hella are actually Rosen*blatt.*"

"We?" I scoffed. "Do *we* indeed believe that?" I think what angered me most was the abuse of legalistic German to discuss something that plainly was not a crime. Not by any stretch of the imagination, not by any cause of logic or reasonable jurisprudence could someone act like they were in a court of law, snap their braces and say, 'we have reason to believe this person is a Jew.'

"Do you intend to charge David and his wife in a court of law?" I asked, highly facetiously, but I didn't care. Eilas glared but said nothing. Nor did he drink. He just sat there, looking down at the floor.

"You know that's not how it works, Anders."

"Yes, I know that, Eilas." I said rather loudly, breaking our cone of silence. "If you have the evidence, you'll execute them without trial, without any semblance of legality, so don't corrupt the language even further with your *reason to believe.*"

How could a man like Eilas think this way? It drove me to the edge of insanity, attempting to understand. My fingers twitched with the urge to flip the table, watch the shards of glass scatter along the street and smash him over the head with my chair. We could put his outranking theory to the test.

In 1939 Eilas had not been like this. What if there had been no war? If Hitler had somehow been deposed by his politburo who didn't actually think invading Poland would be a good idea. Let's even say another Nazi took his place, one slightly less vitriolic on the anti-Semitism scale. What would have come of Eilas then? If he had stayed in Paris, continued working at Citroën, perhaps seen me once in a while. I doubted he would have sought out a job in a genocidal enterprise, making quasi-legal accusations against fellow human beings for the crime of existing.

I could almost understand the ones who believed we were behorned, blood-drinking Bolshevists who were also capitalists who also controlled the world while simultaneously being sub-human. Believing whether they actually believed that or not was another matter, but at least with that as their justification, then there was perverse logic that almost made sense.

But Eilas did not believe that. Not even close. Not even a little bit. He dressed me in a uniform so we could enjoy a day outside instead of our normal fucking in my room, which he also had no problem with.

Perhaps the very act of demonizing an entire people creates enough ripples in reality that, through some kind of habituation, normal, everyday people are infected. Like a virus that spreads to a new continent from one infected rag on a ghost ship drifting across the sea, there becomes no way to protect yourself, no inoculation or prophylaxis will help. The virus is coming to change the world. Even if you yourself do not have it, you must abide by its rules.

"I'm only trying to help you, Anders. Reydrich is desperate to expose Goering's favorite dance parties as being run by a cabal of Jews. This is bigger than you. Reydrich wants to strike terror into half the Wehrmacht high command. If he can get his hands on David, then he can put under investigation every officer who's ever attended their parties, from the Reichsmarshall down. And he'll find a way to murder the Rosenblatts, and you, and anyone else remotely in their orbit to grab some power for himself."

"Thank you, lieutenant," I said loudly and stood up, fixing my hat and draining my drink. "For the conversation." The casual interest one gathers when one exeunts from a public place dissipated, and I held Eilas' gaze long enough to show my utter disgust at him and everything about him. I was liberating myself from his occupation, and willing to sacrifice my life on the battlefield of my own freedom.

"They're Roosevelts, and cousins of the President. Reydrich is of course free to molest them to his heart's content, if he doesn't mind finding himself on an American kill list." That gave him a pleasant shock. "Or you, too, I suppose."

I stepped away from the table and into the street, straightening down my uniform and breathing in a sense of localized power for perhaps the first time in my life. "Shoot me if you want, Eilas. Quite frankly I don't give a damn."

* * *

I marched north, away from Eilas and his café of terrors and soldier friends. Away from the cloud of fear he'd tried to cast over me. It was oddly liberating to walk up Boulevard de Sebastopol as an SS lieutenant colonel. Soldiers scurried out of the way to let me pass, while the French kept their eyes to the ground.

The uniform was like a suit of magical armor, but I knew its spell wouldn't last forever. I would have to get it back to Eilas, or else this would provide him additional casus belli. Although he had given the uniform to me. Should anyone ever question where I had obtained it, an officer called Eilas would be implicated. I'm sure his boss would be none too pleased with him letting a Jew masquerade as an SS staff officer.

I decided to try and enjoy my walk home, along with the unseasonably pleasant spring weather, and resolved to hold on to the uniform for now. I could store it somewhere in the bar, possibly in a crate in the basement. Should it ever be discovered, it was plausible enough to blame it on any of the hundreds of horny degenerates who passed through Giovanni's doors on any given week. Let the SS have fun with that.

I crossed the *Boulevard des Italiens* into the 9th arrondissement, home to Montmartre and me. It made no material difference, but these streets around the storied hill I knew better than most. And I always felt that little bit safer, being close to home. It was likely an illusion, but the streets were a bit quieter, the frequency of soldiers a little less, and there was the added bonus that any German walking remotely in the same direction as I was very likely on his way to or from Giovanni's.

But on this late afternoon, there was a commotion across the street that caught my eye. Two soldiers, privates, by the look of their uniforms and rifles, were standing by a truck with its engine on, and shepherding what looked like a large family clan of multiple generations out of their doorway and towards the waiting van. One soldier carried a list and seemed to be checking identity documents against the names he had.

I saw her face before anything else. In the exact same manner I thought I'd seen my mother as Eilas and I drove past a group of Jews earlier, in this crowd my grandmother seemed to gaze across the street at me, looking utterly infuriated at the indignity of what was occurring.

A few times in Vienna near the end, we would be turned away from a place. It would be the last time we, or a great deal of other high Viennese society would go there, but it happened. My grandmother was an influential woman amongst her diet of society ladies; these spouses of former imperial administrators particularly liked to continue the royalist traditions as if the constitution of the Austrian Republic meant little more to them than a chalkboard menu advertising the schnitzel of the day.

I remember one time, in 1935 I think, we went to our normal coffee house, which my grandmother had helped put on the map back in the 1880s. This was long before Hitler bullied Austria into surrender, though shortly after the SS had attempted a coup when they stormed the Chancellor's office. The Nazi party was still banned; indeed it was a common sight in Vienna to see the police round up groups of Brown Shirt youths. At the coffee house, the white-gloved waiters took my grandmother's and my mother's furs from the moment we stepped inside this metropolitan cathedral, and the maître d' led us under the domed ceiling towards our usual table. My grandmother spoke politely with the head waiter Charles as we sat down, and he brought me a slice of my father's favorite poppy seed strudel before we even ordered, as he'd done twice a week since I could remember.

I stuck the miniature fork directly into the flaky pastry, ready to dive into the greatest cake in the world as my mother and grandmother debated the merits of different strengths of Abyssinian coffee beans with the waiter. The black, sticky clump of a million poppy seeds covered in layers of crunchy puff never reached my mouth. My attention was grabbed by a short, tubby man I knew to be the manager rushing between the tables, directly towards us.

"I'm terribly sorry, madame," he said, wringing his hands, "but given the political climate I think it's best if you... find somewhere else. We don't discriminate here, and I would hate for your presence to cause any uncomfortableness, either to yourselves or to our other patrons."

I'd never heard a man say get out in a more complicated fashion. I think what caused the most offence to my grandmother was the fact he was little more than an accountant in a cheap suit. These were not the grand old days of the maestro-like maître d', the man who elevated coffee houses to an art form. But with the Habsburgs gone from power, these institutions had been taken over by 'business managers.' Grubby little bean counters in drab suits, as my grandmother called them. Interested in profit margins over service. The ratio of waiters to patrons began to widen, mistakes would be made in the order, or the bill, or, of all things, the quality of the coffee or strudel.

We left. The maître d' offered a thousand apologies and said he would be making protestations to the Chancellor's office straight away. Our coats were wrapped around our shoulders. My cake was even wrapped up and thrust into my hands. But we never said a word. Not to each other, and not to them. The second we were on the street, my grandmother smacked the cake from my hand. It fell and splattered on the pavement and we walked on, never to look back.

The next day, the coffee house was empty. It was in the newspapers. Unsurprising as my grandmother had called together an emergency meeting of her closest society allies that very afternoon. The day after that we received a personal visit from the business manager himself, begging my grandmother for forgiveness. But we never returned.

I saw all of this in the woman standing across the street. I saw it in her wrinkled eyes, in her pursed lips, in the way she held her thin neck, in the way she looked down upon the taller German soldiers, opening up the back of the van and expecting this entire family of nine to squeeze inside. This matriarch brought so low.

"What's going on here?" I shouted in German at the two soldiers as I dashed across the street. Their arms bolted upright in a reflexive salute. The family froze with a wash of fear. The one closest to me, the one getting in the back of the truck, was a girl no more than my age. Her sharp, suspicious eyes were locked on the situation.

"*Obersturmbannführer*," the first soldier, the one carrying the list, addressed me after a quick glance at the insignia on my shoulder. "We have orders to take these Jews to—"

"Where did those orders come from, *Obersoldat*?" Confused, he checked his list again, then glanced worriedly at the other soldier who, sensing trouble, shrugged and kept silent. I didn't give either of them a chance to answer. "Did they come directly from the mouth of *Gruppenführer* Reydrich this very morning?" The two soldiers practically fainted at the mention of the name. They were not SS, but clearly knew enough of Reydrich to quickly shake their heads in answer to me.

"These orders were given from our commander, Herr *Obersturmbannführer*."

"L-last week," the other said, attempting to give themselves space to wriggle out of the trap I was setting.

"And you didn't check with SS command each morning, like you are supposed to?" I said, clicking my tongue and shaking my head in faux disappointment. "Do you not understand the imperative of checking orders? Operational priorities can change in minutes. We have thousands of moving parts in the SS which clearly you are both too ignorant to understand. I'm not in the least surprised neither of you have amounted to more." The family looked increasingly restless. One of the babies began to wail, the mother frantically trying to shush her like I might crack open the child's skull at a moment's notice. Only the girl looked on with interest.

The first soldier checked his list again, trying to mumble together a better answer. "Give that to me," I demanded. The first test. He obliged. I glanced over the list. It was a hundred or more names long. All handwritten, with dates of birth and place of residence beside each name, like it had been copied by hand from a census. This family was top of the list, each of their names checked off one by one.

Why in Paris?

Margarite Mendelsohn, 10 octobre 1862
Analise Mendelsohn, 27 avril 1901
Jacques Mendelsohn, 24 juin 1899
Alice Sevitt, 9 août 1910
Isaac Sevitt, 1 juillet 1907
Anna Mendelsohn, 14 octobre 1921
Joshua Mendelsohn, 10 mai 1925
Raphael Mendelsohn, 2 mars 1927

And one more that had been scribbled in, possibly just now as the ink still looked wet: *Ella Sevitt, 9 janvier, 1942.*

"Sir," the first soldier ventured. "Nobody told us to check in with SS. I mean, we were only—"

"Following orders, yes I know. So why don't I wait here while you two run off to *Gruppenführer* Reydrich and tell him why you were rounding up *his* Jews, huh? Without his express permission. Let's see what he makes of that." I set my eyes on the Luger pistol in his unbuttoned holster. "Give me your pistol. Now." I barked.

Immediately he complied, a sudden look of terror on his face. I grasped it and wrapped my finger around the trigger, waving it at him to camouflage my shaking hand. "Go on," I said. "Get the hell out of here before you cause any more trouble between yourselves and the SS." They started backing away towards the truck. "And if I see you anywhere near another Jew, you better have Herr Reydrich sitting in the front seat or I'll shoot your cock off. Now go!"

And go they did. The truck sped away, and I pocketed the gun in my own empty holster.

"*Metumtam*," I said under my breath, but just loud enough for the girl to hear. The Hebrew word for stupid was a favorite saying among Zionist youth leaders' most Jews my age had grown up with. She clocked me immediately.

"It's okay," she said quickly in French to her still fearful family. "He's one of us."

Checking the street was definitely empty, I struck a match and set fire to the handwritten list. I wanted to do so in front of the family, and make sure they knew had some time to flee.

"Disgusting," it was the old woman, my grandmother, and she spat right at me. "Have you no shame? I would rather die on this street than deny myself, deny my people, deny my God—"

"Baba, no," the young girl said frantically, leaping in front of me to block any more spitting. "He's helping us."

"I don't need the help of a filthy Nazi. You should have shot yourself before putting on that uniform. At least die a Jew."

"I'm sorry," the girl said to me while the other members of the family began to understand they were not being sent away, at least not today.

"You don't have long. Get into hiding or leave. And do it today."

She nodded.

I stamped out the last embers of the list and kicked away the ash. The girl started to shepherd her family back to their apartment, speaking quickly to her mother and the woman with the baby that they were leaving immediately. The others didn't look at me as I started back on my way, thinking it best to get out of here as quick as I could.

She looked back and smiled once more, then disappeared inside. I heard the door bolt closed and let out a brief sigh of relief. The adrenaline I never even knew I had started to dilute, and only now I could feel my heart begin to pound.

I kept on walking towards Giovanni's, feeling one millionth better, grabbing onto whatever hope I could find. At least now, if I were to die, I had done something. Tried something. I had woken up every day sick with the occupation, and even sicker with my useless place inside it. What good had shooting Nazi pornography done? What life had I saved? What I'd done could be art, perhaps one day, but what good was art in a world such as this one. So now I'd done something. Given one family one more chance. Yet what good was even that? Another day on the run. Another hiding place they'd eventually be cleared out of. My sense of purpose now fleeing before it was even grasped. The bird had landed in my palm, and I'd killed it with just a touch.

I walked on, lost in my own thoughts, the scenery passing by as I remained bewitched by my magic, yet heavy suit of armor and the helplessness swirling across the horizon like black clouds. I was a bit turned around, had gotten too day-dreamy; the pathway I was on, the cobblestone alley, didn't seem to lead anywhere now.

I stared at the graying sky and the aged buildings of Montmartre closing in. These alleys where Bohemia once lived, now echoing with jackboots—my own. I had wandered too far north. I could see the white domes of the Sacré-Cœur between wrought iron balconies. That stupefying monument to order built atop the birthplace and then graveyard of the Paris Commune. I had to turn around, to get the monument out of sight. I felt sick at the number of pictures I'd once taken of the cathedral. They never hung a swastika on the Sacré-Cœur. They didn't need to.

I was alone on an alley I only vaguely knew would take me back to Giovanni's. Cocteau's philosophy of queer geography was right once again. Eilas's SS uniform itself had the institutional memory of how to find the pit or peak in any city. I would live or die, he would mourn or not, then move on to the next place, the next set of orders. Perhaps with a promotion for having successfully infiltrated a queer Jewish network living in plain sight. The Boulevard de Clichy was ahead, the cobblestones of this narrow downhill lane soon to lead me back. I felt a drop of rain. Cold on my neck.

"*Schweigen*," a voice said from behind, demanding silence in a breath so quiet it could have come from the wind. A blade pressed flat against my throat. A body stood close behind me, a hand heavy on my belt where I'd holstered the stolen gun. "Do what I tell you and make no sound." The voice continued in French-accented German. I raised my hands before I was asked, the blade holding me back from swallowing. Rain started to fall on the Boulevard de Clichy up ahead, only a few drops making it onto the cobbles of this narrow lane, where I was sure my life would end. What a strange state of affairs that the Resistance took me before the Nazis did.

Chapter 13

WITH MY HANDS ON my head, on the cap of an SS officer, the figure marched me into a narrow gap between two buildings. Here we were sheltered from the rain, but the man breathed heavier than the wind. I faced a crumbling wall.

"I'm not who you think I am," I said in French. My captor said nothing, but kept his blade and body close. I sensed him dancing from one foot to the other, nervously wondering what to do with me. This was not the efficiency I'd expected from a Resistance assassination. There was, inexplicably, an opening, a silence to fill. I tried to lower my hands. He twisted the knife from flat edge to blade.

"I swear I'm not a Nazi. I'm not even German. I'm a Jew."

The knife stopped turning. The man stopped breathing, at least so heavily.

"Anders?" The question struck like lightning. The voice made sense. His knife withdrew and he stepped back. I spun around, hands still raised.

"Jean!"

He returned my look strangely, knife in one hand, the stolen gun pointed at me with the other. His hair was wilder than before, curlier, with a stubby black beard surrounding his lips and chin when years ago he'd been smooth-cheeked. His eyes were infinitely more tired, bashed with a bruise under one and a cut above the other. But still, he was Jean. My hands lowered, so did his weapons. Our mouths moved cryptically without speaking; shock.

Questions formed and discarded. There was too much to ask, too much to say.

Before answers could come to unasked questions, we kissed in a swirling mass of flesh and tongue. He held my body against the stone wall, vulnerable and threatened by the street he'd taken me from. I didn't care. And neither did he.

Perhaps this was some fantasy of his forged in the fires of war, wherever he had been or whatever he had been doing, to suck the breath from a German officer, to run his hands under the skull and crossbones cap, rip open the buttons of the feldgrau uniform. If it was, may it never end. Please, God, may Jean never get tired of kissing my lips and thrusting his hands deep inside the stolen skins I wore.

"Stop," I whispered while his lips sucked on my neck, "someone could see." He wiped his mouth but stayed close, as if keeping me here in case I tried to escape.

"Why are you dressed like that? Since when are you a Nazi?"

"I can explain. I swear. It's not my uniform. But… you! What are you doing here? Where have you been? Tell me, were you going to kill me?"

His nose rubbed against mine and his lips twisted into something like a smile. All the insanity and danger, flirting with death and destiny made us unable to leave each other's orbits.

"I heard boots on the cobbles, I was here, hiding out. No one walks down these alleys. My bike and bag are over there." He nodded deeper into the narrow lane. A rusty bicycle rested against the wall beneath a pile of rags to make the ground a little less rough. "Germans alone don't normally walk down here, at least I figured you'd either got horribly lost… or else knew exactly where you were going."

"So what, you were going to blackmail an SS officer on his way to Giovanni's?"

"I was going to try." He slipped the gun into the back of his trousers, but kept the knife in one hand. "I need a uniform. Preferably without blood on it, but that's not strictly necessary." Then he leaned in and kissed me again. Deep and strong. He tasted of many nights out here in the wilderness, and I thought, what a fulfillment it was, kissing him now. A past life fondly remembered. For both of us. I pulled away.

"You haven't been back to Giovanni's. Why did you never come find me?"

"I'm not long back in Paris. I wanted to come. I tried to come, but that place was full of Nazis. Then I tried at David's, and it was the same situation."

"This is Paris. Everywhere is full of Nazis. You should have come to find me, to stay with me instead of… wherever you're staying."

"I can't exactly waltz into a place like Giovanni's. What is it now, Nazi high command?"

"A brothel. David's too, actually. But of a different sort." Jean smiled. It was good to see him smile, even with a face in obvious physical pain. I kissed his bottom lip, if only to give it moisture, and we held each other close. But his hands didn't know what to do with my clothes. "Why do you want this uniform? Actually, I don't care. Take it."

"No, Anders. Don't. I can't take something you need to survive."

"I don't need this." The cap I'd already given him. The evil black jacket came off too, and I bundled it into his hands. My shirt I couldn't unbutton fast enough. It smelled of Eilas. "I don't want it. Please, take it."

"It's for the Resistance."

"Good. I don't care."

"Wait," he said, as I stood in my undershirt, unbuckling my belt. "I have some clothes. You'll freeze."

He brought a satchel from his hideout, pulled out a shirt, sweater and ragged trousers as he stuffed in the uniform.

"You need the boots, too."

"Anders, you'll get a cold."

"I'm not far from home. I'll walk in bare feet, I don't care. Just take this thing away from me and do what you want with it."

I was near naked, shivering in next to nothing as Jean crammed what I'd given him into his bag. He kept looking at me, at my body, measuring it up in the same way I'd done to him so many times. Taking photographs in his mind.

"Let me help you get dressed."

I nodded as he tried to dry my cold, wet feet on his knee, then helped me into the rags. He kept his body close to mine, transferring heat and keeping the worst of the rain away. I was vulnerable, but I wanted to be. Finally, in front of Jean. He threaded my arms into the too-large jumper, and we kissed again. So soon after the first, I feared it may be the last.

"Your letter," I whispered. "I'm so sorry. For everything."

"No. No, let me take the blame. I am sorry. I let myself be carried away when I wanted to get closer to you. I was afraid you'd cast me out if I wasn't the person you wanted me to be. I was never honest. And I wrote that letter in a terrible state."

"You wanted to be a model and I made you a prostitute."

"You didn't make me that. And look, I suppose I was a model of a sort. At least I did something while I could, right? I don't think this world has much use for me as a model now."

"You're fighting?" I asked in fear, holding his cheek rough from the years.

"I'm doing what I can. Fighting, but mainly hiding. Turns out the Nazis don't trust me any more than the French did. But Anders," he glanced back to the empty alley, the rain running down on cobbles. "I must go now, while the streets are clearer. People are waiting for me."

"No, please. Come to Giovanni's. You can sleep there. No one comes up to our room. And the people there won't bother you, I promise. They're more scared of us than we are them."

"You're kind. But there's things happening. I'm in Paris only for one reason. There are things to do... I must go."

I grabbed his back. Felt the gun next to my hand. I could take it. He knew I could. "Maybe... I can help. You know, with whatever's going on. With the Resistance."

"You want to help the Resistance?" It sounded like wishing for suicide. His eyes went wide.

"I can try." I stroked his broken face and he flinched. "Or at least I can help you. Those cuts look bad. Come to Giovanni's. Come to the back alley and knock the door three times. I'll be waiting. I'll bring you in. No one will hardly see."

Jean offered the hint of a smile.

"I will. Tonight. I promise." I watched as he snatched the bike and whipped the satchel across his back. Spurred with perhaps a newfound energy. "You'll get back there all right?"

"I will, it's not far."

On the bike already he leaned in to take one last kiss, then pedaled into the cobbled alley and then he was gone. I'd been stripped and de-armed in the space of twenty minutes, and for that I was eternally glad.

*   *   *

It had been about five hours since I saw Jean, and in that time I'd managed to smoke every cigarette in the building and annoy Giovanni, Madame Framboise, Claude, and numbers eight to fifteen who were waiting for their turn downstairs. Now I paced around Claude's boudoir one floor up from the bar, in the room he used to entertain clients.

"Are you going to tell me why you're trotting around like a nervous bride?" Claude had said while dabbing powder on his balls I'd just watched him shave. "I do have clients waiting, you know."

"Yes… Nazis."

"Yes Anders, they are Nazis. They fuck me in exchange for money and restricted goods, and in return, you, I, and everyone else in this house is protected."

"Are we, though?" I stubbed out one half-smoked cigarette and lit another.

"Hey!" Claude jumped up from his precarious position on the bed, freshly powdered balls flapping around his open silk robe as he snatched his cigarette tin from me. "Those don't come cheap."

"What if there were Resistance people here? Do you think your hole will protect us then?"

"Who's in the Resistance?" Claude said with an unlit cigarette between his lips.

"Jean, probably." The way I said it made it crystal clear I was not referring to Jean Cocteau, or Jean Marais, or Jean the young kid from Normandy who'd been a Giovanni resident for a few months last year before disappearing into thin air like so many others.

"Ah, *Jean*." Claude struck a match. "So, he's ran out of dicks to suck in the Occupied Zone?"

"I don't know. But I heard he's working for the Resistance."

"Sweetheart, everyone thinks they're working for the Resistance, everyone thinks they're fighting for France. And for what? I've never had more money, and you've never eaten better thanks to Hans and his daily deliveries. What is there to resist?"

"I never took you for a nihilist."

"Call it what you want, Anders." He slipped off his robe, held his cigarette above his head and maneuvered onto all fours on the bed with his perky ass up in the air. "Just leave the door open, be a dear and call down for number eight."

*   *   *

"Ouch, that stings," Jean complained again. He was sitting on my bed as I wiped a cloth soaking in bleach across the cuts on his forehead as I'd seen Claude do a hundred times. Sneaking him in had been easy, getting him to stay was much harder. "This is definitely not how Claude would do it."

"Well Claude isn't here, is he?"

"You're pushing against the bruise."

"I can't see the bruise, can I?"

"It's where the cut is!"

"Fine," I hurled the damp cloth at him, got up and lit a cigarette—one of his—from the tin on top of the chest of drawers. "Do it yourself."

Jean wrung out the cloth in the sink, a heady mix of blood and bleach swirled away down the drainpipe and he fixed himself up by the mirror. I smoked in silence, watching him, still not really believing he was here. Like he could disappear in the smoke that whirled out my nostrils.

I looked at his return the same way I viewed the occupation. It happened, and things would change. There was nothing to do but look at it logically, dispassionately, void of true emotion. To do so any other way would let in the abject, absolute, all-consuming terror that Jean might leave again, or might get hurt, or like so many other Resistance fighters found in the Seine, find their invincibility had one day run out.

"Come over here and let me help you with that," I said as Jean threw the bandage onto the floor in frustration.

"I saw David," Jean admitted as I patched up the cuts around his eye with a fresh white gauze.

"Today? Hold still."

"Last week. I came one morning, and we talked. And then today. They're throwing a party," he said. "A big one, tomorrow night."

"I know. I'll be there."

"There's an SS man coming. A man called Reydrich."

I smiled. I had better intelligence than Jean. "I know who he is." I hadn't known he was going to attend one of their soirees, though. I supposed Eilas planned to move against David and the rest of us quicker than I'd thought.

"I'm going to kill him."

I had nothing in my hands to drop, so they fell by themselves. The air seemed to suck out of the room, to disappear between the edges. I could breathe, just about, but it was hard.

"At David's?" I could only whisper. "Jean, you'll get us all killed."

"David doesn't want me to do it there." He touched the bandage I'd put on, and I understood. "He screamed at me and said never return."

"I'm not surprised."

"Anders, this Reydrich must die. He's murdered hundreds, thousands, if not more. He got von Stülpnagel shipped back to Berlin because he wouldn't execute any more hostages. He's a mad man. He'll raze Paris to the ground."

The lack of oxygen led to sweating. And a pervasive swirling in my stomach like I'd swallowed Jean's blood and bleach mixture then sucked the rag dry.

"What are you going to do?"

"Tomorrow night, make sure he stays there until one a.m."

"Me?"

"Reydrich's car will be waiting around the corner. We'll take care of the driver."

"We?"

"Us. The Resistance. It's come together quickly, but it's going to work. Just listen. The hat and jacket you gave me will be inside on the driver's seat."

"How am I meant to keep him there till one?"

"I don't know, but you need to come down at a quarter to one, go around the corner and get into the driver's seat."

"Why me?"

"Because you can speak German!"

"Jean, no. This is insane. First of all, he's going to notice me in place of his regular driver. And second of all…" I didn't have a second of all, apart from repeating how insane this all sounded.

"He won't notice. It'll be dark, he'll be drunk. Or at least tipsy."

I stood up and made a beeline for the window. I didn't even want to smoke. I didn't want to throw the window open either for air lest his treacherous words seep out into the night.

"You can't be serious. This is insanity. Even if he's wasted and strung out on hashish he's going to know I'm not his driver. You can't be serious with this. I know I said I wanted to help but this is suicide. I… I don't even know where to drive him."

"You don't have to drive him anywhere. Just around the corner and out of sight. Then slow down. I'll be there, waiting. I'll open the door and shoot him in the mouth. We'll pull him out the car and put the gun in his hand so it looks like a suicide, then you just need to drive us both away and we'll dump the car and the uniform in the Seine."

His face was utterly convinced of the inevitability of success, and he was desperate for me to join him there, on his plane of satisfaction. To hook me into a scheme he could see only upsides of.

"Jean, listen to me. Even if this works there's going to be reprisals. Thousands of them. Do you know how many people they'll shoot if Reydrich is found dead? Every single one of us at that party for starters."

Jean smiled. How he could smile at a time like this?

"That's the beauty of this." He got up from the bed and stepped over to me. Instinctively, I retreated as one does from an approaching cloud of death, but there was no more back. Jean wrapped his arms around me, and I sank into his shoulder because there was nowhere else to turn. "Everyone hates Reydrich. All our contacts in military HQ can't stand him. They're afraid of him and this vendetta he's been running since he got to Paris. Von Stülpnagel was the tip of the iceberg. Even a casual suggestion of suicide will be more than enough to convince everyone who's looking for something to convince them. Shooting himself outside a bordello when everyone inside witnessed public rejection by a crazed prostitute."

"What are you talking about?"

"One of the girls who'll be there tomorrow is an agent. She's going to slap Reydrich in front of everyone and yell out loud that he impregnated her, gave her syphilis, and demanded she abort the child."

It all kept getting more bizarre. A series of events so loosely connected which absolutely had to work as planned for us all not to die. I thought over the words again, to make sure I had understood each of them correctly, that he was actually suggesting what he'd just said.

"Jean, again, please listen to me, this is not going to work. Who's going to believe what any girl says over Reydrich? Who's going to care? What… what about the driver?"

"I told you, leave him to us."

"Us?" I unwrapped his arms from me. They had got so much stronger than when I'd last saw him. Although I'd never touched him back then, only imagined. In my mind I'd pictured him being a soft lover. A gentle one. His touch like a thousand feathers. But here he was, touching and holding me, and it felt he could snap me in half if he wanted. "You are saying *us* like De Gaulle himself hatched this plan. Like… like the entire Resistance is behind it." I stared at his face, so eager, full of the pointlessness of liberation theory. Claude was right. What was the use? "Is this even sanctioned by anyone?"

"Anders, this is our best shot to kill a high value target with a minimum amount of risk." He said it without answering my question. "We tried just shooting them in the street, but they shoot a hundred of us for every one of them."

"Doesn't killing him make us no better than them? What about a trial? Huh? A conviction? Making him stand in front of a court of law when all this is over and answer to a magistrate for what he's done?"

Jean looked at me like I was the one who'd gone crazy, then burst into a round of wide-eyed laughter on the edge of shock. Then, as if he'd seen an enemy solider hiding under the bed, he dived in there and yanked out a brown paper bag of pictures, the ones I'd shown him of the injured boys earlier that evening.

"Look at these," he said, not yelling like David did, not getting violent to make his point, just presenting evidence to make his case. I took the pictures, even though I'd seen them all. I'd taken them, developed them, and given them to Cocteau who arranged for their transport down to Mélenchon in Perpignan who returned a scribbled diagnosis and what treatment to take. I looked through them once again. Headless images of broken torsos, bruised bodies, deep cuts and scars in amongst the images of swollen tonsils or unsightly abscesses.

"This is what they do, Anders. The ones downstairs. The soldiers, the conscripts, the ones who'll say for the rest of their lives they only obeyed their orders. Who ordered them to do this?" I had nothing to say in response. "They're all complicit. Every single German is as guilty as the other. There are no innocent ones. None left alive, anyway."

"You can't kill them all," I whispered, thinking only of Eilas. What would Jean have me do? Strangle him as he slept next to me?

"You're right," Jean said. "We can't kill them all. But we can kill Reydrich. Every German in Paris hates him. Did you know he had Le Sphinx raided?" I shook my head, wondering whether I could corroborate the accusation with Eilas. "Reydrich's men took down the names of hundreds of the men inside the brothel, barging in on the men who were in flagrante. Two were engaged in anal sex with the women. Reydrich's goons dragged them all out naked into the street. They shot the women and arrested the two soldiers for immoral conduct. The city was on the verge of a full-scale mutiny until HQ commuted the sentences and sent the two men to a labor camp instead and compensated Le Sphinx. Trust me, Anders. There's going to be celebrations in the street when Reydrich is found dead."

"Funny how upset the Germans get when one of their own is treated barbarically."

"Anders, this is happening. It's our best chance, and you can make it happen. All you need to do is come downstairs at a quarter to one. You'll be waiting in the car. He'll get in, and two minutes later he'll be dead. No one's going to shed a tear for him. We just need to tell them a story that makes sense. A fall from grace, public humiliation…"

Jean took me back in his arms. And I let him. Those lips sucked hard on my neck. The room refilled with air like a fresh breeze was coming from an open window. No one knows how they will act when the weight of the world is dropped on their shoulders. If I was to die in Paris, then perhaps it should be like this. With Jean, trying to make the world a little less evil. Eilas might suppose to recognize Reydrich for his madness, but what good did that do? He didn't care. It wasn't evil that led Eilas to facilitate Reydrich. It was something much worse. Conformity. He simply didn't care as long as he made the grade. No wonder I was still alive.

Jean kept kissing me and I kissed him back. Claude was right, this place was as safe as we could get in Paris. A bar full of soldiers with secrets to hide. None of them wanted Reydrich raiding this place either. In fact, to let him live was to put ourselves at risk. The Wehrmacht didn't care that much that we existed. They celebrated the brothels and sponsored the Roosevelt Mansion, Le Sphinx, Le Chabanais and the others. We were tolerated, serving a certain need for certain men. Reydrich's fanaticism was out to destroy that. People could say what they want about the Wehrmacht, but for all their mindless shouting about their *führer* and Reich they ran their army as a professional, rational force. Conformists like Eilas, those willing to adapt to anything, even Hitlerism, have need for rationality. Suddenly a new way comes about and they fit in with it. As long as it's the done thing, the thing everyone else is doing, they could inflict cruelty and violence against their own people as easily as they could against someone else, as easily as they could inflict no violence if that were the fashion. Men like Eilas have no country but the one they look around, bleary eyed, and find themselves in.

My head was spinning again, but that's partly because Jean was undressing me. When I closed my eyes I could not stand, so he led me to the bed, lips still locked around mine. My clothes came off, so did his. All of Jean's hot skin pressed in against mine.

Jean lay me on my back. With his tongue, with his fingers, with kisses on my neck and down my chest, he opened me up, slowly, gently, but deliberately.

The deeper he went, the more I needed him. Like a young bride whose first love is going off to war, this could be our very first and very last night together. I did not want to live another day without having all of him.

Gently, helped by a smear of petroleum jelly Claude kept on his bedside and a large drop of spit, Jean moved in with the first few centimeters. I gasped and hyperventilated, but it was unrequired. The block was in my head. Jean stroked my face and smiled, and I concentrated on relaxing.

"You're doing amazing," he said, even as a drop of blood fell from under the bandage on his face and plopped on my belly.

"Your face."

"Never mind. There's nothing more important than you."

"Are you in all the way?"

"Nearly half."

"Half!" I tried not to panic. Perhaps now was the time to delve into Claude's opium supply. "Just go slow."

The door creaked open, slowly, like someone had been standing outside it the whole time and only now had decided to interrupt us. I leaned my head back to see who it was. Even though he was upside down, I could see it was Eilas, dressed as himself, in a black SS uniform with shining silver lining.

Jean, meanwhile, took fright both at the door opening and at seeing a German standing behind it, clearly looking for me. Instead of pulling out in shock like an adulterer caught red-handed, he pushed himself all the way in.

I yelled at the multiple shocks as my body seized up from the unexpected penetration. Jean collapsed on top of me, as if trying to shield me from an expected shot.

"I'm sorry," Eilas croaked out. "I didn't know you were with a client."

The door slammed shut, and I heard his footsteps rush down the stairs. How long had he been standing there? How much had he heard? I didn't know, but Jean did not seem to care. He pulled all the way out, grinning like an innocent member of a love triangle might.

"The hard part's over," he said, holding me close and kissing my neck. "Now breathe, and we'll try again."

Chapter 14

THE FEAR OF WHAT Eilas had seen, and what he might do, was about fifth on my list of heart-attack inducing possibilities that could occur. I woke from a dream where I'd been screaming into a black abyss to find Jean already gone, Claude snoring, and dark, foreboding clouds of biblical proportions blasted across the Parisian sky.

Downstairs, Madame Framboise was sitting at a table which still hadn't been cleared up from the previous evening. In fact, the whole bar was a bit of mess. And she was drinking cognac, the good one.

"It's a bit early, no?" I asked her, picking up glasses from the neighboring table and taking them over to the bar.

"You have a letter," she said breathlessly. I stopped at the bar, facing the long mirror, all of a sudden struggling to recognize the man who stared back. Never mind that, I thought. Never mind the apparition in the glass.

It was not a letter. The only thing the *Reichspost* would deliver since the occupation were pre-filled cards where the sender could check off the appropriate words 'in good health', 'wounded', 'dead', or 'prisoner.'

"I wrote to the Red Cross last year," she said, not looking at me. "I wanted to know, even if you didn't. I said nothing about you, though. I only said I used to be in her employ."

Carefully, I leaned over the bar to put the glasses in the sink.

"They won't know about me," I said. "I don't exist."

Through the mirror I saw her turn around. "You don't exist?"

"My mother burned my birth certificate when I left Vienna. And she had her friends in the government destroy my census returns and school records."

"But… your papers. They're from—"

"From France. I have the identity card they gave me when I arrived in '36. It cost my grandfather's watch to have them list my place of birth as Paris. I imagine it would be more expensive now. And I have my *Ausweis* David gave us all when they started things up again at the Roosevelt Mansion. We got one for you as well, right?"

The old woman nodded. This war had given her a dogged, aged complexion. Gray and tired, like her core had been frozen for a thousand years, and now thawed and thoroughly spoiled. Perhaps it was the dirty glass of the mirror, but her face looked stained with tears. To say the words out loud gave them a sense of finality. Almost a bubble of security, an insulation from the terror Madame Framboise had grasped in her hand. That's all my mother had wanted for me. To never exist as an Austrian, or as a Jew. To deny everything about who I was, create a new identity paid for by our families' silverware and my father's pension in the hope I might survive.

I sat down opposite her. The woman was crying. In her, however, I did not see my mother. But I saw the woman who had looked after me for the last six years. I leaned across the table and clasped her bony hands. They used to be full and fat, now they were drawn, thin, fragile. The stress and heartache of collaborating, running a circle of hell for demons who devoured the souls of countless young men, the ones we thrust into the fire pits so we might survive.

Their shadows haunted the empty basement bar. Chairs they'd once sat at, jokes they'd once told, pictures I'd once taken of them, leaving this corner of Rue Duperré more haunted than perhaps any other place in Paris. The excuses the Germans offered were pathetic. A boy had allegedly stolen money, or a watch, or given a soldier syphilis. A rowdy, unsanctioned group of Germans would storm in, shouting for Louis, Alexandre, Lucas, Martin, Hugo, Nathan. Whomever had supposedly wronged the solider. *Let him go,* Claude would whisper as we watched, yet protecting us from a punch in the face, or being dragged out to the back alley for a beating.

We let it happen, all of us did. It was part of the job. *Better outside than in*, Giovanni would say as we dragged the broken body of the latest victim back inside, Madame Framboise mopping up blood as we climbed the stairs. That was until what happened to Nathan. I didn't hear the start of the confrontation. I'd been sitting at the bar flicking through a left-over army newspaper *Das Reich*. Nathan stumbled down the narrow stairs in only a thin pair of shorts. Two strong Germans, both in their trousers and vests, came rushing after him, pushing and shoving the terrified Nathan. I looked up. Giovanni ordered them out to the alley. Before I could return to the newsprint, I heard a gunshot. We all did, shattering the silence. Smashing the illusion that we didn't know where the missing boys went. "Survive," I said. "That's what my mother told me when I left. Survive at all costs."

I looked at the crumpled, tear-stained card and noticed there were two. Both had the same box ticked. Both had been sent by the Red Cross. Both had the same place of death written, no, stamped in thick, gothic letters: *Theresienstadt*.

The only thing I could think of was how someone had made that stamp. At some point they'd tired of writing out the word by hand on death cards, and so had manufactured a stamp to ease their burden. I imagined a clerk, a thousand letters piled on his desk all inquiring about missing persons, taking a card, ticking the 'dead' box, then taking his Theresienstadt stamp, dipping it on the ink pad, and stamping the cards.

I spread both letters out. I could see the ink on one was a little more faded. The letters on my grandmother's card were full and thick and black, on my mother's a little less so. The tops of the 'T's,' 'h' and 'd' did not have the clean black lines of their predecessor. I estimated the clerk would have another four or five good stamps left before he would have to dip it in ink again.

Surely it would be easier to print the cards already ticked, and already marked with Theresienstadt. That would truly be the efficient way of responding to such inquiries.

* * *

"What's wrong with you?" Claude asked as we shared some hashish in David's kitchen. It was barely eight p.m. but the sky outside was already dark and threatening the world with rain. Out in the main room the band was striking up, tonight they'd found a brass band to play something as close to, but as far from, jazz as was possible. I worried everything was about to begin far too early. That everyone would arrive in half an hour, David would decide to kick things off before the sun had truly set and we'd all be done by eleven, Reydrich back home before anything had the chance to happen. Most of the girls were already out there, squabbling over which couch to sit on.

I'd tried to identify this alleged double-agent, the collaboratress who was also a Resistance fighter, but short of spilling Jean's plan to a crowded room I didn't know how else to do it.

"Anders," Claude said again, snapping my attention back to him, "don't take anymore if it's too strong." He looked at me oddly. Still trying to uncover what the matter was. Where should I even start. "Any particular targets tonight?" Claude asked, dabbing out the hashish cigarette even though it was only half-smoked.

"Hi boys," a voice said from the doorway. We both spun around.

"Marais! You're back." I dived into his arms, and we spun around together in a tight hug. He was thinner. And bonier, for sure. Where once had been broad, rippling shoulders there was now sharp points. Cocteau looked on from behind with the proud, broad smile of a one whose love has returned from war. But Marais had only been shooting a movie in Rome.

"My God it is so good to see you," I said, moving on to hug Cocteau in congratulation as well. "But you look so ill."

"Acting these days is a hard business," Cocteau said.

"Not just acting. We were making Carmen so I had to sing, too." Marais was in good cheer, but an undercurrent of worry vibrated from him. Cocteau responded with those same notes. Their car had got very off track on the way to the Cape.

In this age of war and whores, it was impossible to hold on to the ones you loved.

"Anders," Cocteau said as Claude re-lit the hashish cigarette for Marais. "Come, I want you to meet someone."

I followed him out of the kitchen, narrowly avoiding being smacked by the trombonist of the eight-piece band in place of the standard singer and pianist.

211

"We're pulling out all the stops tonight, aren't we?" I wondered if this was for Reydrich's benefit.

"The new military commander of France is coming I believe, Carl-Heinrich von Stülpnagel. The cousin of the last one."

I sucked in a breath, suddenly afraid this is who Cocteau wanted to introduce me to, and would make up some horrendous excuse of why I could speak German which the new commander would see through in a split second. But it wasn't a member of the Wehrmacht Cocteau wanted me to meet, but a middle-aged man in a sharp suit.

"Anders, this is my good friend Arno Breker, the official state sculptor of the Third Reich."

The man smiled and offered out his hand with the other behind his back, like he was a waiter. This is who Jean should shoot, the artists who lend their talents to the pursuit of evil. Reydrich was just doing a job. This Breker was actively lending legitimacy to a regime through the bastardization of artistic ideals.

"Good to meet you," I said in French.

"Anders speaks German," Cocteau said, "so if you need anything just give him a wave."

I nodded with complicity.

"How did you come to know German, and have a German name, but find yourself in Paris?" Breker asked me in our native tongue.

"*Meine matter*," I responded sharply. Cocteau glanced at me nervously. The word was pretty international.

"Well… enjoy your evening."

"You too."

After a few more minutes of pleasantries I didn't pay attention to, Cocteau pulled me to one side as Breker went to fix himself a drink.

"That was pretty rude." Cocteau hissed.

"I'm not in the mood."

"Well you better get in the mood. This isn't the time for getting on one's high horse. And I need him on my side."

"Why? What do you care about a Nazi sculptor?"

"Because he can help Marais. And you, too, if it comes to that."

"Ah."

"Ah indeed, Anders. So just behave yourself for the rest of the evening, if at all possible."

I didn't think being involved in the murder of a senior Nazi counted as my best behavior, so I said nothing else.

The Roosevelt Mansion filled up as it normally did. The band played the Nazi anthem, *Horst-Wessel-Lied*, as guests arrived, were given a drink, and began sputtering around the different women like every other night.

It struck me how respectful these senior henchmen of death were to these women, at least on the face of it. The Germans only took a woman's hand when offered. They stood when she did and did not sit until she sat. And not once, not in a hundred or more different evenings had there been a single complaint from any of the women, not even a broken nail.

What made these men so different than the animals at Giovanni's? Perhaps it wasn't the women they respected, as these men had no time for the dignity of human life, but the decorum of being around each other. None of them wished to embarrass any of their comrades-in-arms with a social faux-pas. So would a hysterical woman slapping Reydrich really, reasonably, lead to suicide?

The atmosphere was different than other times. More formal, less relaxed. The men seemed stiffer, like they were on display. No one wants to humiliate himself in front of a brand-new boss.

"Busy tonight," Claude said, sneaking up and handing me a clandestine glass of gin and tonic. I nodded and we watched the guests mingle. What I'd feared just an hour ago—a quick affair—had not come to pass. I glanced at the royal sun-style clock, already after nine. We were running behind normal schedule. I quickly added up all the ways I might delay proceedings even more.

"They're not all here yet, are they?" I said. Claude shrugged. "I don't think we should start till everyone has arrived. Plus, they normally take half an hour to find a partner and what not."

But Claude wasn't listening. His attention, like a growing number of others around us, was distracted by a shouting match of increasing volume and ferocity coming from the corner of the room. Marais was bright red and pointing threateningly at a short, fat, sweaty man with a greasy comb-over who was dismissively batting away Marais' theatrics as Cocteau looked on.

"Who is he yelling at?" I asked Claude.

"Oh fuck, that's Alain Laubreaux." Claude shifted around me to get a better look over and above the band who were now playing louder and longer to cover the shouting.

"Who?" I had to skip to keep up with Claude who was drawn ever closer into their argument. Desperate to overhear while keeping a respectful distance. Truthfully, no one in the room knew how to act. The officers glanced over while continuing their polite chit-chat with the women. I looked around for David who was nowhere to be seen.

"He's a theater critic," Claude explained. "And a terrible collaborator, of course. Just a French Nazi, really. Anyway, I read last week in the paper his review. He called Marais 'the man with the Cocteau between the teeth.'"

I snorted with abrupt, surprised laughter. It was the sort of low-brow innuendo that only landed from the dumb mind of the writer to the equally uncultured mind of a certain type of reader. Neither Cocteau nor Marais had ever hid a single facet of their relationship. Indeed, here they were at the Roosevelt Mansion while Cocteau entertained Hitler's sculptor.

A grubby little man like Laubreaux tried his best to cast Marais and Cocteau in a shade of shame. I remembered what Cocteau had told me in Le Touquet years ago. How they were alone on a midnight road, driving through jungle and desert as those around hoped and tried for them to fail.

Suddenly the shouting took a sharp turn, and Marais grabbed Laubreaux by his starchy-white collar. One officer nearby put down his glass and jumped in, as did Cocteau who, terrified, tried to hold his lover back.

"That's quite enough," I heard David, finally, shout from the kitchen as he burst forth and leapt across the room. "Outside now, the pair of you."

Cocteau had Marais by the arm, and the German officer held on to Laubreaux. They followed David's lead and marched them straight to the door. A short silence followed as we all digested this brief interruption, before the band struck back up and the conversation returned to its flow.

David and the officer returned. He offered profuse apologies to everyone he passed, but they all seemed content to nod it off as nothing of importance.

A slight hiccup in an otherwise flawless evening. Entirely forgivable, completely forgettable. Tempers could run hot during a war. David dashed around being the smiling host, topping up champagne as I heard him say "find your dance partners, we'll start in a few minutes."

"Look," Claude whispered, gesturing me to come over to the window behind the band. I slipped across and we looked out onto the street below, lit only by a few streetlamps marking the entrance to the Jardin du Luxembourg.

Marais was shoving Laubreaux out into the middle of the street. The man was enraged, furiously pushing the short, fat Nazi theater critic who flapped his arms around in a vain attempt to fight back. Then Claude and I both gasped. As did a line of others gathered by the window to watch this most unusual of sights in occupied Paris: a street brawl.

Marais punched Laubreaux so hard we could hear the thwack all the way up here. The critic, his greased-down hair now drastically out of place, collapsed to the ground as blood spouted from his nose like a fire hydrant. Manically, Laubreaux began to laugh.

It echoed around the empty street, wafting four floors up as we watched the scene unfold in stupendous shock. Laubreaux remained on the ground with Marais standing over him—a heavyweight champion standing over an opponent he felled with one punch. The shrieking laughter was the only thing that gave Marais pause for thought. As if, in a cone of silence, he would have finished the job and killed Laubreaux right there in the street.

"You're dead, Marais. Dead like your career was before you began to fall to your knees for a living. Dead!"

"Away from the windows, please," David said to us, snapping his fingers and shoving in between Claude and I to shut the curtains. He dropped his voice to address just us. "Either suck a dick or freshen a drink, do you hear me?"

I started back to the kitchen to pour myself another one, before heading around to offer these Nazis another round, or go and entertain Breker since his chaperone had now disappeared into a street fight. But then, across the room, I saw a sight that tightened up my spine. Reydrich had arrived, complete in his pitch-black and sword-silver SS uniform. Thin hair, almost white, neatly parted. Skin stretched over his face like the skull on his cap.

But I knew it was him purely from the reaction of the room. The mood sank as soon as he entered, like this man had the power to suck out any modicum of joy from the places he went, such as demons are wont to do.

But something more terrifying was standing beside him, dressed also in the formal black and silver killing colors of the SS. It was Eilas, and he was looking right at me.

* * *

"*Heil* Hitler," I said to them both.

"*Heil* Hitler," Reydrich repeated with a casual, waving gesture like his arm got tired of doing this fifty times a day.

"This is Anders, my contact I was telling you about," Eilas said to Reydrich in German, presenting me like a prize exhibit in a museum of things soon to be dead. "The one I'm hoping will join us soon."

Reydrich nodded with approval. I dug fingernails into my palm. Eilas would simply not give up on trying to recruit me into the SS. He stared at me, Eilas, flashing wide eyes my way, silently screaming *do it, save yourself.* I acted better than Marais had ever done in his life, swallowing the bile burning a hole in my throat and maintaining a sharp, professional smile while sweat flowed openly down the curve of my back.

"*Sprechen sie Deutsche?*" Reydrich asked, casting a casually suspicious eye over me.

"*Jawohl,*"

"Your mother was from Vienna, right?" Eilas offered, and I could see he was attempting to be helpful.

"Yes, she came to Paris after the Habsburg monarchy was overthrown. Her first husband fell in the Great War, and the Republicans confiscated their lands and titles."

"A tragedy that befell too many noble families," Reydrich said, shaking his head like this lie was one of the saddest things he'd ever heard.

"Indeed. And then she met my father... here in Paris, of course." Eilas was standing behind Reydrich, whose black, soulless eyes were trained only on me. He was making some sort of face, Eilas, trying to communicate whatever story he'd spun to Reydrich. Why the hell hadn't he told me before? Or told me he was coming?

"But, uh, my father died. In the Spanish Flu."

"And your mother?"

For this performance, I should have won every award for acting given out. Without my consent, tears pricked my eyes. The weight of this mornings' letters seeped out of my body, how could they not?

"She passed… just recently." I sniffed away the flood. "It was a shame," I looked away, turning to wipe my eyes and hoping to catch Claude's attention to come and rescue me. "She wanted to be buried in Vienna so much, on her family's land."

"This war is hard on us all," Reydrich said. "Give Eilas the details and we will arrange for her to be reburied back in the Reich as soon as possible."

"Thank you, sir." I wiped away the emotion that was acceptable, if not expected, of someone who had lived in France all his life but was bordering on the unacceptable for a German. "Excuse me, I do apologize."

"Not at all."

"Can I get either of you a drink?"

"No, thank you Anders. Nice to finally meet you. I hope you will be working with us soon. We could use a man of your obvious talents." Reydrich held out his hand. Eilas, behind, looked terrified. That I might throw the whole thing overboard on a handshake, storm off, reject his outstretched palm, not even protected by a glove.

"A pleasure," I said, gripping the cold hand of evil.

"Eilas, come. I want to speak with Arno."

The two men walked away, both with their hands clasped behind their back. Eilas threw me the slightest look, as casually as one man who knows another might nod as they pass each other by on a busy station platform. No time to talk, but secrets being said nonetheless. '*You did well.*' I breathed out flame and fire, panting until I grabbed a drink from a uniformed waiter. The champagne burned my well-bitten tongue.

Then finally the mood shifted. David called for the dancing to begin and women and Germans took to the floor as Claude started to shift the couches and chairs.

"Come," he shouted over to me. But I could not. Eilas had arrived with Reydrich. He would be leaving with him too, surely. Our mission was… impossible. Unless Jean proposed to shoot Eilas too.

Couples were starting to dance. Claude had enlisted David in shifting the furniture out the way as the band started up a foxtrot.

"Thanks for your help," David called over to me, stuck in the middle of dancing circles of hell. I was looking out for Reydrich, for a woman who looked like a friend of Jean. Oh God, what did that even look like?

"*Achtung.*"

"*Pardon, monsieur.*"

"Anders!" David shouted over the music, "get out of the way."

The couples were dancing, spinning. Nazi generals and colonels and majors whacked into me from every side. Women with faces of gold when turned towards their men cursed me under their breaths.

"Move, you dumb fuck," one woman said to me. I watched her face as she danced with a fat German. Her eyes were not on him, though. Which was fine because his were on her chest. She was looking through the crowd, looking for someone. Her brunette hair was tied up in a smart bun held in place by a couple of sharp sticks which I could easily imagine being plunged through a rib cage. Her face was smooth and her skin seemed soft compared to the other women who had a certain haggard, worn-out look about them.

By the collective force of having no space to stand, I was expelled from the make-shift dance floor. Much to David's visible relief. But I did not take my eyes from the woman with the sticks in her hair. As David called out for the partners to swap, she made a beeline for Reydrich, grabbing him by the waist and practically smothering the man in her barely contained bosom. I had to tell her to abort.

There was a hand on my back, and it was edging down to my trousers.

"Don't turn around," Eilas whispered. I kept staring straight ahead, at Reydrich dancing with the French agent, and I realized Eilas must know exactly what was happening. How easily he could have been waiting outside my bedroom door last night, listening in as Jean laid out his treachery. "Meet me in the second bedroom from the left in five minutes."

He brushed my ass with the palm of his hand like one might grace a vase in someone else's manor house. He touched me in a way that felt forbidden, here in the presence of so much evil ideology. This touch was designed to make me know he was different, to pull me back into his orbit, or lull me into a false sense of security before bundling me off in the back of some SS car.

Ten minutes later, I found him in the bedroom primed for use during the dancing breaks. The bed was perfectly made. Fresh cut flowers were even in a vase on the bedside table, one of Hella's delicate touches that perpetuated the illusion this was not actually some seedy sex room.

Eilas was pacing. I closed the door, and the next second he was on me. His kisses were rough and sloppy. Less a kiss, more licking my face while his hands grabbed at my belt. But this was one-sided.

"Stop a second," I managed to squeak out and push him off me for a moment as I gasped for breath. "What's going on?"

"I need you." His hand pulled my head to one side, and he sucked hard on my neck. Not in the way Jean did, though. Not even close. "When I saw you yesterday with… him. I couldn't handle it. I don't want you doing that job. I can't."

"Job?"

"I'll pay you whatever you need, whatever you want, I'll take care of it. Just… please, Anders. Don't sleep with anyone else. I need to have only you. Only. I wanted to kill that man yesterday. I can't… I can't go around shooting every man who fucks you."

I wanted to burst out laughing at the sheer absurdity. Couldn't he?

"Eilas, wait. Please wait for a moment." My trousers were already pooled around the floor. His dick was out. He spat on his hand and turned me around. We could not do it here. No way. Not in this room. I heard the music stop and a round of applause flit around the main room. The first dance was over. Now was the break. Germans would be filling the hallway. Women would be knocking on doors. He couldn't be doing this to me. Not now.

"*Nein,*" I said as he flipped me round and pushed me up against the door. "*Nein, Eilas, Nein.*"

Then the door pushed against my face. It pushed harder as it met the resistance of my body, with Eilas pressed against mine. But the door kept pushing. I had to move back, holding on to Eilas to keep myself tripping over my own trousers.

"Herr Reydrich," Eilas said first, in absolute shock. Then the hellish skull with skin, the man demon, appeared from the door, into the room. Reydrich watching aghast as Eilas quickly stuffed his dick back in his uniform. Seeing what was going on, Reydrich quickly moved into the room and slammed the door shut as the voices of polite chatter filled the hallway.

I never had a father, so I did not know, but I could imagine this would be exactly how a father would react when walking in on his favorite son, the paragon of athleticism, his pride and joy, on the verge of penetrating the boy the father had assumed was just a good mate. It wasn't only about being caught in the act now. In fact, it would have been more of a relief, or less of a trauma probably, to see his son with a stranger. That could be written off as a one-time thing. A momentary lapse in judgment that would never happen again.

For a father to see his son about to bugger someone he *knew*, who he had been introduced to, dined or holidayed with the family. Eaten at their table, slept in their guestroom, gone on hunting trips and drank together, well that was the sort of trauma fathers never got over.

I shuffled over to the bed before pulling my trousers up, not particularly wanting to bend down around Reydrich.

"This…" Eilas started to say as Reydrich looked on at him, almost looking forward to the explanation. "Anders has been… giving me, us… advice. Help, sir. Identifying possible Resistance agents. Jews."

"Well," Reydrich sighed. This was clearly not something he wanted to deal with, at least not now. Only then I noticed a bright red mark across his cheek. Like he'd just been slapped. "Thank you, Anders, for your assistance." His tone was ice cold.

I nodded, but kept watching Eilas, how the fear rippled through him. How awful to live with such terror. How great a toll the work of evil exacts on the evil doers.

"Anyway, Eilas, I shall be departing now. I've had quite enough embarrassment for one evening."

"Sir, no one knew that we were—"

"Not that, although the hostess was quite aware you had gone into this room which is why I could find you. No, I was accosted out there by a screeching harlot. A filthy slut. Good only for spreading her legs." He wiped his otherwise clean hands with a white handkerchief, then dabbed flecks of white hate from his lips.

What was she playing at? It was barely—I glanced at the clock beside the vase of flowers—quarter to ten. Jean said keep him here until one.

"Shall I drive you, sir?"

"No thank you. There's no need. I'll go with Opperman in his car. Just pick me up in the morning. And early."

"Very good, sir."

Reydrich looked at us both in turn. He smoothed down his uniform, nodded curtly at Eilas, then, somewhat reluctantly, at me, and opened the door. "Don't spend all night in here, Eilas. You wouldn't want to blow this boy's cover."

I'd already let out the tight, heart-crunching breath as all of Reydrich save for the heel of his boot left the room. The door was closing, closing… then it opened again.

"Oh, and Eilas, shoot that girl, will you? Have Altmeir help you escort her out. She's the one with the Chinese sticks in her hair. I'm sure they can point her out to you."

"Of course, sir."

Then the door closed. The way Reydrich said it was beyond an afterthought. A nota bene to a postscript on a letter he had barely remembered to send. A nothing. A banal, beige throwaway to end a life.

"Eilas, where are you going?" I leapt off the bed and held the door shut with my back.

"Anders, out of the way."

"Where are you going?" I screeched. Eilas tried to grasp the door handle, but I lashed out and kicked him in the thigh.

"Ow, Anders. Get out the way."

"No!" I kicked again, with much greater force, but he moved out the way and glared at me.

"This isn't the time. I've got a job to do."

"Don't kill her, Eilas. Please. Please…don't."

"Anders, stop it. I have to. And I'm not exactly in a position to argue with him now, am I?"

He tried again to get to the door, but I dropped to my knees and hugged his legs, wrapping myself around him with every last iota of energy I had left in my body.

"No, Eilas. Don't. Please. Say she got away. What difference does it make? Just send her away. I'll send her away."

"I can't do that, Anders. She's out there now. Reydrich wants it done."

"Do it tomorrow. Why can't you? What difference does it make? Do it tomorrow. I promise. I know where she lives. David will know. I'll come with you. Just… let her live tonight. Please. Please let her go tonight."

I looked up at Eilas. He looked down at me. But…kindly. He cupped my cheek with his hand. I didn't know what I was saying. What difference did tomorrow make? Likely none at all. But she could run. Maybe. I could tell her. Jean could say the mission is off, time to run. Maybe Jean and I could run too.

But Eilas was saying nothing. Not giving in. Not even close.

"Anders…"

"Please Eilas. I'm begging you. And you can have me. Tonight, now, always. Think about it. Reydrich is gone for the night. We can be here, together. All night. The whole night together."

"You heard what he said. People saw us go in here. They need this room for… you know."

"There's another room," I said without thinking. "It's secret. Inside the study. No one knows about it, only David. We can be alone there until morning. Wouldn't you like that? The two of us? Please Eilas. Just let her leave tonight. Who knows what will be tomorrow. But at least you can have the night with me. We can be together in there and no one will know."

I hugged his legs as tightly as any human could. If I was a stronger man, I might have snapped his kneecaps. But I was not strong. I was the one denying who I was, hoping for death when all I had to do was survive.

"Stand up." He took my arm and lifted me up. He was gentle, but firm. He kissed my cheek. Then, with a growing smile, said: "Where's this room, then?"

The door to the study was across the hall and a bit further up. I wanted to take him straight inside before he changed his mind. But it was locked.

"Fuck."

"Maybe someone's inside?" Eilas asked, and looking around the hallway at the couples softly chatting and the door to the room we had just left snapping closed as a couple went in shrouded in laughter.

"Wait right here, okay? Do not move."

I bounded down the hall and back inside the main room. The band was drinking, couples were chatting, all looked normal. But a mist hung over the room. The cloudy aftermath of excited drama. Quiet questions spoken between groups of people; words traded as gossip in a group that was trying to come to terms with two bizarre incidents in the one night.

"David," I yelled across the room, skipping between the guests like only someone who seems to be staff can do at an event. He was about to step inside the kitchen. "I need the key."

"You need?"

"To the study. I need it. Now."

He dipped into his breast pocket and placed it furtively in my hand. "Who's going in?"

"Me. I am."

I darted away again, leaving him by the kitchen. He could try to wiggle his way into the crawl space if he wanted. I didn't care. I just needed to keep Eilas occupied until dawn.

I saw her. The brunette. She was sitting on the green couches in the middle of the room being comforted by Hella. If I deserved to win best actor for my performance this evening, she certainly deserved best actress.

If I had known nothing, I would have said her flushed cheeks and hands wrapped tightly round a glass of water would suggest her Nazi lover had left her pregnant and with syphilis. Hella saw me approach and jerked her head to get me to go.

"Mission aborted," I whispered into the agent's ear. She did not turn around to look at me. Hella was staring death at me, but I was confident she could not hear. Nor did I have to say much else. The agent got the message, but I repeated myself. "You're compromised. Flee. Now."

223

I leapt away. Rushing towards the hallway as I heard David call out from behind.

"*Meine damen und herren*, round two is about to start. Grab your partners for the Lindy Hop! But with a Berlin twist! It's Hitler approved; I promise you that. The Führer loves nothing more than Lindy Hopping around the Berchtesgaden to this one. I myself had the privilege of…"

Eilas had not moved from the doorway. He was leaning against it, hands in his pockets, waiting for me. I smiled at him. Finally, we could all breathe. Jean wouldn't put himself at risk tonight. The agent could disappear from Paris. No one would be marked for reprisals. Although perhaps Marais would. But that was a worry for tomorrow. For now I just had to get through tonight.

"Drink?" I asked Eilas as I conspicuously locked the door. Rain battered against the window slit. The sort that one would find in a hidden room of a glowering castle as co-conspirators kissed by the light of a crackling fire.

"Why not," he said, gripping me by the middle, throwing his hat onto the chair and kissing me deeply.

*   *   *

I woke with the dawn. Eilas had his naked back against mine, snoring as a man satisfied. I turned and traced my fingers along his taut skin. A smooth curve of beauty, eggshell skin, freckled, toned, smelling of uniform, of leather, of gunpowder. Almost of blood.

He did not smell like evil. Neither did Reydrich. Nor any of the Germans. He did not touch me like he could commit acts of unspeakableness. Neither through sound, not touch, nor smell, nor taste… nor even sight, could I identify Eilas as a henchman of heinous, hideous acts. What was I meant to trust?

I could hear rain thwack steadily on the window in the study. We had left the secret door open. There had been no reason to feel confined in a small, cramped box when the door to the study was firmly locked.

"Good morning," Eilas said, surprising me. He flipped around and gazed at me, face smashed up against the pillow, lips pursed and wrinkled, one eye lost deep in the sack of white goose feathers.

Another morning waking up beside this man. With no uniform, no lies, no terror, no Reydrich or Jean, what could we have been?

"Is it raining?" He asked.

"I think so." I wondered if the rain had washed away Laubreaux's blood from the street.

Eilas propped himself up with one arm, his chest twisting as he sat, stretched, and looked around the unfamiliar room. I played with the hair on his chest, pulling gently on brown nipples, indicating I wanted to have him once again. Once more before he left, and the day would take whatever unpredictable turn that it might take. The surrealism which held this occupied city together felt on the verge of passing with the rainstorm, like something was about to come and wash our unreality away, here in 1942. Perhaps it could all be over.

I was his dream, or he was mine. None could tell. Or perhaps we were all still players inside the warped mind of Salvador Dalí.

"I don't think it's rain," he said.

"What do you mean?" The light flooding in from the study was bright, suggesting the storm had passed and revealed a cloudless sky.

Eilas got out of bed, bits flopping against his leg, the line of his buttocks perfectly carved. I knew his body well by now, but this felt like the first time we had actually made love, as odd as it seemed.

I expected Eilas to go out into the study to investigate the alleged rain, or at least gather up his uniform which I had relieved him of long before we got to the bedroom. But he didn't, he went to the wall, and straight for the butchered Picasso that had been staring directly at us all night.

"Eilas... what are you doing?"

"Something's behind this wall, maybe a leak or a pipe."

I was too slow. I should have never let him get out of bed. I should have slammed the study door shut, or hurried us out, or covered his face as I hopped back on for another ride. But he was up now, tapping the wooden wall, fingering the painting. I froze to the bed, unable to say something. He was right, though. It wasn't rain. The sound was clicking, methodical, metallic. Like a Vinten Model H which had run out of film, but had not been turned off.

Eilas lifted the painting off its hook, and I found my voice.

"Eilas, stop! I can explain." Another mistake. Ignorance would have been the better option. At least he wasn't listening.

"What the fuck…"

I could not see because of his naked, muscled body standing in the way. Would it be too late to throw myself at him?

He threw the painting onto the bed, then, with bare hands, ripped the cheap, flimsy wood which served as a wall. The entire middle section came off with barely a flex of his bicep. He didn't have to even break a sweat, or grunt, or use his body weight or push against the wall with his foot. It just came apart. Our years of secrets ripped to shreds by with all the strength of a toddler.

Eilas stepped back. He could not go far though; the bed was right behind him. Two pieces of wall as strong as cardboard in his hands, and the Vinten Model H staring at us both like a Martian, its motor whirring with an empty reel, clicking like rain from a cloudless sky.

* * *

"Eilas. Eilas, come back. It's not what you think."

"Where's my uniform?" he shouted, throwing the table over and kicking the chairs with his big, naked foot like a furious bull. "Where's my clothes? Where's my gun?"

I genuinely didn't know. We'd left it on the chair when I undressed him last night. His gun on the table, the door, we assumed, was locked. Like he assumed no one was filming us. What an idiot David was to do that. What a complete—

"Anders. Give. Me. Back. My. Clothes."

"I don't have them. I don't know where they've gone."

"What are you people playing at? What the fuck is going on here." Eilas tore around the small study, pacing around and around again and looking in all the places it clearly was not. Only David would have another key. What the hell was he thinking, stealing an SS officer's uniform. Did he think Eilas wouldn't notice?

Sick of pacing around the shrinking room, and decidedly not caring about being naked anymore, Eilas threw the study door open and stormed down the hall, shouting the house down. I crept out after him, well beyond the embarrassment of also being unclothed, my only intent to calm Eilas down.

"What the fuck is going on here? And where the fuck is my uniform? I am an officer in the Schutzstaffel under the command of Gruppenführer Reydrich." He kicked over a chair and punched the metal telephone receiver box attached to the wall with his bare fist, his entire body burning red with rage.

Down the corridor I saw Claude emerge from the main room, standing calmly, watching Eilas' brush with madness. Once Claude was sure he'd caught my gaze, he shifted around to show me what he was holding behind his back—a shining butcher's knife, glinting in the early morning sun.

"What's going on here?" David said from behind, emerging from their private rooms, with Hella in tow. David yawned and tied his dressing gown tighter around him. "Anders, what's wrong with him? Oy, you, stop whacking my wall."

"Give me my fucking uniform back," Eilas screamed, marching straight towards David, his finger menacingly out and cock flapping between his thighs.

"I don't have it," David pleaded, and he sounded sincere.

"So why the fuck is there a camera in there fucking filming me? Huh?" Eilas's furious face now turned to me. I was trying to shield myself behind the door, but he grabbed my wrist and yanked me out into the corridor. Immediately, Claude primed his slight body to leap out to my defense. But I pleaded silently with him to stay back, and not make more problems. There wasn't much Eilas could do now but give me a slap.

"Look," David said, slowly approaching us with his hands out and up, as one might coax a roaring tiger to drop a child from its jaws. "The camera was a mistake. It's mine. Totally mine. Anders had nothing to do with it."

"You've had half the officers in Paris in that room, haven't you?" Eilas yelled, now screaming in German. David looked lost. He was trying to follow the words. "And what have you done? Hm? Given the reels to the Americans? The British? You'll hang for this; do you understand me?"

"Anders, what's he saying?" David said, increasingly exasperated.

"And you," Eilas roared at me, yanking my wrist so hard I almost fell in the middle of the hallway. "Tricking me when I only tried to help you. When I scrubbed your stupid name from Reydrich's list, do you know that? I saved your fucking life, and this is how you repay me?"

I didn't see the slap coming, but I felt it. It reverberated around my skull and left a sharp ringing in my left ear.

"Leave him," Claude yelled, joining the fray and displaying his knife. It didn't phase Eilas, but I could see Hella gasp and David raise himself high, arms out wide to bring us all to order.

"Calm down. Anders, tell him to calm down. We'll find his uniform and his gun. The camera we'll explain. Claude, get that knife away."

Eilas must have understood that fine, because he slapped me again. "Don't you fucking dare tell me to calm down. I'll run naked through the streets if I must." Then he lunged for me, fist clenching around my throat and forcing me back, all the way to the wall.

"Get back, now." A new voice yelled. Not Claude nor David nor Hella. It came from behind Eilas. He kept a hold of my throat but turned to see the newcomer, and now I saw as well. Jean had burst through the front door, a Luger pointed straight at Eilas.

Jean looked awful, like he'd spent the night crouched behind a bush waiting for the signal which never came.

Eilas spread his broad shoulders, natural biceps flexing as he raised his hands in the air. A sinister smirk crept across his lips, like he'd now figured out our entire game.

"The whore?" Eilas hissed at Jean.

"That's right," Jean gasped for breath through a grin, "me. Now shift to the corner." Jean kept the gun pointed at the direct center of Eilas' mass and stepped further inside the hallway, kicking the front door closed with the back of his foot in case someone downstairs on the street might question all this shouting. "Anders, Reydrich is here. I saw him, right now. Someone dropped him off. He's come for his car. We can still pull this off."

"Pull what off?" David said sharply. "Anders, what is he talking about?"

"Anders," Jean commanded, "I hid this Nazi's uniform in the cupboard over there," he nodded towards where Claude was standing, never taking his attention from Eilas for even a split second, as if he was desperate for any reason to shoot. "Put it on and run down to take Reydich to his car."

"Jean, no," I pleaded. "He's seen me. He saw me last night. He knows who I am. This will never work."

"Just do it," Jean barked, pointing the gun at me now. "Run fast so he doesn't see you. Now."

I edged closer to Claude, my hands also raised for some reason.

"Anders," now it was Eilas gasping to give me commands. "Don't go anywhere. These people are all going to die, but I can still save you."

"Anders, uniform, now. We don't have time."

I heard a banging, we all did. From outside. Eilas looked shocked. Jean kept the gun trained on him. I glanced at Claude, who stared at me, just as confused. The banging got louder, heavier. Footsteps. Someone coming up the stairs and a voice calling out... in German.

"Eilas? Are you still here? I had to find out from a Sturmmann where my car was. I need you to drive me to..."

Reydrich entered. I gawked at Jean. Jean sensed the man behind him but didn't take his eye nor gun from Eilas. Eilas started to point at Reydrich. No, behind him. Hella screamed, and David yelled at Jean to put the gun down.

Reydrich turned to see Claude coming from the other room, knife out. Reydrich moved for his own gun. Eilas writhed like a caged animal, slinking towards his boss. Jean screamed at him to stop. Reydrich was the threat. He was loose.

There it was again, that disappointed father look. That not only was his son a fruit, but had allowed himself to be so easily cornered. Then I saw Reydrich's eyes drop from my face, down, down my naked body. I could lie about who I was until the end of time, but this was one thing I could not lie about.

Reydrich's face changed, utterly transformed, like he'd felt the presence of evil. He no longer just disapproved of Eilas' sexuality; he was morally, righteously repulsed by the fact his favorite little officer had been fucking a Jew all this time.

In the precious shards of a second that he took to acknowledge my circumcision, his hand missed the grip of his pistol. Just by a hair, though. The thumb banged the gun, but he was way off. I didn't think an SS man could blunder like that. He looked down to see why he'd missed it, as baffled as I was, then I lunged at him.

Muffled in the background of the chaos, Claude was calling my name. He was running, too. Towards Reydrich, towards me. But I was closer. I didn't even see him throw the knife, I just saw it coming towards me, pointing down, the silver handle floating through the air. I could take it. I was that close.

One foot forward. One hand up. I gripped the knife, caught it out of the air. Words came all at once, a babel of shouts in the chaos. I saw only David's face, though. Drawn out in shock.

David and his stupid camera. His insane ideas that had brought us all to the edge of ruin. David and his dumb Bohemian Revolution, pushing the artistic boundaries of…

The knife went into Reydrich's chest like he was made of soft butter. Like the butter they'd stolen and made scarce. I could taste butter, in fact. Perhaps I was dying. Vaguely, I noticed my arm lift, the knife dragging out a long, bright red streak, like a clown at a circus might pull out a trick handkerchief, all of them tied together. Down, my arm flew again. I'd been wound up like a toy monkey, and was now jabbing, jabbing, jabbing at the heinous Reich.

More screaming in the background, outside the circus tent. How odd. What was so funny? German, French, English. How different laughter sounds in each language. How close laughter is related to the sound of terror, especially when the one doing the hearing is so busy stabbing Reydrich in the chest, again and again.

But all the scuffling and yelling and laughter, it all ceased with the crack of a gun.

Act III:
The Center of the World

Chapter 15

"MY GOD," DAVID SAID, his arms folded as he peered down at the mess. "This carpet is utterly ruined."

Reydrich's body was a butchered corpse—blood, bones, lung, and leather all spilled forth freely onto the once soft carpet I'd so admired when I first stepped foot in the Roosevelt Mansion. But Eilas hadn't made a mess. His body had simply crumpled, from one, deep black hole in the center of his chest. Funny, I thought, how no red handkerchiefs seeped from his wound. Just dark smoke puffing out of his punctured chest.

Jean lowered the gun. Hella openly wept.

"Oh fuck," Claude said, as if he'd misplaced a pocket watch. "I'm meant to be meeting Hans this morning. He was going to take me for a drive, and we were going to get croissants for all of us."

"Claude, my dear," David said through gritted teeth. "There's two dead Nazis on my carpet and you're worried about missing a breakfast date?"

"It's just...I told Hans if he didn't find me at Giovanni's, then he should come..."

"Here?" I offered. Claude was beside me, gaping at Reydrich's corpse. He was white. Far whiter than usual. And he nodded. "Are you feeling all right, Claude?"

Eilas was by far the most handsome of the two corpses. By a long shot. He looked peaceful now. Lying there on the carpet, a perfectly chiseled body.

Germanic, Aryan, soft, beautiful features. Yes, I thought, if it wasn't for Jean being the true beauty of this age, I could have loved Eilas.

David was starting to pace, running his hands through hair and looking down at Reydrich's body. I noticed now, irrelevantly, how considerably David's hair had thinned since we first met.

"Could I perhaps have some clothes?" I asked, calmly. I realized I was still very naked, and spattered with Reydrich's blood.

Claude, his eyes unmoving from the body by my feet, walked sideways to the closet where Jean had stuffed Eilas' uniform, then handed me the dead man's trousers and coat.

I thanked him.

"Claude," Jean said. He was still armed so we all listened. "Go to Giovanni's and meet Hans."

Claude nodded, but David slammed the front door shut.

"Oh no. You're not going anywhere. None of you are. Not until we sort this mess out."

"We'll put the bodies in the car," Jean said, "and drive it into the Seine. That's what I was going to do, anyway."

"How convenient that you had this little operation so well planned out, Jean."

"Don't pretend you didn't give your tacit approval, David. You wanted me to kill Reydrich."

"I wanted two dead Schutzstafflen ruining my moquette?" David said while Hella howled louder, as if the true devastation was the stains of blood soaking the cream carpet.

"Shh," Claude hissed. "Do you hear that?"

We stopped moving. Stopped talking, stopped breathing. Voices came from the street—loud, casual, chatting. Then footsteps came closer. And banging like when Reydrich had come up the stairs. But the bangs were quicker, rapid, a firing squad doing target practice.

"I'm telling you," a muffled voice said in French from behind the door, "Arno will sort it out, you've nothing to worry—"

The front door tried to open, but it smacked against Reydrich's lifeless skull. If none of us moved, maybe whoever it was would leave? But no, he tried again, and harder, this time shifting the body and causing even more guts to spill out onto the carpet.

Cocteau entered with Marais close behind. At first, he seemed not to notice the dead Nazis, just our shocked faces. Then he saw Eilas' naked body, and Jean's smoking gun, and finally Reydrich's congealing blood which was threatening his shoes.

"David," Cocteau said, "what on earth happened to your carpet?"

* * *

The consensus was we should flee. It was Marais who saved us, in fact. Perhaps he was the one most used to seeing dead bodies, but after bolting the doors both upstairs and down, he took us all into the kitchen to concoct a plan.

Being away from the immediacy of the corpses helped us all to focus. We stood around the countertop in the morning light, a cluster of people who had survived this long. Surely, we could survive a bit longer.

"Let's go to Perpignan," Cocteau said. "Mélenchon is there, and the Nazis know him. He supplies a great deal of their opium and methamphetamines. If we tell the high command we're heading south, all of us, for a spring break, it's at least plausible."

"How do you expect us all to get across the Demarcation Line?" David said with an air of unearned satisfaction, like he wanted to be proved right. "It's impossible to get into the Free Zone. We should go to Le Touquet. It's closer, and, who knows, maybe we can get a boat to England?"

"You cannot flee over the Channel," Cocteau shot back. "Vichy is the only option. And anyway, I have an *Ausweis,* you and Hella have your American papers, and don't you still have those *Ausweis* papers we gave out to the women for the first event here?"

David looked like he'd been struck by lightning. Without saying a word, he left the kitchen. We were quiet, all of us, still wondering if this could work. And, if we had too quickly dismissed the first idea of disposing of the bodies and pretending that none of this had ever happened.

"I still have to meet Hans," Claude said, "or at least stop him coming here."

"Don't worry," Jean said, "there's plenty more bullets in this gun."

Perhaps it was a joke, but it made Claude go even whiter.

David returned, rushing back into the kitchen and dropping a stack of brown cards onto the counter.

"*Ausweises*," David said with a broad grin. "All of them signed by Otto von Stülpnagel." We spread around the dozen cards, blank where the photograph and the name should be, but true enough they were signed, and would promise the bearer unfettered passage around France.

But as each of us handled the precious passes like they were pure crystal, suddenly my heart dropped. Our victory was seized away. "Otto von Stülpnagel isn't the military commander anymore though, is he? Carl-Heinrich is." The others joined me over the crestfallen cliff.

"We all have a reason to leave," Cocteau said quietly, flinging the brown card with its Nazi insignia onto the table like some mogul dropping a weighty note onto a game of roulette. "Laubreaux has you marked for death, my love," he said to Marais as a matter of fact. "I've offered to Arno to prostitute myself to Hitler and the Reich to save your life, but who knows if it will be enough. David, Hella… neither of you can stay here, not while two SS men are about to go missing. I doubt if you'll ever be able to return to this house." Cocteau began to walk around the kitchen, running his hands over the marble countertop, telling each of us our fortunes if we stayed.

"Jean, Anders, you must leave Paris, even France, if you can, as any one of us could turn you in should our own lives require it." Jean looked on, uncomfortable at the truth Cocteau was telling. If any of us wanted to protest at the eventual accusation, we did not. This was simply the rules of engagement in this dadaist nightmare.

"Anders, you must doubly leave. The nets are closing in around every Jew in this city, and you do not have the stolen name of Roosevelt to protect you, or American citizenship. But that is not why you'll go. You'll go because Jean must, and you will follow the man you love."

I sucked in a breath, but I could not argue.

"And me?" Claude asked. "Am I the only one that is condemned to exile in this god-forsaken city while the rest of you flee?"

"No, not at all. You will go because you are in love with Anders. And you will go wherever he does."

The words hit hard, ricochet off the silence. Maybe that was the farce at the center of all this tragedy, an unrequited love triangle between us.

"Now," Cocteau said, grasping all of the *Ausweises* back together in a pile. "It's not about one individual lie, it is about the complete illusion."

David snorted. "Are you suggesting we all flee dressed as women?"

Cocteau ignored him and continued. "A superb photograph is nothing but an illusion, isn't it, Anders?" I listened, but said nothing. "It's not about the figure or what they're doing, but the feeling it gives. Indeed, a single frame can show emotions unseeable to the naked eye. That is what we must do. All of us. Dazzle them with artistic brilliance until we're all safely in Barcelona, and they realize the picture they're holding is nothing but a cheap copy." Cocteau turned his nose up with obvious derision at the art affixed on David's walls.

"Have we quite finished with the lectures?" David asked. "Meaning, do you have any practical idea of how we can escape with out-of-date passes, or should I just whip up a batch of poison right now?"

"Save us your Gin Rickeys, David. My point is, we cannot rely on these cards alone, but they can help. So what if the old commander signed them? That won't matter if everyone believes they are real. Look at this place. For how many years did the Germans think this was a place they were safe?"

Some shared sense of purpose shivered around us, like hearing an oracle, or when God spoke to Abraham or Moses or Joan of Arc. A glimmer of hope. A sense that all of us, together, just might be able to pull this off. Individually, it was doubtful, because there was no illusion. Why would one, even two people go south if not to flee?

Yet all of us together, this group which worked hard to entertain the German high command heading to French Catalonia for a spring vacation with our good friend Doctor Mélenchon, official drug dealer to fascists, well, it was more than plausible.

"First things first," Cocteau said, taking a pen from his coat pocket and scratching out a list on the back of one of the precious *Ausweis* cards. "We need suitcases, for each of us, and filled to bursting with clothes. Only our best outfits. They must believe we are a rich group of avant-gardists." Cocteau looked at me. As if this entire escape rested on my shoulders. I gulped, straining at the desert dryness in my throat.

"I can pretend to be that," I said, nodding gently at first, but then furiously, as the others looked on me, dressed in a dead man's SS uniform. None had said how this was all my fault, but I felt it. "I can act."

"You don't need to *act,* darling. You need to *be.* You don't *act* as if you're a photographer. You *are.*"

"I, don't have anything very nice to wear." Jean said, the most disheveled amongst us in his Resistance threadbares.

"Don't worry," Claude said, throwing an arm around his nemesis, "I have enough for all of us."

"Claude," Cocteau continued, leaning over the counter and adding more items to the list. "Go home and collect all of your clothes. Everything. And deal with Hans. Anders, you take pictures of us for the *Ausweis.*" The instruction struck hard. It was only a simple portrait. Tiny, lifeless, but it had to do so much. It had to save our lives. "You can do it."

"Okay," I hadn't stopped nodding. "But my camera is at home."

"I'll bring it," Claude said. "But how will we get south?"

"David, that telephone in the hallway, is it an ornament?"

"No, not at all. It's hooked up to the military HQ."

"Anders," Cocteau grabbed me by the wrist, "come with me."

He pulled me out of the kitchen and back into the hallway where the two bodies had been laying now for over an hour. I tried to ignore them, but they gave off the strangest feeling in the world. That of being watched, judged, actively spited by the souls of two people whose departure you caused. They weren't the only ones watching me, though. Everyone else had followed us out.

My chest pounded, but Cocteau thrust the receiver into my hand before I even had time to process what he wanted me to do.

"Ask about the trains," he said quietly, as the voice of a female German operator squeaked through my ear.

"*Hallo,*" I said, for want of anything better to say. My mind fuzzed. But they were all watching, and waiting for my performance on this stage they'd made. "This is, uh, SS-Untersturmführer Eilas Bahr. When is there a train to Marseille?"

"One moment please, Untersturmführer." I waited as Cocteau watched, breath bated. So did the rest of them. I stared at Eilas' body, and had the strongest urge to cover him up with his jacket now suffocating me. It was so utterly unseemly to leave his naked body laying there on the floor. I didn't know if to cry tears for a dead lover, or joy for a defeated enemy. "*Hallo?*" the operator said again.

"Yes, I am here."

"There's a troop train coming into the Gare du Nord in an hour. It was scheduled to return to Lyon today, but we will inform the driver to take you to Marseille, Untersturmführer. Departing at noon. How many in your party?"

I gave the number so forcefully. "*Sieben.*"

"Including Herr Reydrich?" Reydrich and Eilas were more famous than I thought.

"No," I turned away from his mutilated body which now attracted flies from somewhere. I sucked in iron-tinged oxygen, and breathed out crippling fear. Eilas's uniform smelled of him. My mouth still tasted of the body dead on the carpet. I inhaled, but it was a herculean task. I tried to focus back to those early days in Paris, those simple days when Claude and I could waltz into three tailor shops in an afternoon, and trick them all. "He will not be joining us, no."

"Very good, Herr Bahr. Noon at Gare du Nord. Platform four. The guards will be expecting you. Travel well."

"Goodbye."

I hung up and breathed for a long, silent moment.

"That seemed too easy. The train is at twelve, today."

"But the bodies?" David said, "my carpet."

Cocteau motioned for me to give him the receiver while he pointed to Claude, and then the door. Carefully, Claude stepped over the body, looked us all over once more, then ran down the stairs like he would never return.

"*Bonjour,*" Cocteau said to the operator. "Le Sphinx, please." He waited, tapping on the metal box and smiling at us all. "Oh, hello. Is Madame Piaf still there? Yes… I'll wait… Édith, darling. How's things? Uh huh, how was the show? A bit early for that, no? Well, anyway, you know that hideous carpet at David's…"

David looked appalled, like he'd rather keep the bodies there than have his taste criticized.

"Yes, well I've *finally* convinced him to have them removed. Your friend, the hardwood floor man, can he come today? Uh huh, yes, okay. Oh, but it must be today. Yes, that would be perfect. Thanks Édith, you're a star."

Cocteau hung up the receiver. "Problem solved." David looked even more aghast. "Oh, don't worry. Her upholsterer is one of us. Do you think this is the first bloody carpet we've gotten rid of? Now, my darling Jean, shall we dispose of these mannequins?"

* * *

All of us were shocked by how quickly things came together. Jean hot-wired Reydrich's car as Cocteau, Marais, David and I rolled the bodies up into old curtains Hella had. Jean reversed the car right into the doorway, and the easiest way to move Reydrich and Eilas was to slide them down the stairs, their heads banging on the wood, then stuff them directly into the boot.

Jean kept hold of the gun and drove straight off to dump the car in the Seine. There was no time to say goodbye to Eilas. No space to mourn the man who I was expected, apparently, to become.

"Don't worry," Cocteau said with a hand on my shoulder as the car roared into the early morning. "A tragic end to a first love only makes it easier to spot the next one. And he'll come, in time. But first you must live."

Fortunately, when we got back upstairs, Hella had soaked the carpet in bleach, which at least covered the smell.

Claude returned by ten, dropped off at the door by Hans in his car with a clutch of hastily packed suitcases which Hans had wanted to take up for him.

Jean had waited behind the door, gun at the ready, in case Hans had decided to come up. I most of all breathed a sigh of relief when only Claude appeared, a suitcase in either hand.

"Dear me he's clingy. Jean, you must promise to shoot me in the head if I ever become sentimental like that. There are more bags downstairs."

Jean stuffed the pistol back in his waistband and rushed down the stairs to collect more cases as we heard a car drive off.

"Guess what," Claude said with a grin as David and Cocteau hurried into the hallway to gather the suitcases. "Hans has arranged a military escort for us to the station."

David's face released a touch of the tension it held, then he returned to rushing from room to room, throwing several books and various papers into an open suitcase in the hall alongside tins of caviar and anchovies.

"My God, Hella," David cried, investigating the overflowing case. "How many of Gertrude's love letters do you need?" She hurried out from the living room, the spot of so many countless triumphs of hosting, a flustered mess and holding a de-framed painting. "I said the Matisse. The Matisse!" Hella reacted with confused concern, glancing down at the white-clothed woman sitting by the sea.

"Isn't that a Picasso?" I whispered to Cocteau, but David overheard me.

"Christ! Even Anders knows the difference. What good is a damn Picasso if we need to sell it." Hella hurried away.

"Is it wise to take *all* your art to Perpignan?" Cocteau asked.

"Just the valuables," David said as he fiddled with a suitcase clasp. "Sorry darling. I'm afraid your work didn't quite make the cut."

Cocteau unhooked a cubist painting to make a few inches of blank space on the wall. "Be a dear and hide this in the cupboard. We don't need to give the Nazis any more cause. We've already invented homoeroticism on film." I took the painting, but didn't stop staring at Cocteau.

"What do you mean inventing?"

"Well, not only film. Your photographs were always rather good. Why stick to one medium, I always say. For instance Édith is just as good an actress as a singer. And even better at hiding a couple of dead bodies. We should have brought her round first thing. Never mind. Camera ready, darling? We really should start."

At eleven thirty, we were ready to go, all seven of us standing on the street with our luggage. David and Hella had dressed like when I first saw them—over-the-top caricatures of Americans in Paris—David in his linen suit and Panama hat, Hella in lacy gloves and a parasol despite the rolling clouds.

We decided Marais should dress in the spare SS uniform, the one Jean had stripped me of two days before. Word had likely traveled about him punching

Laubreaux last night, and at present he was likely the most wanted out of the lot of us. Claude decided to dress in memory of a geisha.

"When you're as fabulous as I," he'd told us when Jean and I cast a wondering eye over his choice of travel outfit, "hiding oneself is not an option."

Jean had been harder to dress. Marais was concerned he'd have trouble at the border, despite the hastily finished *Ausweis*. Much to Jean's disgust, we'd decided the backstory with the best chance of success was that Jean was actually from Louisiana, and a servant of David and Hella. Cocteau even had me scribble it on his *Ausweis*.

"The Nazis understand slavery," Cocteau concluded. "Carry the bags, wear this cap, and keep your eyes down."

"If you expect me to so much as pour you wine in Perpignan I'll crush your balls with my bare hands."

"Oh my. Don't promise me such a good time."

It was only me who had refused to accept my role in this peculiar parade. As the haze of the morning faded, the weight of what happened replicated around my body like a cancer. All of them, even Hella, had shouted at me to get Eilas' uniform on, convinced it was the ace up our sleeve.

"He's not from Vienna," I had protested more than once. "Speaking German is not enough. They'll know I'm not him."

No one cared. And so, as Hans' convoy of three Mercedes cars pulled up outside the Roosevelt Mansion, it was left to me to chat with the driver.

"This lot are friends of the SS?" The young private asked me as we careered through the empty streets of Paris towards the station.

"Friends of Herr Reydrich."

"I didn't know he had friends, that one." The private said to me with a grin bordering on cheeky. I smiled back, lulling him further into this fraud.

"You know him?"

"Heard of him. We all have. He did a surprise inspection of my friend Michael's barracks. I didn't even know the SS could do that. They found an American magazine, you know the kind, and Reydrich went insane. Demanded to know whose it was. No one owned up, so he had the entire unit strip naked and stand out in the freezing cold. Brought in this giant

Alsatian. It must have been some demon dog, I tell you, 'cause it caught the scent of some poor guy just from the magazine."

We pulled into the train station, crowded with German soldiers stretching out in the Parisian air, yawning from a long journey but clearly excited for their 'once in Paris.' The private meanwhile looked upon his comrades with pity, like he didn't have the heart to tell them how, at least thanks to Reydrich, Paris was nothing but a tortuous trap.

"Then what happened?"

The private glared at me as the other soldiers who made up our escort started to lift the luggage out. He'd turned a sickly shade of cream. "Reydrich commanded the dog to rip off the guy's gonads."

They were quite something, these Nazis. The horror and shock they felt at the mistreatment of their own was matched only by the callousness of their ambivalence to any life that wasn't theirs.

"Thanks for the ride, private," I said, getting out the car. I walked around to his side and leaned into the window. "I'll make sure to let my good friend Reydrich know exactly what you think of him. Enjoy the Russian front."

I only saw his eyes enlarge as I walked away to greet the others.

"Right," I commanded in German, snapping the men with our bags to attention. "Platform four. Quickly now."

As Cocteau said, it was all about the illusion. Even if we were as ragtag and disjointed as an overstuffed drawing room, we could at least hold together the fantasy that, once upon a time, we were something marvelous.

*   *   *

The train sped through the countryside, rolling hills seemingly untouched by war. Fields of wheat bowing in the breeze and Frisian cows grazing across rolling hills. After so many years in Paris, first under the cloud of a coming war and now battered by the storm of occupation, passing through the unmarked country, laying right out here, unscarred by war, untouched by terror. It was like watching a movie. It looked so real, but we knew in our hearts it was false. France was fake.

Hans had gone to the trouble of packing us a lunch hamper, filled with cheese, pate, biscuits and even miniature bottles of Merlot allegedly requisitioned from the ration stores for French officers. But none of us wanted to eat. The clattering sound of the pistons running us along the tracks gave the perfect cover for silence.

The train was made up of a grand eight carriages, but it was practically empty, save for the remnants of the hundreds of soldiers it had dropped off in Paris that morning: empty ration wrappers and bottles of mostly drunk beer. We had picked up a few passengers just south of Paris, but other than that we steamed through villages and empty stations like it was our private passageway on the railroad out of hell, the final destination still unknown.

Claude, Jean and I sat in one cabin, with Marais, Cocteau, David, and Hella in the other. We thought it would be better for Marais and I to divide ourselves between the cabins in case… well, in case of what we weren't so sure. There were no ticket inspectors because there were no tickets. At the station the guards had waved us through with only a brief glance at the *Ausweises* we'd fretted over so much. All I had to do was tell the guards on the platform we were all together, and give them my sharpest glare in this black uniform, to keep up the illusion.

Outside, the monotony of travel wound by. Every so often a detail would leap out, an odd-shaped tree, a cottage, a donkey, a ruined village, a corpse swaying from gallows outside a still-burning village, a dead donkey, a collapsed cottage, a blackened tree. Scars of war.

Jean sat against the window, arms folded, and eyes closed, the 'servants' cap draped down over his face. No one wanted to say yes, this was all his fault. But I was glad no one had taken to blame me, either.

Jean, however, did not hold a hint of blame over himself. He'd done what he'd came to do, he'd done what he'd said he would do: kill Reydrich. And he'd done it with the added bonus that I'd been the one to do the actual killing, plus he had the satisfaction of shooting Eilas dead. Fleeing Paris was merely a natural consequence to required actions.

"I'm not in love with you," Claude said without any apparent reason or purpose. He was sitting beside me by the window, as Jean had his feet on the other seat. Claude had been staring out of the window for hours. Saying those words had steamed up the glass, and he wiped it with his sleeve.

"I never thought you were in love with me."

"Good. Because if they come for you, I don't want you to expect me to sacrifice myself. Or be disappointed when I don't." I didn't know quite how to respond, so I just nodded. Claude acknowledged my nod through the reflection, but it didn't seem to satisfy him. "I... I have a confession." Jean's breathing pattern suddenly switched. He'd never been asleep, just resting. But now he was paying attention, although Claude didn't seem to notice.

"What's your confession?"

"I told Giovanni you were dead."

"What? Why?"

"He saw me taking your camera and throwing clothes into a suitcase while Hans waited downstairs, and he wanted to know what was going on. So I told him, last night at David's, the SS had dragged you outside and shot you in the street when you tried to get away."

"Oh."

"Anders," Claude turned to face me. "You can never return to Paris, do you understand? Giovanni told the Germans about you."

"He... did?" I tried to be shocked, but I couldn't quite muster the surprise.

"Some time ago."

"Huh." So Eilas was right. He had protected me, or taken my name from whatever list the Germans had kept. Claude handed me a small scrap of paper.

"Keep this safe."

"What is it?"

"An address in Barcelona. An apartment. Dalí owns it, but this man who lives nearby looks after it for him. He has the keys. All you have to do is go to him, say you are a friend of Dalí, and the place is yours."

"Where's Dalí?"

"America. I'm going to get you to Barcelona, do you understand?" I nodded, memorizing the address then slipping the paper into my sock. "There's a route the Republicans came... it's how Jordi and Iker came." Claude said the name with a heft of sadness. I remembered the name from his letters back in '39, the Catalan fighter he'd fallen in love with and watched die, and the brother who comforted him in the loss. "You can take the route back and slip across the border through a covered-up mountain pass. It's a few days walk to Barcelona from there, or less than a day if you can find a bicycle."

Claude turned back to the window as the train began to sputter and slow. But my mind was racing. No return to Paris. I hadn't even considered it. I wasn't ready to say goodbye. Not to Claude, or David, or Cocteau and Marais, and certainly not to Jean. I stared at the pretend sleeping man who'd so suddenly shaken my life once again. He cracked open an eye and looked right at me, then winked, and closed his eyes again.

I went out into the corridor. I had to walk, or do something. I could not just sit and wait to be dumped at the border. The train was slowing anyway, and I wanted to find out why.

"Papers all, papers." I heard a voice announce from the other end of the carriage. My instinct was to hide when I saw the two uniformed and armed Germans peering into the empty cabins. But then they saw me, and their instinct seemed to be to hide as well.

"Sir," one said, approaching me as the other peered into our cabin and the uniformed Marais stepped out of his.

"They all have papers." I told the two soldiers. Marais was taller than them both, and had taken to his role of playing a scary soldier with aplomb. "This is SS business," I added. "If you have a problem you can take it up with my superior, Herr Reydrich."

The name did the job. The two men glanced at each other, then back to me.

"Very well, sir. No problem. Have a good journey."

Chapter 16

MARSEILLE IN THE EVENING was a dream. A foreign land where the war seemed so far off. My uniform had quickly secured us a late-night taxi, and we'd taken a few rooms at a beachfront hotel thanks to a fistful of Reichsmarks which we had more of than we knew what to do with.

The south was an hour behind the north, and there was no curfew, so it wasn't even ten p.m. when we took a stroll along the beach among couples and families enjoying a warm spring evening, untouched by the troubles of Europe for now. I was wearing some of Claude's clothes, hoping to never put on a uniform again.

There weren't even any Germans around. Not that I could see. Some Italian soldiers who were hanging out on the promenade smoking and whistling at women, but that was about all the signs of occupation we could find.

Claude was walking farther ahead on the shore, talking with Marais and Cocteau, and Jean was beside me, carrying both our sandals as the warm waters splashed our ankles.

"I want to come with you," he said, and slipped his fingers around mine. The promenade was more distant, the lights of the cafés and dance halls some way off. But I had never felt less alone. A hand in mine, an arm to protect me from the evening wind. The others went ahead to eat or sleep, but we stayed on the beach, our shoes off and trousers rolled up, letting the soft waters of freedom lick our toes.

I had never been to a beach at night. Never seen the sky painted with so many stars while black waves rustled up against a sandy shore in a primordial eternity. As it had since Romans rested their sandled feet upon this sand. A hundred empires over thousands of years had all risen and fallen while the simple froth of sea rushed in, then out, the lungs of the world breathing in and out.

Between Jean and I there were no words. We had lived those missing years and filled the empty memories with enough excitement over a few short days to last us into the next lifetime. We sat on the sand, almost alone, next to the black waves and sharing the warmth between our bodies. Cocteau was not here to quote Arnold so I suppose it fell to me.

"The ebb and flow of human misery…The sea of faith." The words were smothered by the waves. "I can't believe you found me again." The lights of the enemy boats drifted around at sea. The war was just there across the Mediterranean, but all I felt was peace.

"Why? You were right where I left you."

"I suppose so."

"Do your people believe in souls?" Jean asked. I had to think for a moment what he meant.

"I… don't really know."

"My father's people do." Jean leaned over, his elbow buried in the sand and touched the bottom of my lip. Through the darkness I could only make out his eyes, staring deep into mine. Was this a soul?

"There used to be two moons in the sky," he said, looking upwards as the length of his body laying against the length of mine. "But then the Great Mother had her heart broken, and she shattered the second moon. Millions of pieces rained down from the heavens as her tears filled the seas and rivers. Those pieces of shattered moon brought to life people to walk the earth. Inside each of us," Jean laid his hand upon my chest, feeling my heart race, "is a tiny piece of that broken moon. We're drawn to those whose pieces fit together with ours. And by coming together, we bring a little bit more wholeness to the world. One day, when every piece of moon has been reunited, the second moon will rise again in the sky, and the Great Mother will smile on us again."

248

We stayed on the beach while the soft, foamy sea washed our feet clean from the million steps we'd taken apart. His strong body, my shield, rolled onto mine as we kissed beneath the light of a second moon that shone down on only us.

*   *   *

Barcelona seemed an age and a world away. The border an impossible horizon to reach. I wondered if Francoist Spain would merely be another trap. A false aura of security like the Roosevelt Mansion. The stop off we'd decided to take in Perpignan felt like hosting a party while Eilas and Reydrich decomposed in the hall cupboard. But there was no other way. I'd studied the map of southern France in the hotel lobby, counting the distance with my fingers. Three hundred and fifty kilometers from Marseille to the Spanish border was a long way to travel, unseen, by foot. But if we ever made it west to Mélenchon's house in Perpignan, freedom was a mere day's stroll away.

The hotel manager was so happy we'd come to stay and paid in far more hard cash than was necessary, that he and his son offered to drive us all the way to Perpignan the next morning. As the brilliant blue coast ebbed towards purple mountains, I started to fill the void in my heart with something akin to hope. This time, I dressed in Eilas' uniform without complaint. That death half a continent away.

I had a place to go, a man to love, and a plan to get there. I hadn't told the others about it, but I figured we would have time. Although the reason for our trip was escape, it didn't mean we couldn't actually enjoy some time away with Mélenchon, and Jean and I could say our goodbyes—in our own time—to this crazy little family.

By evening, we arrived at Mélenchon's place just outside Perpignan. Place didn't cover it. He lived in a chateau. High stone walls, an iron gate, and a gravel stone driveway that led to the kind of palatial residence that would put an English country gent to shame.

Mélenchon stood on the stone steps as our cars pulled up, every bit the greasy little man I remembered from before. David and Hella rushed out to greet him like a long-lost brother, while Claude and I untied the suitcases which had been secured on the roof with rope.

"I'm so glad you made it," I heard Mélenchon say with an air of worry. I almost scoffed. It hadn't been hard.

"Why not?" David said, slapping the doctor on the arm. "You underestimate our abilities. We weren't stuck in Paris; we could have left any time! It's just more fun up there, you know."

"The city's been locked down." Mélenchon said with the bitter smile I remembered.

Claude threw the rope over the hoteliers' car to me, but I let it drop onto the gravel when I heard Mélenchon say that.

"Oh my goodness. What happened?" Hella said, a bit too dramatically, but it's not like we had to hide ourselves from Mélenchon. Even as that thought passed through my mind, I forced myself to stamp it out. I was no longer solely among friends. Although, I never really had been. If it wasn't for Eilas, Giovanni would have got me out of the picture long ago. I wondered, from this group, if any would have stuck their necks out for me. I could imagine David leaning against the doorway when the Gestapo came knocking, shaking his long head, puffing on his pipe and saying: *Never heard of the fellow.* Claude? I almost laughed. A toss up at best. I figured Cocteau would be my best bet. It was hardly heartening to trust one's life to an artist. And a famous one, at that. Amazing how war hits the psyche.

"Two SS men have gone missing in Paris," Mélenchon said, the worry taking over his own voice. His eyes wandered across my black and silver uniform, and Marais'. "The Germans are taking hostages all across the country. And not just in the occupied zone, either. The Vichy police are under the same orders, too. Every town, every village even. Thousands of them. It's all over the radio."

"How do they know?" I heard Cocteau ask.

"It's the Germans broadcasting it. They say they've taken thousands of prisoners already, and they'll shoot ten at random, every hour on the hour, from midnight tonight, until the missing SS men are found."

"What do they think?" Marais said it like a line from a movie, and he was the villain, "the Resistance have taken them as hostages?"

"Quite likely," Mélenchon said. "But it's a dark night across France. I can only hope whoever took those men will be smart enough to let them go unharmed, before the massacres start." The words fell long across our group, the two stolen uniforms that had allowed us here like red flares shot into the sky. Only to rain down and cause untold death to thousands.

From the other side of the car, Claude stared at me, and I back at him. Jean was kicking around gravel, smoking anxiously, having heard it all.

Mélenchon clasped his hands together and painted a strained smile across his face, "But come, come in all of you. I've got dinner."

We took the cases from the car to let the drivers head back to Marseille, then went inside into the ornate hallway as the others spoke quietly with Mélenchon over drinks. Jean stayed outside as dusk gathered to darkness. And the darkness out here was all-encompassing. They had tried, in Paris, to darken the city of lights. But like the soul of the city itself, it could not entirely be darkened. There was always some streetlamp which stayed alight, one house that never closed its windows, one German car speeding through the city. One was never in complete darkness, unlike out here. There was not even a star in the sky. Clouds had gathered above us out of nowhere, and they threatened thunder.

I could barely see the steps to get into the house, let alone where Jean had got to. But he struck another match down by the gate we'd arrived from.

"Aren't you coming?" I called out to him. He waved me away and sucked on his cigarette.

"I'll come in a bit," he said, crunching gravel and smoking through the darkness. I knew all I had to expiate, and considered how much more Jean had, so I left him awhile with his confessional cigarette.

"Funny," Claude said to me as we went inside. "Dalí always banged on about this place being the center of the world." Claude took a last look outside, like he was in mourning for the sun which could never break through this wall of darkness again. "Feels like the end of the world."

*　*　*

The villa must have had a dozen rooms, but Mélenchon gathered us in a wood-paneled private dining room barely bigger than the study at the Roosevelt Mansion. The table was almost too big for the room, so our chairs were pushed up against the wall, meaning someone would have to get up and leave the room to let another one out. It was as if the room was made for mutual destruction, for those who did not trust each other to dine collectively, assured that no one could slip out unnoticed. I'd taken pictures of us all as we entered, somewhat deliberately, a form of mutual guarantee that we had all dined together on the night of Eilas and Reydrich's death.

Claude, Cocteau, and I were at the back facing the door which faded into the paneling of the wall, with David and Hella on the left, and Marais then Mélenchon on the right. The camera obscenely taking up space on the cramped table. The empty seat by the door saved for Jean. Unless he too was out to betray us all.

Thunder landed outside, and when the door was open for Mélenchon and Hella to bring the food in, a hefty rain struck the windows loud and clear. The food was plentiful, and better than any of us had eaten since the fall of Paris. Despite a crowded table of meat, cheese, bread, roast chicken and wine, our mood was edged.

Claude had been describing the route I would take to Barcelona through code, talking in great details about the route his lost Catalan love Jordi had taken. As if our escape was still some great secret we had to keep from someone. Mélenchon, I assumed, but the faces surrounding me no longer held any familiarity. I understood, finally, the feeling my mother tried to soothe by sending me away.

"Every time Jordi and Iker came to a break in the beach, they would need to go inland for a few hundred meters to cross the stream." Claude practically painted the route on his plate with breadcrumbs and olive oil. We were so engrossed in our conversation I hadn't picked up on the growing row between Cocteau and Mélenchon. "It's a mistake to cross them by the shore. The road though is far, and they didn't need to worry—"

"But surrealism is a profound rejection of logic for the sake of itself," Cocteau said, pointing at Mélenchon angrily with a chicken bone. "Hitlerism is no different. It rejects the logic that we don't murder people for no reason. We don't wage war because we can. We don't condemn millions to death and plunge the earth into the fiery pits of hell because we're angry at the state."

"Look, what's the difference between Hitler and Napoleon?" Cocteau continued. "Both men seized advantage of a nation spinning into chaos. But Napoleon wasn't living in an age of fucking Dalí and Emmanuel and Duchamp and the rest with their rejection of what it means to be a human. They reject humanity, they reject art, which, in turn, makes it so much easier for Hitler to reject humanity. When there is no objective truth, objective beauty, objective art, then the objective value of a human life is also up for debate."

Mélenchon sat back in his chair with a cynical smirk.

"That's quite a leap, don't you think? To suggest our artistic friends, my friends, your friends, are what... the shock troops for Blitzkrieg? Do you honestly think they have that much influence?"

"They might not individually, but art is the whole game. The power of art is terrifying. Why else is Herr Goebbels number two in the Reich?"

Neither David nor Hella seemed to be buying Cocteau's point. Even Marais looked skeptical.

"I understand we live in a surrealist age," David said, trying to calm the tempers, "but dadaism... it's one of the most respected, renowned artistic movements since... I don't know." He looked at Hella for support.

"Expressionism, probably," she said.

Cocteau scoffed, and knocked back wine like we were at a half-price absinthe hour.

"Imagine, if you will, a radio station run by surrealists. Nameless ones, it doesn't matter. But confirmed followers of Dada nonetheless."

Mélenchon was not keen. "Why a radio station?"

"Why not?" Cocteau continued. "Dadaism influenced poetry, art, sculpture, literature, theatre. Why not modern mediums too?" Mélenchon rolled his eyes, but Cocteau continued.

"This radio station spews nothing but distortion and lies, simply for the sake of it. For the *art*, as some might say. Or the anti-art. These are not necessarily huge lies, but obvious ones. The sky is red. The King of England is a vole in a trench coat, FDR's wheelchair is oiled with the blood of German children, that sort of thing. The avant-garde understand this radio station is serving an artistic purpose; it is for entertainment, as distasteful and baffling as this entertainment may be.

"But this art form is not confined to a gallery, only to be seen by those who understand the rules which are being broken. Oh no, this bizarre nonsense is being broadcast on the radio waves twenty-four hours a day, for anyone and everyone to hear. That, my good doctor, is why I am referring to a radio station. Because the masses, who, through no fault of their own, are utterly unfamiliar with the ways of surrealism, or even the existence of such a thing hear these broadcasts. Endless speeches. Prima face lies spewed as truth. The twisting of facts into mere opinions. Questioning reality, the value of objective truth. Spouting narratives, an endless, twisting narrative, conspiracy theories they want turned into national policy, all of it repeated ad nauseum across the airwaves. You hear what Ezra's doing; you're not sickened?"

"And what?" Mélenchon cut in. "The people will think it's truth?"

"Perhaps not at first. But as time goes on, there would be some. Contrarians, comedians, witless men who feel left out of the joke, who rally to these falsehoods, and just as the surrealists propagate surrealism for the sake of it, so the listeners of this radio programming repeat the falsehoods they hear as facts, purely for the sake of it.

"What is fact? A fact is something objectively true. Quantifiable and proven. Now imagine you had never heard this surrealist art played on the radio before. You would tune in as you switched between the weather and jazz, and then come across this broadcast of lies. You ask your friend in the butcher's shop has he heard of this perplexing station playing these outlandish claims, and your friend says to you, with the utmost seriousness, 'why, it is the truth.'

"And this disease spreads. In a matter of months, the Spanish Influenza crossed oceans and seas, and so do rumors and lies. Thus, fiction becomes fact. The very nature of objectivity is up for discussion. People start to feel fulfilled by a surrealist narrative that shows them their own personalized truth they believe should be above interrogation."

"Like Jews have horns," David added quietly.

"Do you see horns?" Cocteau demanded of Mélenchon.

"Well… no, but—"

"But you looked to check!" He said, full of excitement. "You've heard it so many times now, that you think 'well I must see for myself, maybe he cut the horns off.'"

"That's the distortion surrealism perpetrates on reality. Truth and objective beauty turned inside out. And they congratulate themselves for it. Did they really believe this would cause no consequence on the world? Can I stand atop the Eiffel Tower and throw pennies for fun, then shrug my shoulders if people are injured down below?"

"What are you suggesting?" Mélenchon shot back, "artists should stick to watercolors and lilies? Art must have walls and boundaries in case someone takes a painting the wrong way?"

"Not at all," said Cocteau. "But art either reflects the world as it was, as it is, or as it could be. The only responsibility an artist has is to finish his work. Is he creating a hellscape where nothing makes sense? If so, finish the thought. What is this hellscape he has painted? Does he believe this is the world as it is, or some aspect of it or himself he is attempting to highlight? Or does he want the world to be this way. Does he want death and destruction to rain down upon humanity, burn everything we have created in order for us to start again. If so, say it. And let others who disagree respond with art that shows the beauty in the world worth saving. Will you, Mr. Artist, sweep away the righteous with the wicked? What if the number of righteous should lack five? Do you understand what I mean? If you create something, anything, then for God's sake tell us why. Tell us what you think it means. At the very least to you. Because if you don't, then someone else will."

We all looked upon Cocteau as he gulped down wine. I did not know if Mélenchon was convinced. He seemed a hard character to persuade of anything, but I could only apply Cocteau's theory to my own life. What had I created, what impact had it had on the world? Semi-nude portraits of Jean which had led to movie reels of him stripping and simulating sex, which led to hidden cameras and blackmail, and pictures of young men having sex, some of whom had died, and now two dead Nazis and a thousand innocent hostages preparing to die. How could I explain any of that?

But it wasn't the case. The 'art' we had created was secret, subservient to a nefarious purpose. Art to embarrass, art to destroy. No wonder no good could come of it. I slunk lower in my seat, trying to avoid Cocteau's gaze in case he accused me of inflicting a new artistic medium on the world which was nothing but homoeroticism writ large, come to tear apart the very fabric of the world, given the wild, sprouting branches of his logic.

"Why did Anders come to Paris?" I jumped at the sudden twist of attention to me. "I'll tell you why," Cocteau continued, "because it used to be the most open and vibrant and exciting and free city on earth. There he could be himself, could find love, could become who he wanted. But he never told anyone that. So how do we know? And how do we know that is something worth saving? Do we want a world where any young person can wake up, travel to the place their soul takes them and become the person they always want to be? If so, we must defend the places we find it, and fight those who seek to destroy it. Because those places will not defend themselves. Why, my friends. Always ask why. Why this art? Why this place? Why this man or this woman, or why does this piece of music or line of poetry stir your soul? And don't stop asking until the answer is true. Why is the most powerful word in the world. Why will reveal the truth of all things."

Then there it was. A knock at our dining room door.

I assumed it was Jean.

It was not Jean. It was a tall Gestapo man in a wet trench coat and a soaked hat, flanked by two mustachioed Vichy police officers. And the Gestapo man was staring directly at me.

"*Guten abend,* Eilas Bahr."

*   *   *

The Gestapo man took his time to come inside the narrow, cloistered room. He took off his soaking coat in the hallway, and, uninvited, swung it over the back of the empty chair at our cramped and crowded table. The two Vichy police officers stood over his shoulder just outside the dining room, peering in, like two immovable bishops on a chessboard. And we had been check-mated.

"May I help you?" Mélenchon asked in English. The clear-faced German was a thin man. Wiry, spindly, like a tree which had been struck by lightning. But he wore the confidence of an omnipotent being, for that's what he was. The power was with this one man.

"I am investigating the disappearance, two days ago, of *Untersturmführer* Bahr and *Gruppenführer* Reydrich. My enquiries have led me here, and to this man," the Gestapo officer pointed at me, and they all looked. "Eilas Bahr." I adjusted my tightly knotted black SS necktie. I was sitting in Eilas's uniform. Markings and all. He could check the size of the trousers if he wanted. What if I played along? Pretended that I was truly him. What would they do to a deserting officer? A few years in a labor camp?

Nobody said a word. They didn't come to my defense, nor rat me out, either. I didn't dare glance at another soul. I stared straight ahead, slightly beyond the Gestapo man, with an expression of utterly unbothered neutrality on my face. I had never in my life been inside a casino, let alone gambled on a deck of cards, but I imagined this was pretty similar, except instead of money, my life, and the lives of all my friends, was in the ante.

Nobody knows what they will do in these situations until they happen. I never knew I would run across the street in Paris to intervene when the Nazis tried to take away the family of Jews. I never knew I would see Jean again, and perhaps I wouldn't have if I hadn't done that, or left the true Eilas alone in the café. Perhaps none of these things would have occurred with a difference of five minutes here or there, but here we were.

"And who do you claim to be, sir?" I asked in German, straightening the jacket that still commanded the respect of an officer in the SS. If the Gestapo man was surprised, he didn't show it.

"*Kriminaldirektor* Menzner."

"Well, *Kriminaldirektor,* what can I do to help you?"

Menzner sat back in his chair, Mélenchon's chair, and poured himself a glass of wine. None of us moved, but the Vichy officers looked uninterested in the theatrics, or perhaps they were just bored of the story that was about to come and wanted to hurry up to the end where they shot us all.

"I'm not normally here in France," he told me, still in German. "So I don't really speak French. I'm based in Vienna. Have you been to Vienna?"

I shrugged. "Maybe."

"Your accent is certainly Austrian. Well, anyway, six weeks or so ago, I was in Vienna, working as normal," he took a sip of the wine, crossed his legs and stretched out like one might at the end of a very long day, or very long search. "I was overseeing the arrest of a Jewess and her mother from quite an expensive apartment in the city center. It turns out this Jewess was something of a politician in her day, and her mother was practically an aristocrat. Anyway, after they departed for Theresienstadt, I had a look around their apartment. A nice place. Expensive, you know. Full of knick-knacks. Very Jewish. A lot of photographs. A lot. Some of the husband that had been killed in the Great War, some of the mother's family, and quite a few of a young man, clearly this woman's son, who looked quite a lot like you, actually."

Menzner swirled the merlot around in the glass to investigate its legs.

"Good vintage," he said to Mélenchon in English, waiting for me to say something. The rest of us had to sit and listen to this strange crossing of ending paths, translating in their heads if they could, I said nothing, and so he continued. "It was strange to see so many pictures of a young man in this house, when the records made no mention of a son. No birth certificate, no death certificate, no school records, nothing at all to suggest we should have arrested anyone else but this woman and her mother.

"You can imagine, Herr Bahr, how odd it was for me, a perfectionist in my job, to discover that perhaps an oversight had been made. Some clerical error, a problem in our records, or the Austrian census, who could say. But I do enjoy I good mystery. Particularly one with such high stakes. After all, who wants to spend all day shooting fish in a barrel? These days we have plenty of men for that job. But this case confounded me. I couldn't sleep, Eilas. Not for days thinking about this possible missing Jew. I was obsessed. Where had he gone? What had become of the sweet, cherub-cheeked boy whose pictures covered the house, yet no trace of whom existed?

"I returned to the house and decided to conduct a more thorough investigation. And under the mattress of this woman's bed, I found a stack of letters. Dozens of them, actually. All from this one address in Paris. Paris, can you believe it? Of all places. What was this woman with the missing son doing with a stack of letters from Paris? And they were all signed 'your loving son, Anders.'

The Vichy officers crept inside the room and stood on either side of Menzner. Their heavy presence sucked up more oxygen than the rest of us combined. Marais breathed heavily on my right, something shiny resting in his lap. Claude kept his hands still and in sight on my left. Cocteau was as unfazed as ever. Only Mélenchon as the head of the house openly showed his nerves.

"Aha, I thought to myself. So this mystery boy has a name, and I have an address. Before the war I found missing persons. That was my profession. Heirs to fortunes, renegades from the law. I'm exceptionally good at it. And my superiors, naturally, agreed that it was worth heading to Paris to see for myself. After all, Vienna is nearly Jew-free, these days. The only ones remaining were lucky enough to have abandoned their race and married non-Jews. But their time will come. As will Anders's. We can't let a criminal roam the continent. Well, what do you know. At this address in... where is it... Montmartre, I believe it's called, I found the oddest little man there called Giovanni."

Claude sucked in a sharp breath. I didn't need to look at the others to know they very well recognized one name in this story they were struggling to follow.

"Do you know what Giovanni said to me when I asked him about this Austrian fellow Anders? He said 'what took you so long? I told you people months ago about him.' Giovanni was exceedingly helpful. He informed me this Anders did in fact live upstairs from his bar, but spent an awful lot of time across the river at the home of a couple, David and Hella Roosevelt.

"Now who in Paris hadn't heard of the legendary parties at the Roosevelt Mansion? How interesting a strategy for this Anders to adopt, hiding in plain sight in a place catering to the most senior officers in the Reich. I thought I should alert the SS about my investigation, and that's when I spoke to... well, you, apparently.

"You, Eilas, you told me yourself there was an SS operation taking place in the Roosevelt Mansion, and Reydrich had given explicit orders for no one to interfere. This person called Anders, you told me, was under SS jurisdiction and I should leave him well alone. You had some rather choice words for me about what you might do and have done to me if I disobeyed, and I thought, 'now there's a man dedicated to his work.' I can respect that. So I let it be. I let this Anders go for the time being.

"So it was quite a shock when I heard a few days ago that both Reydrich and Eilas Bahr had gone missing, and both had last been seen at the

Roosevelt Mansion where this Anders, the Jewish double-agent, spent his days. Fortunately, I wasn't far away when I heard the news—in Belgium actually—and I drove straight to Paris and to my good friend Giovanni. Well, he told me Anders was dead. And after a bit of investigating, I discovered that a phone call had been placed from the Roosevelt Mansion the morning after a social event at the Roosevelt Mansion, commandeering a train bound for Lyon all the way to Marseille, for seven people, under the name of Eilas Bahr. These things all get recorded somewhere, you see. Seldom checked, but always recorded."

"The guards at the station remembered this group. Of course they did. Two SS officers with a collection of rather odd-looking individuals. The final destination on the manifest was listed as Perpignan. This address, in fact. And all had permission to travel. So, here you are. All seven of you have fled Paris, and I want to know why."

Did he say seven? I counted out of the corner of my eye. Minus Jean, we were seven. Jean wandering around outside smoking—another escape for him. One thread in a knot of tension snapped. At least Jean had made it out; he was safe.

"So perhaps you might enlighten me, then." Menzner continued. "Because the Gestapo believes one of two things. Either you are Eilas Bahr, and have fled Paris after the death, somehow, of Herr Reydich. Or, you are Anders, a Jew from Vienna, who has assumed the identity of Eilas Bahr after presumably killing the real Eilas and Herr Reydrich."

"Does it make a difference?"

"To the manner of your death?" Menzner answered in English for all of us to understand. "Not particularly. To the manner of theirs? Perhaps. If they can shed some light on what transpired."

It was a little strange, having all the attention on me. I'd never considered myself a lynchpin, of this or any other group. David a lynchpin, Cocteau a lynchpin, even Claude in some circles, but me no. Your life flashes before your eyes when you die. No one ever said it to me, but I heard it is something people say. Sitting across from Menzner, with his wine and his power and his two Vichy policemen standing guard, all the moments of my life when I felt the outsider came back to me.

Yet here I was, the center of the world, as it so happened. Our lives hanging in the balance. Still, no one said a word. Food remained uneaten and wine undrunk. The Gestapo man looked ready to bring the discussion to a head, until Claude cut him off.

He didn't address Menzner, but the two Vichy policemen standing behind. And he didn't speak in French, nor English nor Spanish, nor any other language I could immediately recognize. I never knew at the time what Claude said to those two officers. Only many years later did I find out what he said to them, in Catalan, the common second tongue of French and Spanish Catalonia, where we now sat.

"There's ten thousand German marks in a brown leather suitcase in the hallway, the one marked Claude. Leave now and you can take it. Take the suitcase if you want; I don't care. If we survive until morning, there's another ten thousand marks waiting for you here."

Menzner waited for someone to translate, but no one did. The two Vichy men listened. "And I know every whore in Paris. Come and find me on the Rue Duperré and I'll bring you the best women in town, without end. These Germans will be gone one day, but Paris, and whores, are forever."

Now Menzner was getting angry. He turned to look at the policemen, to get some insight into what was going on. I held my breath—we all did— wondering what Claude had said to them with such certainty, and if they had even understood. But the officers swapped a glance at each other, and then the rest of us. We were a disparate group, unlike in age or appearance, but now, as I looked around us and imagined what another must have seen, there was a power to our group, an energy I had not known, and it whispered survival.

The two Vichy men were uneasy, staring at each other over Menzner's head. Then at us again, then Menzner.

"*Quel est le problème?*" he asked. They whispered a few indistinguishable words, one to the other, and then the words were quickly returned. Menzner looked up at them both from his seat by the door, annoyed at their insolence and the whiff of insubordination. The Vichy men did not look back at their master, but at Claude, who remained steadfast in his gaze and what he'd promised, of which we all wondered.

"We, uh, must... to go now," one of the policemen said to Menzner. Proving the bonds of Catalan brotherhood transcended whatever borders or nations or dictators tried to contain them. Without waiting for an order or counteroffer, one of the men maneuvered through the wood-paneled door and squeezed out of the small space. The other shifted behind Menzner's chair and hurried out as well, slamming the exit closed. Suddenly the room was lighter, airier without the presence of two great hulking French Catalans. It was only us. Seven of us around a dinner table, the narrow walls at our backs, against just one German, sitting alone, clutching a half-drunk glass of wine, his back to the door.

The Gestapo man was a pro. He showed no sign of concern, at least not outwardly. In fact, he swirled the wine in the glass, not taking a drink but not giving it up either. I wondered if the next words out his mouth might not be to ask if there was a plate for him. Then in a move much sharper and more elegant than Reydrich had managed, Menzner pulled a gun from his belt and held it above the table. In the same instant, Claude snatched a bread knife, Hella a corkscrew, Cocteau the bottom of a wine bottle, and David a fork. Marais lifted his own gun above the threshold of the table. It had been sitting in his lap the entire time.

"Eilas, Anders, whoever you really are, why not tell me what happened to Reydrich? We can make a deal." His gun remained poised, as did our own weapons. Only I lacked a proper implement to defend myself. "There's no need for anyone to die today." He understood this position was nowhere near strong enough to finish the game in a few quick moves. Nevertheless, that inbuilt sense of German superiority would not let him resign. A draw was on offer. To cut his losses, come back and finish me off some other time, in some other place.

Menzner gripped the handle of his gun tighter. He could shoot me, yes, but that would be the end of his story. All this glory for catching the runaway Jew would be meaningless if he were dead to spend it.

I wondered how we might get out of this impasse. Whatever I told this man, he would return with a hundred more Germans the moment he walked out of here, no matter his promises. But I figured the odds were looking increasingly poor for him.

"How funny," I said in German, not bothering to disguise my Viennese accent in the slightest, "that you frequented Giovanni's bar. Claude, do you remember this man?" I said it slowly, so Claude could follow with his rudimentary understanding of the language. I wanted Menzner to hear every word too. "Do you remember this man sniffing around for a boy to fuck? Taking a number and waiting in line, perhaps?"

"Do I?" Claude asked himself, pointing the bread knife straight at the German, lips pressed thinly together. "I don't think so. I only remember the faces of men with big cocks." Menzner's eyes widened, and a gap appeared in his mouth. I filled the silence, though.

"I suppose you were never important enough to get invited to the Roosevelt Mansion, Herr *Kriminaldirektor*. If you were, I might remember your face. In fact, I'd likely have a record of it. On film. In a photograph. Alongside your perversions. The ones you only ask whores to inflict." Menzner gripped his gun tighter, face leaving behind the calmness of before, bringing anger to the table while I reveled in the obscene joy of the reversal. "Did you know the German ambassador to Paris likes his bottom spanked? Or that the Landgrave of Hesse, Prince Philipp, can take a man, a Black man, I'll add, thirty centimeters deep? I know. Because I filmed it all. Hundreds of hours of footage, captured and stored for safe keeping."

A nervous twitch afflicted Menzner's left eye. I could see he wanted to run. The room was cramped with the guests hanging onto to the words, translating what they could in their mind. If he wanted to move, he'd have to shoot first. And only get one of us, before a bottle was smashed over his head, corkscrew jammed into his throat, and on and on.

"*Es ist richtig,*" Cocteau joined in, then added in English: "The boy is right: you are not important enough to warrant your own homoerotic movie. *Kriminaldirektor.* But we can change that, what do you say? Shall we take a few snapshots of your perversions now?" Cocteau nodded to my camera perched on the table. "But why limit yourself to just one of us? Perhaps a group romp would be more to your fashion?"

"Oh goodie!" David clapped his hands together. "I haven't been to a good orgy since... well, not since Herman Goering was last in town."

"*Stille!*" Menzner shrieked, the gun waving so wildly he might fail to hit any of us. "Enough from you all." The mechanism rattled inside the weapon. We cocked our own weapons, bottles and corkscrews and silverware, as if a single floating feather might fall and crush us all. One shot, that's what I kept my mind on. The sweating German could get one bullet into one of us before he was clubbed to death. He had to have known it.

The gun settled on David. His thin blond eyebrows raised no more than if a guest had vomited into a potted Ficus. Mélenchon and Cocteau edged closer to the Gestapo man, but Menzner had his target. It wasn't a silence that held us, but raging tension, until Hella, of all people spoke, as if waking us from a tortured dream.

"I wouldn't be so quick to pass on my husband's offer. He's rather talented, so the boys tell me." False lashes flicked in the direction of Claude and I, turning us both a shade of uncomfortable pink. No more than Menzner, though. Every word he heard left him more disgusted. Hella spoke with Athenian serenity, addressing Menzner like a lady who lunched. "This war has changed us all. I never imagined I could serve Gin Rickey's without any limes, but needs must. I'm sure you can appreciate we've all had to do things we'd rather not discuss in polite company, Herr *Kriminaldirektor*. Perhaps we should let sleeping dogs lie, hmm? No need for such a fuss."

Her face remained flawless. The gun remained on David, as Marais' weapon remained on the German, but the whitened anger had faded from Menzner's eyes. He turned back to cold and calculating, weighing up the offer of a truce. I gulped down nervous balls bubbling up my windpipe. Menzner slinking away might save us for now. During the hours it would take for him to return to a reliable station, we'd have to all be on our way fleeing south. But I feared the Parisians among us would rather martyr themselves than live life on the run, and I feared I had become Parisian enough to agree. The best outcome was a dead Menzner, but the matter of sacrificing one to save the many still hung there.

"Give me the Jew, and the rest of you can leave."

"Well I'm the Jew," David said immediately.

"Perhaps he has a thing for us Jews," I said, dropping a weight into the room. The gun swung to me. Hella shuddered a desperate breath, as if her own child was now in the crosshairs. I raised my empty hands above my head. Menzner gripped the gun tighter; the others were half raised from their seats, ready for whatever might come. "I have something to show you, that's all." Slowly, I rose from my chair, hands in the air. Menzner rose at the same speed, as did each of the others in a quick screech of moving chairs and re-gripped weapons. "I'm only reaching for my billfold." With one arm still in the air, I kept my hand firmly visible as I carefully slipped my thin wallet from my pocket with two fingers.

"You didn't need to go hunting around Europe," I said, slipping a much-creased paper from the leather. "You could have come to Paris and just asked to see my art. I would have gladly made you a copy." I unfolded the picture, looking at it first myself. I hadn't looked since I'd learned the news, so I took a moment, inside the well of chaos. Just one moment, when the room's attention was drawn not to me or to Menzner nor any of our weapons, but the contents of the photograph in my hand. I held out the picture, still turned towards me, reaching across the table, nodding for Menzner to take it.

The opportunity was obvious. Now on his feet, Cocteau barely a hair's breadth away, wine bottle raised. David drew the fork comically closer Menzner's eye. Marais had his gun aimed straight at the German's head. His long arms making it practically a point-blank shot.

"Go on," I said, waving the paper. "It's a photograph I took. I'm an artist, you see." Menzner took the picture and stared at my family. I wondered if he remembered these women he murdered. He considered the photograph, and I considered him. He seemed—for the better part of one second—affected.

The others watched. I was ready to say it. *Take me.* An age of seconds. The scene stirred me. The murderer confronted by the black and white ghosts of his victims.

"Your family…" Menzner said, still looking at the picture. But I didn't hear the rest. I reached for my camera on the table, savoring the touch of black leather and cold chrome like buttons on another man's uniform. The world twisted again, like it had been doing more and more.

The camera's mechanical trigger startled Menzner. His gun rose in sudden defense. The feather landed, and the house collapsed. Before Menzner could look at me, or decide who to shoot, Cocteau's wine bottle smashed across his head. Mélenchon jumped back and yelped as blood and red wine spurted across the table, spattering the butter dish and pate rinds. The German wobbled for a brief second, stunned, perhaps wondering why we were all splashed in red. No one dared do more. The scene a fresco frieze. All of us perched, waiting, holding aloft our last lines of defense. Marais a gun, Claude a knife, Hella a corkscrew, David a fork, Cocteau a broken bottle and me a camera. Maybe I could throw it at his head. Finally, Menzner stopped wobbling. The color drained from his cheeks, and he fell face first onto the table.

I could not breathe at the thought of another dead Nazi. But we did not leap away. The clattering of dishes and cutlery rung through our ears while Cocteau—broken bottle still in hand—attempted to unhook the gun from Menzner's fingers. But the fingers still gripped back. The man was not dead. Relief rushed up my spine as a garbled, growling groan proved the point. Perhaps some semblance of a deal could still be reached. Hella could make it all better. Get this truce back up and running.

She scuppered the thought. Menzner tried to stand while she lunged forward, driving the corkscrew under the Gestapo man's collar with a rage I'd never before seen from her. She pulled the spiraled metal out, doused in red, then jammed it back in again, and again, and again. Taking her lead, Cocteau thrust his jagged bottle into the man's soft underbelly, returning with a hand soaked in blood. He too kept going. David came forward, drove the fork he'd held half an inch into Menzner's back. It stayed up with a twang, then he snatched Claude's bread knife and drove that deeper into the lifeless dud. Out and in again, stabbing through the brown Gestapo coat flooding with burgundy.

Endless years of our misery pounded into the corpse. Pent up fury and tragedy seeping out as fast-congealing blood from the flayed body. Finally the bloody butchers stepped back, at last fallowed by their red-handed work.

Marais rushed around the table, jabbing the dead face with the point of his gun, checking whether to waste a bullet. No need. Even Mélenchon did his part, prying the German's gun from his loose fingers. Only Claude stood back, hands covering his open mouth, then staring at me. I stood dumb with a camera, only partially aware I was taking shots. I clicked and suddenly found there was no film left.

"He's already dead," Mélenchon said, *tsk-tsk*ing at the sight of blood drenched wood-paneled walls.

"Thank you doctor for the diagnosis," David said. The others were strangely calm. Wiping blood with chicken-stained handkerchiefs. Only Claude shook.

"What have you done?" He tried to scream, but his voice was broken. Words were being spoken. Bloody napkins were peeled from Menzner's face. I watched it all through a camera lens, a terrible ballet in costumes of death. I was the only one to see the door handle move. It swung open, or tried to, hard and heavy. Pushed by one who didn't know another person was on the other side. The door smacked straight into the dead Menzner's backside. His body slid more into the table, the dead hand still holding the bloody photograph of my mother and grandmother.

"Any food left?" Jean asked, squeezing through the door. He saw me, he saw the body, and he nodded. I willed him to go. To run and to flee from this. To save himself and leave us to our fate. He could have never been here. The others barely registered his presence.

"Go," I said as a whisper.

"Jean!" David said, dropping Menzner's bloody arm back onto the table where it smacked on a plate. Jean edged inside the room.

"Go!" I yelled. But no one was listening. Mélenchon and Hella were stripping the blood-stained clothes from his body. Cocteau and Marais were shoving the table back to give more space to maneuver. Claude stood against the wall, dipping the only unstained corner of a white cloth into a half-drunk drink and dabbing spatters of blood from his clothes. Jean stared at me through the chaos with a look I couldn't comprehend. With something close to pride.

"There's a magnum of Rémy Martin Louis XIII in the cellar," Mélenchon said to Jean as he struggled with Menzner's cuff links. "You can drink it straight from the bottle if you help us."

"Don't waste it on him," Claude called from the corner. "He'll do it for a bourbon."

*   *   *

"Dig!" Jean yelled at me through driving rain. He'd dug his side of the hole three feet deep. Menzner was already stripped to the waist, his filthy soaked clothes left on the trimmed hedge, ready to be burned with the rest of the evidence. I'd managed enough space for perhaps the man's head. The ground was soft and wet, easy digging though I made long work of it. The rain barreled down as every clap of thunder frightened us. The only thing I was glad for was that it covered our aching yells. Claude kicked mud away, cursing us for his ruined clothes. David, Cocteau and Marais struggled with carrying the body through the rose garden.

"Lift his arms," Marais yelled through the driving rain.

"It's going to come off," David said. "Cocteau severed his damn tendons."

Hella and Mélenchon were still inside scrubbing the room and sweeping everything into sacks to be destroyed. But we were running out of homes to murder in and flee from.

"Get him in the hole!" Jean yelled. "Anders, for fuck's sake dig faster. It's filling with water."

Time completely washed out and abandoned us out here. This surrealist haze we'd all been locked up in was being rapidly undone with every thwack of the shovel into the soft mud. This was not the Center of the World, as Dalí had said, but the Center of Worlds. With realistic pain and consequences. If someone murders your family, the ancient duty of vengeance falls down upon you.

"That's enough," Jean said after we were all soaked to the core. The hole was not large, but it would fit a man if his legs were pulled up. The body was crammed in, but one leg would not bend to go inside. It stuck out, a flag in the soaking field. "Give me that." Jean snatched the shovel.

Torrential rain continued to lash us all. We watched like a solemn funeral procession as Jean remained alone, grave-digging to perfection. He finally fit all of Menzner down in the hole. Now tapping down soil, stamping out ruffles in the earth. The whites of his eyes shone through the storm. I looked at nothing else. Staid and silent, saying nothing, feeling nothing but that we were at the end of the world, another dead Nazi at our feet. Now it was time to run.

Why in Paris?

* * *

In the hallway, Claude had quietly prepared three satchels for himself, Jean, and me so we could flee as soon as we were dry and dressed.

"They shouldn't go anywhere tonight," Jean said to Mélenchon as he laced up his cleaned boots. Mélenchon stood in a silk dressing gown and slippers, rolling the cognac around a glass. "Stay here, keep the house locked and the lights off. The grave is well covered over, but check it again first thing after the rains."

"It's long past midnight," Mélenchon said, looking at the clock. You shouldn't go anywhere at this hour." David, Hella, Cocteau and Marais were in the lounge, talking in low voices and clinking glass from the cognac we'd shared while washing death and mud from our bodies. Their plans were as vague as they were terrifying to countenance. *Wait it out* David had said as Mélenchon popped the cork on the bottle of Louis XIII, the others erupting in a celebratory cheer. *They think we're here for a holiday, why suggest anything to the contrary?* Cocteau and Marais thought exactly the same. Marais talked of a return to Rome for the summer, and suggested I might find a use for myself working for his friends in Italian cinema. Jean, Claude and I silently agreed through nervous glances that simply pretending we hadn't just killed and disposed of our third Nazi in one day wasn't the best way to survive.

Let them drink in an ignorant bliss. They didn't know we were leaving now, but I silently agreed with Jean it was better this way. Even if only in our minds.

"Here," Claude said, stuffing a roll of Reichsmarks in Mélenchon's free hands, "Give this to the Vichy men tomorrow. Tell them the Gestapo came and took the three of us away."

"Yes," Jean agreed. "Tell them that."

And then we went out. Claude took us over muddy grass around the other side of the house to a shed, the rain dancing through the light of his torch. It was already open and inside were a clutch of bicycles.

"Take," he yelled over a crack of thunder. "If we get separated, head downhill, you'll end up at the beach and we'll meet there."

269

In another moment we were out of Mélenchon's estate and cycling along the country road as wet as a river. Trees bent and waved, and it was a battle to keep steady in between gusts of wind. We followed Claude and his torch, cycling at full pelt through the blackness. Even if the Nazis were out searching for us, who could find a soul inside this storm?

"Wait," I shouted as we came to a crossroads. My bike fell to the ground as I ran through the rain to reach what I thought I'd seen. Yes, it was a telephone box; I pushed into it and prayed it was working.

Inside, there was no relief from the rain. The glass panels above were missing and the ground inside was a pool of mud. Everywhere, war. And we three were still a continent away from freedom. Years, decades might pass before the shoots of spring returned to Europe, if ever. The dead Germans did not weigh a single gram on my conscience, but all the boys of Paris we had lost, and all the ones we would lose in the aftermath of this, did. All the lives that had been lost. My mother, my grandmother, my own. There was no fear left in me. It had fractured with the stab of a knife into Reydrich and crumbled with the crack of a gun. Not fear of myself, fear of David or Cocteau, Claude or Jean, and certainly no more fear of the Nazis. I grabbed the receiver and started yelling in German:

"HQ in Paris. Put me through to HQ in Paris. Now."

"One moment, sir."

"This is Paris command. Who is this?" A gruff man with a Bavarian accent demanded to know.

"This is Eilas Bahr." The line went silent, as if we had lost connection. But I thought I could hear the sound of activity in the background and the clicking of half a dozen receivers listening in. I imagined this man in a control room, covered in maps and death lists, motioning for everyone around to hear from someone claiming to be one of the Germans the entire country was looking for.

"Eilas, where are you? Are you safe?"

I could have said a hundred things. I'd been kidnapped by the Resistance. Or the Brits had killed Reydrich, or the Gestapo attempted a mini-coup. But there was only one story I wanted to tell. A story that pushed the boundaries of artistic freedom. That shocked as well as titillated, shaming the audience while refusing to let them turn away. That was art too, I knew. Not another painting or piece of clay, a cinema reel or photograph. Those which we are bombarded with incessantly. Art is what makes us stop, which forces a reaction, makes us confront and feel... something. In the Germans' case, shame and shock and a thirst for bloody revenge. In my interpretation, my reaction... well, I smiled while I spoke.

"I killed Reydrich. I stabbed him in the chest. Go to the Roosevelt Mansion on the Royer-Collard, that's where I did it. The carpet was ripped up, but there's probably still splatters of his blood on the wall. I killed him because he found out I'd been having sex with a Jewish man." I gulped and sucked down a breath. My heart was pounding, my head too. I was soaked to my soul, my hands already wrinkled, and my shoes were caked in mud and Menzner's blood, but I had never felt like this. On the thin edge between artistic madness and greatness. There was nothing more Parisian than that.

"In the study, third door on the right, there's a hidden door behind the drinks trolley. Inside there's a camera, a Vinten Model H, with a reel still inside. Play it if you want, but I can also save you the trouble. There are hundreds of these reels recording every perversion of every officer who ever stepped foot inside that place. They documented everything. They filmed and photographed every one of us who ever had sex with one of their degenerates, and the Allies have it all," I lied. "They have everything. From Herman Goering to the Landgrave of Hesse. For every hostage harmed, the Allies will release another reel. It will be in every movie theater in the free world. Every Tommy, every GI, will eat popcorn and laugh as they watch Reichsmarshall Goering being spanked with a wooden paddle."

Shocked, sharp intakes of multiple breaths came through the receiver. But then I hung up. I wasn't ashamed of what I'd spent these years doing. Not any more. Not when it might prevent a massacre. I didn't care for my part in it, for there wasn't much more of a 'me' to consider. Those who knew me, who'd loved me, were gone and fading from this world. I'd be a distant memory to most quite soon. So there was no shame in sharing the existence of those reels. Nor in lying about who had them. For all the shame I'd felt in my life, heavy clouds that had forced fear through my veins where clear waters ran for others, let my enemies feel one part of that. Let shame fall on those who see themselves as shameful. Not me. Not when Claude and Jean were waiting outside, living beyond shame, and beckoning me to follow.

"You tried," Claude said as he handed me the bike. Jean kissed me on my soaking cheek. "It's all you could do."

"Let's get out of here. Spain is not that far," I said. And we headed downhill, in the direction of the rainwater as it flows to a river which flows to the sea.

Chapter 17

Paris, 1947

WE PULLED UP OUTSIDE the Ritz. Jean was driving the Rolls. I was in the passenger seat, wiping dust from the *Place de la Bastille* off my camera lens as Claude and Señora Perón shrieked with laughter in the back seat.

"Claude, you are awful!" she said in Spanish, playfully slapping his arm. The Paris phase of the Argentinian first lady's Rainbow Tour had begun only that morning with our little outfit arriving from Barcelona. While the President went off to meet with de Gaulle, we took over as semi-official photographer, driver, and personal shopper.

"There's more bags in the back," Claude said out of the window as he gathered up an armful of packages from the Avenue de Foch.

"The Argentine Republic must be doing well," Jean grumbled to me in French, our mostly secret language after so many years in Barcelona.

"Jean, my dearest," Eva said. "Can you drive me to Coco Chanel's this afternoon? I have a dress fitting for the State dinner tonight and I… well, I wanted to offer you some help."

"Help?" Jean said, turning around as the Ritz men glared at our car obscenely parked outside the hotel entrance, blocking any arrivals or departures.

"To be a proper model! Anders told me. He showed me some of your photos from Barcelona. My, they were utterly wonderful."

Jean cut me an angry look. *What the fuck?* I cut one right back. *Yes, I told her. Too bad.*

"Now Eva," Claude said. "I wouldn't say so much modeling career as 'aspiring to not live on the streets.'"

"Well I can appreciate that. Coco is just going to love you. In fact, I won't rest until you're on the cover of every magazine. Come pick me up at three, darling, and we'll make you a star."

With a great deal of force, Jean popped open the trunk. Ritz men rushed towards us, carrying off bags and boxes.

"We'll see you this afternoon then," Eva said, her white gloved hands waving at us through the passenger seat window. Her luscious blonde bob seemed to bounce and sway with its own consciousness as she linked her fur-coated arm through Claude's.

"Where to now then? The Champs Elyse?" Jean asked. He knew the answer already.

* * *

Five years ago, we had slipped from one world into another, and now we were back. Claude left Barcelona in early 1945, after France had been well and truly liberated. By then, he had exhausted about every opportunity a whore could have in a city of that size. Like a true Parisian, Paris was calling him home, and home he went. When he arrived three weeks later, he wrote us, explaining in lurid details about the diversions and re-routes he had taken with various members of the Allied forces in Europe. When he finally got to Paris, he found Giovanni's had been marked as a hotbed of collaborators. The doors and windows boarded up, the inside looted and empty. Giovanni and Madame Framboise long gone or dead. He didn't know. Our home a hollowed-out shell, devoid of sentimentality even.

Over the course of weeks, Claude dedicated himself to restoring the bar to its former glory. He even changed the name: *Claude's.* Soon enough, the Cocteau principle took hold, and the queers of the occupying armies found themselves drawn to this little basement bar on Rue Duperré in Montmartre. Madame Framboise at least returned. Shaken, but unperturbed. And even some of the boys who had survived the rest of the war. But Giovanni never did, although Claude kept a gun under the counter, just in case.

After the escape, our first few months staying at Dalí's hastily commandeered apartment in Barcelona had been an uncomfortable dream. We were squatters in an abandoned hotel, and the art gave me nightmares. Eventually, the three of us found ourselves a little two-room apartment in Eixample, just south of La Sagrada Familia, handily enough above a bar known for our sort of company.

Franco's Spain was an odd kind of dictatorship. A lot of things the state simply did not care about, or couldn't be bothered to police. Photography being one, queers seemingly another. To an extent. I founded a studio and quickly became in demand of every cabaret star and would-be actress in Catalonia. They said I could capture the subconscious of a person in one portrait. I could drive an audience wild with desire through a single snap of a fully clothed model. It wasn't simply camera magic, nor were my supposed talents the obvious product of long years taking pictures under literal fire. Taking pictures to save my life. It was because I looked at the subjects—businessmen and their proud families, singers posing on a couch, rich newlyweds having their pictures taken down by the beach; I looked at all of them and I did not see war, nor scandal, not sex. Just pure normalcy tinged with happiness. It was a pleasure to lose myself in those images. To see my pictures staring down from a gossip magazine in a newsstand, instead of posted down to Mélenchon for a diagnosis or stapled to the corner of an *Ausweis*.

It was only natural when Evita came to visit Spain and she asked for the most fabulous photographer in the land, the knock came on Jean's and my door. After she invited us to come to Paris on the next leg of her Rainbow Tour, we no longer had an excuse to put off the inevitable. We had to return.

"It was along here, no?" Jean asked, peering out the window on the search for Linda and Roland's studio I had once been the custodian of.

"Up there by that lamppost."

Jean stopped the car and I stared at the wooden door and the silver nameplate affixed to the wall. The anxiety rose in my throat like bile.

"Do you mind?" I asked, squeezing my lover's hand. "I'd rather limit the number of emotional reunions today to the minimum."

"Of course not." Jean leaned over and kissed me before stepping out the car. I closed my eyes and dozed in the once familiar sounds of French being spoken by passers-by, imagining the last five years had never happened. When Claude and I had been reunited this morning, I knew he knew what had happened to the others, but he had not said a word. We'd promised Eva the most spectacular time of her life in Paris with Claude, the most unique guide the city had to offer, and that had not been the time to sit and compare lists of whose funerals we had missed.

Although, he did tell me one thing. Late in 1946, the Americans dredged a car out of the Seine that had been caught in an embankment and was collecting considerable algae. Inside were the decomposed bodies of two men, one wearing the uniform of a senior SS officer, the other naked. Rumors had abounded around Claude's bar as to the identity of the drowned Nazis, and the mystery twisted even further when an autopsy revealed they had not drowned, but died before and their bodies, along with the car, had been dumped in the river.

I shot back to life with the opening of the car door and Jean jumping back in, a broad grin across his face.

"Enjoying the leather seats, I see?" He said as I wiped the exhaustion of days on the road from my forehead. Photographing the most famous Argentinian in the world and her husband took its toll. "Here." Jean dropped a thick brown envelope onto my lap.

"What is it?"

"Photos. Yours, apparently. Linda collected everything you took and stacked it altogether when she returned. And she gave me this to give to you." He pulled a smaller envelope from his pocket. Inside was a stack of American dollars, the total running into the hundreds.

"Dear Anders," I read from a letter attached. "Claude tells me you are well, and I am so glad to hear. Thank you for looking after my studio during the occupation. I can't tell you how much of a surprise it was to return and find it had been so well used, with so many incredibly moving images. I've kept everything together, and I've even sold a few of your shots of Paris to the news magazines. Here are all the dollars I have to give you as earnings. Please come and see me before you leave Paris, if only so I can pay you for the rest. All my love, Linda."

Why in Paris?

I peeled open the large brown envelope and inside must have been every picture I'd ever developed at her studio—all the injured boys from Giovanni's, and the landmarks of Paris, so innocuous-looking, until one peered at the image to catch the little bump in the ground where treasure had been buried.

"Are you ready to go there?" Jean asked, lighting a cigarette in anticipation of my silence. He was right. I said nothing for ten minutes or more. I just went through every photo, more than two hundred, again and again.

"Why else are we in Paris?" I said eventually. But we were already driving.

* * *

Jean parked the car on the other side of the Jardin du Luxembourg. When we had imagined this day, the Great Return, while laying on the beach on a lazy Catalan afternoon. He asked if he should come, but I said no, and sent him off to get ready for his meeting with Madame Chanel. Perhaps she and Eva Perón could convince him to properly take up modeling, a thing I'd singularly failed to accomplish over all these years. He wouldn't even pose for me. Not that I asked any longer after the first dozen times being shouted down. My photography became like the night Menzner had died. A thing we both vividly remembered, but never talked about again.

Despite that one smudge in the reel, we had spent many nights, as three, then as a duo, and then me, alone, reflecting on the events which had led to our exile. Like a circle of hell, the blame kept passing from one of us to another. At least in the early years. Some months Jean was to blame for anything in our new lives that went wrong. That Claude had syphilis yet again, or I couldn't get my tongue around Catalan.

Yet equally it could be argued, as it was at length, that Jean was not the cause but merely the effect. He was the neutral object swayed by outside forces and delivering the inevitable blow. The true blame lay with Claude. He'd encouraged and willingly participated with David in the secret filming. He'd been key in the planning and operation of hundreds of such events at the Roosevelt Mansion; he had even handed me the knife with which I had stabbed Reydrich. And as the fate of the others was unknown to us, Claude would have to be the scapegoat for the sins of the Parisian avant-garde.

Then, the blame passed to me. Neither of them said so out loud, at least not at first, but I knew they thought it. I knew they talked on it. I felt that they felt it. Many must have felt the same. Hence why I was digging under a certain statue in the Jardin du Luxembourg with a spoon stolen from Eva Perón's breakfast table, in broad daylight.

The park was busy. Busier than I'd perhaps ever seen it in my life. Strangely, the *toilette* I remembered had gone. Blown up or knocked down. A small part of me was eternally grateful it was no longer around to taunt me.

Freedom was still new to the people of Paris, or so I felt. When one lives under guard, when freedom returns, it will always feel sweeter, and one will always appreciate it more. The memory of those stolen years still scarred the city, as it must the people, for Parisians are unlike any other citizens in the world; so I had come to understand.

Paris is the center, and the savior of the world. It seethes with a rebellious smirk at all times. It is the only capital I have ever heard of where the government not only sits but lives in constant fear of the citizens of the locality in which it resides. The occupation of Paris so strongly left its mark because for most of its history, Paris has occupied France. But there is no France without Paris, just as there is no Paris without France. Paris is Jean. I have always thought so. It is the rich and the poor. It is the up and the down. The moneyed and the not. The foreign and the local. The working class and the avant-garde. Jean is Paris, and Paris is Jean, and I love them both equally.

* * *

I rang the doorbell of the Roosevelt Mansion, completely without thought of what I would find. The brass bell and gold-plated name plate were still there, and I traced the edges of the stone outside the heavy, bolted door for signs of forced entry or recent repair. Then the door unlocked, and I was let inside.

Upstairs was like stepping into a museum that had permanently closed. The floors in the hallway were now wood, and I assumed had been since that fateful day in 1942. The paintings and pictures were still there, mainly, and perhaps even more than before, but the furniture I could not find. I wandered into the main room I remembered so well, sunlight catching the raincloud of dust which floated in the air.

Old sheets covered all of the furniture which was left, and that was not a lot. Only one of the green couches in the center of the room remained, and it looked old and tired, as if it should be covered up too like a dead body after a massacre.

"Oh," a voice said from the door while I recreated in my mind the scene of Jean laying naked on the same place Hermann Goering had once danced. "It's you."

Hella made us tea in the private kitchen. It felt very much like this was the only room in which she lived. Everything was crammed inside. Newspapers covered the kitchen table; something was cooking on the stove and even more remnants of baking and boiling littered the not altogether large space.

I sat at the table and watched as she made the tea on autopilot, filling the kettle while simultaneously preparing mugs and sugar. I looked over the days' news in French and English, while we both steadfastly refused to talk about the things I had come here to say, and to ask. I had wiped the dirt from the reel before I came in, but still it did not feel right to put the object on the table. Underneath was the envelope, which I wasn't sure if she had even seen.

David's absence was palpable. I could understand why she only wanted to live in this part of the house, and the rest seemed so empty and dry.

"How have you been?" Hella asked as she brought tea to the table. Real tea, with real milk. Even after the war it was still not easy to find. But knowing her, she would have sold whatever furniture and jewelry was necessary to keep the house stocked with real tea.

"We've been okay. Barcelona has been good to us."

"I can see. You look well, Anders." She stirred lifelessly, like she was exhausted already by the things we hadn't even said.

"You knew I was there?"

Hella smiled. "Claude told me, after he came back. To be honest, we thought you were all dead for quite some time."

"And David..."

"As my best friend always said, 'fall in love with your friends.' And I did. Every day, I fell in love with him. In a world where everyone wants you to be someone else, he let me be me, and I let him be him."

I reached out and held her hand. She held it back. If it was forgiveness I wanted, this was it.

"I always told him those movies were dangerous. I would hate to think you—"

"Don't. It wasn't you. David would always do whatever he thought was best. I knew better than to think I could convince him otherwise."

"How did he…"

"Protecting me. Protecting this home we built together. It was after Paris fell. The vacuum was… terrifying. People were angry, and rightly so, at those they felt had helped the Nazis. We were only trying to survive, but that didn't mean we weren't also guilty." Hella was not crying, although I was. She spoke calmly, and with certainty. But it was too much for me. I felt my face break apart.

"Someone…?"

"No. He took his own life. We were not the only ones with our reputation in tatters, but for David, it was his *raison d'etre*. Without it, what was he? If you think war makes people into hypocrites, you should see what an outbreak of peace does."

"I feel so…"

"Anders, stop." She leaned over and wiped my tears. "We had no other way to make it through. And neither did you."

We sat quietly for a while, drinking the tea which was getting cold.

"What will you do now?" I asked.

"Probably return to America." She sighed. "Not that I want to. Once they've lived in Europe, Americans can never be truly happy again. Which is a problem when happiness is all we have."

"Why do you have to leave?"

"Money, I suppose. I've sold as much as I can to keep going with this place. Even the curtains. But what will I do? Paris will never be what it was. I'm not like Marais or you. I don't have a skill or a job. My life was being with David, because he let me live my life the way I wanted. Without him, without money,

I have only Paris. I've known for quite some time it's not enough, although I can't bring myself to leave."

"You know what David did once... the blackmail?" Hella nodded. I placed the round metal can I'd been holding on the table. "Pass me a knife, please."

Slightly confused, she got up and brought me one. I popped the can open, getting a hit of stale air sealed inside since 1941. Carefully, I cut off the last frame of the reel, and held the negative up to the light to check my memory served me well.

"This is Erich von Manstein, Claude, and your husband." I held onto the negative, feeling ashamed to show her the image even though she knew everything that had ever gone on here. "He gave testimony at Nuremberg."

Hella nodded. "I saw it in the papers. I thought he looked familiar."

"Take it," I whispered, sliding the negative across the table. "Take it to the Americans, the Russians, the press, to anyone." I had to stand. The weight of memory was getting too much. "They'll pay to keep this buried. I know they will."

Hella held it up to the light, nodded enthusiastically, and smiled. It was worth the entire war to see her smile. I laid the envelope on top of the reel.

"There's more reels here. Where they are, I mean. Take the image of Paris and stand in front of it. Directly in front so the image exactly matches your vision. Because wherever you're standing is where a reel is buried."

"Anders," she said, peeking inside. "There's a hundred or more in here. And... dollars. Is that yours?"

"It's yours. From Linda and Roland's studio. She's publishing a book of my pictures, actually. But I want you to have the rights. You and David."

"Anders, I don't know what to say."

"You don't have to say anything." I made for the door, leaving Hella flicking through the landmarks of Paris where the reels were buried.

"I was thinking *Hidden Treasures of Paris,*" I said after some time. "To call the book."

Hella pulled back and grinned. "I think that would work." She gathered up the pictures from the table, and the money and handed me the envelope. But the cut out negative she dropped in her purse. "You take these back, Anders. I'll wait for the book."

"No, please. I want you to have them." But she held up her hand in protest.

"I'll be fine. And anyway," she said, tapping her purse, "I think this little thing will be more than enough for a first-class passage to New York."

"And a Park Avenue apartment to go with it."

Hella started for the door alongside me. "Can I give you a ride somewhere?" I shook my head. "Very well. Walk me out though, will you?"

"Of course, where are you going?"

"Allied command." We shared a long, cleansing laugh. "Where are you going, Anders?"

She was probably expecting me to say Claude's like I used to say Giovanni's. Or Barcelona, or America, or England, or Austria, or a million other sides of this world I had not been.

"Always back to Paris. Before I came, after I left, it doesn't matter. I'm always on my way back."

Hella took my hand as we walked down the stairs that everyone who was ever anyone in this city had once climbed.

"That's why we're here," she said. "That's why you and I..." Hella paused to wipe away one last tear under a sparkling sun. On the street, life unfolded before us. Gone were the dead days of the war. Here were the cyclists, the old ladies, the men with pipes and flat caps, the babies being pushed in carts, the women in fur coats carrying Chanel bags, the American soldiers gawking like tourists, the exiles, the refugees, the escapists, the Jews, the gays, the people like us who had only two states of being. Either in Paris, or fighting to make it back. I gave her hand one last squeeze.

"To seek out beauty, then follow wherever it may lead. That's why we're here. That's why we're in Paris."

Acknowledgments

NO BOOK IS BORN without a constellation of people, fluttering in and out of the author's life. Some can be named and thanked, as I'll attempt to do so here, but most remain nameless. They are faceless conversations offering kernels of ideas and fragments of lines which weave themselves onto the page many years later. For all the people I cannot thank by name, thank you.

For those I can name, I owe an incredible debt of gratitude to Craig and John who have been instrumental in helping me build my confidence and career as an author. They have always offered a safe and welcoming space to explore ideas and provide the invaluable currency of feedback authors crave. Without their support and influence over the years I couldn't have put this book together.

Thank you to Criz, who knew I had something many years ago. You gave me far more than pen, paper and a room of my own. You saved my life.

An incredible thanks to the wonderful group of people on the WriteNow 2020 program. You are all a depth of wisdom, advice and searing energy and because of you all quarantine was far from an isolating experience.

Thank you to Kayla, who took a chance on this story. I sincerely appreciate the efforts you made. And thank you to Tabatha for believing in me as an author and for getting this book over the line.

Last but not least, a bursting waterfall of thanks to Michael at Encircle. You were one of the first people to believe in this story, and more importantly, kept that faith which brought us to a happy ending. You grasped the truer story I wanted to tell and together we reached its heart. Thank you for bringing Anders' tale to life.

About the Author

HARRY F. REY IS an author and lover of gay-themed stories with a powerful punch. He writes tales that explore fantastic yet realistic queer lives and loves, from the deep past to deep space or wearing a crown. Harry strives to deliver plot-twisting, action-packed, edge-of-your-seat queer stories he wished he had growing up gay in Glasgow.

Alongside *Why in Paris?,* his other works include the queer space opera series The Galactic Captains, and the gay royal romance series The Line of Succession. He's also penned a teen romantic-comedy, *All the Lovers*, and has been featured in a number of anthologies including *Queer Life, Queer Love* and *Not Meant for Each Other.* Follow Harry F. Rey on social media for his latest release or chat about gay literature.

If you enjoyed reading this book,
please consider writing your honest review
and sharing it with other readers.

Many of our Authors are happy to participate in
Book Club and Reader Group discussions.
For more information, contact us at info@encirclepub.com.

Thank you,
Encircle Publications

For news about more exciting new fiction, join us at:

Facebook: www.facebook.com/encirclepub

Instagram: www.instagram.com/encirclepublications

Twitter: twitter.com/encirclepub

Sign up for Encircle Publications newsletter and specials:
eepurl.com/cs8taP

Lightning Source UK Ltd.
Milton Keynes UK
UKHW010817220422
401896UK00001B/40